W9-BBP-690

HARRISON RAINES CIVIL WAR MYSTERIES:

A Killing at Ball's Bluff

"Kilian offers clues for anyone wishing to guess the identity of the murderer, but also indulges in a case of misdirection that might nag at a genuine mystery buff for months."
—*Publishers Weekly*

"Raines, a relentless but all-too-human hero, is an intriguing character who can withstand the scrutiny of subsequent episodes in what promises to be a fine series of novels. Both Civil War and mystery fans will appreciate Kilian's grasp of the genres of historical fiction and mystery." —*Booklist*

"A can't-put-it-down book. The plot is like a jigsaw puzzle, and you are never sure where the pieces fit. The characters are many and the conflict constant. Harry is intelligent, sensitive, and loyal. . . . A sense of urgency keeps the pace racing."
—*Rendezvous*

Murder at Manassas

"Harry is an engaging character, and he and his freed slave Caesar Augustus are an amusing pair as they try mightily to disguise their underlying ideals and bravery with a cloak of cowardice and greed." —*The Denver Post*

"[Kilian] successfully combines the genres of historical novel and murder mystery. [He] captures the chaos, confusion, and horror of war, and he effectively handles the irony of a quest for justice in the midst of mass killing. He has provided a slick, engrossing mystery dominated by an interesting and attractive sleuth." —*Booklist*

continued . . .

"The story line is strong and the research is impeccable, so this is bound to please fans of mysteries and historical novels as well."
—*Romantic Times*

"Kilian blends fiction and history, using real people to establish a believable context and create an absorbing period piece."
—*San Antonio Express-News*

"Michael Kilian has triumphantly opened his Civil War mystery series. The story line reflects strong research that includes trivia that adds period depth to the plot. The flawed and guilt-ridden Harry is a wonderful hero. The author's Herculean task, to write a series of mysteries that chronologically follows the war to its conclusion, gives this series a fascinating twist."
—Harriet Klausner, *Midwest Book Review*

"The series seems on the whole a promising notion."
—*Kirkus Reviews*

"Absolutely brilliant. The authenticity is splendid and the plot is stunningly rich in deceptions. It's a rare find that must be read—an exceptional mystery by an exceptional author."
—*Old Book Barn Gazette*

"History buffs as well as mystery lovers will enjoy this innovative new series. Readers who enjoy this book in the series can look forward to many more battles."
—*The Stuart (FL) News*

"Intriguing . . . a must for mystery fans."
—*Rendezvous*

A KILLING AT BALL'S BLUFF

A HARRISON RAINES CIVIL WAR MYSTERY

Michael Kilian

BERKLEY PRIME CRIME, NEW YORK

If you purchased this book without a cover, you should be aware that this book is stolen property. It was reported as "unsold and destroyed" to the publisher, and neither the author nor the publisher has received any payment for this "stripped book."

This is a work of fiction. Names, characters, places, and incidents either are the product of the author's imagination or are used fictitiously, and any resemblance to actual persons, living or dead, business establishments, events, or locales is entirely coincidental.

A KILLING AT BALL'S BLUFF

A Berkley Prime Crime Book / published by arrangement with the author

PRINTING HISTORY
Berkley Prime Crime hardcover edition / January 2001
Berkley Prime Crime mass-market edition / January 2002

All rights reserved.
Copyright © 2001 by Michael Kilian.
Cover art and design by Tony Greco & Associates Inc.

This book, or parts thereof, may not be reproduced in any form without permission. For information address:
The Berkley Publishing Group,
a division of Penguin Putnam Inc., 375 Hudson Street,
New York, New York 10014.

Visit our website at
www.penguinputnam.com

ISBN: 0-425-18314-9

Berkley Prime Crime books are published
by The Berkley Publishing Group,
a division of Penguin Putnam Inc.,
375 Hudson Street, New York, New York 10014.
The name BERKLEY PRIME CRIME and the BERKLEY PRIME
CRIME design are trademarks belonging to Penguin Putnam Inc.

PRINTED IN THE UNITED STATES OF AMERICA

10 9 8 7 6 5 4 3 2 1

Acknowledgments

My thanks to William Seale, John S. D. Eisenhower, Kristie Miller, the late Cleveland Amory, David Elliott, and the splendid National Park Service rangers at Fort McHenry. A very special thanks to Gail Fortune and Dominick Abel. I am grateful to my wife, Pamela, and sons, Eric and Colin, as only they can know.

For David Elliot, "Wise Anselmo,"
and old New Almaden

A Killing at
Ball's Bluff

Chapter 1

HARRISON Raines did not want to talk to the small, dirty boy who darted into the Palace of Fortune and headed directly for his table.

Harry was holding four eights in a high-stakes poker game with some of the best cardplayers in the federal city. It was the only good hand he had drawn that night, or that week. But the boy's presence portended more than the abandonment of a rare gambling opportunity. Harry guessed that an altogether different game was in the offing—one that would see a beautiful and gracious lady, a good friend of his and his family's, hauled off in irons to a jail cell.

And he would be asked to play a part.

The small boy, whose name was Homer, tugged at Harry's sleeve.

"Please, mister," said Homer. "He says to come."

"Yes, of course. After this hand."

The boy relinquished his grip on the sleeve of Harry's expensive linen coat—his grubby fingers leaving their mark—but didn't budge from the spot where he stood. The conditions of Homer's employment were that he would not receive his due compensation until the recipients of his messages responded to them.

Harry ignored the boy for the moment, taking his gold-rimmed spectacles from his coat pocket to better assess his situation in the card game.

Raines was as vain as any Southern gentleman of his youth and agreeable countenance, and not fond of wearing eyeglasses. Normally, he used them only when reading, or attending theatrical performances that featured comely actresses, of which wartime Washington City now had substantial supply. He sometimes left his spectacles off even when aiming a firearm, trusting to instinct.

He almost always wore them when engaged in a game of poker, a serious business with him. Gambling was one of several occupations he had taken up after breaking with his slave-owning Virginia family. Lately, he hadn't prospered at it much.

This hot August night he wondered if he might need stronger lenses. He still did not quite believe the four eights in his hand.

The others at the table were serious players as well. Big Jim Coates was a bearlike, cheerful, professional gambler who'd come to the capital from the western territory of Colorado in hopes of greater profit. He liked to joke that there was too much fighting and brawling out on the frontier and he preferred the peace and quiet of the Potomac during wartime. Certainly there wasn't much fighting around Washington, not with General George B. McClellan having taken command of the army after Irwin McDowell's disaster at Bull Run the month before.

The celebrated English war correspondent William

Howard Russell was another notable gambler at the table, and a friend of Harry's as well, who had been with him as a spectator at the Bull Run debacle. Next to Russell was Colonel Phineas Gregg, an army surgeon at the Union hospital in Georgetown. Gregg was Harry's mentor on almost all matters, but most especially on chess. The war had not interfered with their weekly games.

Adolph Webber, a whiskey seller and notorious Washington swindler, had few friends—and Harry was not one of them. But Webber was always welcome at the poker tables because he had a large pocketbook and, oddly, small talent for the game.

Templeton Saylor was a dashing young captain serving with the 3rd New York Cavalry. He had graduated from Harvard College three years before. Though Harry sometimes found it hard to abide Saylor's unfortunate snobbery—he liked to say that he and Harry were the only "gentlemen" to be found in the Palace of Fortune, if not all of Washington—Harry liked the man and counted him a friend. They shared a passion for the theater and were often invited to the same dinner parties. Saylor was a terrible poker player. Harry sometimes wondered if he truly examined his cards before making his bets. But the captain frequently won, if not by the intimidating size of his wagers, then by his willingness to see every bet and draw cards to every hand.

Saylor's father was said, without too much hyperbole, to own most of New York City and Saylor had little need of the money he won, or much care for that which he lost. He was a generous fellow who, despite his snobbery, always had a coin or two for the poor.

The remaining player at the table was Sam Buckeys, a Maryland horse trader whom Saylor quite openly despised—mostly for his uncouth appearance and horrible manners, but also because he was the sort of man who'd rob grandmothers on their deathbeds. A man who'd rob them *of* their deathbeds.

And rob the federal government as well. Harry had seen some of the mounts Buckeys had sold to the army. He could only hope the Union cavalry would not have to ride into battle anytime soon if they had Buckeys's nags beneath them.

Also engaged in horse trading, Harry sometimes held his nose and did business with Buckeys, though he thought the rough fellow to be a Confederate spy. Buckeys held a similar notion about Harry, which Raines of course encouraged. Harry was an agent, to be sure, but with a much different employer.

"Bet's to you, Raines," Webber said. The whiskey dealer had taken only one card.

Harry brought his hand into closer focus. The four eights were still there.

"It's a dollar to you, Sir Harry," reminded Saylor, using an appellation inspired by too much attendance at Shakespearean theatricals.

"He must still have his mind on that English actress," said Coates. "The one he took out to Bull Run and nearly got killed."

"Was the other way 'round," said Dr. Gregg. "She was the one keen on seeing all the heroes lay waste to one another."

"A splendid-looking woman, Caitlin Howard," said Russell. "And an actress of prodigious talent. But, do you know? I've only seen her perform here in the United States. Never once in London."

"'The grass stoops not, she treads on it so light,'" recited Saylor.

"She's in New York now," Harry said, swallowing away a pang of sadness. "Preparing for a play."

True enough, but as everyone in Harry's circle knew, she'd gone there with another man—the actor John Wilkes Booth—a fellow Harry also did not count among his friends. The beautiful Caitlin was enormously fond of Harry—and had demonstrated this on numerous public occasions. But she was madly, hopelessly in love with Booth, who, beyond his considerable acting talents, enjoyed enormous fame as "the handsomest man in America." It was perhaps not true, as had been said, that all the women in the country were in love with Booth—but all the women in Washington certainly seemed to be.

"Damn it, Raines," said Buckeys. "See the bet or throw in your hand!"

Quickly, with little further thought upon it, Harry pushed forth a silver dollar. He'd leave the raise to someone else.

That did not take long. Saylor, rich as Croesus and sitting to Harry's right, tossed in a five dollar gold piece with an elegantly accurate flip.

"The Virginia gentleman is too reticent," he said, with a nod to Harry. "Northern blood is stronger stuff."

Coates and Dr. Gregg folded their hands. When the bet came 'round to Buckeys, the horse trader grumbled, but then raised Saylor's offering another dollar. The pot now held more than even an actress of Caitlin's stature and celebrity made in a month.

Harry was now ready to hike the wager even higher, when he felt another tug at his sleeve. He looked down at the small, dirty face.

"You're to come, mister," the boy said. "You got to come."

"Not now, Homer," Harry said. "Have to finish this hand."

"Damn it, Raines," said Buckeys. "Bet!"

Harry merely saw the previous raises. Saylor raised another five dollars.

"He says come now," said Homer. "He says the horse is sick."

Those particular words were a signal. Harry glowered at his hand.

"Soon," he muttered. "Very soon."

Raines gave the boy a penny and a friendly shove toward the door, then tried to return his attention to the game. There were only three of them in it now—the raises having intimidated the others into folding.

Harry glanced at Saylor. He wasn't at all certain whether the young officer was bluffing, playing recklessly, or had something very good. That was never clear.

Buckeys was a different matter. Greedy to a sizable fault, he always played shrewdly. He was by far the table's biggest winner that night.

A small shiver ran up Harry's back. Who could beat four eights?

Another tug from Homer, which Harry struggled to ignore. He'd leave with the boy the instant the hand was done.

"I call," Harry said.

Saylor flamboyantly laid down his hand, which boasted no more than three jacks.

Harry set down his own hand faceup, separating the magnificent array of eights from the lone queen. He was about to reach for the pot when there came another tug at his sleeve. It was Buckeys. He'd set out four tens on the table.

Harry straightened his spectacles and stared at Buckeys's hand with great deliberation. Then, sadly, he shook his head, quickly downed his glass of whiskey, and pushed back his chair. It was barely nine o'clock, and he'd already lost most of the money in his wallet.

"Sorry, gentlemen," he said. "Have to see a man about a horse."

"The South in retreat," said Saylor.

"I ain't retreatin'," said Buckeys, raking in his winnings.

Dr. Gregg was looking at Harry strangely. He seemed about to speak, then thought better of it.

WITH Homer nipping on ahead, Harry hurried across the muddy expanse of Pennsylvania Avenue, dodging considerable street traffic and carousing soldiery, happy to reach the brick sidewalk on the other side. From there, he made his way west toward the President's Park and the Treasury Building, proceeding to the corner opposite Nailor's Livery Stable. Careful to keep out of the glow of the street lamp, he waited.

Not long. The line about a sick horse was a coded message for him to come to this place at once for a rendezvous with one Joseph "Boston" Leahy, a former Massachusetts police detective who now shared with Harry the distinction of discreetly serving the Union cause as an agent in the new U.S. Secret Service, formed just after the North's Bull Run defeat. When the term "sick horse" was used, it meant a matter of some urgency that needed immediate attention.

Leahy was taller even than Harry, who stood six feet. The Irishman was also so powerfully muscled his habitual cheap black suits seemed never to fit, especially about his shoulders. Leahy had a large head, and the bowler hat he always wore seemed similarly undersized.

He stepped out of the shadows behind Harry so quietly, he made Harry jump.

"Major Allen's got a wee job for us, Harry," he said softly.

"Something tells me it's not quite as wee as I should like."

Leahy looked both ways along the dark street. "It's Rose Greenhow," he said.

"I thought as much."

"Let's hope she has not. The night's game is to catch her unawares."

ROSE O'Neal Greenhow was one of the most influential and socially prominent hostesses in the federal city. Maryland born, she had married a prosperous Virginia lawyer who had become even more moneyed through successful land speculation in far-off California. In 1854, he'd fallen into a street excavation in San Francisco, a misfortune that had enriched Rose's sizable holdings by ten thousand dollars when the claim was settled. She'd afterward reestablished herself in Washington as might a noblewoman at a royal court.

James Buchanan had been her close friend before her husband's passing and remained an intimate of hers after Buchanan had ascended to the presidency. Senator Stephen Douglas had married her niece. Her friends and admirers in the Lincoln Administration included several high-ranking generals and, in great particular, Secretary of State William Seward. Her power and position in Washington were such that she'd been emboldened to snub the president's wife, Mary Todd Lincoln, at a dressmaker's.

Now past forty, Mrs. Greenhow was at the outer edge of what had not so long before been a brilliant beauty. Age had abated none of her charm, which could be magical in its effect.

Harry's plantation-owning father, now a colonel in the Virginia Cavalry, had been so friendly with Mrs. Greenhow that it caused some embarrassment for the family. Harry called upon Mrs. Greenhow to pay his respects upon moving to Washington two years before, and had been thoroughly smitten, though she was fifteen years his elder.

Leahy's summons meant Harry would be calling on her once again, to much different purpose. Both men knew, as did their leader in the newly formed U.S. Secret Service, that Mrs. Greenhow was more than just another of the capital's many highborn Southern sympathizers. She was thought to be the Confederacy's principal spy in Washington. It had apparently been decided she could no longer be tolerated.

"She's to be arrested?" Harry asked Leahy. They were moving along the north side of the avenue toward the Willard Hotel. "Tonight?"

"That's not clear, Raines. But the Major indicated some urgency in the matter."

"Major" E. J. Allen actually did hold that military rank, but he was no soldier. His true occupation was detective. He had been the first detective on the Chicago police force and later was chief detective for the Philadelphia, Wilmington & Baltimore Railroad. Now he headed the newly formed U.S. Secret Service, reporting directly to General McClellan. His real name was Allan Pinkerton.

He had a number of offices and hideaways in Washington from which he worked, and kept living quarters at the Willard, the city's finest hostelry. It was also the hotel most favored by supporters of the Union. Mr. Lincoln had stayed there in the days before his inauguration.

Harry's quarters were down Pennsylvania Avenue at the National Hotel, still a hotbed of secessionism. Its other residents included some of the most ardent Southerners in the federal city—as well as Harry's rival for the affections of Caitlin Howard, John Wilkes Booth.

Before knocking at the door to Pinkerton's rooms, Leahy went back down the hall to the stairs to make certain no one had followed them. Enemy agents were as thick in the capital as the prostitutes and drunken soldiery in the streets.

Pinkerton admitted them quickly. He was a short, stocky, strongly built man with broad face and nose and a brushy, closely cut beard, though he lacked a mustache. He was friendly enough, but seldom smiled. Never broadly. Yet Lincoln was always telling him jokes.

"Where were you?" Pinkerton asked. "Idling in the abodes of criminals again?"

"The Palace of Fortune," Harry said. "Yes."

"You are not a virtuous man, Raines. Happily, you are a useful one. I trust you will prove so tonight."

The gaslight in his parlor was very low. Going to the window overlooking the street, Pinkerton parted the curtains carefully, observing the passersby below. Satisfied that no one was taking an interest in him or his window, he let the drapes fall back into place, then came to the center of the room, where Harry and Leahy stood waiting. Pinkerton's dark eyes darted from one to the other quickly.

"You both have your revolvers?" he asked.

Leahy nodded. Harry started to nod as well, then stopped in alarm. "We're to shoot her? Mrs. Greenhow?"

Pinkerton shook his head. Harry almost detected amusement.

"No one wishes her dead, merely that she be removed from her mischief," the detective said. "That will be up to us. We need proof, and tonight we shall have it. She has dangerous friends. I want you prepared."

Harry had joined the Secret Service with great reluctance, compelled by circumstance to abandon the neutrality he had clung to after Sumter. Had he not joined the federal service, he'd been persuaded that he might well end up arrested on suspicion of being a Southern agent. His father was a good friend of both Confederate President Jefferson Davis and his chief military adviser, General Robert E. Lee. Harry's brother was also a Confederate officer, and the family plantation in Charles City County down in the Virginia Tidewater was home to more than a hundred slaves.

It was the matter of slaves that had driven Harry from his family and into residence in Washington. He was a supporter and admirer of Abraham Lincoln and all that the president stood for—including especially abolition of "the peculiar institution."

But before swearing his oath to the Republic as a newly inducted member of the Secret Service a few weeks before, Harry had made a point of warning Mrs. Greenhow that she would be arrested if she remained in the capital. He intended no treason to the Union cause by this. Like many, he wanted her gone from the capital for the good of all concerned, but wished this to be accomplished without her suffering harm or discomfort. Despite his hatred of slavery, he was still an adherent of the Virginia gentleman's code of chivalry.

"If there's no proof," he asked, "why are we so intent on this?"

"Because of what we know but cannot yet prove, Raines. This woman has done a powerful lot of damage." Pinkerton went to the window again, then settled into an armchair. "My people in Richmond report the most boastful talk of her accomplishments. It's said she sent no fewer than three messages to the enemy relating General McDowell's plans before Bull Run. Three! And they say they all got through. All of this in time, I need not add, for General Beauregard to transfer his army from Winchester by railroad to join General Johnston at Manassas. There's a reason for our defeat at Bull Run, Raines. That dreadful, traitorous woman! And yet she invites Secretary Seward to dinner to tell him the Union Army got its just deserts!"

"I was there at Bull Run, Mr. Pinkerton. It wasn't Mrs. Greenhow who caused that panic on the Union right."

"It was Mrs. Greenhow who had those Rebel troops sent to the field, and they who caused that panic!"

Pinkerton's burning gaze unsettled Harry considerably. He wondered if his participation in the entrapment of Rose Greenhow was some sort of test on which his future career in the Secret Service depended—if not his liberty to walk the streets of Washington a free man.

"There's more," said Pinkerton. "We've had at least a dozen sightings of her encounters with suspected Confederate agents. She has such bold contempt for us she meets with them in Lafayette Park, directly across from the President's House! People ask why General McClellan does not attack. Among the reasons is his having to change his plans. He tells me she knows them before Mr. Lincoln or the cabinet. Four times he's been compelled to change them because he's heard she learned of them."

Harry suspected McClellan changed his plans whenever Mr. Lincoln or the Congress suggested he put one of them into action.

"In Europe, the English would hang her and the French would cut off her head," Leahy said.

Harry sighed, accepting reality. He supposed Rose was lucky to have been tolerated for so long. It was a vexing question to him whether she was driven to spying by the fanatical nature of her loyalty to her "cause"—or if she had some inner drive to destroy herself.

She had a child, a little girl of eight years, also named Rose.

"How do you propose we acquire this 'proof,' Mr. Pinkerton?" Harry asked.

"In two steps. We go to her house and wait for something suspicious to occur. Then we obtain a warrant, arrest her, and scour her house until we find the proof."

"And if there's none?"

"There'll be proof. This woman is not only incorrigible, she is flagrant. If it weren't for her social position and connections, I'd not need to waste time gathering proofs at all."

Harry took out his pocket watch. "And you want to go now?"

"Yes, now."

A tremendous downpour commenced almost the instant they stepped from the hotel onto the street.

THE Greenhow house, one of the most stately in the capital, sat on a corner at 398 Sixteenth Street just north of Lafayette Park. Harry thought Pinkerton would want the three of them to skulk in the lampless shadows across the street, but the stout little man led them instead directly up to the house's front windows. The main floor was on a level considerably higher than the sidewalk, making it impossible for them to have a view of the interior—not Harry, who stood six feet in height, or Leahy, who was a good two inches taller.

"Raise me up," Pinkerton commanded.

"Sir?" said Leahy.

"Up! Up on your shoulders. Both of you. I want to look within."

"Mr. Pinkerton," said Leahy. "No disrespect, but you are no athlete."

"I'll use the wall for balance. Hurry!"

With the rain falling in sheets, it was a struggle, but the doughty little Scotsman was determined. After two unsuccessful tries, they had him shakily standing on both their shoulders. Happily, he had removed his shoes.

"What do you see?" asked Harry, whispering loudly over the drumming rain.

"The parlor."

"What's she doing?"

"The room's empty."

Holding Pinkerton's ankle with his left hand, Harry turned his head to wipe some of the water on his face with his sleeve. As he did so, he saw a glimmer of movement down the street near Lafayette Park.

"Someone's coming," he said, whispering as loudly as possible.

"Quick, then," said Pinkerton. "Get me down."

Lowering the detective to the ground, they scurried around to the other side of the front steps. There was an alcove beneath them, with a floor of dirt, now rendered mud. They crowded into it.

Harry lifted his head from this refuge to look down the street. The approaching figure wore a military hat and a military cape. He strode along with some speed, his boots splashing water, then abruptly stopped in front of Mrs. Greenhow's house, looking sharply both up the street and down.

The three of them hugged the darkness as they heard him ascend the stairs above them. The door was answered very quickly after his knock.

"Again," said Pinkerton, still in stocking feet. "Up on your shoulders."

Unable to hear any of the conversation inside because of the loud drumming of the rain, or see much of anything aside from Pinkerton's sodden stockinged foot on his shoulder and the brick wall before him, Harry reflected on the dashing life of the U.S. Secret Service agent, and how his decision to take a side in this war might have been more nobly rewarded. He thought of Caitlin Howard, imagining what she might think to see him now.

Not at all the heroic figure her beloved Wilkes Booth habitually cut.

Whatever Pinkerton had in view through the window, he seemed transfixed by it—to the point where he was paying insufficient attention to his balance. He began to wobble, compelling Harry to hold his leg with both hands. Harry was relieved when a pedestrian came hurrying along the walk, necessitating a return to the shelter beneath Mrs. Greenhow's stoop.

"What did you see?" Leahy whispered heavily.

"The officer bowed," replied Pinkerton. "He smiled. I think I know the devil. A Captain Ellison. He's regular army, an infantry officer in charge of one of the provost marshal stations. He must know every strong point in the federal city—all of Washington's defenses."

"Secretary Seward knows them, too. And he calls upon her regular," Harry said, shivering slightly. He doubted there was now a dry square inch of skin upon his entire body.

"Bet he doesn't smile at her like that. This fool must be besotted."

They hushed for the passing of the pedestrian—a nondescript man doubtless hurrying home. He paid them no mind.

Leahy nodded, and with some effort, they returned to the window and got the detective back up onto his perch again. He began shaking once more, but this time the cause seemed to be indignation. He was swearing oaths under his breath. They were compelled to lower him again as a carriage turned the corner from H Street.

"He's showing her a map!" said Pinkerton, when they were beneath the steps once more. "Do you hear me? A map! By God, we've got her now."

"You'll need the map before you can say that, sir," said Leahy. "It could be of London."

"No. I heard a few words. It's Washington."

The carriage, drawn by four horses, splashed by, the coachman hunched on his seat like a right-side-up bat.

"Again," Pinkerton said. "Hurry."

No sooner did he go up than he slid down again, using their heads for support.

"They've gone," he said.

"Where?" said Harry.

"Now, that's a question with an interesting answer," Pinkerton said. "Pity we don't know it."

The three endured their rainy misery for nearly an hour, pausing every so often to hike Pinkerton up for a quick glance to the parlor—each time finding it empty.

"I left a very nice, dry abode of criminals for this," said Harry finally. "Can't we let it go for the night? It would seem that they have."

"Shhhhh," said Leahy.

"Once more," Pinkerton ordered. "Up."

This time the effort bore considerable fruit. Mrs.

Greenhow and her Union Army swain had returned—as Pinkerton observed in a whisper—arm in arm. And then even closer.

"Down!" he said quickly.

They reached their sanctuary beneath the stairs just as the door above them opened. Barely breathing to keep their quiet, they listened through the rain as the couple spoke words of farewell—pauses between the words indicating some very demonstrative exchanges of affection.

The captain sauntered from the house, walking away as cheerily as though beneath blue skies and a bright sun. The rain had slackened, but the air was thick with mist and all about was mud. As the officer's figure began to recede in the gloom, Pinkerton set off after him—the detective still in stocking feet. Harry followed. Leahy looked about for his leader's shoes, then gave up and followed.

Twice the officer paused to glance over his shoulder. Each time Pinkerton shrank back into the shadows, with Harry and Leahy quickly doing the same.

The captain quickened his pace, heading for the provost marshal station that lay just ahead. Harry pulled out his watch, holding it close to see it clearly. The hour was now well past midnight.

Reaching the provost quarters, the captain hurried inside—but not to get out of the rain. In a moment shouting was heard. The officer reemerged at the head of a squad of soldiers. Pinkerton turned to Harry with alarm.

"Go, Raines. Or they'll have your name. Go! Run!"

"What about you?"

"I want to make certain of this man. Go!"

Harry did so. Reaching the nearest corner, he flung

himself around it, then crept back and peered around the wall.

The captain and the soldiers had surrounded Pinkerton and Leahy. Harry watched in amazement as the two federal detectives were marched away under Union Army guard.

·Chapter 2

LEAHY appeared at Harry's rooms at the National the next morning with a bizarre tale to tell.

He and Pinkerton had been arrested by the amorous captain, who had them thrown into a cell with an assortment of drunks, thieves, and other common criminals. Rather than protest, and run the risk of revealing his true identity, Pinkerton quietly accepted his incarceration, but managed to get a message out to General Winfield Scott, the army's commander-in-chief, by bribing one of the soldiers of the provost guard with a silver dollar. Scott quickly responded with orders for Pinkerton and Leahy to be brought at once to his quarters. After hearing the detective's unfortunate story, Scott summoned the traitorous captain. Failing the general's interrogation, he was relieved of his post on the spot and placed under house arrest. Pinkerton had since resumed his surveillance of Mrs. Greenhow's.

"Are we to join him there?" Harry asked.

"I am," said Leahy. "Not you. Not yet. Just carry on as usual."

"In the 'abodes of criminals'?"

"Wherever Homer can find you."

HARRY was in the dining room of the National, enjoying a lunch of ham, stewed carrots, biscuits, and coffee when the boy appeared before him.

There was no nonsense about sick horses. The message was open and direct.

"They got the lady arrested in her house," he said. "You're supposed to wait one hour, then come callin' on her like you don't know nothin's happened."

Harry gave Homer five pennies and a biscuit covered with jam, then went upstairs to change clothes. A Southern gentleman didn't call on Rose Greenhow in anything less than his very best finery. The coat he chose was tight fitting, so he left his Navy Colt revolver in its case, confining his armament to a small, two-barreled derringer he slipped into his breast pocket and the sheath knife he customarily carried in his boot. Washington was now more than ever not a city to walk around in unarmed. There'd been a man murdered over a gambling debt in this very hotel the previous week.

HE was greeted at the door by Pinkerton, who immediately began to enact a loud charade.

"Mrs. Greenhow is not receiving guests," Pinkerton exclaimed, almost loud enough to be heard at the President's House on the other side of the park.

"I am a family friend," Harry replied. "Where is she? What is happening here?"

"Who are you?" Pinkerton asked, raising his voice still more.

"My name is Harrison Raines."

"Who?" The detective gestured to Harry to make himself better heard.

"Harry Raines! A family friend! I demand to see Mrs. Greenhow!"

"You do, do you? Come with me!"

He led Harry into the parlor, the same room in which they'd observed her entertaining the unfortunate Captain Ellison, then closed the door and drew Harry away from it.

"We have her, Raines," he whispered. "We have her squarely. Haven't searched the entire house. But we've found enough to hang her. Letters, Raines. Some from a United States senator! He signs himself 'H' but we know who he is. She has traded the fruits of amour for secrets—military secrets!"

"Where is she?"

"Upstairs. In her bedroom. I've posted a guard at her door."

"If you have so much on her, why isn't she in irons? Why haven't you hauled her off to the Blue Jug?"

That was the common name of the oddly painted building that was the city's awful municipal jail.

"Not there. The president thinks that no fit place for a lady. But the Old Capitol Prison, that'll be her home soon enough, I should think."

"What do want of me?"

"More evidence, Raines. More facts. A confession. She has powerful friends, and this will not sit well with them. Go upstairs. Be her friend. Draw her out. But don't betray yourself."

MRS. Greenhow was facing away from the door when Harry entered her room, her hands busy over a vase of flowers. She turned toward him abruptly, her eyes widening in recognition.

"Harrison Raines. It *was* you I heard downstairs."

She rushed to him and embraced him fiercely, pressing her face against his shoulder and her breasts against his chest tightly enough to cause discomfort. He patted her back, almost politely, then gently pushed her away.

"I am sorry to see you in this distress, madam. What has happened?"

"The vile, bastard Yankees have denounced me as a spy. I am under arrest. I fear the worst."

Harry stepped back, but not far, for she now gripped his hands. Her lovely eyes were fixed hard on his. Aging or not, her allure had not yet abandoned her.

"I tried to warn you, Mrs. Greenhow."

"Yes. You sent word through your cousin."

She meant the young Belle Boyd, who was Rose's frequent houseguest in Washington but lived in Martinsburg, Virginia, not far from a small farm Harry owned outside Shepherdstown. Harry and Belle were related only distantly through a marriage between distant kin, but the girl made much of it and called him cousin.

"Why did you not heed it?"

"I could not comprehend how you might know such a thing. You are a Virginian. Your father is a colonel in the Confederate cause. What Yankee would trust you with such intelligence?"

Harry smiled—he hoped disarmingly. "I play at cards with high-ranking Union officers. There was talk."

"Talk, indeed." She dropped his hand and turned away, her voice becoming tremulous. "I fear I am informed upon."

"Madam—"

"It's true, Harry!" Her eyes were on him again, brightly. "They have intercepted my messages—one for certain. The note I gave to Betty Duvall to take across the Chain Bridge to General Beauregard. She sewed it in her hair in a silk bag. No one knew of it. She wasn't caught. Yet now I hear talk of it. I am spied upon, Harry!"

He took a step closer to her, wishing he could tell her how sorry he was for his role in this. "Mrs. Greenhow. You've entertained known Southern agents right there in Lafayette Park. You denounced Lincoln to Seward's face. Everyone talks of it. This was inevitable. I warned you."

Her eyes held him back. "Where are your loyalties, Harry—on which side of the Potomac?"

Harry made no reply. Telling her of his neutrality would enrage her as much as hearing him express his admiration for Lincoln.

"You move so freely on this side. Do you still have that Negro—that Caesar?"

"I emancipated him—as you know. He works for me. I pay him a wage."

"Yes. Very curious, Harry."

"I am no less Southern for my generosity to him, madam. No less a Virginian. And I'm here as your friend."

Her eyes dropped away. She came against him again, her cheek against his. "What am I to do, Harry? What will become of me?"

"I'll find you a lawyer."

The lady looked up at him, the brightness in her eyes now that of anger. "Lawyer? They have no law! They use no courts! No writs! No charges! They just haul people off to their dungeons. Now me! And my little daughter! She has done nothing."

"I am so very sorry, Rose. I'll do whatever I can."

Her voice fell to near a whisper. "I heard you enter

the house," she said. "But there was such a long delay before you appeared. What happened?"

"They took me into your parlor."

"What for?"

He needed a lie, quickly. "To search me. For arms."

"Are they so afraid of one frail woman?"

Mrs. Greenhow was about as frail as a Parrott rifled cannon.

"It's wartime," he said.

She moved in a sweep of skirts to a bookshelf. From behind some large volumes she snatched up a large revolver.

"If they lay a hand on me or my daughter, Harry. I'll kill them. I'll shoot the first wretch who comes near me."

"That would mean the gallows, Rose. Let's keep you alive."

She slipped the firearm into a pocket of her skirt. "You'd best go, Harry. I need to think."

"I'll get you out of this. I promise."

"Go, Harry. Please."

This time she kept her distance. He bowed, then turned for the door, closing it quietly behind him. Descending the stairs, he pulled Leahy aside.

"She has a pistol," he whispered. "Don't let her know you know."

Leahy nodded. "Do you have anything for Major Allen?"

"Later, perhaps. Just don't hurt her."

Going down her steep front stairs, he paused to look up at what he guessed was Rose's bedroom window. There was a glimmer of a face, framed by a pane. Then it was gone.

Chapter 3

ROSE O'Neal Greenhow's arrest turned into an ordeal that lasted longer than a week. She was kept under guard in her own house, an ill-advised arrangement that Leahy said had her scuffling with an officer of the provost guard in one nasty incident and losing her revolver to a female detective's search in another. At one ludicrous point her little daughter ran out into the backyard, climbed a tree, and began screaming: "Mama has been arrested! Mama has been arrested!" One of Pinkerton's men dragged her down again, but not before she had half the neighborhood persuaded her mother was being tortured.

Harry had run into Templeton Saylor in the bar of the National, where Rose's house arrest was the talk of the establishment. This was mostly very angry talk—including threats to form a mob and free her—but the National was the hotel most favored by those sympathetic to the South, and Saylor said he didn't take them seriously.

"'Words, words, mere words; no matter from the

heart,'" he said, from his boundless mental archives of Shakespearean quotations.

Harry wondered if he'd studied much else at Harvard.

The search of Rose's house, which some in Washington were calling "Fort Greenhow," yielded prodigious amounts of damning material. There was evidence of her warnings to Beauregard before Bull Run, of her sending Richmond messages and maps detailing the defenses of Washington, of reports of actual Lincoln cabinet meetings. One unsent letter provoked her erstwhile friend Secretary of State Seward to a towering rage. She had described him as the only gentleman in Lincoln's "black Republican cabinet," but also as a craven toady who would truckle before anyone to advance himself politically.

There were names recovered as well. It appeared she'd been able to destroy some incriminating documents and lists, but enough information survived and was found for arrests to be made all over Washington within days.

Rose had been allowed a number of visitors after Harry paid his respects. Some were detectives and Union agents, some were genuine Southern sympathizers, and some just friends, including more federal army officers. All these conversations were clandestinely listened to by Pinkerton's people. None produced the kind of confession Pinkerton sought, but it was clear now to all that, in Rose Greenhow, they had in their hands the ringmaster of the Confederates' espionage network in the federal city.

The pressing question now was what to do with her.

Through all this, Harry had kept his distance, attending to his various businesses during the day and passing the nights at the Palace of Fortune or the bar of the

National. It was there that Booth kept a suite of rooms, and there, presumably, where Harry might best learn of Booth's whereabouts and plans. He'd not had a letter from Caitlin Howard in weeks. He could only assume she was still with the actor.

Maddox, the Welsh-born bartender at the National, had no word of either.

"He'll weary of her, Harry. Don't worry."

"His wearying is not my worry."

Harry did not make another visit to Rose. The confession he had failed to procure from her now hardly seemed necessary, with the lady safely under lock and key and piles of evidence in safekeeping at the War Department.

"WE'VE limited her visitors," said Leahy, joining Harry at the National on another afternoon. "And we search 'em good. 'Major Allen's' afraid someone will manage to get another firearm to her."

"We should set her free," said Harry. He sighed, then drank down his whiskey in a swallow and signaled Maddox for more.

"Don't be daft, man," said Leahy. "We've only just locked her up."

"I don't mean free to walk about Washington City. I mean sent through the lines to the South. Into exile. Deported. You could transport her in chains if you like. She'd probably be grateful to you for the martyrdom."

"Can't be done."

"We exchange prisoners of war, don't we?"

"Aye, and a bloody damn stupid thing it is to do. The Union has far more men to draw on than the Confederacy. We ought to take advantage of it. Even at that, laddy-buck, those prisoners we exchange are soldiers who were serving honorably. A spy's in a different kettle. A rifle ball or a rope is the prescription."

Harry had seen a man hanged once—bulging eyes; swollen, protruding tongue; purplish face; twitching limbs. He couldn't imagine Rose Greenhow looking like that—not in the most horrible of nightmares.

Yet he'd probably helped put her head in such a noose.

"She's a woman," he said.

"Aye, she's made that clear enough to a number of susceptible gentlemen."

"But the government has never before hanged a woman. And she's harmless now. She's been exposed. Everyone knows she's been spying for the Rebels."

"Harry m'lad. She'd shoot you down right here in the tick of a clock if she thought it would help the Southern cause. Leave her fate to the proper authorities and stop worrying about it."

"Mr. Leahy, I think I'm going to resign from the Secret Service."

"You're not serious, man?"

"I think that I am."

"You only just joined our ranks."

"If this is what we do—then I want no part of it."

"You can't quit, Raines. *Captain* Raines. You signed the papers. You took an oath, in front of the president himself. If you were to turn quitter now, you'd have to head south and waste no time about it. That'd be the only place you'd be welcome. And given what you know, we might not let you. Secretary of War Cameron or some such might clap *you* into prison, too. That what you want?"

Harry stared down at the polished bartop. "I want to stop feeling guilty about what we've done."

Leahy put down his glass of lemonade and turned,

gripping Harry's shoulder. "More than two thousand men dead or wounded at Bull Run, Raines. You saw some of them go down. That blood's on her hands. You've got no reason to feel guilty. Anyway, she won't be lonely. We've arrested some other ladies of the Rebel persuasion. Pinkerton figures the Greenhow house is as good a place as any to keep 'em in."

He stood up straight.

"Got to be going," he said. "I'll see if Mr. Pinkerton can't find you something to do—something not involving herself. Something to take your mind off her. McClellan needs good intelligence from the field."

"What for? He's always preparing, never attacking. They say he may not move the army before fall."

"Careful how you talk about the man. You may count me as your friend, but the general has other agents not so well disposed toward you."

HARRY had established his horse-trading business in an old, commodious barn and paddock near the Swampoodle neighborhood just to the north and west of the Capitol. He'd placed the management of the concern in the hands of a worthy fellow: his former slave and lifelong friend—Caesar Augustus.

The same age as Harry to within a month, the black man had been raised as a childhood companion to Harry and then given to him as a present on his twenty-first birthday—as if he were a good horse. Harry's father had been furious when Harry took Caesar Augustus into Richmond the very next day and arranged for the man's freedom, complete with two sets of papers recording the fact. Harry's estrangement from his family and eventual remove to the federal capital dated from that event.

Caesar Augustus was properly grateful for his liberation. But he had not forgotten any of the indignities and injustices visited upon him during his plantation servitude. He was not an admirer of most white folk. Sometimes, he merely suffered even Harry.

He gave Harry a dark look now as he entered, an assertion of his independence. But his manner quickly mellowed.

"Ain't seen you in more'n a week, Marse Harry. I was beginnin' to think you had maybe given the business over to me but just forgot to say so."

Harry smiled, with deliberate impertinence.

"In time, Caesar Augustus. You get some new stock in?"

"Yassuh, massuh."

"Stop that."

"Come out back."

There was a string of new cavalry mounts in the paddock, which abutted the rear of the barn. They looked to be excellent animals, unlike much of what was being peddled to the army.

"Some goin' to call us fools, Marse Harry," Caesar Augustus said, resting his elbows on the paddock fence.

Caesar Augustus had continued to address Harry with the "marse" that had been obligatory on the plantation, but he did so sardonically—a commentary on his freedom and also on the nature of their link to each other. It rankled Harry to hear it but there was no persuading the African to abandon the term.

"Who's going to call us fools?"

"Everyone. That son of a bitch Buckeys sells the army broke-down nags that can't hardly walk for dollars more a head than we ask for prime animals."

"We ask a fair price. We're making money."

"We ain't gettin' rich, Marse Harry. A lot o' work here for not gettin' rich."

Under their arrangement, Caesar Augustus got a white man's salary for running the livestock business, plus half the profits, which, for all Harry and Caesar's fairness, were not inconsiderable in wartime. Few black men in any Northern city could boast such compensation.

But the fact remained that Caesar Augustus did all the work. Harry's involvement now was mostly to use the business to mask his activities with the Secret Service.

"Mr. Buckeys's cheating ways will catch up to him," Harry said.

"He been by here, Marse Harry. He waited for a time you weren't around."

"What for?"

"Partnership. His company's gettin' a bad name. He asked me to front for him for a quarter of the profits. You weren't supposed to know."

"He wanted to use our name?"

"Your name, Marse Harry. I was supposed to let him do it—for twenty-five percent."

"My good name."

"He seemed to think you wasn't goin' to be around much at all."

"What'd you tell him?"

"Ain't wise to be disrespectful to a white man—but I was disrespectful."

Harry glanced over the many horses in the paddock. "You want me to hire more help?"

"Only good horse handlers in this town aside from you and me are all white men. No white man goin' to work for me. Can't have a black man as a boss man."

"Let me know if you want to change your mind." Harry lit one of his long, thin cigars, careful to make certain the match was fully out before dropping it to the straw-littered barn floor. "I have a favor to ask of you."

The black man turned his attention back to the horses in the paddock.

"Fine with me, Marse Harry, long as it ain't nothin' that's goin' to require me gettin' shot at again like out at Bull Run."

Harry let this pass. "I need you to drive an army ambulance. From the Union hospital in Georgetown upriver a bit—maybe as far as my farm out by Shepherdstown."

"The army is providin' this army ambulance?"

"No, sir. We're going to do that. I want you to fix up the feed wagon with a new top—make it look like an army ambulance."

Caesar Augustus spat. "This sounds more like somethin' goin' get me shot at."

"Nothing of the sort. I just want you to wait outside the hospital until I bring out a patient—then take her up the river road."

"Her? What kind of patient be a her? That's a soldiers' hospital."

"She'll be a patient until she's in the wagon. Then she'll become a nurse and I'll be the patient. I'll have bloody bandages prepared."

"Marse Harry, you sound like you already *are* a patient—in one of those lunatic asylums."

Harry patted his friend on the shoulder. "I'll tell you more about this when I figure it all out."

DR. Phineas Gregg was in the rear yard of his hospital, sitting in a wooden chair tilted back against the wall with his booted feet up on a barrel. His white coat was soiled with blood and grime, as were his hands. He looked asleep, but there was smoke coming from his cigar.

"Hello, Harry," he said from beneath his hat. "If you've come looking for a chess game, I'm afraid I've not the mind for it today."

"I wouldn't take advantage of your fatigue," Harry said, seating himself on the stone steps at the hospital's back door. "You know I prefer to win on the merits of my play."

"Which is why you lose so much of the time."

Gregg routinely took Harry three games to one.

"I'm getting better."

"You're not getting better at poker," Gregg said. "How much did you lose in that last hand the other night?"

Harry shrugged. "Almost fifty dollars."

"Very strange hand," said Gregg. "Strangely played." He took a small flask from a breast pocket, lifting it in Harry's direction. Getting a polite shake of the head in response, he pulled the cork and took a long draft. Harry caught a whiff of cognac.

"Was there a battle today?" Harry said, taking a long look at the crimson drips and smudges on the doctor's coat. "A skirmish or some such? Have you been doing surgery on more wounded?"

"Surgery on a boy wounded last month at Bull Run," Gregg said, returning the flask to his pocket and taking a few puffs of his cigar. "Took off one leg then and today I took the other. Trying to keep ahead of the deadly humors."

"I'm sorry."

"So am I. He died a few minutes afterward. I need not have bothered."

"You needed to try."

"It's all I can do. A few make it, don't they? But that's more the work of divine providence than of my poor labors."

"They'd all die without you, Doctor. All of them." Harry hesitated. "Are there empty beds here?"

"Too many, now."

"Is there an unused chamber? Where a woman and her daughter might be restored to health?"

"This is a military hospital, Harry. Full of men. No place for a woman."

"There are women here—Miss Barton, others."

"They don't stay the night—unless they're on duty." The doctor smoked a moment, then turned his head and gave Harry a very hard look. "Has this something to do with that Greenhow woman?"

Gregg was a very smart man. "She is ailing, Doctor. She cannot long abide in her present circumstances."

"There are more comforts there than here, m'boy. I would not wish residence in this charnel house on that miserable Jefferson Davis himself."

"It would not be for long."

Another hard look, thinly veiled by cigar smoke.

"I get your meaning, Harry—and I do not like it. There's a smell of treason."

"Not treason. Charity. She would be sent south—where she belongs."

"She belongs in hell, damn it! Got blood on her hands!" He lifted a corner of his coat. "This blood!"

"She could be hanged. The child would be orphaned."

They sat in silence. Finally, startling Harry, Gregg abruptly got up.

"The doors to the hospital are open to all," the doctor said gruffly. "I have never turned my back on a patient—or a friend. And I will not." He tossed his still-smoldering cigar end onto the dirt, then ground it out with his boot. "But neither will I be a party to treason when my country's at war. If she comes here, so be it. But I won't help you in any mischief, Harry."

"I'm not asking for that."

"She should be cleaning the wards, that's what she should be doing." He started back inside, halting on the stoop. "Collecting the sawed-off hands and feet. Scrubbing away the blood. That should be her fate."

The door closed behind him.

Chapter 4

HARRY labored into the night on a carefully worded letter to Rose, which he signed only with the letter *H*. An ingenious ploy, he thought. Her jailers would think it was another *billet doux* from her mysterious swain. She, upon reading it, would know it was not. He'd carefully inserted some references to past conversations they'd had to give her a clear idea as to who her correspondent and benefactor actually was.

But he received no reply. In all the weeks that followed—nothing at all.

He next sent a message by means of Rose's good friend Lily Mackall, who memorized what he had to say about a transfer to the Georgetown hospital and conveyed it to Mrs. Greenhow by spoken word. Rose did at least respond to Lily. It was to ask Harry for money. He was to deliver it by Rose's sister, a Mrs. Leonard. She said nothing more.

Harry did as asked, sending Rose fifty dollars. A few days later a male prisoner over at the Old Capitol was shot by a guard he tried to bribe. A suspected Confederate spy, the unfortunate fellow apparently used the same fifty-dollar banknote Harry had given Rose. How she had gotten it to him was another of the mysteries of her murky calling.

The sister was arrested and held at the now very crowded "Fort Greenhow" for several days. She held her tongue, confessing nothing and implicating no one, and was released. She fled from town without saying a word to Harry. He would have been so happy if Rose had done just that when he'd asked her.

Finally, Harry decided to risk all and visit her again—suspicions and consequences be damned. It didn't surprise him upon arriving at the prison to discover that she had thoroughly charmed one of her jailers—a young lieutenant named Carleton—who seemed to hold every wish of hers a command. If she wished to see Harry, Harry would be admitted at once, the lieutenant told him. If not, then not.

Harry was taken to a side room and told to wait. They closed the door behind him and he shortly began to feel a prisoner himself.

When it opened again, Leahy came in.

"Come with me, Raines," he said.

"Am I to see Mrs. Greenhow?"

"No. We are going for a walk."

Leahy led him back out onto the street, his rapid pace drawing them swiftly away in the direction of Lafayette Park. Harry tried pausing, as though to look at the work under way at the neaby War Department, but Leahy hurried him on. The hammering of the laborers echoed behind them, sounding like slow, carefully fired musket shots.

"Mr. Pinkerton is persuaded that you are only trying

to regain Mrs. Greenhow's confidence, that you hope to learn some more from her before her fate is decided. That all this letter writing and such is in the line of duty for a captain in the U.S. Secret Service."

"The first part's true."

Leahy shook his head. "I am not persuaded, Raines. I know what you're up to. And it riles me, lad. This lady is the enemy."

"Mr. Leahy . . ."

Leahy preferred to be called simply "Boston," as most knew him, but Harry still found the name odd upon his tongue.

"What is all this concern about her health?" the Irishman asked. "That damned woman has a stronger constitution than any horse in your stable."

"I fear for her nonetheless. I want her under the care of Phineas Gregg."

"He has agreed to this?"

"To treating her. In principle."

"Colonel Gregg is very busy at his hospital. Why would he take the time to come all the way over here and bother with a Confederate spy?"

"It was my hope she could spend a few days there—at the hospital—making it less inconvenient for him."

Leahy snorted. "Not likely Mr. Pinkerton's going to stand for that." He paused. "Has she agreed to this?"

Harry shrugged. "She hasn't yet said."

"She hasn't replied?"

He decided not to mention the incident involving the fifty dollars. "No. Not in person."

"I think you'd better back away from this, Raines. I don't think this woman is your friend. And if you don't do as I suggest, Mr. Pinkerton's not going to be your friend, either."

Two days later Leahy sought Harry out again, this time in the bar of the Willard, where Harry had been drinking with the writer Nathaniel Hawthorne—an antislavery man, to be sure, but a Democrat who'd held political patronage jobs in the administration of his childhood friend, the unfortunate Franklin Pierce.

They'd been arguing about what Harry considered Pierce's fecklessness, especially on the slavery question, when Leahy approached. The writer seized upon the opportunity to make a hasty departure, leaving Harry to pay for the drinks.

"That man writes about sin," Leahy said. "Without redemption."

"The most common kind."

"This might interest you," Leahy said, accepting a lemonade on the house. He took a sip of his drink, then set down the glass. "Mrs. Greenhow's daughter has taken sick."

"How sick?"

"She's not near death. It's the measles. Pinkerton has agreed to let her have another doctor."

"Mrs. Greenhow has asked for Gregg?"

"Never mentioned his name. She requested a Dr. MacMillan—brother of a major in the provost guard. She says he's a gentleman—as Dr. Stewart is not."

"Nothing about Dr. Gregg?"

"Not a word about him; not a word about you. Best put her from your mind, Raines."

Harry nodded, staring at his glass. "Your advice is duly noted, Mr. Leahy."

"The Rebel spies we should be concerning ourselves with now are the ones who *aren't* in jail—yet."

"That's likely half the city of Washington."

"So, lad, we should get to work." Leahy finished his lemonade.

"What does Pinkerton want me to do?"
"For now, just stay out of trouble."

HARRY finally figured that, at the least, he had done his duty by Rose Greenhow as best he could. If nothing was to come of his effort, that was her fault. It wasn't very damned easy rescuing a damsel in distress if she persisted in preferring the dragon to her knight in shining armor.

It occurred to him that might be what Rose Greenhow really wanted. Martyrdom was a role infinitely preferable to mere espionage, effective as she might have been at the latter. Martyrdom was public, as spying was not. Mrs. Greenhow loved drama, loved the stage, loved attention. She should have been an actress.

He lingered in the bar for more than an hour after Leahy had left, thinking that as good a place as any to stay out of trouble. He was pondering the wisdom of lingering another hour or more when he felt a familiar tug at his sleeve. He looked down to find once again the grimy face of Homer where he wished it wasn't.

"What's he want now?" Harry asked. "He was just here."

"Wasn't him," said Homer. "Wasn't no man. Was a woman. Real pretty woman, mister. She say come quick."

The boy handed Harry a small, folded note. It was written on very fine paper, in a fine hand, though it had been dirtied and crumpled somewhat in Homer's care.

There was only one word on it: *Ella*.

MOLLIE Turner ran one of the better whorehouses in the capital, rated among the first class of Washington's bawdy establishments by the provost marshal's office, which attempted to regulate them. Though her enterprise occupied a rather large and shabbily elegant house at 62 C Street, she employed only three prostitutes—all beauties and much in demand—deriving a substantial portion of her income by renting out bedrooms by the night and hour to couples who paid well for her discretion.

One suite of rooms on the third floor of the house had no part in Mollie's business, however. These were the quarters of a lady who was an inmate of the house solely because she was Mollie's sister.

Only eighteen, just a few months older than Harry's rambunctious cousin-by-marriage, Belle Boyd, Ella Turner was as worldly and self-possessed and well read a woman as Harry had ever met. She had hair the color of burnished gold, large green eyes, a patrician carriage, and a figure worthy of the artist Ingres's *Grande Odalisque,* whose classical, small-featured face her own much resembled. She was esteemed by some as the most beautiful woman in Washington—an assertion Harry could not fault, though proper society in the city faulted everything about her.

It was well that she was so blessed, for the love of her life was held to be "the handsomest man in America"—the actor John Wilkes Booth.

And, though Booth's conquests were said to be numbered in the hundreds—and included Harry's inamorata, Caitlin Howard—the only woman Booth was said to truly love was Ella Turner.

Ella had saved Harry's life once, shooting down a drunken criminal bent on staving his head in with a club in a late-night encounter on C Street near Murder Bay, outside her sister's house of horizontal "refreshment," but he had otherwise been in the woman's company only three times before.

She was where she was usually to be found when not with Booth, in her richly furnished sitting room, occupied with a book. Harry was admitted by a maid, who scurried away as soon as he stepped through the door to what Ella called "her apartments."

"Shut the door, Captain."

He did so, carefully and quietly. There were only a very few people in the federal city who knew of his government employment and rank. It bothered him inordinately that Ella Turner had become one of them—even to the extent of his rank. She had sworn to him she would never reveal this knowledge, offering as well to keep him supplied with information. Certainly she was aware that Harry's superiors had the power to shut her sister Mollie's business down and pack the both of them off to the horrors of the "Blue Jug" city jail. They could do so on their own whim, without recourse to writ, warrant, or any other legal nicety.

Still, Harry didn't quite trust her, and viewed her frequent references to his Secret Service rank as an implicit form of threat. She had a disconcerting ability to make a man feel powerless in her presence. He wondered if she had the same effect on Wilkes Booth. Certainly no other woman did.

"You have something for me, Miss Turner?" He put it that way to avoid acknowledging that he had been summoned, as though by royal command.

"A glass of sherry, if you like. If not, I would like one, if you would be so kind."

As usual, she was dressed in green—a cotton dress this hot night, and not the satin she had last worn in his presence. It was cut low, and it seemed unlikely she wore anything beneath it. She reclined on a chaise longue near her shuttered window, the gaslight bright. Without his eyeglasses, Harry could not quite tell the title of her book. He was curious, as this woman made him feel about so many things.

He poured for them both. As he handed her a glass, her fingers brushed his—a deliberate occurrence. He took a seat in the chair across the room from her, crossing his legs in gentlemanly fashion. After a small sip of the excellent sack, he sat back and waited. Her eyes, like a cat's, watched his every motion.

Suddenly she smiled, lowering her eyelids.

"My beloved Wilkes would like to return to this city," she said.

"Surely he is free to do so."

"You know that he is not. Certain persons are suspicious of his loyalties."

"Suspicious? He goes about damning the Union and smuggling contraband to the Confederates and calling Virginia 'my country.' Wish he'd stop that, Miss Turner. He's a Maryland man. Spent less than two years in Richmond. At all events, his celebrity should guarantee his liberty wherever he goes."

Her eyes lifted to meet his. "It's a dangerous time, Captain Raines. Civil liberties suspended in Baltimore. Elected officials jailed on military order. Secret police everywhere. He is worried he'll be molested in this city. He also has business in the South—and theatrical commitments."

They stared at each other for a long moment.

"Mr. Booth is no friend of mine," he said finally.

"He's not interested in your friendship. He is aware that you are connected to powerful men. He wants to make use of the friends you already have."

"I would more readily help you than him."

She colored slightly. "I fear he's aware of that. I told him of our last encounter, and it did not please him."

"The handsomest man in America, jealous?"

"He is also the vainest. And when angered, he can get a little crazy. Please, Harry. Do him this favor, and you will do us all one. Me, and your friend Caitlin Howard."

Harry sighed. "What does he seek?"

"He wants a guarantee that he will not be molested by authorities here."

"I can't guarantee that for myself," Harry said.

"Harry, please. I know you are well acquainted with President Lincoln, and many other gentlemen of consequence. You can help Wilkes. You know it."

"But I have no inclination to do so."

She hesitated. "You may. Your friend Caitlin is with him. If you agree to this, you will have her back here with you soon—as I will have him. All he asks is a guarantee."

"Where is he?"

"In Detroit. A theatrical engagement. From there he goes to Buffalo, and then Cincinnati, and then he would like to return home. To here."

"I cannot be ordering the president about—or making promises in the name of high officials. Surely not for some corrupt bargain between you and me involving affairs of the heart."

She swung her long legs over the side of the chaise and sat up, stretching out her bare, slender arms. "Very well, Harry, I'll offer you a different kind of bargain. I said I would keep you informed of important matters if I could. Guarantee Wilkes's safety, and I will provide you with knowledge of a very important matter."

"But what sort of guarantee? How can I guarantee anything?"

"A pass, Captain. An official military pass permitting him to come and go as he requires. In and out of the city. Across Union Army lines." Her eyes held him. "A pass signed by President Lincoln or General McClellan. One that will not be questioned by anyone."

Harry stared down at the floor. "That's no small thing to ask."

"I told you I'd trade for it. Information."

"And what is that?"

"There is someone in Washington City who wants you killed."

A small tremor ran down Harry's back and his flesh turned everywhere cold.

"Who?" he asked.

"It sorrows me, Harry, that I do not know. But there is someone out there, and this person has put a bounty on your head. I don't know how much it is, but it is generous. Thugs in the street are talking about it. One of them may get brave enough to take up the offer."

"Do they say why I'm to be killed?"

"No. These are perilous times, Captain Raines, and the city is full of desperate men. You have enemies on both sides of this war now."

"Are you suggesting I leave Washington?"

"That's for you to decide. I am only warning you, in return, I trust, for the document I mentioned, so that Wilkes may return."

"So you'd have him here and me gone."

"You vex me, Harry Raines. I would have the both of you alive and safe."

He set down his glass and rose. "I will take my leave of you."

She stood as well. "Your word, sir?"

"I'll make inquiries about it." He paused. "As long as

Booth breaks no law and raises no hand against the Union, there may be no problem."

"A pass."

"I'll see."

He kissed her hand. She continued her hold on to his, then rose on tiptoe to kiss his cheek. Unlike many women in Washington, especially in her sister's profession, her breath was very sweet.

"I have affection for you, Captain. I hope you live, as I know we will have further business."

"We shall see, Miss Turner."

He had taken note of the book she had been reading. It was a bound volume of Edgar Allan Poe's *Tales of Terror and Detection*.

OUTSIDE, he glanced warily to either side, deciding to proceed to the respectable precincts of Pennsylvania Avenue by the most direct route possible. Stepping off the curb and out of the reach of the street lamp, he looked left and right again. He had reached the other side and nearly turned the corner when there came the crack of a gunshot and the whistle of a bullet seeking its mark.

Chapter 5

HARRY sat in the shade of the porch of his farm near Shepherdstown, looking up from the rifle he'd been cleaning to observe the galloping rider who had turned into the lane from the Martinsburg Road without slowing his horse.

Back in Washington, only Pinkerton, Leahy, and Caesar Augustus knew where Harry had gone—and none of them had found a reason to disturb him in nearly two months of exile. He'd done nothing more on behalf of Rose Greenhow, and they were content to keep it that way—and keep him out of harm's way. They'd not taken happily to gunshots fired at members of the U.S. Secret Service in the nation's capital.

Now this rider, moving with such speed and purpose.

All Pinkerton had asked Harry to do while holing up in this refuge was to watch for Confederate agents trying to cross into the North, and to assist fugitive slaves attempting precisely the same thing. Before the war, Harry had allowed one of his barns to be used as a way station for the "Underground Railroad," which was run locally by a Shepherdstown blacksmith named Jay Hurley. The farm was close to a good Potomac ford and the short distance from there across a narrow stretch of Maryland into the free state of Pennsylvania made it very useful to such visitors.

These fugitives were still turning up—if not at Harry's place, then at Hurley's blacksmith shop. He was a friend of Harry's, and informed him whenever he had African visitors taking shelter in his cellar. Harry had talked to perhaps two dozen since coming here. Pinkerton set great store by the intelligence to be had from these people, though Harry was dubious. They very naturally avoided any contact with Confederate soldiery while on the run, and could have no very precise idea of troop movements and numbers. When they did encounter Southern military, and survived to tell about it, they tended to exaggerate the numbers. Harry had done the same thing the first time he'd come under enemy fire.

Pinkerton's habit was to send such raw intelligence directly to McClellan, but Harry was reluctant to encourage this, fearing it would only aggravate the general's already excessive caution. He consequently had sent few such reports to Washington. Now he wondered if this rider had come to reproach him for this lack.

Upon reflection, he hadn't really made much of a contribution to the Union effort since joining the Secret Service. His only real accomplishment, he supposed, was the one he'd tried to undo: Mrs. Greenhow's arrest and imprisonment. He owed Mr. Lincoln's cause more than that, especially when other men were dying for it, not taking their ease on a country horse farm.

The rider was intruding upon an incomparably lovely and peaceful day, the autumn air pleasantly warmed by the sun, the sky a clear and gentle blue except for a line of haze lying over the long ridge to the east called South Mountain. Migratory birds were calling in flight. Harry's large herd of horses was browsing and grazing quietly in the meadow that stretched from his house down to the Potomac. He'd not heard a cannon or musket shot in all these weeks. He wished this rider would go away.

Pinkerton had provided Harry with an excellent pair of army binoculars. Putting them to use, he noted that the man was wearing a coat that was either gray or covered with dust.

It was difficult to determine the man's flag. At least two of the Confederate units Harry had seen at the Battle at Bull Run had been wearing blue, and there was a Union cavalry troop operating in Maryland across the Potomac that favored gray. Some Massachusetts and New York units wore gray as well.

This confusion of uniforms would present a problem only if the Northern forces moved to engage the South in actual battle. There seemed little danger of that. General McClellan was still using the army for little more than martial drills and parades.

The rider disappeared briefly behind a stand of trees, emerging in a cloud of dust and pounding on, ever nearer. Instead of halting to lower the bar of Harry's snake rail fence, he jumped it, clearing the top nicely.

Harry's young "cousin" Belle Boyd was seated on the porch with him, sewing.

"I'll bet you that is a cavalryman," she said. "A Southern cavalryman. No Yankee can ride that good."

She spoke with some authority on horsemanship. Harry had seen her ride her horse Fleeter at full gallop while standing on the saddle.

"If he's Rebel, it could be a message from my father," Harry said, still following the rider's progress up the lane. "In which case, I'd have to wonder how he found out I'm here."

Harry's father and brother commanded cavalry units with Confederate General James Longstreet's corps, somewhere in northern Virginia near Washington.

"Oh dear," said Belle, who sometimes used stronger language. "Now I think he's a Yankee."

Harry couldn't tell. "You sure? That's a gray coat."

"Harrison. I see lots better'n you. He's wearin' Yankee pants and Yankee boots and he's settin' on a Yankee saddle."

Squinting, Harry focused the field glasses. The rider had red facings on the lapels of his uniform coat, which was gray, but definitely Union. He'd seen the like many times in Washington.

"Better get yourself inside, Belle. There are some in the Union Army who'd still like to see you strung up for what you did Independence Day."

Belle had shot a Union Army sergeant to death at her mother's house at Martinsburg that July Fourth. Her plea of self-defense against the marauding, threatening rogue had been accepted by the local Union commander, but she had bent the truth—and then bragged about the deed to Southern newspaper reporters far too much in the ensuing weeks.

"You mean hanged like our friend Rose Greenhow?" Belle said.

"What do you mean? Have you heard anything?"

"Just wouldn't be surprised they hang her, now she's in the clutches of that beast Lincoln."

"My neutrality in this quarrel," said Harry, dishonestly laying claim to something he'd resolutely abandoned three months before, "does not extend to tolerance of remarks like that. I can't believe the president would order the death of a woman."

"Why not? We're the equal of men. Rose and I are, sure enough. And if she goes to the gallows, Harry, I'm going to blame you. I may even shoot you. I don't believe you played a part in this, but I'm guessin' you could have stopped them."

"Now, how could I do that?"

"You know all kinds of important Yankees."

Belle knew Harry did some work with the federal government but thought it was pretense—a cover for what she considered his real role as a Southern spy. She couldn't believe that the son of a Southern planter could be a foe of secession.

"I warned her, Belle. You were my messenger. She wouldn't listen and paid the price. Now go. Another fence and he's here."

She rose obediently—though there was never any guarantee that she'd stay obedient—and retreated into the parlor.

Harry stood as the man trotted his mount up to the porch, amazed to see the splendidly arrayed fellow once again.

"Well, I see you've been promoted," Harry said.

"I'm afraid it's my father's doing," said Templeton Saylor as he dismounted. "It was his notion I should enter the army a colonel, if not full brigadier. As our regiment has a superfluity of those, he was disappointed, but seems to be trying to get me there with a promotion a week. I started this war a second lieutenant."

The captain's bars on the shoulders of Saylor's well-tailored uniform had been replaced with a major's insignia.

"Do you want to command a regiment? I thought you liked cavalry patrols. Operating on your own."

"Want to do the honorable thing, Harry. Whatever that may prove to be."

The newly minted major had allowed his horse to become lathered. If the ability to compel an animal to do what it didn't want to do was the measure of a good horseman, then Harry judged Saylor to be among the best. The poor beast he'd just taken over all those fences looked unwilling, if not unable, to step across a single fallen log.

"Where'd you get that nag?" Harry asked. "Not exactly what I'd expect to find you aboard on a morning ride through Central Park."

"Bought it from Sam Buckeys. At any rate, my regiment did."

"Pity the poor beast didn't go to the other side. I'd like to see this Jeb Stuart so badly mounted."

"Might buy another from you while I'm here."

"A business happily arranged, sir," Harry said. "Your visit comes as a surprise."

"The army is on the move, my friend. At least my small portion of it is. And it would seem your assistance is required."

He smiled. Saylor was not yet twenty-five. Harry could not imagine him a major, but there were generals in both armies as young.

"The army is here? McClellan?"

Saylor stepped onto the porch, dropping his dusty hat onto Harry's table and sinking onto a chair.

"At Poolesville, Maryland. Downriver. Only a division—under General Stone. McClellan's still in Washington."

"Poolesville's a long ride from here. How did you know where to find me?"

"Instructions on where to find you came with this." He reached into his tunic and produced a letter. "I've no idea who it's from."

"They send a major to deliver my mail?"

"I volunteered. I was getting bored. Thought I'd see a bit of the country. Not far from Pennsylvania, are we?"

"About twenty miles—due north across the river and that little strip of Maryland." Harry took the letter. For a foolish instant he hoped it might be from Caitlin, but she'd have no access to the military post. As he should have supposed, the letter was from Pinkerton, which was to say, it was signed "Major E. J. Allen," Pinkerton's nom de guerre.

Captain, it said, employing the military rank Harry had been given in the Secret Service. *You are to proceed directly to Stone's Division. Attach yourself to Colonel Baker. Safeguard his life with your own. He has a most important friend. Tell no one of this.*

"Who is Colonel Baker?" Harry asked.

"Surely you've heard of him?" Saylor said. "Edward Baker? Until the war he was a senator from Oregon. And California before that. They offered him a major generalship—he fought in the Mexican thing—but he turned it down. Took a colonel's rank with a Pennsylvania regiment instead. They're at Poolesville with us."

"Pennsylvania? But he's a Westerner."

"Baker's the man who kept California and Oregon free states. He's from Illinois. He is Mr. Lincoln's very closest friend. They grew up together and were in Congress together. The Pennsylvanians have become so fond of him they renamed the outfit 'the California Regiment' in his honor. Certainly looks the part of the noble warrior. You'd almost think him a gentleman, and not a rustic, like his friend Lincoln."

"Baker's in Poolesville now?"

"Yes. Do you have business with him?"

"This message suggests that I do."

"Really?"

Pinkerton had said to tell no one.

"It's from a mutual friend, who asks me to do Baker a small service."

"This friend must be a man of some consequence. The letter was given special priority. Didn't know a Southern gentleman could be so highly regarded by the federal service."

"I'm not highly regarded. That's why I'm out here." Harry thought Saylor looked a little dusty. "May I offer you refreshment? I have lemonade, fresh cider, and whiskey."

Saylor smiled. "Obliged, Harry. Obliged. I'll have all three, if I might, in the order you spoke them."

Harry gave a quick nod of a bow and went inside, quickly dragging Belle away from the window where she'd been lurking, and taking her into the kitchen.

"Much as I've enjoyed your company, 'cousin,' I want you away from here," he said.

She stood at the cupboard. There was a crimson paper rose in a small vase. She took it out, twisting it back and forth in her fingers.

"What's that Yankee son of a bitch want?" she asked.

"I think they want me to provide them with some horses," he said, keeping the truth from her as well. "I'm going to sell one to this officer. Nothing to do with you. Let us endeavor to keep it that way. For your own good."

"Maybe he's got news of Rose Greenhow."

"He's from New York City. With a cavalry regiment. Very much a Yankee. I doubt they've met."

"Is he a friend of yours?"

"Yes."

"Then he's a lucky man, for otherwise I would shoot him down for a dog."

A few minutes later she was thundering over the meadow on her horse Fleeter, heading for the Martinsburg Road.

WITH Harry leading the way, he and Saylor took a back road down to Harpers Ferry, crossed the Potomac on the Baltimore & Ohio Railroad bridge, and followed the Maryland shore downriver by means of the C&O Canal towpath.

They passed a number of Union pickets. Because of Saylor's rank, none challenged Harry. They encountered no sign at all of a Confederate presence, though Harry was sure there were Rebels all along the Virginia side of the river.

"You ever been under fire, Harry?" Saylor asked as they slowed their mounts to a walk along a lonely stretch of canal upriver from Licksville, Maryland.

Harry had sold him a big bay gelding with a particularly smooth gait. He himself was on his favorite horse, Rocket, hoping he would not endanger the big animal by getting caught up in some battle.

"Haven't made a career of it. Had a few rounds come my way at Bull Run, but none that seemed truly aimed at me."

The shot fired at him outside Ella Turner's had missed him by only a foot, but that had nothing to do with battle.

"I was in the rear at Bull Run," said Saylor. "The affair turned into a rout before I could reach the line."

"Then you were fortunate."

"I think we will see battle soon."

"Would you like that?"

"That's why we're in uniform."

"The honorable thing."

"Yes."

"President Lincoln wants a battle soon as well. You have something in common."

"Well, he's certainly common." Saylor gave a small laugh. "Not much of a gentleman, is he?"

"Not much of a Harvard one."

"But he's an educated man. I've heard him speak. Brilliant."

"Yes, he is."

"Yet to read the newspapers, you'd wonder."

THE Poolesville encampment was considerable. General Stone, who commanded, had close to two thousand men gathered there. He'd had reports of Confederates gathered in some strength on the other side of the Potomac—most of them said to be collected around the town of Leesburg—but no one had any idea of their number. Harry supposed there were enough waiting at the ready on both sides for any kind of forward movement to precipitate a battle.

During the journey, having a care not to reveal the reason for his interest, Harry tried to draw Saylor out about Colonel Baker and why the officer might be in danger beyond that expected for army officers commanding combat troops in the field. His friend, alas, was of little help.

"If you mean is Baker rash and incautious," Saylor said. "I've heard that. If there is a fight, we'd best stay clear of him."

UPON learning of Harry's presence in the camp, General Stone sent for him. Entering the farmhouse Stone had taken over as a headquarters, Harry was impressed by the man's martial appearance. He looked more a shining example of a professional soldier than even General McClellan—erect bearing, perfectly groomed hair and beard, an honest face, and bright, quick, intelligent eyes. A career officer who had graduated from West Point near the top of his class, Stone, too, had fought in Mexico, commanding a unit in which Baker had served as a mere lieutenant.

Harry inquired whether the general was interested in fresh mounts and began an encomium on the many merits of those he might have available in Shepherdstown, but Stone cut him short with a commanding gesture of the hand.

"Already have new animals," he said, "though from the looks of them, I may be in need of newer before long." His eyes narrowed slightly. "I know who you are, Raines."

"Sir?"

Stone rose from his camp chair, went to the opening of his tent, glanced out, then turned back to Harry.

"I'll say it this way," he said. "I know who Major E. J. Allen is. You got a letter he forwarded through this command. And you are with us now because Pinkerton bids it. Isn't that so?"

Harry decided against blurting out anything about protecting Colonel Baker from peril. At best, it would sound as though Lincoln were playing favorites to the point of providing bodyguards for friends among the officers. At worst, it might sound lunatic. Officers advancing with their regiments against massed musket fire were not easy to protect.

"I'm not sure why I'm here, other than that I'm

directed to be so, sir," he said. "Perhaps Major Allen is concerned about the Confederates across the river, and thinks I may be of help to you."

"You know this country?"

Harry nodded. "I grew up down at the Tidewater end of the Potomac and have a farm up the other end near Shepherdstown. Rode a lot between them over the years."

Stone went to a map. "You are familiar with the area around Leesburg?"

"Yes, sir."

"I'm putting a few men across the river tonight. Would you be willing to guide them?"

"Certainly. But where?"

"Wherever there's Rebels. I need a better idea of their strength—and whether there's good ground over there to put a large force across tomorrow. The Confederate commander is said to be a fellow named Evans. Colonel Nathan Evans. Know him?"

"No, sir."

"Shanks Evans. West Point man, from South Carolina. They say he was the one who held the Stone Bridge at Bull Run against us."

"Then he's an able officer. I was there. The men who held the bridge kept the Union assault from succeeding. It wasn't all this fellow they call 'Stonewall.'"

"Heroes are a thing for the newspapers to decide, Raines. No concern of ours. 'Specially Rebel heroes." He frowned, glancing at a map. "Find the Fifteenth Massachusetts. Colonel Devens. They'll be moving onto Harrison's Island. Look for a Captain Philbrick. Captain Chase Philbrick. He'll be taking a picked group the rest of the way across to Virginia to scout the opposite shore. You join 'em."

Stone spoke the words as orders. Nothing was voiced as request. Harry was supposed to answer only to Pinkerton. But the Scotsman answered directly to McClellan, who doubtless had directly ordered these movements—at long last.

Harry wasn't about to argue.

Chapter 6

THE Union camp was not preparing for battle. Gambling, drinking, and rowdiness were as much in evidence as good manners were not. Harry might as well have been in Washington's Murder Bay district on a Saturday night.

Though it was not long past sunset, brawling had begun in earnest and Harry heard a musket discharged up the line that he doubted very much had been fired at the enemy. No one had seen any enemy. The common joke here was that the smell from the Yankees' open garbage pits and latrines had driven all the Rebs out of northern Virginia.

As Saylor understood matters, General Stone had for several days been reluctant to make any reconnaissance across the river to look for Confederates. A Union spy named Francis Buxton had reported Rebel strength around Leesburg, only a few miles distant, at twenty-seven thousand. That was better than ten times Stone's force. The number seemed so exaggerated to Harry that he wondered if the source of Buxton's information was General McClellan.

But now, apparently, Stone wanted better information. He gave orders to Colonel Charles Devens of the 15th Massachusetts to procure it. Devens had decided to send Captain Philbrick and a small group of about twenty men to make a foray onto the opposite shore and look for Confederates. If they found any, they were to count them, map them, and hurry back.

Unlike Devens, a patrician Boston lawyer with the beard of an ancient Persian potentate, Philbrick was not one of the ubiquitous Harvard men in this little Poolesville army. Neither had he much military experience. He commanded a company of the 15th but had begun the year as a stonecutter in Northbridge, Massachusetts. His second in command, a lieutenant named Church Howe, had been an accountant.

There was a Harvard man in Philbrick's reconnaissance group, however—a friend of Saylor's and a first lieutenant all of twenty years old named Oliver Wendell Holmes. Though in a class three years behind Saylor, he'd gotten to know the New Yorker through the amateur theatricals they'd both participated in at college. Holmes had received his commission only three months before—six days after graduating from Harvard. He belonged to the 20th Massachusetts, which was camped a little downriver at a place called Edwards Ferry, but he had heard about the scouting mission and volunteered.

"My father didn't encourage me to enlist so I could sit around in camp picking up bad habits," Holmes had said.

The father, also named Oliver Wendell Holmes, was famous as a poet and essayist and the author of something called *The Autocrat of the Breakfast Table,* a work of which Harry was ignorant. He liked the young lieutenant, however, and was agreeable to accepting the man's offer to share an "A" tent with him and two other junior officers during his stay.

It didn't seem likely he'd be spending much of the night on an army cot. They were supposed to cross the river on their patrol directly after the midday meal, but Colonel Devens had been at church and missed the initial orders. By the time Devens returned, received General Stone's instructions, selected and organized his party, and sent it off toward the river, the sun had left the sky. There was some illumination from the twilight and rising moon, but essentially the patrol was going to have to look for the enemy in the dark. The more sensible thing would have been to use daylight and some commanding height to survey the Virginia landscape for movement. The leaves were thinning in the advancing fall.

"The fighting at Bull Run, did it last into the night?" Holmes asked as they prepared to leave the shelter of the Maryland shore for the assembly point on Harrison's Island.

"Only the running part. The battle itself was over well before sundown."

"I should hope not to run—should we have a battle."

"I fear swimming may be more in order tonight," Harry said.

They waded from the Maryland bank across a wide shallows to the near shore of Harrison's Island, which would serve as a forward base for their undertaking. Philbrick had scouted the isle some two weeks before, finding only an old Negro named Old Phil, an unfortunate fellow as decrepit as the few, crumbling buildings on the elongated, forested island.

Old Phil had been sent north into Maryland—with luck, to a happier situation—and Union pickets had moved onto the island, digging a few entrenchments. There were also three boats beached there, large enough to accommodate Philbrick's small party, but woefully inadequate for any sizable force to cross in. The main river channel between the island and the farther Virginia shore was deep, and the current swift.

"Why cross at this place?" Harry asked. "Why not down at Edwards Ford, where we can wade across and then move on Leesburg from the east?"

"Raines, you ain't even in the army," said Philbrick. "Leave this to us who are."

In the moonlight, the steep bluff opposite was clearly defined, as were individual trees. Harry put on his spectacles and scanned the high ground, but could see no movement.

"That's Ball's Bluff," he said. "The slopes are steep. The trails up the ravines are narrow. If there are Rebel pickets up there, we're dead."

"It's close to this island, and we got that for our own," said Philbrick.

"But you don't know what's up there."

"That's what we came to see—and what you're supposed to find out for us. Let's go, Raines. Stop your complainin' and get into a boat."

There weren't oars enough for Harry to have to handle one, so he sat quietly in his seat, up near the bow, his eyes steady on the tree line silhouetted against the night sky. There was a bit of mist gathering. Harry guessed there'd be fog along the river by the time they returned—whenever that would be.

NOT a shot was fired against them. Not a word of alarm or warning was sounded. The water was deep and Harry had to slosh in up to his coattails to get ashore on the Virginia side. The soldiers parted to let him pass, expecting him to lead the way. Harry asked for young Holmes to accompany him.

"Have you good eyesight?" Harry asked.

"Yes, I do, indeed, sir," Holmes said, with great eagerness.

Harry raised a finger to his lips, then spoke more softly. "Then stay close and look sharp. And don't speak unless you see something."

As they started up the trail, Harry noted that Philbrick was staying about a dozen men back in the file.

They startled a night bird and a brace of deer, but nothing that might give a whoop for Jeff Davis. Harry had been to this place only a few times before—riding between Frederick, Maryland, and Leesburg and taking Nolands Ford instead of Edwards. Still, the trail leading up from the shore was easy enough to follow. A tiny stream burbled alongside it. One could ascend the path by sound alone.

At the top there was a small clearing, but the woods around it were thick and full of noisy leaves.

"Well, damn all. We've invaded the Confederacy," said Philbrick, drawing near finally.

"A few feet of it," said Holmes, prompting a quick, dark look from the captain.

"I want to go on to Leesburg," the captain said.

"All the way to Leesburg?"

"Yes!"

Harry could guess Philbrick's goal here—a triumphant return to camp, a welcome due a hero. All the way to Leesburg and back. A daring exploit. Massachusetts newspapers please copy.

"I thought the goal was to locate the enemy," Harry said.

"Go to Leesburg, and I'm sure we will."

Harry vaguely remembered the route, and in the few places where he didn't, the moonlight allowed him to just keep moving west until they at last came to a narrow lane that bore south obliquely.

"As memory serves," he said, "this reaches a good road, and the road leads due south to Leesburg."

Philbrick grunted. "You go on ahead. Take Holmes with you. If you run into anything, send him back to us fast."

AT length, the meandering lane reached a parting of the woods and they emerged on a farmer's harvested cornfield. The bunched corn stalks startled Harry at first, for they looked so much like men in the moonlight. But their formation was wrong. There was too much distance between the forms. Real soldiers would be in close formation, as centuries-old tactics required.

If there were some Confederate pickets about, however, they would more likely be in hiding, perhaps up in a tree with a view of the lane. There were two white-barked sycamores directly across the shorn cornfield, both of them broadly limbed and looking eminently climbable. They possessed a view of all the open ground.

Harry hunched down a little lower, wishing Caesar Augustus were with him and not this Harvard boy.

Holmes was looking at Harry, as if waiting for a decision.

"What do we do?" the lieutenant whispered finally.

"We need to get to the other side, but I don't like all this open ground," Harry said.

"Why don't we skirt the field?" Holmes said. "I'll go 'round along the right and you take the left. We'll meet on the other side."

This was sensible. Harry said so, adding, "If someone takes a shot at you, hit the ground and find some cover. I'll come at him from the flank. If the shot's fired at me, you come up on the flank."

"And if there're shots fired at both of us?"

"Then we run like blazes back down the lane."

Harry watched as the young Holmes slipped off to his right, hugging the tree line. Whatever stealth he managed by staying out of the open was undone by the sound of his stepping on the dry-leaf-strewn ground. Moving to the left, Harry encountered the same problem himself.

Finally, he took to the open field, where the ground was clean and quiet. Darting from corn stalk to corn stalk, he reached the far side ahead of Holmes. When the younger man rejoined him, they huddled by the brush for a very long moment, listening.

"Now I'm wondering if there's a Confederate soldier within a mile of here," Harry said finally, in a whisper. "This is good defensive ground and they haven't even posted a picket."

"They may have patrols out."

"Have you been in combat, Lieutenant?"

"No, sir. But I've been reading about it. Crimean War."

"I hope this won't be anything like that. If you'd be so kind, would you fetch up Captain Philbrick and the others?"

AFTER he was rejoined by Philbrick and the rest of the detail, they made their creeping way on down the road, which was well rutted, pausing finally on a slight wooded rise that looked upon a crossroads.

"Where are we?" Philbrick asked.

"About two miles from Leesburg. That should be Edwards Ferry Road."

"Two miles from Leesburg? Or possibly only one?"

"Possibly, but I don't think so."

Philbrick had brought a pair of field glasses. He raised them to his eyes, leaning against the tree to steady them.

"I see a light," he said.

"Could be a farmhouse."

"Could be Leesburg."

Harry saw where this was heading. "I can't say it's not," he said.

"We'll go back," Philbrick said, lowering the binoculars. "Orders were to make a reconnaissance." He stood up. "I want to return by a different route. See more ground."

"There's a trail that runs nearer the river, but it curves a lot and we'd have to cross two deep ravines."

"Sounds agreeable to me, but let's make haste. This patrol has taken too much time as it is."

HASTE they made. Every man in the group had volunteered for the mission, but no one seemed reluctant to be getting back to camp. As Harry and Holmes led the way, they could hear the rest of the men close behind. But crossing a sparsely treed hilltop, the captain called to them to stop.

"Over there to the left," Philbrick said. "What's that?"

Harry turned in the direction indicated, looking west between two trees to a large field in the distance. The night haze had thickened and the moonlight was not so useful.

"I'm not sure," Harry said. He glanced at Holmes, who shrugged.

Philbrick had the field glasses up. "It's an encampment!"

Harry blinked, then put on his spectacles and took the binoculars from Philbrick. He saw some distant shapes, set in rows, but there were no campfires, was no movement.

"I believe those are haystacks," Harry said.

"Clean your spectacles. I see tents. About thirty. If they're Sibley tents—and they certainly look like Sibley tents—that's twenty men a tent. Six hundred men—and the only Rebel force we've encountered."

"We didn't go very far, sir," said Holmes.

Philbrick shot him a look like a cannonade. "We've gone all the way to Leesburg, Lieutenant. Within a mile anyway."

"Those are haystacks," Harry said. "I was looking at the ones on my farm just yesterday, taking note how much they looked like tents."

"These look like tents because they *are* tents!"

"Would you like me to scout the position?" Holmes said. "Make certain what they are?"

"No," said Philbrick. "We'd be obliged to wait for you, and there's no time for that. I must report to General Stone as soon as possible." He hesitated, as though about to change his mind, then shook his head. "No. We go to Poolesville. Now."

IT was past ten o'clock when they crossed back to Harrison's Island and they consumed nearly another hour after that getting to Stone's camp. The general accepted Philbrick's report with great seriousness, going to his tent table to write a hurried note.

"I'll telegraph this intelligence to General McClellan," he said. "I expect we'll make a reconnaissance in force in the morning. Send in a full regiment. Maybe a brigade. If these are the only Rebels on hand, Captain Philbrick, we can push 'em back hard. Swing 'round and take and hold Edwards Ford. Establish ourselves on the Virginia side of the river, outflank Joe Johnston, and maybe open a new route to Richmond."

"Sir," said Holmes. "Mr. Raines here says they weren't tents. Just haystacks."

Stone looked at Harry unhappily. Philbrick spoke before Harry could manage a word.

"I rejected that assessment," the former stonecutter said. "Raines may know the ground 'round here, but he don't know the military or military equipment. Besides, it was gettin' a little misty and he needs spectacles to see good."

Turning away without giving Harry opportunity to comment, Stone dismissed them with a gentle wave of the hand. "Thank you, gentlemen. You must be tired." He stopped. "Colonel Baker wants to see you, Raines. Better go to him directly."

THE colonel had left his tent and was seated on a box in front of a campfire, reading a Washington newspaper. He continued to read it as Harry stood before him, and so Harry sat down himself, choosing a nearby log.

"You were across the Potomac?" Baker asked, without lowering the paper.

The principal story was about a clash at some place in Missouri called Lime Creek, where more than a hundred Rebel soldiers had been killed, wounded, or captured. The paper was treating it as a major engagement.

"Yes, sir."

"Any sign of the enemy?"

"Captain Philbrick thinks there was. I think what we saw was haystacks."

The paper came down. Baker turned to look at Harry with considerable steadiness. "Haystacks?"

"Philbrick's reported seeing a Rebel camp with about six hundred men in it about halfway between Harrison's Island and Leesburg."

There was a burst of laughter at some distance behind them, nervous laughter, exaggerated by drink. Baker frowned.

"Six hundred men? That's all?"

"Yes, sir."

"If the captain's correct, there will be strong sentiment to move there in force tomorrow and engage them. I expect Stone's already informed General McClellan."

Harry didn't ken how informing McClellan would engender strong enough sentiment in the man to budge even an inch in any direction. He merely nodded.

"Why do you think it's only haystacks?"

"I own a farm, Colonel. I may not know military equipment, but I know hay. Also, there wasn't a single campfire. I can count a dozen or more here in your regiment even at this hour."

Baker leaned back, draining his canteen cup and setting it carefully down on the ground.

"If they're not there, where are they?"

"It's only a guess, for we encountered none of them, but I'd say back at Leesburg. They've got to protect the town from three directions. There are Union forces down in Dranesville, up in Harpers Ferry, and here. They have to be able to meet any threat."

"And if we attack?"

"They'll come running."

"But you saw no sign of them."

"We didn't get very close to Leesburg. No matter what Philbrick says."

"You seem pretty knowledgeable about military matters after all—and you're a farmer?"

"I'm not a farmer, sir. I merely own a farm."

Someone near the camp was having trouble with horses. Harry could hear whinnies and snorts—and then swearing.

Baker took a piece of folded paper from a pocket, read it over quickly, as though familiar with its contents, then put it back. He stared at his coffee, then lifted his eyes to Harry.

"The president sent you here, didn't he, Raines?"

"No, sir."

"The truth, please!"

"It was a detective. Somebody who works for General McClellan."

"Are you known to Mr. Lincoln?"

"I am, sir."

"And you are in his service?"

"In a manner of speaking—as are we all, sir."

Baker looked about the camp, somewhat warily.

"I've received a telegraph. I believe it's from this same subordinate, though sent in the president's name. The man warns me there's a plot afoot with the president's friends the mark. I'm to be on guard. He says I'm to receive protection. Would that be you?"

"I guess so, sir."

Baker rose, slowly and majestically, his eyes on the darkness on the side of the camp nearest the river. "Mr. Raines, I command a brigade here. If I wish it, there's a major general's commission awaiting me, which would put me in command of this entire force. We're about to cross the river and I expect to do battle. Are you proposing to protect me from several thousand Confederate soldiers? How could you do that?"

"I can't, sir. I suppose my job's to see that the deck's not stacked against you, that you're at no more risk than any other Union soldier. I think the president would prefer that you accepted the general's stars and remained in a headquarters on this side of the river. It would make my job much easier."

"That is preposterous."

Harry said nothing.

"Get some sleep, Raines."

"Yes sir." Harry got up. "Good night, sir."

There was a splatter and hiss as Baker threw the remnants of his coffee into the fire. "Good night."

IT took a while for Harry to find Holmes's tent again. The other two officers were asleep but the lieutenant was sitting on the ground, reading a small book by the light of a candle.

They'd given Harry a blanket and he had his saddlebags to use for a pillow. He laid his head down on the latter, grateful that he'd have at least a few hours' sleep. Despite his fatigue, which weighed heavily upon him, slumber eluded him. Partly it was the cold, partly the odors. Harry was not taking to this soldier's life. He yearned for a bath and wished he'd brought more than a change of shirt and linen.

He lifted his head. Holmes was still at his book.

"What are you reading?" Harry asked politely.

"Something of my father's."

Harry's own father had never given him books—or read many himself. It was another thing that divided them.

"It's nice—your father sending you books."

"He didn't send it. He wrote it. It's poetry. He writes poetry. This one is called 'The Last Leaf.'" Holmes leaned closer to the candle flame, then began.

"The mossy marbles rest
On the lips that he has pressed
  in their bloom;
And the names he loved to hear
Have been carved for many a year
  On the tomb."

"Cheerful stuff," Harry said, putting his head down again.

Actually, as he thought upon the words, they were quite beautiful.

He closed his eyes. Tomb. Death. Colonel Baker.

Harry sat up. "I'm sorry," he said. "I appreciate your hospitality, Holmes, but there's a duty I'd better attend to."

Blanket and saddlebags in hand, he trudged through the encampment back to Baker's tent, finding the colonel just where he'd left him, sitting hunched by the fire, staring into it.

Harry laid out his bedroll not twenty feet behind the man, took pistol in hand, and slid under the blanket. Baker paid no attention, scarcely moved at all.

Harry watched the officer for as long as he could, but sleep finally overtook him.

Chapter 7

HARRY awakened to painfully bright daylight and someone shaking him insistently by the shoulder. Squinting, he saw a gray coat with red facings and then a lieutenant colonel's leaves on shoulder straps and for a moment he thought it was Baker. But that was a very bad guess. The president's friend was a full colonel and wore a more regulation blue.

"Stir yourself, Harry. We're off to war."

Harry blinked against the light. "Saylor?"

"You've an uncanny eye."

As Harry sat up, Saylor handed him a metal cup of steaming coffee, hot to the handle. Holding it gingerly, he took a stimulating sip, then squinted again at the young officer, his eyes moving back to the man's shoulders.

"You've been promoted again?"

Saylor smiled. "Brevet rank. I've become a staff officer. Temporary posting. Still haven't commanded more than a cavalry troop."

"You need not worry. I'm sure they'll have you replacing General McClellan himself by next week."

Harry drank some more coffee. It was hearty and good, not at all like the gritty muck he'd been served in this camp before.

"The staff I've been assigned to is Colonel Baker's," Saylor said. "I outrank everyone else on it."

"And your job is to bring civilians coffee?"

"That's just a gentlemanly courtesy. Mind your manners. My main reason for stirring you from your inordinately long slumbers is that you're wanted across the river."

"Across the river? I just got back from there. What's afoot?"

"Reconnaissance in force. McClellan's under pressure to get something going and he seems to have decided on General Stone to do it. Colonel Devens has taken five companies of the Fifteenth and Twentieth Massachusetts across to Ball's Bluff, where you were last night. Stone's sending him a few cavalrymen to scout the way to Leesburg and he wants you to accompany them. They've got a New York regiment and a Pennsylvania one going over, too."

Harry hesitated, listening. "I don't hear any firing."

"They've found no enemy. That camp you said was over there turned out to be a line of trees or haystacks or some such."

"It was Captain Philbrick who said there was a camp. I said it was haystacks."

"Well, I'm sorry, Harry, but it's you they're blaming for the bad report. Philbrick must have pointed a finger at you."

"Yet they want me to scout today?"

"Stone maybe figures you can see better during the day. Devens is going to move on to Leesburg."

"How much time do I have?"

"About enough to finish that coffee, visit the latrine,

and check your revolver loads. The cavalrymen are waiting for you on Harrison's Island with an extra horse."

"I'd rather ride my own."

"No time to fetch him."

Harry took a last, large sip of the coffee and stiffly stood up. He started toward the latrine then abruptly halted, looking anxiously about the camp.

"Where's Colonel Baker? He's not across the river, is he?"

"No. Only Devens for now. Baker's at Stone's headquarters. Why do you care so much about Baker?"

Harry looked to where a small column of infantry was marching out of the camp, heading toward the river.

"Just curious," he said.

CROSSING the river in one of the three boats they had used the previous night, Harry pondered the fact that for the first time in his life he might actually be going into battle as part of an army. He'd attended the great debacle at Bull Run merely as a spectator, putting himself in harm's way on the battlefield only once and briefly at that, extricating two frightened women from the field who had gotten caught in the mad retreat.

One of the women had been Caitlin. He wished now he'd taken the time to write her a letter before joining Stone's little army. *Should I not return* . . . or some such. He doubted she had any idea where he was. He had to wonder how much she cared.

He'd manage the letter later. Saylor could carry it for him. He was among Caitlin's many admirers and would be pleased to visit her on so romantic a mission.

Morbid mission.

"Here we are, sir," said a man at the oars. "Have a care gettin' out. It's deep."

Harry looked to the shoreline. The high water had receded somewhat, leaving the bank very muddy. "Where's the cavalry waiting?"

"Up on the bluff, I guess. Not easy gettin' a horse up there."

Harry climbed over the side of the boat and sank into water and ooze up to his waist. "Or a man," he said.

THERE were ten riders in the little cavalry unit that Harry finally located at the head of a ravine that cut through the bluff. They were under the command of a nervous young second lieutenant who seemed far more in control of his mount than he was of his men. The troopers seemed respectful of the fact that Harry presumably knew what he was doing—or at the least, where he was going—and readily moved their horses into line behind him once he was in the saddle, having beforehand been milling uselessly about. Without further comment, he spurred his borrowed animal into a trot down the remembered lane. With a jangle of spurs and sabers, they followed. The affair seemed more a parade than a patrol through enemy territory.

The patchy gray-and-black gelding they'd given him was willing enough, but moved with a slight wobble. For all he knew, another purchase from the swindling Sam Buckeys. Come a battle, and the cavalry would quickly become infantry.

Even at a trot, it took Harry's little mounted group nearly half an hour to catch up with Devens. The colonel seemed relieved by their presence, but an anxious look remained on his face.

"Can you find us a way to Leesburg?" he asked Harry.

"This is it," Harry said, with a nod down the trail toward the south. "Only road around unless you want to go a long way west. There's a trail closer to the bluffs, but it's narrow and rough. Take twice as long."

"No, no. I want to get to Leesburg fast as possible. Do you think we'll run into Rebels? That 'camp' you and Philbrick found was only trees."

"Haystacks. But we'll find Rebels."

"We haven't seen so much as a farmer with a shot-gun. And Lieutenant Holmes informs me you two didn't encounter a single Confederate last night."

Harry reined in the gelding, who was fidgeting in an irritable and irritating way. "Now they know we're coming, Colonel. And they're not going to give you Lees-burg without an argument."

"Don't want Leesburg, Raines. Just want to locate the Rebels, run them back, and get some good ground to hold this side of the river." He looked at Harry's little band of cavalry. "Only ten of you?"

"Suffices for a scouting party."

"Not if you run into more than their pickets. I'll detail one company to follow close behind you."

Unfortunately, the company he picked was Captain Philbrick's. The officer glowered at Harry as they moved on, but followed his orders and kept his men in place. Harry was pleased to have him come along in one respect. They were near the place where Philbrick had decided to turn back the night before. Now he'd see firsthand how close to Leesburg they hadn't been.

As things turned out, he was to be denied that oppor-tunity. As they ascended a gentle rise crossing an open meadow, two Union riders the young lieutenant had sent out ahead suddenly wheeled about and bolted back toward Harry and the others. A moment later a massed musket volley on the horizon produced a long, sparking line of flashes and smoke. A flight of lead balls came whistling and singing overhead, fired too high.

The young lieutenant was fighting with his horse, which had been spooked. Harry looked to a corporal mounted nearer.

"Ride back to Colonel Devens! Tell him we've run into Rebels!"

Harry had no authority to be issuing orders, but the man was happy to go. He spurred his mount hard, goading it into a full gallop. It stumbled, and almost buckled, but he kept his seat, heading for the bluff and the river landing.

The enemy having been found, there was little now for Harry to do. Engaging the Confederates they had encountered was a job for Philbrick and his infantry.

To his credit, the captain didn't shirk, nor did his men, though most of them were green recruits. Philbrick moved them at the double-quick, holding their muskets before them in the "make ready" position as they trotted over the meadow and up the slope. Harry expected more firing from above, but amazingly there was none. As Philbrick's troops, now spread out across the field, approached the top of the rise, Harry moved to join them.

Dismounting, he walked with the infantrymen to the top of the slope, peering through the high grass down the other side. He didn't want to make himself too visible to his fellow Southerners, and not just because they might send a few musket balls his way. He presumed this was a Virginia outfit, and there might be someone in its ranks who'd recognize him. He'd diminished his usefulness to Mr. Lincoln enough as it was.

The Confederate commander, still in his saddle, had begun pulling his force back off the high ground down to the tree line at the bottom. Once they reached it, they stood there, man and boy, watching and waiting.

Philbrick waved his men on over the rise. Keeping ranks, they stepped on down the slope, but still there was not so much as a pop of Rebel fire. Instead, a mad thing happened. The Confederate officer in charge down there stood up and shouted, "Halt!"

Wavering uncertainly, Philbrick's men complied. One of them shouted, absurdly, "Friends!" Others picked up the cry. "Friends! Friends!"

Did neither side recognize the other?

Philbrick, at least, seemed to know what he was about. Swearing in healthy stonecutter fashion, he waved his sword and started walking forward, bellowing, "Advance!" just once. Harry was impressed, especially when the men quickly followed.

Then it happened again. The Confederate officer below shouted out, "Halt!" Philbrick's company called out, "Friends!" The Union men stopped, then Philbrick ordered them on once more.

When it happened the third time, Harry slunk back and sat down in the grass, reducing himself to mere spectator. If this bizarre tableau ever did turn into a battle, he didn't want to be caught in the middle of it. This would be a fight between lunatics.

Finally, the advancing Union line reached to within a few dozen yards of the Rebels. The federal uniforms were dusty from the hike down the road, but the men looked like Yankees to Harry. Perhaps the Confederate commander was even more shortsighted than he.

Now at last the inevitable occurred. The Southern officer, looking at Philbrick's men face to face, realized his mistake and ordered his own first rank to kneel. A moment later both first and second Rebel ranks fired.

Three or four Northern men fell, but most of the Southern rounds, triggered nervously and too quickly, completely missed. Philbrick ordered his company into a retreat back up the slope—an order eagerly obeyed. As the federals drew back, the Confederates began moving from their position as well, but in reverse, pulling back into the shelter of the trees.

Harry got to his feet and began walking away from this daft combat. This would indeed be a long war.

Coming over the hill was another Massachusetts company sent forward by Devens as reinforcement. At the head of these troops was Lieutenant Colonel Templeton Saylor, though he seemed not to be in command.

"Good to see you still standing," he said, striding up to Harry with pistol in hand. "I feared that as scout on point, you'd take the first bullet."

"The battle started oddly. Words before the bullets. That Philbrick's mad. You'd better take over here."

Saylor scanned the field below. "I'm not sure that's in order. I was sent forward to observe—report on the enemy strength."

"Well, Templeton, observe."

The Confederates at last had decided to advance and were now coming slowly up the slope as Philbrick's men continued their uphill, backward withdrawal. Harry borrowed Saylor's field glasses, making a quick study of the Rebel line from flank to flank.

"They've been reinforced," he said. "At least two companies. Probably more on the way."

"The battle's on, then."

"They know this is no roving patrol. They'll be bringing up more troops as soon as they can." Harry handed back the binoculars. "Judging by the dust they're raising, we may already have four or five Rebel companies in front of us."

Saylor made a quick assessment, nodded, then strode over to Philbrick, as nonchalantly as asking a lady to dance at a Harvard cotillion. "I'm going to make a suggestion, Captain," he said, with some flourish. "Withdraw your men from this position and re-form back with Devens."

"We are withdrawing."

"A bit faster, then."

The former stonemason scowled, but did not question his superior—not openly, at all events.

As the Union men began hurrying back toward their main body, the Confederate firing abruptly ceased. Harry looked to see the Rebels again in retreat.

He reached into his now filthy coat for his flask.

"**W**E have one killed, two missing, and nine wounded, Colonel," said Philbrick, after saluting.

Devens, who had come up with still more Union reinforcements, frowned, more out of concern for what he should do next, it seemed, than for the losses, which were remarkably light.

"Where'd you leave the enemy?" the colonel asked.

"In possession of the field," Harry said, removing his hat to wipe the sweat from his forehead. "And heading this way."

Philbrick now gave Harry the darkest look he'd seen yet.

Devens looked to Saylor. "We'll form along this rail fence—anchoring the left flank around that house there. What's it called?"

An aide consulted a map. "Doesn't say, sir. Not on the map."

"I believe it belongs to a woman named Jackson," Harry said, stepping up from just behind Saylor.

Devens nodded, then looked up as an enlisted man came running up from the direction of Leesburg.

"They're comin' again, Colonel! They got a heap of reinforcements."

Devens glanced around him, then settled on Harry, who apparently was the most expendable of those present.

"If you would recross the river, sir," he said. "My respects to General Stone. Tell him I am engaged and the enemy is attacking."

Harry started to salute, then caught himself. "Where is Colonel Baker?" he asked.

"Your concern is with General Stone, Raines. Go find him."

Leaping onto his borrowed army horse, Harry hurried back to the bluff, finding the place aswarm with fresh troops who'd just come across the river and seemed not sure where they were to go. They were Massachusetts men, commanded by a Colonel Lee.

"Are you Raines? Raines the scout?"

"Yes, sir. Bound for General Stone across the river with a message from Colonel Devens. Are there boats there still?"

"Not enough, damn all." The white-bearded colonel relit his cigar, shoving it to a corner of his mouth. "Take a message back for me. Tell him if he wants to open a campaign here, now is the time."

Harry dismounted, moving down the steep bluff trail on foot. He had been too long absent from Colonel Baker, who he hoped was sitting safely and snug in General Stone's headquarters.

He had to dodge and scramble down the path to the river landing, as more troops were coming up—mostly single file, but sometimes in bunches. He was almost to the bottom when someone sliding on the dirt collided with him from behind. Harry picked himself up to see that it was Philbrick's man, Lieutenant Howe, the accountant.

"Battle over already?" Harry asked, helping the man to his feet. He could hear the faint rattle of musketry coming from somewhere over the bluff, though he guessed it was at some distance.

"No. Colonel Devens sent me after you—to make certain you weren't detained. You being a civilian, he was afraid someone might grab you for a Rebel."

"Obliged," said Harry. "I suppose."

"He also gave me the same message to deliver to the general."

"Then let us deliver it together so he need hear it only once."

The three large boats were plying the river between the Virginia shore and Harrison's Island like ferries, returning empty—though Harry had the uneasy feeling that might not be true for long. Reaching the island, and then the Maryland shore beyond, they proceeded down-river along the C&O. Canal towpath, which was as thick with soldiery as the Ball's Bluff trail.

Too thick by one. Coming around a bend of the canal, they encountered a tall, noble figure astride a large horse, scanning the bluffs opposite with field glasses: Colonel Edward Baker.

Looking at the two, he accepted Howe's salute, but turned to Harry when he spoke.

"You've been over across the river?" Baker asked. He seemed intensely interested, but there was no sign of fear, or the troubled look that had sat upon his counte-nance the night before.

"Colonel Devens is in a fight, sir," said Howe. "The

Rebels broke off, but they're coming up again— reinforced. We're on our way to report to General Stone."

"You're going to Stone?" Baker's question was addressed to Harry.

Harry hesitated. "Yes, sir."

"He has just placed me in command of the troops on the Virginia side," the colonel said. "I am going over there with my full force." He gave Harry an odd look. "Join me across the river, Raines, when you've made your report." He turned and spurred his horse, cantering up the towpath nimbly between the files of soldiers. Turning at a bend in the towpath, he disappeared.

"Let's go, Raines," said Howe impatiently. "Colonel Devens wants his message delivered swiftly."

"Which I'm sure you will do," Harry said, backing up a step. "I'm going back to the bluff."

"What for?"

"I think Colonel Baker would wish me to."

BAKER, unfortunately, was no longer to be found. Not on the towpath or on Harrison's Island. Clambering aboard a small boat—a river skiff that had been found somewhere and pressed into service—Harry recrossed the Potomac. Regaining the top of the bluff again, he found it swarming with Union soldiers, but none of them Baker and none with news of him.

There was loud, continuing noise now to the front— rolling volleys of musket fire near and far. This would lapse into sporadic individual shooting and then reintensify into a rattling din. An ever-thickening haze hung between the trees, lacing the air with an acrid smell. As he moved closer to the combat, a twig came spinning down from a tree above him and struck him stingingly in the ear. He'd been carrying his hat in his hand. He returned it to his head.

Devens would know Baker's whereabouts. Dodging between groups of Union soldiers, he headed toward the woods-bordered field where he'd left the Massachusetts men.

They'd been reinforced now by the Pennsylvanians who called themselves "the California regiment" and were holding firm along the line of the snake rail fence.

He found the long-bearded colonel standing with sword in hand, looking forward with great intent. Harry pulled down a rail and crossed the fence, crouching as he went up to Devens's side.

"Got us a fight all right, Mr. Raines." Devens was staring through his field glasses at the gauzy smoke before him. "You report to Stone?"

"He's put Colonel Baker in command over here," Harry said, avoiding a direct answer to the question.

"Baker?"

"Yes, sir."

"Well, where is he?"

"I don't know."

The colonel gave Harry a quick, unhappy look, then returned his attention to the battlefield. Harry was dismissed.

Devens had established a perimeter on the Virginia side that encompassed the whole of the bluffs and had both flanks anchored on the river, but was bent inward at the middle to conform to the contours of the wide and deep ravine that cut through the top of the bluff. It made for a poor position, exposing part of the Union line to flanking fire and offering little room to maneuver in the rear. Harry was no soldier, but his own notion would have been to move the little army as far forward from the river as it could get.

Many of the men had taken off their heavy coats and jackets, and he was pleased to see that most of them had taken cover behind trees or fence. A number were firing their weapons lying prone on the ground—a sensible disposition in the circumstance.

He moved along the line toward the right flank, still hoping to find Baker or word of him. The musketry seemed to diminish the farther right he went. At the end of the Union line, there was none at all. At length, pushing through a brambly thicket and emerging at the summit of a wooded knob, he found himself overlooking the river again.

Traffic on the water was now heavy and steady. Several more smaller boats had been acquired from elsewhere on the river and put to work. But there seemed to be sizable confusion. Two of the boats were being rowed to the Virginia shore only half full, though there were crowds of men waiting on the Maryland bank for transport. A flatboat being launched from the island overturned, sending its blue-coated passengers struggling to regain the shore. Harrison's Island was now teeming with soldiers, resembling an insect mound. But they were mostly standing idly.

Harry paused to rest. He'd had next to nothing in the way of breakfast and no lunch. It was hot now, and he was feeling dizzy.

He pulled out his flask, took a reviving nip of whiskey, then followed it with a swig of river water from his canteen. He didn't know how long it would last, but he felt a little better.

What he needed more than sustenance was Baker. Once he was back with the colonel all else would fall into place.

Moving urgently now, he came back along the line, keeping almost at a crouch to avoid making himself too attractive a target. Confederates had advanced to the other side of the ravine and some of them had attained the top of a small rise overlooking the Union center. Leaves and bits of wood were falling regularly here, a sort of rain.

He kept his head low as he maneuvered along the ground, then at once lifted it. A young Union soldier was standing out in the clear just ahead of him, looking down at his leg very curiously. The cloth of his pants on that limb was dark. The other pants leg was light blue. The soldier took a step, wobbling, then reached to clutch the thin trunk of a young tree.

Harry lunged forward and went to the soldier's side. He was young—still a boy—with a beardless face. He looked to Harry, then took another step. His features twisted a moment in some sort of pain, but he did not cry out.

"I'm wounded," the youth said, marveling at the word.

"Your leg looks bad. Can you walk at all?"

"Depends on which leg." The youth grinned at his joke, but his face drained of color when he took his next step. Holding him by the waist, Harry got the boy off the firing line and over to two stretcher bearers, the first he had noticed.

Continuing on his own toward the left flank, moving through a sooty veil of gun smoke, he stumbled, regained his balance, and stood straight. A hand reached from some unseen place and pulled him rudely down just as a musket ball came clipping through the branches.

"Got to have more of a care for your head, Mr. Raines," said Lieutenant Oliver Holmes.

Harry nodded. "So I detect. What's happening?"

"We're stopped dead here. Too many Rebels across that ravine. There was some sort of plan to push south from here and meet up with a regiment attacking across the river at Edwards Ford, but that appears somewhat a shambles now."

"We seem to have moved some cannon up here."

"Won't do much good in all these woods."

Holmes had taken off his gray coat with red facing. The Massachusetts boys were going to need some redesign in their uniforms before they fought a battle again, as would Saylor and the regiment he represented.

A man in some bushes not twenty feet away yelped and stood up as though propelled by a coiled spring, then fell back, clutching at empty air. Another man popped up near him and set about dragging him away.

Holmes's eyes went to the wounded man. "Is he badly hurt?" he shouted to the rescuer above the battle racket.

"He's daid, Lieutenant," came the reply.

A cannon shell exploded off toward the left flank. It was impossible to tell if it was federal or Rebel.

Harry decided it might be best just to find Devens again and inquire once more after Baker's whereabouts. With Confederate musket balls striking all around him, he leaped up and pushed on through the trees. More Union soldiers were coming up, brushing past him.

"Raines! Over here!"

He looked to his left. Standing by a sycamore, as though resting, was Lieutenant Howe. As Harry went to him, he could hear the young man's rapid breathing.

"Ran up the trail," he said, struggling to regain his wind.

"Seen Baker?" Harry asked.

Howe nodded, then took two more deep breaths. "Took us hours and hours yesterday to get our little party over the river. Yet I've been back and forth across it two more times just since I left you."

"Where's Baker?"

"Still on Harrison's Island. He had a work party trying to get a canal boat out of the canal and into the river."

"Isn't that something a sergeant could do?"

"Baker takes a personal interest. But Stone's ordered him to attack, so he should be here soon."

There was a loud crack of an explosion not far distant. Harry realized it was a Union artillery piece being fired, not an enemy shell. He looked at his watch. It was nearly two o'clock.

COLONEL Baker's arrival on the bluff was announced by the sound of cheers. Harry looked back to see Baker emerge from the woods on horseback, his bearing that of some mythic hero.

"Do you boys want to fight?" the colonel shouted to the men along the rail fence around Harry.

A few shouted back, "Yes!" Most seemed confused, as there'd been firing along the line for nearly two hours.

"Then a fight you shall have!" cried Baker.

There was more cheering. Baker nudged his mount forward, continuing his slow walk. He gave the impression of wanting to tour the entire battlefield in this manner, bringing encouragement to the troops like a circuit-riding preacher spreading the Gospel.

But that was not his job, and it could get him killed. The Rebels hadn't had such an attractive and imposing target all day. Baker was within sharpshooter range.

Harry hurried to the colonel, positioning himself to the front of Baker's horse to prevent the officer from moving any closer to the Confederates. Baker regarded him, not happily.

"Well, here's the battle, Mr. Raines. Can you keep me safe?" He spoke with some derision.

"Yes, I can," said Harry, "but it would be of great usefulness, sir, if you would dismount and go back to the rear."

"Now, how could I do that?"

Without waiting further for an answer, Baker nudged his horse's flanks and pushed ahead, leaving Harry to follow. A party of officers was coming toward them on foot. In the midst of them, Harry recognized Colonel Devens. A bugler sounded officers' call, and a crowd of shoulder straps began to gather around the new commander, who insisted on remaining in the saddle. Harry wished the whole lot of them back on Harrison's Island.

Moving up close to the edge of the group, Harry heard Baker bark out a few orders and words of encouragement. As best as he could make out, the colonel was rearranging the line—giving Devens's men the center and shoving the other Massachusetts regiment farther to the right. The "1st California," the Pennsylvania unit given a Western name to honor Baker, was placed to the left of Massachusetts men, extending from a sharp angle. The extreme left went to New York boys, the rough and tough "Tammany regiment." The cannon were repositioned as well, shifted to cover both flanks from points near the center.

Harry supposed it all made good military sense, but still didn't like the sharp angle at the center.

Holmes was nearby, seeing to the ammunition supplies of his men. Mindful of the continuing fire still whistling through the trees, Harry went to him.

"I have a request to make of you," Harry said. "Could you detail three or four men, your best shots, and have them keep between Baker and the enemy?"

Holmes finished checking the musket load of one of his privates, then handed the weapon back to the man. "You're a fine fellow, Mr. Raines, but I'm afraid I have orders from my captain, and they're to hold this position against Confederate attack. I can't spare men to form a praetorian guard."

The truth was now in order. He drew Holmes aside.

"Mr. Holmes. I will ask you to reveal this to no one, but I am a member of the U.S. Secret Service and I've been sent here to see that Colonel Baker lives through this campaign. He has frustrated this task at every turn and I need help. This man is the president's best friend."

The lieutenant eyed him speculatively, then shook his head. "Raines, we're in the middle of a damned battle. The president appears to have granted Senator Baker his wish, and that is to lead this fight. I'm sorry."

Harry clapped Holmes on the shoulder. "Have a care for yourself, then." He trudged away, keeping low, his revolver in hand. He would have to serve as a praetorian guard of one.

He caught up with Baker by the Tammany regiment, where the president's friend was talking to the commander, a colonel named Milton Cogswell. Saylor had introduced Harry to him the previous day. A handsome fellow with a magnificent blond beard, Cogswell was a regular army officer who'd been a captain at the time of Sumter and been promoted to colonel even more rapidly than Saylor. Cogswell's father happened to be a New York State Supreme Court justice.

He'd gotten his troops close to the edge of the deep ravine that cleft the face of the bluff. An equal number of Confederates were arrayed on the other side of the divide. Worse, others of them had occupied a high hill just beyond.

Of a sudden, a withering volley of Rebel musket fire snapped through the position like a whip, toppling Union soldiers as if they were toys. A following volley was just as devastating. The Confederates were in good cover, and even with his eyeglasses on, Harry found it difficult to make out where they were. The Rebel officers were taking good advantage of that hill.

"I want artillery on that high ground!" Baker bellowed.

"Can't, Colonel," said Cogswell. "My cannoneers are down!"

The regiment had two howitzers in support but both crews had been shot up badly by the massed volleys.

Baker dismounted, which pleased Harry enormously. Then, to his amazement and alarm, Baker took Cogswell in tow and started walking toward the guns. As Harry watched in horror, the two officers and some infantrymen they dragooned into service began loading one of the field pieces.

It took them forever to ready the gun, and when they fired, the shot carried high, clipping branches off a few trees but missing the Rebels on the hill. The Confederates, like hornets stirred to anger, began concentrating their fire on the Yankee artillery position. When one round rang soundly off the barrel not an inch from Baker's hand, the colonel gave a start. Two men next to him fell, one screaming. Baker appeared stunned. He stared at the screaming man, as though in disbelief. As stretcher bearers came up, he and Cogswell wearily abandoned the cannon and headed farther down the line. Very frightened now, Harry followed, coughing in the thick pall of gun smoke.

Moving left, closer to the river, the two colonels came upon a third, lying wounded, who seemed to be an old friend of Baker's. His name was Isaac Wistar, and he was still in command of the "Pennsylvania" regiment. Blood was flowing through the bottom of his boot, where he had cut a hole.

"I need you to send two companies across the ravine," Baker said. "Clear those Rebels off that hill and find out how many we're up against."

"Ned," said Wistar, barely making himself understood above the din of musketry. "That's murderous fire."

"We have to know!" Baker thundered. "There could be five thousand—ten thousand of them—coming up from Leesburg!"

The wounded colonel sent a runner for two of his captains, who came running up quickly. They listened carefully, looked to the ravine, and looked back to Wistar. He looked to Baker, who extended his arm toward the Confederates.

Both companies moved out smartly, but to Harry, crouching near Baker and the fallen Wistar, what followed seemed to occur with an odd and painful slowness. Despite the hot and heavy firing, a fuzzy quiet came over his hearing. The Union soldiers one by one disappeared over the rim of the ravine, then returned to hazy view, the same way, creeping up behind trees and rocks on the opposite slope. Some stopped moving entirely. A few of the remainder reached the Confederate side, then faltered and fell back, leaping with that same unnatural slowness down into the ravine.

There was an odd flicker of motion to the side of Harry's field of vision. Turning to follow it, he saw Baker lean sharply over the fallen Wistar, who was grimacing in great but silent anguish, clutching at his now shattered elbow. Baker called for stretcher bearers again, in words Harry could not quite make out.

He closed his eyes. He supposed his lack of food and water all that day was beginning to tell on him. He wasn't sure he could bear much more than another minute of this. When he opened them again, the two companies Wistar had sent into the ravine were struggling forward again. There were fewer of them now, but the Confederate gun flashes were much more numerous.

Movement to his right. It looked to be Holmes, though it was hard to tell in the smoke. As if to distract some of the Rebel musketry, he was leading a company of Massachusetts infantry obliquely to the head of the ravine. Sword in hand, charging into mist of battle, he looked the picture of a veteran—anything but a fresh-faced youth only a few weeks out of classes at Harvard.

There was a searing, ripping sound in the air and then the ground shook and shuddered. The Confederates had moved up more artillery of their own. A riderless horse trotted by, stepping daintily over and around wounded and dead bodies.

Wistar's men reached the other side of the ravine one more time, with the same lamentable result. Baker was standing now, watching the action intently. A musket ball struck a near tree, festively scattering wood dust and splinters into the air. Harry clutched at Baker's arm.

"Please, sir," he said, perhaps a little insanely. "Lie down! Lie down!"

Baker's words came clearly to his ears now, sharply. "I will not lie down," the colonel said. "And when you are a United States senator, you will not lie down either."

Harry decided the man had gone mad, but fittingly so, for the battle itself had become all a thing of madness. Harry had never experienced anything like it. Bull

Run, which he'd witnessed mostly at some distance, had been a sort of macabre but splendid pageant, smoke and glitter and rank upon rank of colorfully uniformed troops—at least until the panicked retreat. Here was squirting blood and screams. Here were awful smells. And great confusion.

Over to the right, where Holmes's platoon had been positioned until it moved forward, another bunch of men were moving slowly toward Harry. They were not retreating, but advancing. Confederates!

Harry shouted the word, but no one paid any mind except for a bearded man a few yards away who'd been firing steadily toward the ravine and enemy hill. He rolled over and took a bead on what appeared to be a Confederate officer on a white horse, but he didn't shoot. The officer had a revolver out, but the Yankee stayed frozen.

"What's wrong?" Harry shouted.

"Can't pull the trigger!" the man shouted back. "Finger got shot off!"

Harry had an impulse to rush up, grab the man's musket, and take down the officer himself. But what if it was his brother? Or his father? There were hundreds of Virginians here. How had he gotten himself into such a fix?

The senator, as Harry would now always think of Baker, continued his heroic pose, observing dispassionately as the remnants of Wistar's two companies came struggling back from the ravine. Another artillery shell exploded somewhere to the left.

An officer behind them called out to Baker. "Colonel! Will you not come out of that fire and get behind my men?"

"See to your company, Captain!" Baker replied, without turning his head. "I'll attend to myself."

Harry had witnesses. Baker had lost his mind. There was no way of protecting him.

The Confederate officer on the white horse had somehow vanished. What looked to be another Rebel— a red-haired man—was leaning against a nearby tree, his eyes on Harry.

But he raised no weapon. The intruder appeared to be an enlisted man. Yet he was holding a revolver in his hand, an officer's weapon, letting it hang by his side.

The daintily stepping horse came by again. Stymied as to where to go, it stopped and began munching on some strands of grass.

Holmes and his men were returning from their foray, pushed back by a Confederate rush. As his troops went streaming past, Holmes stood his patch of ground, sword in left hand, pistol in right, firing into the smoke.

At once he stood up, rising in a backward arc, his hand going to his chest. He seemed to lift, his feet off the ground. Then he went flying onto his back, with such force his body threw up bits of leaves and dust.

Half a dozen men ran to his rescue. He was a brave and well-liked officer. Most of the officers on the bluff were. The Confederates were in great and increasing strength, but there was no mad panic, no retreat. This was no Bull Run. Not yet.

Indeed, on open ground barely visible beyond the ravine, Harry saw small dots of the enemy pop up and get shot down, much like targets in a marksmanship contest. This was not all one-sided. Both the Massachusetts men and the Pennsylvania "California" regiment were showing considerable mettle.

But none such mettle as Baker. Sword in hand now, he was wandering along the line, exhorting his troops with, "Stand fast, boys!" and "Reinforcements are coming! We'll beat them yet!"

Not a bullet had touched him. Harry stumbled along behind the colonel, trying desperately to work up the courage or lunacy to whack Baker on the head and drag him out of danger. The officer was performing no useful function here. He issued no orders. He was carrying on like an actor in a play.

But then at once he did issue a command. Summoning the captain who had been exhorting him to get out of danger, he yelled at him to get to General Stone and bring more troops across the river by the bluff.

"Tell him we are stopped here, and may not hold. We must have more men or we are lost!"

The captain looked to his company, somewhat desperately. He was a line officer, responsible for those men, not a courier. If anyone should go, it was Harry, but Pinkerton would kill him if he did that—flying for the rear while his charge strolled about among whizzing musket balls as he might wade in a stream.

The younger officer departed. Harry looked at his pocket watch, amazed to see it was almost five o'clock. He looked to the west and saw the sun was lowering.

Turning back to the front, he realized now that the mission Pinkerton and presumably Lincoln had sent him on was doomed to failure. Baker was striding directly forward now, waving his sword, bellowing words at the air in front of him. Perhaps he thought he would single-handedly hold off the Confederates until Stone came to the rescue.

Harry pulled out his flask, took a deep draft, then staggered after the colonel. He was just catching up when he heard a muffled crack and felt a tear at his sleeve. Looking down, he saw that a bullet had passed through it. But the sound had come from behind. Looking up again, he watched Baker's sword fall, and then Baker himself.

Whirling about, his revolver in hand, Harry saw the red-haired Rebel, standing in shirtsleeves. He heard yelps and hollers. Several Confederate soldiers came running out from between the trees. Lunging on, hoping to at least cover Baker's body with his own, Harry was happy at least to see that the colonel was alive. His head was up and he seemed to be grasping for his sword. With his other hand, he gripped his wounded left leg.

Reaching him, Harry raised his own revolver, prompting the onrushing Rebel soldiers to come to a sudden halt. For some reason, they did not shoot at him, but a bullet from somewhere cut close to his head.

And then he heard a thunder of hooves. Out of nowhere, appearing in a flash between two trees, came the Confederate he had seen before, on the white horse and at full gallop, heading straight for him and Baker.

Harry loosed a shot, but it was hasty and went wide, even though the mount and rider now seemed to tower over him. The officer yanked the animal to a sudden stop and, ignoring Harry, leaned down over Baker, his horse's chest almost in Harry's face.

There were five quick gunshots from the Confederate's weapon, and then the white horse and rider leaped and dashed away. Harry flung himself down to Baker's side—far, far too late. Every one of the five shots had found its mark. The president's friend was as dead as any man on that field.

Chapter 8

THE argument could be made that Colonel Baker's fate had been inevitable from the moment he had come across the Potomac to take command on the bluff. He could not possibly have long survived in the reckless manner he had conducted himself. Harry told himself this over and over.

But, in the end, there was still the inescapable fact. Baker had not simply died of wounds. He had been murdered. The colonel had been down, flat on his back, helpless and wounded. Then this phantom of a rider had swooped in from nowhere and extinguished the senator's life as one might crush a bug. The bloody deed had been in violation of every code of honorable conduct in war. It was a crime, an atrocity. The war might reach a level where such barbarism was commonplace, but it had not yet done so.

And Harry had let this murder happen. He had stood there, pistol in hand, taking more notice of a chance bullet through his sleeve than the welfare of the eminent personage in his charge, and so Baker had perished.

Harry Raines, freshly minted captain in the United States Secret Service, had failed in his first real mission.

He shook his head, as though to clear it. There was one small fragment of duty left he might still perform: capture the phantom rider. He could still accomplish that. If it came to it, he could kill the miscreant.

First he had to find him. Harry looked wildly about the field, noticing at length a flicker of motion between the trees in the distance to the right. A white horse. Gray-coated rider. The fellow was moving away with the same incredible speed with which he'd descended upon his victim.

A horse. Harry had been paying no attention, but there were several at hand among the trees of the battle-field, most with officers in the saddle but a few wandering loose. Nearest was the dainty-footed beast, still munching at what greenery it could find in the fallen leaves and brush despite the whiz of bullets and crash of shell.

Harry ran for him. It seemed he could hear every musket ball in the symphony of them crisscrossing the ravine in both directions. Two in quick succession came very close to his head, as though following the same trajectory. Some sharpshooter had marked him.

But what rifle could be fired so rapidly?

Another shot struck the ground near his foot as he snatched at the dainty-footed horse's reins. If he ran out of luck, he could be dead in just seconds.

Turning the little horse, putting foot to stirrup and hand to saddle, Harry flung himself aboard. The animal bolted forward before he had quite gotten his seat, but that kept him low and less a target. His grip on the reins was desperate and too hard, but he got the animal aimed in the right direction, obliquely away from the ravine and west toward the lane he and Philbrick's men had

followed the night before. It was the most direct way off
the battlefield, and he was sure the gray-coated rider
had been riding fast toward it.

Bullets were still zinging overhead and smacking
into trees, but none yet sang home into Raines's bones
or sinew. As his agitated but remarkably agile beast
leaped and darted across the leaf- and body-strewn
ground, dodging tree trunks and soldiers, it occurred to
Harry that he might actually survive this. The combat-
ants seemed to be losing interest in him now. He was
heading straight for the Confederate line, which probably confounded both sides—at least briefly.

Suddenly a man with a great black beard rose up
from the Confederate position, as if to grab Harry and
haul him off his mount, but Dainty Foot swerved easily
away to the side. Then Harry was into and among the
Rebels in all their force. Hoping his clothes might con-
fuse them about his loyalties, he smiled at them as his
horse leaped and jiggered past. Something then struck
him as a remarkable oddity. All the men in this patch of
woods were wearing civilian clothes. He guessed they
were either local militia who'd lent themselves to this
fight, or regular soldiers in the Confederate Army who
hadn't yet been issued uniforms.

They appeared perplexed by his passage through
them, and he took comfort in this, hoping they'd conclude he was one of them. But even at that they might
take him for a Rebel soldier on a skedaddle. Deserters
in either army were shot on sight.

None proved so bold or decisive. Dainty Foot danced
along and headed of his own volition for the lane, leaving the bulk of Rebel soldiers behind, though one fellow
finally became resolute and sent a musket ball chasing
after Harry.

Wherever he'd gone, the phantom rider clearly had

no interest in remaining with his Confederate comrades. He had left the field of battle with as much speed as Harry had seen in this war.

But Harry had one advantage. He knew this country—a knowledge that had been greatly enhanced by his wandering foray with Captain Philbrick the previous night. If he left the lane at the cleared cornfield he had scouted with poor Lieutenant Holmes, and bore off instead into the trees and over a rolling ridge to the west, he'd come out on the main road between Leesburg and Frederick, Maryland. Depending on which way the villain was bound, he might yet cut off his prey.

Revolver stuck in his belt, he let Dainty Foot trip along until the clearing appeared ahead, then turned him sharply right and down to the end of the cornfield. The leaf-covered ridge that climbed steadily to the west from that spot was slippery and steep, but when he at last attained the summit, he could see the Leesburg Road. He missed his big horse Rocket. That good steed could hold a strong pace from here all the way to Richmond.

Descending to the road, he looked both ways, seeing hanging dust in each. Guessing left, he urged Dainty Foot into a canter, only to discover at the next rise that the dust had been stirred up by a small procession of Confederate army supply wagons, heading south. Turning Dainty Foot around, Harry whipped him into a gallop, north, toward Nolands Ford and the town of Frederick, Maryland, beyond. After a mile of hard riding, reaching the top of a saddle between two hills, he saw dust ahead, though no rider.

Harry kept on, following the wisps of dust cloud up and down hills, around curves to the left and to the right, across streams deep and shallow. Finally, coming into a long straight stretch, he saw in the distance, just at the edge of some woods, the rider himself. The man had stopped. He appeared to be reconnoitering, as though he were lost. Then he flashed off to the right into the trees.

If Harry went galloping recklessly toward that spot, he might find himself facing a waiting gun. If he held back, the assassin would make his escape. He could be as good as gone already, given his head start.

Warily, revolver in hand, keeping Dainty Foot to a walk and staying close to the side of the road, Harry proceeded forward. He could still hear the sounds of battle behind him, the tinny rattle of musketry, the thumps and cracks of cannon.

Reaching the place where he thought the rider had entered the woods, he dismounted and led his horse into the trees on foot, tying him finally to the back side of an old oak.

Standing perfectly still, Harry listened with care. He thought he heard a noise or two coming from a glen that lay just ahead, partially hidden by a clumpy mound of earth and boulders.

A squirrel bounded off the mound at his approach, scampering up the trunk of one tree and leaping to the extended branch of another. Sticking his revolver back in his belt, Harry moved carefully to the boulder-strewn little hill and began to climb. His foot slipped on a rock, causing his knee to bang down and his trousers to rip slightly, but he quickly found better purchase and made his way to the top. Crawling up beside a brambly bush, he edged forward and looked down below, to where a wide opening between two trees gave a good view of the glen.

The white horse was there, edging about nervously, its reins simply dropped to the ground. Dumped upon the leaves were pieces of gray cloth, glints of brass and gold braid indicating a uniform, and near them, what might be female things—including, as best Harry's experienced if shortsighted eyes could reckon, a petticoat and camisole.

Just beyond these—her back to him—stood a naked woman. He thought at first it might be a small, slender man, but no. He couldn't quite make out the color of her hair, which was done up tightly. But the skin of her back was the whitest he had ever seen. A most prized attribute of ladylike beauty in Southern society. She had a form and figure to match.

He had put his spectacles away lest they be jarred off in his mad ride. Reaching into his coat, he pulled them out again and set them carefully in place. The lady was leaning over now, picking something up from the ground, something white.

Watching her don the garment, he thought he heard a stirring in the leaves behind him, but assumed it was the squirrel, his eyes on the lady's still mostly naked form.

A mistake. A moment later something very heavy came thunking down on the top of his head.

Chapter 9

HARRY awoke to darkness, which confused him until he realized that a sack or cloth had been put over his head. Trying to shake it loose made his head hurt all the more and accomplished nothing, for the cloth had been tied securely around his neck. His hands and ankles were bound as firmly. And he seemed to have been thrown sideways over the back of a horse or mule, at any rate a strong-smelling animal with a damnedly uncomfortable gait.

He wondered what had happened to his hat—a gift from Caitlin, now a casualty of war.

An attempt to pull apart the rope binding his legs was also unsuccessful, producing only chastisement in the form of riding crop or stick thwacked down on his shoulder.

"Keep still, you dumb son of a bitch," came a gruff and very male voice, "or you'll strangle yourself." There was a pause. "'Fore we get to do it for you."

Listening to the horses' hooves, Harry guessed he had two captors, one leading his horse from ahead and this outrider alongside. He had another pistol in his boot—a small two-shot derringer—they did not seem to have found. If he could free himself from his fetters and blindfold, he might yet win this game.

They jerked his horse into a rapid trot, which served to make his bonds tighter against his flesh. Then all at once they seemed to come free. He had an odd sense of flying. Then there was a sharp, sudden pain at the back of his head and the smell of dust, strong in his nostrils. Again he slept.

HE awakened slowly, finding himself reclined upon a cool ground. There was no dust. He was in a different place. The hood was still over his head. Stirring, with great discomfort, he sat up a little and called out, "Hello, hello!" The response was a sudden rush of noise that his mind had somehow held away. It was gunfire, a lot of it, to one side and the other.

There were shouts, but not directed at him. No one paid him any attention. Perhaps he was dead. He began to drift into sleep.

HE felt a hand on his shoulder, gently placed.

"You all right there, prisoner?"

"Are you addressing me?" he muttered from beneath the cloth.

"Yes, you. I am addressing you, sir." The voice was soft and cool, much the opposite of the angry one he had heard before.

"No, I'm not all right. I feel half dead."

"Scoot back a little. There's a tree right behind you to lean back against."

He did. There was.

"Thirsty," he said. "Near parched."

"You can't drink through that sack."

"That's very true. I congratulate you on your acute powers of observation. Could you perhaps remove it?"

"Why'd they put it on you?"

"I've no idea. Punishment for looking at a woman without her clothes, maybe."

"Where'd you do that around here?"

"Please. I'll do you no harm. The hood."

There was a long pause, then he felt a tug at the neck rope. For a few seconds he thought he might indeed find himself strangled, but then the rope came loose and, with a jerk, the sack was pulled off. The air was cool upon his face.

Blinking, he opened his eyes, and found himself looking straight into another pair—very large, dark eyes.

He blinked again. The dark eyes belonged to a Confederate lieutenant. Agreeably situated in a youthful, dark-complexioned face, adorned with an improbable and theatrically long moustache and full goatee. They were staring at him intently—and, as it oddly struck Harry, with some concern.

He looked about. It was night, and he was in some army camp—the wrong army's.

"Where are they?"

"Who?"

"The people who brought me here."

"Those cavalrymen?"

"Was one a woman? Was there a white horse?"

"They was just cavalry."

"Where'd they go?"

The lieutenant gave him a sharp look. "You're the prisoner, you know. We're supposed to be asking *you* questions."

"But you're the one with the answers," Harry said. "Who's winning the battle?"

"I guess everyone but you would know that by now," the officer said. "It's pretty near won. 'Nother victory for the Southern cause, looks like."

The lieutenant had an odd accent, part Southern, part something else. The Southern part sounded different than a Virginia accent, perhaps from a part of the Confederacy far away. The Deep South. The Far West.

"Union boys back across the river?" Harry asked.

"They were tryin' to reach it, last time I was up there. A lot of 'em probably wish they'd never come over in the first place. A lot, I think, didn't make it." The officer's eyes narrowed. "Where'd you see a naked woman?"

He was an infantry lieutenant, wearing an extremely new and clean gray uniform that was a bit too large for him.

"Back up the road," Harry said. "I think she was meeting someone, someone who disapproved of my presence."

"Her husband?"

"I wish I knew who it was. I would have words with that person."

The lieutenant stared all the harder, increasingly interested.

"You were following her?"

"Him. I was following a rider on a white horse. He went into the woods. I went after him, but I found her."

"On the road north to Frederick? Toward Nolands Ford?"

"Yes."

"What'd you want with him?"

"I believe he murdered a man."

"Where?"

"Up on the bluff."

"You mean in the battle?"

"Yes."

"Hell, war ain't murder."

"Sometimes it is. This was. The man was wounded and helpless. You don't shoot wounded."

"I've seen it done. At Bull Run."

"Then it was murder."

"Maybe so, but you're goin' to see lot more of it before this thing is done. Was it somebody in uniform did it? A Confederate soldier?"

Harry nodded. "Some of the Rebels up there didn't have uniforms, but this one did. Was an officer, like you. On a white horse."

"You're not in uniform. Were you in the battle?"

"Got caught up in it. I'm a horse trader."

"Sell horses to the Yankees?"

"To whoever buys 'em."

The officer leaned close to Harry's face again. "You took a blow to the side of your head. And there's a cut at the back. There's been some bleeding, but it doesn't look too serious. You feel all right? A little dizzy?"

"A little. Do you know about wounds?"

"I do indeed, sir. This company lost all its officers, so I had to take command. I'm a lieutenant in the Independent Scouts, sometimes attached to the Loudon County Militia, but I was traveling with these men. They're the Eighth Virginia. Now who be you, sir?"

"Harrison Raines. Private citizen. I own a horse farm a ways upriver, near Shepherdstown. As I say, I got caught in the middle of this battle."

The lieutenant finally offered him a canteen of water. It was very warm, but Harry was grateful.

"Secessionist?"

Harry replied with a deceitful nod. "My father and brother wear your uniform."

"Then why'd these boys take you prisoner?"

"I wish I knew. Maybe they thought I was going to harm that woman."

The lieutenant rose. "You don't look like a man who'd do much harm to women. You don't look much like a farmer, either. I'll be back."

The lieutenant's face was in short time replaced by another—older, more masculine, and black. The man wore a fieldhand's clothing but hefted a musket. It was an amazement, an armed Negro in the midst of the Confederate Army.

"Are you a slave?" Harry asked. "Or a freeman?"

The black man simply glowered.

"Help me get away from here and I'll get you to freedom."

"What'd you say?"

"I can get you out of here. If you want. To the North."

"Slavery's still the law in the North," the man said. "Same as the South. Slavery all the same."

"No, it's changed," Harry said. "There's a general named Ben Butler who's got the Union Army to adopt a new policy. All escaped slaves are now contraband of war. They never have to go back."

"What happens to 'em?"

"They work for the army. For pay."

"Doin' what? Diggin' trenches? Haulin' wood?"

It was the truth. Harry said nothing.

"I stays here," the black man said.

Without further word, the Negro moved back a little, shifting the musket away from Harry. A moment later the lieutenant was there.

"What're you botherin' my man about?" he said.

Harry smiled. "Just passing the time." He glanced to his left and right, seeing no fellows. "I'm the only prisoner?"

"There's others—the other side of those trees." The officer gestured at a group of Union soldiers in shirt-sleeves seated on the ground in a slight decline behind a line of live oaks, their faces bright in the firelight. A couple of the federals were eyeing Harry speculatively—and not happily. "They want you kept separate."

"Why?"

"They're soldiers. I think you're being held as a spy." The lieutenant smiled and moved away again.

"Spy?"

"Runnin' around behind our lines. Spyin' on that woman you talked about."

"I wasn't after military secrets."

"My man's name is Bob," said the lieutenant, busying himself with the contents of a knapsack. "I bought him in Alabama on the way up here, but he is as loyal to me as a man can be. And he's not interested in any truck with abolitionists, in case that's what you were talkin' about."

"Why do you think that?"

"Bob stays with me, wherever I go." It was a pronouncement. The lieutenant handed Harry a chunk of bread and a slab of roast meat, then began to busy himself about the little camp again.

"Thank you."

"Last meal, maybe. Colonel Evans deals with spies meanly."

Harry watched the officer quietly. The firing was more subdued now, as though the battle was moving away. At this hour at Bull Run, the Union Army was halfway back to Washington in what became known as the Great Skedaddle. Here on Ball's Bluff, they'd have no place to go. Only the river—cold, swift, and deep. With night upon them.

The lieutenant's movements oddly reminded Harry of something pleasant—the last time he had been to the theater. The play had been *Twelfth Night,* with Louise Devereux playing Viola and Caitlin, the countess. In the play, Viola disguises herself as a man after a shipwreck.

"Are you married?" Harry asked.

"No, sir. Not no more."

"Was your husband killed?"

The lieutenant stopped, angry and flustered. "What're you talking about?"

"It is clear you are a woman," Harry said.

The officer's head snapped around, the dark eyes like the mouths of cannon.

"My name is Harry T. Buford," she said, sharply, her voice cracking slightly as she lowered it. "I live in Leesburg. I am a lieutenant with the Independent Scouts, attached to the Loudon County Militia, as I told you. I think they cracked you on the head a little too hard."

"I do not think that is truly your name," Harry said. "I think your name is one better suited to a gentler nature. I do not think you belong here as a soldier."

"You are damned wrong!" Anger in the eyes now. "I am a soldier. I was at Bull Run. I brought two hundred thirty-five men from Arkansas—recruited every one. Brought to Florida through Alabama and up to here."

"You are a woman. As much a woman as the one I saw up along the Frederick Road, only she had very white skin. If I had my hands free, I should be able to prove my point quick enough."

"If you had your hands free, I should be obliged to shoot you."

"That would impair our friendship." He smiled. "Don't worry. I won't report you."

"Who'd believe you if you did?"

"If I accused you of being a Union agent, I think I could find an officer curious enough to want to make certain."

"No, you wouldn't."

"Yes, I would. If I told them I was one, too—that we were both Northern spies."

She took a long barreled revolver from her holster, aiming it at his head. The dark skin of her hand was broken by a line of white, a scar that ran diagonally back from the forefinger.

"Before I shoot you," she said, "you tell me. Are you a Union agent?"

"No. My father's a colonel with General Longstreet."

"How'd you know I was female?"

"It's a knack. I go often to the theater. I know actresses. I've watched them play men on the stage."

"I'm no actress."

"On the contrary."

"What do you want of me?"

"Your help."

The lieutenant now appeared weary and exasperated. "Mr. Raines, I am not going to let you go. They would shoot me, too, for that."

He thought about this. "I understand. But I would be forever obliged if you could get word to someone for me, someone who could intercede on my behalf."

"Who would do that from around here? Since I expect you really are a Yankee spy."

"A lady in Martinsburg. Her name is Belle Boyd."

The revolver barrel lowered a little. "I know about her. She is much celebrated hereabouts. Killed a Yankee on the Fourth of July. How do you know her?"

"She's a cousin."

"That's true?" she asked.

"Yes, ma'am. Cousin by marriage."

"What does that count for? There's brothers on both sides of this war."

"You get word to her that I am held, and she will come."

"But if you are a spy . . . ?"

"I tell you no. That's a mistake."

She studied him. The gun barrel lowered further.

"I go back to Leesburg soon. I'll send Bob over to Martinsburg as soon as it's practicable, but that's all I'm going to do for you. You may find yourself hanged before Miss Boyd gets here."

"In that case, tell me your name."

"What if you're not hanged?"

"Then you will have a grateful friend—and a discreet one." He smiled.

She smiled back, then gave two quick looks to either side. "It's Loreta Janeta Velasquez. Colonel Evans knows—I think. I don't know who else does. But not many. I don't want it widespread. I'm breaking the law, and they'd send me home for good. Or do something worse, like make me a company laundress."

"Why have you become a soldier?"

"My husband was an officer. Federal first, then he became a Confederate. He was killed. My three children are dead from sickness. This is my life now."

"You fight to avenge your husband?"

"He was killed in an accident, in Pensacola. He wouldn't let me serve as a soldier in his company when I asked him to. Now he's dead and there's nothing to stop me." She hesitated. "Were you fixin' to kill that woman? The one with the white horse?"

"No, ma'am. Just talk to her. I need to find out what happened. The dead man was a U.S. senator. There could be a lot of the wrong kind of trouble, once you get into political assassinations. I need to tell Richmond."

"Richmond?"

Sewn into the cuff of his shirt was a much-folded pass signed by Jefferson Davis that Harry had managed to acquire earlier in the war. He wanted to save it for when he truly needed it to stay among the living. He wasn't sure yet this was that time. He decided to leave it where it was.

"Richmond was where I was headed when I got caught up in your fight."

"Aιe you tellin' me you're a *Confederate* agent?"

"I'm a horse trader. Out of Martinsburg."

"I can tell you this. There was a woman come through camp yesterday on a white horse. Had a man with her—civilian. They were headed north."

"Where?"

"Who knows? Once across the ford, that road goes to Frederick, Hagerstown, Burkettsville. Eventually Baltimore.

"They asked Colonel Evans for a pass, but he was not willing to give one. He didn't like 'em much. I don't think he trusted them."

"Baltimore," Harry repeated.

She rose. "You're going down to Leesburg. All your talk ain't changed that. I'll get you some eats. Then Bob and I are goin' to take you on down. Sorry, but you'll have to be wearin' that hood again. Until someone decides otherwise, you're still a Union spy."

"Haven't you decided otherwise?"

"What I decide don't count."

SHE rode alongside him for a small bit of the way, then moved on up ahead, leaving him with Bob, who was not much of a conversationalist. There was other traffic on the road, but with the hood on, Harry couldn't tell much.

When the hood came off again, he found himself in the charge of a Confederate provost guard, on the main street of Leesburg. "Lieutenant Buford" had vanished.

"I'm a civilian," Harry said.

"You're a prisoner of war," said the sergeant of the guard.

They took him to a feed store, which Harry discovered was being used as a temporary prison for Union officers. There were more than two dozen of them in there, by Harry's quick count in the lantern light. Given the relatively small numbers engaged in the fight at the bluff, this was bad news. The Union must have lost this little battle in a very big way.

A filthy-looking Yankee captain, his uniform colored with mud, dust, and blood but otherwise seeming unharmed, offered Harry his flask.

He accepted, with profuse thanks.

"You're Massachusetts?" Harry asked.

"Aye. The Twentieth."

"I'm Harry Raines." He handed back the flask. "Civilian scout."

"George Weatherly." The captain extended a filthy hand and Harry shook it. His own was not much cleaner.

"The battle ended badly, then," Harry said.

"A disaster. You don't know?"

"I was taken early. At the ravine."

"With the Forty-second New York?"

"I was with them," Harry said. "Near them. Yes."

"They got the colonel."

"Cogswell? He's dead?"

"Not dead. Prisoner. He's right over there."

The captain pointed to a small clump of officers seated glumly on hay bales, near a man lying on his side on a blanket. Harry recognized Cogswell by his shoulder-strap insignia and the immensity of his beard. It made him seem older than his years, which were probably about forty.

Cogswell had been nearby when Baker had gone down. Harry wondered if he might recall something useful about the mysterious assassin, something that in all the confusion Harry might have missed.

Thanking the captain again, he rose and went over to the hay bales. Cogswell was the picture of defeat and weariness. He did not appear seriously wounded, but was badly beaten.

"Colonel?" said Harry.

Cogswell didn't stir. Perhaps he was asleep.

"Colonel Cogswell. It's Harry Raines."

With that, the colonel's head slowly rose. Harry was reminded of an artillery piece being trained.

Cogswell's eyes were hard upon him. "Raines?"

"Harry Raines, Colonel. I was with Colonel Baker."

Cogswell studied him a moment, as though doubting Harry's existence. Then at once he became livid.

"You son of a bitch! You shot Baker! Shot him down where he stood!"

"What?"

Harry stepped back, but a major grabbed hold of Harry's arm.

Cogswell looked about at his brother officers. "This man's a Rebel spy! A Rebel agent! An assassin! They put him in here to spy on us!"

Harry supposed he might well have been killed right then and there, stomped to death by Union boots. But there were Rebel sentries at the front of the building, and two of them came scurrying back with bayonet-fixed muskets at the sound of commotion.

"Get him out of here!" yelled Cogswell. "The rules of war call for officers to be held separate. I will not tolerate this contamination! Get him out! We've enough vermin in here!"

Chapter 10

COLONEL Evans appeared to be a drinking man, one who might have been at his whiskey earlier in the day, perhaps all through this battle. The hard-fought contest seemed to have concerned him little. One would have expected strutting and gloating at this point. The man had won the engagement, with sound tactics and skillful use of ground and maneuver. But he looked as though he'd spent the afternoon sitting in his chair, sipping and musing.

He was alone in his headquarters, his face deeply shadowed in the dim lantern light. He had a large, very black moustache but a scraggly beard and thinning hair fringing a high forehead. His small, shifting eyes, though troubled, had a brightness to them. If he was a drunk, he was in no stupor.

"You're Raines?"

Harry stood before him, having not been invited to a seat.

"Yes, sir."

Evans glanced down at some notepaper before him, then looked up.

"Harrison Raines? From Tidewater? Your father's a colonel with Longstreet's cavalry?"

"Yes, sir. Brother, too."

"You look like hell, Raines. You look like you've spent the day with pigs."

"Not quite, Colonel."

"What're you doing here? How'd you end up my prisoner?"

Harry took a deep breath, for he was feeling wobbly. He told his same tale about having a horse farm upriver and becoming caught up in the battle. He left out his time with the Union Army, his crossing the lines during the battle, his encounter with the naked woman. Evans would be a very busy man this day. It wouldn't help Harry's case to complicate things.

Evans leaned back in his chair. Harry thought he might topple over, but the officer caught his balance on the brink of doing so, as though much practiced at this. He had remarkably thin legs. If he'd been a horse, Harry would not have bought him.

"Why'd you get turned out by the Union officers?" Evans asked.

"They took me for a Southern spy, sir."

"Are you?"

"No, sir. Not really. Been helpful, here and there, but mostly I'm just a man with a horse farm."

Evans went back further, studying Harry's face with great intent.

"You sell mounts to the Yankees?"

"Sometimes. Sometimes south of the Potomac. I sell to who buys."

The colonel came forward hard, the chair legs striking the floor like a gunshot. He held his notepaper to the lantern light.

"Those federal officers say you shot the federal commander, Colonel Baker—shot him in the back as he led his troops forward. You do that, Raines?"

The door to the room was just behind Harry. His answer would likely serve to take him back through it, but to where from there?

"To my knowledge, sir, Colonel Baker fell in battle."

"Knowledge? Weren't you there? It says here you were there. Says Baker fell and you stole an officer's horse and bolted for our side of the fight."

"I stole a horse. I came through your lines because I live on this side of the lines. I don't know who shot Colonel Baker."

"A good soldier, that man. Not a West Pointer, but served commendably in Mexico. He deserved better."

"Yes, sir."

Evans leaned forward, taking up a pen and reaching for a scrap of clean paper.

"I'm going to take you at your word, Raines, and set you free. You've been vouched for, in more ways than one. I suggest you clear out of here and get back to that farm of yourn. If you come around Confederate troops again, I suggest you have your father handy." He looked up. "Unless you want to join up with us. I need more cavalry."

"Want to get back to my farm, Colonel."

Evans finished his scribbling, then thrust the paper into Harry's hand.

"That'll get you out of this camp."

"Thank you. I haven't a horse, sir."

A sort of grin came over Evans's face. "Well, Mr. Raines, that's a predicament you share with most of my men. I haven't mounts to spare for what cavalry I do have. If it's a horse you need, I suggest you get yourself back to your horse farm. Or steal another from the Yankees."

Harry hesitated again. It was worth a try.

"Do you know a Lieutenant Velasquez, Colonel?"

Evans frowned. "No."

"A Lieutenant Buford?"

"Maybe. Got a lot of lieutenants. What you want with him?"

"Not a 'him,' Colonel."

He turned to fetch a bottle from the floor and refill his cup. "You'd best go, Raines. If you are on our side, I'd say your usefulness here is pretty well done. Just git."

He spared Harry not a drop, nor another word.

Harry stepped outside. There was light from a lantern hanging from a tree limb, and off to the left a great roaring campfire. Lacking a horse, he headed on foot, as quickly as he could, for the darkness in between.

HE knew Leesburg, knew exactly which of its taverns would be the best to go to for information about the female inhabitants. No one in it knew of a Loreta Velasquez, or any kind of Velasquez. None of the rough drinking men were familiar with a Lieutenant Buford, either.

But several knew of a beautiful, dark-haired widow woman named Mrs. Buford and directed him to the house.

It was on the very edge of town, a fair-sized white house with a porch across the front and a barn in back. Behind it was only the darkness of fields and woods.

The front windows glowed brightly with what appeared to be the light of oil lamps and a large fire on the hearth. The windows to the side and rear were dark. Harry crept from the street along a white picket fence, then hopped it and came carefully up on the porch. A board creaked slightly, but when he came to the window and peered carefully around the edge of the frame, he saw her sitting by the fire, bent over some kind of work.

Her hair was down, lying long over her shoulders and of a lighter color than Harry had expected, noting the darkness of her complexion. She wore a prim gingham dress with a high-buttoned collar and shawl. As best he could see, Loreta Velasquez was in all respects a remarkably attractive woman. It was an amazement how much a simple soldier's suit and false moustache had disguised the fact.

Harry stepped back, then put on his spectacles. Returning to the window, he found his initial impression of her comeliness only enhanced. He also noted that the task she bent over was the cleaning of a gun, presumably the same revolver she had aimed at him earlier on the bluff.

She continued at her labors. Harry watched her awhile, glancing about the room, which seemed simply furnished. Then he moved quietly off the porch, around the side of the house, and back toward the barn. There'd been no sign of the slave Bob. He wondered if she had sent him to Martinsburg in search of Belle. She'd made a promise of it, and she seemed to have taken kindly to him.

The barn door was not locked. Opening it a few inches, he heard the thump of hoof on wooden floor.

Inside, moving away from the door, he struck a match. The barn was small and contained only three stalls. There was a horse in only one, barely visible in the shadows.

He blew out the match to keep it from burning his

fingers. Fumbling, he lit another, looking for a saddle and tack, finding none. When this match burned short, he extinguished it, but the illumination remained.

She stood in the doorway, a lantern in one hand. Looking to the other, he saw that she had reassembled the firearm.

"They set you free, Raines—or did you escape?" She spoke softly, but not pleasantly.

"I am at liberty, Miss Velasquez—by order of Colonel Nathan G. Evans."

"Well, what are you doin' in my barn?" The voice was no longer so soft. He couldn't make out her face too well, as she held the lantern to the side, but he could imagine her expression.

"I was looking for a place to pass the night. I didn't think you'd invite me into your house."

"You're damned right on that one. How come you were looking so curiously at my horse?"

"Just admiring it."

"The hell you were." She shifted to her right, blocking the doorway. "I think you were fixin' to steal it. You've got no mount, no saddle. You came here on foot."

"Borrow, maybe. Just to get back to Martinsburg. I own a horse farm. If something happened to yours, you could have your pick of my herd."

He heard the click of the revolver hammer being pulled back. "I like my horse, Raines, and I do not much like you. I could shoot you and I don't think anyone on either side of this war would much care."

Harry moved to the side a little. He saw the revolver barrel shift to follow and so he stopped, holding himself motionless. They stood like that, with no sound but the horse's flicking of its tail.

He still had the little gambling pistol in his boot. He could drop to his knee and have it in hand in an instant. He could shoot her dead. Maybe. He had a reason now, and it wasn't simply his own survival.

She moved, lowering her arm, sighing unhappily.

"Don't know why I should be so good to you," she said, stepping back. "Don't know why."

"Whatever your reason, I appreciate it."

"You know the roads around here, Raines? A right at the crossroads down the street'll put you on the one to Charles Town. From there it's straight on to Martinsburg."

"I remember."

"Go the other way from my house and you'll come to the main street and the road north to Frederick and Baltimore."

"Why should I want to go there?"

"You're snoopin' around here looking for that naked woman you saw, aren't you? That's what brings you here."

He made no reply.

"Well, you're in the wrong place. That lady was bound north, from what you told me. North I'd go."

"On foot?"

"You're a resourceful man, Mr. Raines. I'm sure you'll do better than walkin'. But whichever way you're goin', go now. I want you off my property. You strike me as nothin' but trouble. Git, 'fore I wake my man Bob."

"Very well." He bowed. "Thank you for your kindnesses, ma'am."

"I don't mean to be inhospitable."

"Understood."

He moved quickly from the barn and hurried into the

dark. He did indeed know the roads around Leesburg. He chose the one that led back north, toward Frederick.

It had been a little difficult to tell in the darkness, but the horse in Loreta Velasquez's barn was white.

MOVING steadily along, guided by the rising moon, he found the lane that led back to Ball's Bluff and turned into it, finding it strewn with the detritus of war. Happily, this included a discarded rucksack which proved to contain two apples and a few chunks of bread.

Thus fortified, Harry continued on, feeling the deep autumn cold of night. Traversing the well-remembered cornfield, he thought he saw movement among the distant trees, but no one challenged him. Pushing on through the woods, he found himself shivering beyond all ability of will to stop it.

There were odd sounds in these trees, night birds and skittering creatures and low moans that seemed to come from everywhere. He stumbled over several dark lumps upon the ground that, looking closely, he discovered were the unremoved dead. He could hear shouting, seeming to come from below the bluff, down along the river, or possibly across it. There was no way of knowing which army was making it.

He stopped before another dark form on the ground and, steeling himself, prodded it with his foot, amazed at the hardness that greeted him. He shoved more emphatically, again without response.

It was a struggle, but he managed to remove the poor man's coat, and found a rolled gum-rubber blanket as well. Curling up in both at some remove from the motionless soldier, he took the small derringer from his boot that his captors had not noticed and, keeping it in hand, closed his eyes, trying to move his mind to

another place. The moans and continued shouting by
the river held him where he lay.

He awoke about dawn, painfully stiff, opening his
eyes to a misty scene of dreadful horror. In the pale
light, he could see bodies lying all about him, some
twisted grotesquely, others lying straight and serene.
One man had fallen between two trees and was held
there erect, though his head hung straight down. All
seemed to be Union men. The Confederates had taken
away their own dead and wounded before nightfall,
leaving the task here to this day, if not another.

Harry rose, caught his breath against the cold, then
looked about, seeking and finding a place to relieve
himself at a respectful distance from the fallen soldiers.
When done with that, he rummaged among the army
goods strewn about the landscape, rejoicing in biscuits
and salt pork, as well as three more apples, two of
which he pocketed for a later meal.

Washing this down with the last of his flask, he got
his bearings and headed east and south, coming
presently to the ravine that had been fought over with
such desperate resolve. Again, the Rebel dead had been
dragged away, but the Union victims lay where they fell.

The place Harry sought next was easy to find. He
remembered the nearby tree. The artillery piece Baker
and Cogswell had worked was where he had last seen it,
its wheel and carriage smashed by Confederate shot or
shell, but the gun otherwise intact.

Pulling out his spectacles, moving over the ground
slowly, then on his hands and knees, he located the
exact spot where Colonel Baker had gone down. Even
in the gloom, he could see that it was soaked with
blood. The leaves were in disarray from when they'd

removed the commander's body, but brushing them
aside, Harry was able to locate the holes in the hard
ground made by the assassin's bullets. Five had been
fired, in a close grouping. Digging with his boot knife,
he was able to pull out two bullets from the dirt. The
others, apparently, remained in Baker's body.

There was a sound, distant, but nearing—and familiar: the jangle of harness, the clump of hoof. Looking
toward the lane he'd come up, Harry saw a team and
wagon approaching. There were several men upon it
and others walking alongside. A Confederate burial
detail, turning at last to the grisly task of Union dead.

He began edging away backward, keeping low, when
his right hand, reaching back, came into contact with
what felt like the hair from a human head. Yanking his
hand away, barely keeping himself from crying out, he
turned to look at the body he'd so unintentionally disturbed, discovering to his shock and amazement that
there was no body. His hand had encountered only hair.

Moving back a few feet more, he gingerly lifted it
before his eyes, recognizing its like from a hundred
nights he'd spent backstage with Caitlin, Booth, and
actors more. It was a theatrical wig, a bright orange
red even in that gray gloom. The only soldier to have
been on the scene in hair that color had been the Rebel
he'd glimpsed when the first shot had wounded and
grounded Baker, leaving him vulnerable to the swift-rid-
ing killer.

That soldier, it now seemed, had been wearing a wig.

Harry stuffed the hairpiece into his shirt, then kept
backing away. Finally, coming to the edge of the ravine,
he slid down into it, banging his shoulder and knees.
Once out of view of the burial party, he began hurrying
as best he could manage down the trail that led to the

foot of the bluff, wondering if a rifle bullet might find his back before he got there.

He could not imagine a sight more horrible than what he had seen atop the bluff, but at its base he found one far worse. The tide of battle had turned swiftly. Hundreds of Union soldiers had been trapped on the shore because of the lack of boats, and the Confederate victors upon the height had sealed their triumph by firing down into the helpless mob. Bodies lay everywhere on the muddy beach, in some places in piles.

There were corpses in the water as well, arms, legs, and clothing caught in the rocks and submerged fallen trees. Here and there along the beach were little heaps of equipment and personal possessions, including wallets and purses containing gold and silver coins. There seemed to be enough discarded muskets, pistols, swords, and bayonets to equip a regiment.

Amazingly, there was a boat, run up onto the beach with its sole occupant, a young sergeant, lying half over the side with his face in the mud, a large hole blown out from the back of his jacket. He was without boots or shoes. Harry figured he had probably managed to swim across and then come back in this little skiff to rescue either belongings or comrades.

Harry wondered if Colonel Evans, CSA, had any idea of the true picture of his grand success, or if Jefferson Davis and Abraham Lincoln could imagine it.

Remembering his few encounters with the president, he supposed Lincoln probably could—and doubtless did.

Pausing, Harry looked back up along the rim of the bluff but saw no movement. Across the river, on Harrison's Island, there were patches of blue—Union pickets watching and waiting for Evans to follow up his victory with an invasion to the north. That seemed the least likely eventuality to Harry. The Confederate commander would be snoring soundly at this juncture.

Borrowing one dead man's foraging cap and another's cloak for warmth, Harry walked along the beach, gathering up wallets, lockets, and other possessions and putting them in a sack. This he dropped in the boat. He started to haul the sergeant's body out of it, but it occurred to him the man deserved better, especially if he had come back after comrades.

Gently now, he rolled the man onto the skiff's forward seat. He was about to shove off when he heard an unexpected sound. It seemed a groan, but sounded more a growl.

Whirling about, he could not find the source. Bounding to the body of a fallen officer, he pulled forth the man's revolver, looking up and down the beach. Some hundred feet or more distant, a hand rose, and then fell.

The man was older than the general run of soldier and more muscular, with thick black hair and beard. A private, he'd been wounded twice. A musket ball had grazed the top of his head and another had gone through his right arm, from the looks of it, shattering the bone. He'd likely lose the limb, but the head injury did not seem serious. The man's eyes were fully alert, and fixed on Harry.

"Give me water, Reb."

"I am not a Rebel, sir," said Harry. "I'll fetch you some. Then I must get you across the river. There is a boat."

As Harry feared, one of the Union pickets became panicky and fired at the little skiff as Harry approached—missing by many yards, but then firing again, much closer to the damn mark.

"You damn fool!" shouted Harry. "Leave off! I've got a wounded man here!"

The shooter ran off, returning shortly with what looked a full squad, happily in the command of a corporal far less worried about whatever threat Harry might pose. While two of the soldiers stood guard with weapons at the ready, the others pulled the boat in from the water. Harry nearly fell getting out.

The wounded man was tended to and carried off, then Harry was led to an encampment on the other side of the island where he was given coffee and a bit more breakfast. Then, placed in a wagon, he was taken down the C&O Canal towpath to Edwards Ford, where he was transferred to a horse and escorted to Poolesville and a small white farmhouse with a sentry by the door and soldiery lounging about the yard.

Motioned inside, he entered half expecting General Stone, but the smiling officer behind the table there was only a colonel.

Named Templeton Saylor.

"Harry! By God, you're alive!" He came 'round the table and gripped Harry's arm.

"More or less," said Harry. "Mostly less."

He sank into the only other chair in the room.

"I daresay, you look something dragged forth from a New York sewer. We must attend to that—and soon. We can't have you going back to Washington looking such a monster."

"Washington? I've no interest in going to Washington."

"I'm afraid that's out of the question, Harry," said Saylor, looking more somber. He sat down on the table's edge, arms folded. "Whiskey?"

"Yes." He watched as Saylor poured. "Why, do I have no choice?"

Saylor handed him a full cup, then retrieved a piece of paper from the tabletop. "I'd no idea whether you were alive or dead," he said. "Or where you were. But now that you're here, I'm afraid I must inform you that I have orders to find you and place you under arrest. For the murder of Colonel Edward Baker."

Chapter 1 1

Harry had been given decent food, his chamber was warm and comfortable and he'd been able to wash and shave. But he'd not been allowed clean clothes or, though the rules of the Old Capitol Prison supposedly permitted it, any visitors. Several had come to his door, but even Templeton Saylor had been turned away.

He'd been decent enough about Harry's embarrassing and discomfiting predicament, arguing with the jailers for better food, an extra blanket, and books to read. When they'd neared the outskirts of the federal city on the ride in from Poolesville, Saylor had actually offered Harry a chance to escape, suggesting he might send the rest of the army escort on ahead to give Harry opportunity to make a dash for the Chain Bridge to Virginia and whatever refuge might be provided by his Confederate kin.

"We admire the same woman, do we not?" he said. "I should be much happier to have a hundred miles or more and a war between us."

Caitlin had mentioned Saylor's ardent pursuit of her when she was performing in a long engagement in New

York in the fall of '59. Poetry, flowers, chocolates, and champagne—and his own handsome, charming, and wealthy self. But all these things distracted her from her purer passion for Wilkes Booth no more than Harry's own small attributes and offerings had done.

"I'm not the rival you need fear, Templeton. The lady directs her affections elsewhere."

"Perhaps, but your absence would increase my odds."

"Well, I thank you for your offer of freedom, sir. But I would not be very free with such a cloud hanging over my name."

"Ah, the Southern chivalry. Honor to the end."

Actually, for a brief moment, Harry had considered taking his friend up on the offer. It could be managed without great difficulty or hazard, despite the Union Army's occupation of Arlington. Harry knew every pig track and rabbit hole in this reach of northern Virginia. Once across the bridge, he could vanish.

But he was not a Confederate. He was a Union man and an antislavery man. He was not going to give that up because of this trumped-up charge of murder. Once he crossed into Virginia, he doubted very much he'd ever be allowed back, and he'd be leaving a mark on his name forever.

HEARING voices and the rattling of keys outside his door on his second night in the Old Capitol, he sat up on his cot, struck a match, and pulled out his watch. It was nearly three A.M.

The door swung open with a sudden creak and a slam. The voice was that of the sergeant who seemed to be his principal jailer. Behind him was a private with musket and bayonet.

"You're to come with me," the sergeant said unhappily. "Rouse yourself."

"Am I being set free?" Harry asked, swinging his stockinged feet to the floor.

The sergeant laughed.

THE room he was taken to was on the floor below, windowless, small, cold, and furnished only with a table and a single chair. Harry had never been in it before but had heard of it. Pinkerton, among other dark powers of the capital, used it to question prisoners. It was probably the most private place in Washington, outside of Ella Turner's boudoir.

Motioning to Harry to seat himself in the chair, the sergeant set his lantern down on the table, then, without further explanation, walked out and locked the door.

Harry waited. The candle in the lantern burned down to near its nub. When it finally went out, he simply put his head down on the table and went to sleep. He was so tired he was sure he could find slumber strung upside down by his heels.

When he awoke, it was to someone shaking him with great vigor. A second person was pacing back and forth on the other side of the room.

His Scots accent was unmistakable. So, as Harry noted finally, after some blinking and squinting, was the short, stout body and the craggy face with fringy beard but no moustache. One could spot the chief of the U.S. Secret Service miles away, though he'd resent hearing Harry say that.

"You are unique in the annals of federal service, Raines. Not three months on the job, and first chance you get, you shoot the president's best friend."

Harry rubbed his eyes. "That's not true, Mr. Pinkerton."

"Well, sir, you've been officially charged with that offense—along with treason, espionage, aiding and comforting to the enemy, sedition, and misappropriation of government property."

"Government property?"

"A U.S. Army horse, which you took into the Confederate lines and did not bring back."

The man who'd been agitating his shoulder, as Harry might have guessed from the painful force of the shakes, was his erstwhile fellow Secret Service agent, Boston Leahy. He gave Harry a sad look evidencing mostly displeasure and exasperation.

"I didn't steal the horse," said Harry. "I borrowed him for government business—riding after the Confederate who gunned down Colonel Baker. The misappropriation was by the Rebels. They took us both prisoner and they still have the horse."

Pinkerton began to pace. With head down and shoulders hunched slightly, he looked more simian than ever. Stopping at a corner of the shadowy little room, he thought a minute, then resumed the conversation.

"Are you saying Colonel Baker wasn't murdered?" Pinkerton said. "That he simply died in battle?"

"I wish I could say that. It's what most likely would have occurred, given the way Baker exposed himself to the enemy. But I don't think that's what happened. He was wounded and went down—but his wound was in no way mortal. Then this fiend out of hell in Confederate uniform came galloping up out of nowhere and emptied a revolver into the colonel's chest and stomach. I was right there. It was the most bloody-minded killing I've ever seen—an assassination. Outside all the rules of war."

Pinkerton turned around. "And no one shot at you? You were next to him and not a round came your way?"

Harry held up his sleeve and stuck a finger through the bullet hole there. "There's this."

"Why in hell didn't you shoot that son of a bitch, if you were that close?" said Leahy.

Harry shook his head. "I was taken by surprise. By the time I collected my senses, he was pounding away for home."

"That's all you can tell us?" Pinkerton asked.

"The Confederates opposite us hadn't been issued uniforms yet. They were fighting in civilian clothes. I remember a red-haired soldier in shirtsleeves. But the one on horseback, he was splendidly uniformed. A lieutenant or captain—I'm not sure which. He didn't stop when he'd gotten back among his fellows. He rode hell-for-leather away from Ball's Bluff."

"How do you know that, Raines?"

"I snatched this loose horse and went after the son of a bitch. Took a shortcut and caught up with him in some woods, but when I got to him, he wasn't there. Only his clothes. And a naked woman."

"A naked woman?" exclaimed Leahy. "On the battle-field?"

"Near it. Up the Frederick Road from there. I watched her from hiding for a while. Failed to notice somebody who must have crept up and hit me from behind. Next thing I knew, I was a prisoner of war. My captor was a woman, in uniform."

"In uniform?" Pinkerton was clearly fascinated, but slightly incredulous.

"Disguised as a man. Lieutenant in the Independent Scouts, with the Leesburg Militia. I think the Confeder-ate commander knew about her, but didn't seem to mind."

"This wouldn't be the same one you saw naked in the woods?" Leahy asked.

"I'm not certain. To recognize her, I should have to examine a part of her anatomy not normally apparent."

"Preposterous."

"But it's the truth. Mr. Pinkerton, I did not shoot Baker."

Pinkerton stood staring at the floor, looking unhappy. Then his shrewd, suspicious eyes lifted back to Harry.

"Raines," he said, recommencing his pacing. "Even without any women in it, your story is about as much at variance with the official report on this tragic affair as it's possible to be. According to that document—a copy of which has been sent to President Lincoln—you shot Baker in the back, then emptied your revolver into him when he was down. A Confederate officer came up, and the two of you rode off to the Southern lines. Some would like to credit you with the Rebel victory."

"How'd you get free of the Rebels," Leahy asked, "if you were taken prisoner?"

"Colonel Evans, their commander, he let me go. He seems to have gotten the same official report you did, only I doubt he credited me with the victory. The outcome likely would have been much the same if Baker lived. Both sides fought well, but the Confederates had the good ground. Once the Union men started to retreat, they were doomed. Backs to the river. When they tried to get back across, they were slaughtered."

"Some of the bodies have washed up all the way down here in the federal city," Leahy said. "The populace is in a bloody big uproar."

"Populace be damned!" said Pinkerton. "It's the Congress that's our problem. The newspapers are screaming 'blunder' and the House and Senate are demanding someone's head. Roscoe Conklin, that meddling rabble-rouser from New York? He plans to introduce a resolution calling for a full-blown congressional inquiry on the conduct of the war. That means a standing congressional committee that will do its damnedest to run the damned army, the entire war effort. The president might just as well recognize the Confederacy and spare the North any further bother and embarrassment. The cause is fairly ruined."

They were interrupted by screams—the source unknown, but possibly from somewhere on the floor above. They lasted only a minute or two, then abruptly stopped.

"Was that the president, or the Congress?" Harry asked.

Pinkerton was not amused. "Our concern here, Harry, is for the survival of the Union."

Harry looked dutifully sheepish. "I understand, Mr. Pinkerton. May I go now?"

"Go?"

"Go free. Be released from this hellhole."

Leahy gave him a hard look. "You've got to understand the seriousness of your situation here, laddybuck. You've been officially charged. There's a witness. An eyewitness."

"How can there be an eyewitness to something that did not occur?"

Harry stood up. He found himself unable to bear this chamber and his incarceration another minute.

"The man is highly reliable, and of good repute," Pinkerton said. "Lieutenant Oliver Wendell Holmes, of the Twentieth Massachusetts."

"Holmes? Holmes is dead!"

"He lives," said Leahy. "He's in the Union hospital in Georgetown. But they say he will not live long."

"And he made a statement?"

"Apparently so," said Pinkerton. "General McClellan has a full report."

Harry sank back into his chair. "I don't understand."

Pinkerton moved toward the door. "I will discuss this with the president. As you might imagine, he has taken an interest in this case."

"Is there a conspiracy afoot?" Harry asked. "A plot against the president's friends?"

The Scotsman paused. "What in blazes are you talking about?"

"The letter you dispatched to me. Telling me to protect Colonel Baker."

"I sent you no such letter, Raines. No letter at all."

"That can't be."

"No letter. No telegraph. No communication. When I heard you'd turned up at Ball's Bluff, I had no idea what you were doing there. Your orders were to stay on your farm."

Pinkerton was at the door, looking impatient.

"But you did send a letter! By military courier. General Stone saw it. So did Baker—and Colonel Saylor. It ordered me to Poolesville to attend upon Baker—to guard him against assassins. Ask Saylor. He's around Washington somewhere. Ask Stone! He read it! He said he knew who you were—who Major Allen was."

Pinkerton looked a little pale, even ghostly. "If there was such a letter, I did not send it. If I had, I would certainly not have sent it through General Stone and his staff to read first."

"But you did, Mr. Pinkerton!"

"Show it to me."

Harry looked down at his wretched clothes. Between the Confederates and the Union jailers, he'd lost most of his possessions.

"I don't know what happened to it."

Now Pinkerton opened the door. "If that's your explanation, Harry, I fear you are doomed. There are perils in war, and you surely have come upon a heap of them."

In the morning, not too many hours later, his chamber door banged open to admit Leahy, bearing a large bundle, and two military orderlies, lugging in a large, steaming bucket of hot water.

"Do you remember baths?" said the Irishman. "You are to take one, such as you can, right now. I have also brought you clean clothes from your rooms at the National, and a razor. You are to attend to your appearance. And be quick about it."

"Am I going on trial?"

"No."

"Direct to my hanging, then?"

"No hanging. Not yet."

Leahy apologized for the shackles, applied to both ankles and wrists, but insisted it would not do for Harry to depart the Old Capitol Prison in any other fashion. The coach they boarded was closed, with black leather curtains rolled down over the windows. Leahy followed him in, with pistol drawn. A soldier armed with a musket rode next to the driver and an escort of four cavalry troopers followed. For whatever reason, Harry was being accorded a signal honor, or at least distinction.

The Old Capitol Prison was at First and A streets, Northeast. Noting the descent down Capitol Hill and a turn to the right onto a bumpy, boggy road, Harry tried to guess their route. When they made another right onto a smoother, seemingly broader thoroughfare, he realized they were on New York Avenue, which meant they were heading out of the city. Unless there was some rendezvous in mind out in the Maryland farmlands, he had a fair idea now of their destination.

"Why are we going to the Soldiers' Home?" Harry asked.

Leahy stared at him, then removed his derby hat and set it carefully on the seat beside him. The slightest smile came to his lips as he returned his revolver to the holster beneath his coat.

"You would make a good spy, Harry," he said finally. "But then, that's what you're accused of being. For the wrong side."

"You're not going to tell me what this is all about?"

"I gave my word I wouldn't, and you know I am a man of my word. You'll find out soon enough. We go but four miles."

"Has Lieutenant Holmes been taken there? Am I to confront my accuser?"

"No. Only his accusation."

Harry heard hoofbeats approaching on the left, horses moving at the trot. As they came by, from the opposite direction, there was the loud jangling of many spurs and sabers. The sound diminished—a cavalry troop heading into Washington.

"Tell me about the conspiracy in Baltimore," Harry said.

The warmth of the day had stirred the city's superabundance of flies and one had made its way into the carriage, settling for an instant on Leahy's cheek. It quickly died from a slap. Leahy fastidiously removed the remains.

"And which would that be?"

The team was slowing, for the effort of climbing a hill.

"There was a plot there," Harry said. "To assassinate the president. Before his inauguration."

"So Mr. Pinkerton believed. It was supposed to happen when Mr. Lincoln passed through the place on the way from Philadelphia to Washington."

"And he disguised himself as a woman?"

"Not true, Harry. That's a calumny spread by the secesh press. And I should know, for I was with 'Major Allen' and Mr. Lincoln on that one. The president wore no disguise and was dressed as a man. But it was fierce cold, and he had on a shawl and a deerstalker cap. We got through that hellish place by arriving on an ordinary train unannounced and making the transfer to the Baltimore and Ohio in the dead of night."

"But you believe there was a plot?"

"I'd believe anything of that town. You saw what happened when we tried to bring troops through there last spring. That riot killed ten soldiers and eleven civilians. Could have been a massacre."

The driver quickened the pace, adding jolts to the ride. They were well out into the country now.

"Do you have names of the suspected conspirators?"

Leahy shook his head. "If we had, they'd be locked up at Fort McHenry."

Lincoln had put Baltimore under martial law. Union commanders had been arresting and holding citizens there without benefit of habeas corpus for months.

"That whole city's a secesh conspiracy," Leahy continued. "But the worst of it's to be found among the fine folk up around Mount Vernon Square and the monument. When General Butler wanted to regain control of the town for the Union, he trained his guns on that square. That quieted things mighty fast." He studied Harry a moment. "What interests you in Baltimore?"

"Naked women."

Leahy grinned, but sadly. "I'm afraid, Mr. Raines, that given your situation, you're not going to be looking upon any of those for a long time."

"Unless . . ." Harry sought Leahy's eyes. "Boston, I need to ask a favor."

"I can guess what you have in mind, Raines, but I'm afraid the only favor I can grant you is to remove you from those irons when we reach our destination—which will not be long."

Chapter 12

LEAHY was true to his word, unshackling Harry just as they turned into the gates of the Soldiers' Home and, as an added nicety, allowing him to peek through the window from behind the leather curtain. Still, Harry felt much the condemned prisoner, and the coach as good as a tumbrel.

The home served as a residence and hospital for aged and ailing military men on pension and was a suitably tranquil place, with seemingly no connection to the war. Its principal structure was a large brick three-story building with a square, crenellated tower. The grounds were ample—woods and gardens—crossed by intersecting circular drives. As they rolled along, Harry saw few men in uniform. The patients and attendants alike appeared to be largely in civilian garb, though one old fellow had about his thin, racked frame a uniform he might well have worn serving with Andrew Jackson at the Battle of New Orleans.

When they pulled up in front of a large gabled house near the main building, Harry was surprised to find a troop of young cavalrymen, brilliant in dark blue tunics with shining brass buttons and ornate yellow stripes, sitting astride their mounts in a long, very military line to either side of the house's front entrance. Their sabers were unsheathed and held upright against their shoulders. From the look of them, they had been waiting in that general position for some time.

They were obviously an escort for a very important personage, but there was no other coach in view. Only a lone black horse with a large and comfortable-looking black saddle. Harry assumed it was a high-ranking officer—possibly General McClellan himself. The great man was, among other things, the nominal head of the U.S. Secret Service and Harry's immediate boss above Pinkerton.

"Are they here for me or am I to meet someone?" Harry asked.

"Why would such splendid examples of soldiery be here for the likes of you, Raines?"

"Perhaps a firing squad?"

The carriage had stopped.

"If you please," said Leahy, reaching to open the door and sounding suddenly weary. "We're expected inside."

THE president's Swiss-born secretary, John Nicolay, was seated in the entrance hall, dealing with some sort of correspondence. He gave Harry only a glance—and a markedly disapproving one.

Harry was not going to be dealing with a mere general.

It was a sunny and mild day outside. Inside, the shuttered house gave the aspect of a wintry place, very dark, with a low fire glowing on the grates.

Moving on into the sitting room at Leahy's prompting, Harry saw Pinkerton standing by the mantel. Seated in an armchair near him, staring into the fireplace, was Abraham Lincoln. His natural melancholy appeared to have deepened, evident in the shadows beneath his eyes. His mind seemed fixed on some faraway place. Harry wasn't certain his arrival had been noticed.

But it had.

"Come seat yourself, Captain Raines," said the president, still without turning his eyes to Harry. "I know something of what happened out there at Ball's Bluff. But I would like to hear more. Most particularly from you."

Harry thanked him and took the armchair opposite. There was a book on the small table beside him, a translation. The author was Julius Caesar.

"I am truly sorry about Colonel Baker, sir."

"So am I. I understand you have been accused of murdering him, and I would like to hear your version of the how of it."

Harry unhappily told his tale yet again, placing great emphasis on the mysterious rider who had come and gone so swiftly. When he came to the part concerning the naked woman in the woods, a sort of smile crept onto Lincoln's face, illuminated by the fire. The president leaned back in his chair, looking less pained, almost comfortable.

"That reminds me of a time I once met a woman riding horseback in the woods," he said. "As I stopped to let her pass, she also stopped and, looking at me intently, said, 'I do believe you are the ugliest man I ever saw.' I replied, 'Madam, you are probably right, but I can't help it.' 'No,' she said, 'you can't help it. But you might stay at home.'"

He did not slap his knee or cackle or guffaw, as he had done on previous occasions in Harry's presence, but the smile increased at the corners of the president's mouth and a spark of amusement danced briefly in his eyes. Then he abruptly became solemn again.

"You are far from the ugliest man anyone ever saw, Raines. But that woman in the woods must have wished you'd stayed home."

"Yes, sir," said Harry. "My very thought, after I got knocked in the head and woke up a prisoner of war."

"You think the man who hit you was the one who killed Senator Baker?"

"I do not know, Mr. President. I wasn't given a chance to look at him. Next thing I knew, I was slung blindfolded over a horse and bound for the Confederate camp. But I learned there that the people I sought went north—maybe to Baltimore."

"Learned how?"

"Camp talk." He'd promised Miss Velasquez he'd not betray her. "An officer. Forgot the name."

"You told Leahy here that officer was a Cuban woman."

The president was eyeing Harry as though he had said the Confederate lieutenant had been a visitor from the moon.

"That's correct, sir. In disguise."

Lincoln looked to his Secret Service chief. "You ever hear of such a thing, Pinkerton? Is this what military arms have come to?"

"We've got a dozen Confederate females under guard now at Mrs. Greenhow's house," Pinkerton said. "One of them was arrested for wearing men's clothing. A lady from Philadelphia named Mrs. McCarty. They caught her passing through en route to the South. Found her carrying explosives, medicine, and a pistol. Nice lady. Mrs. Greenhow seems to like her, though she despises that Mrs. Onderdonk we've got there. Calls her a woman of ill repute."

"Is she?"

"Yes. She's also my spy."

"There was a woman served eight years in the British army and the Royal Marines in the last century," said Leahy. "Joined up as a man to escape her husband, who used to beat up on her regular. When he died, she revealed her sex and left the service. She fought in so many battles they gave her a pension."

The president had enough of this digression. He waved his hand to end it and gave Harry a hard look.

In their previous encounters, Lincoln had evidenced some friendliness toward him, an almost fatherly concern for Harry's welfare when he'd inadvertently gotten himself in trouble with Union authorities. There was none of that now. All the president was showing him was his mind.

"No matter how you look at this, Captain Raines, even the bumblingest prosecuting attorney in the land would seem to have a pretty ironclad case of conspiracy, treason, and assassination against you here," Lincoln said. "Consider the facts. A forged letter bearing Mr. Pinkerton's code name gets into dispatches and consequently you're brought into General Stone's camp and to Colonel Baker's side, where you are when he dies."

"But, sir—"

The president raised his hand again, then continued.

"You are a Southerner, from a slave-owning family. Your father and brother are officers in the Rebel army. You have a cousin in Martinsburg who is suspected to be a Confederate agent and actually killed a Union Army sergeant." Now his eyes narrowed, as if better to see Harry's.

"You are a friend of the notorious spy Rose Greenhow," he continued. "I know you assisted in her capture, but I'm told you also attempted to effect her escape by having her transferred to a federal hospital. When that failed, you turn up at the Ball's Bluff disaster—first as a scout who may have led our forces into a trap there, as some contend, and then as the suspected assassin who may have shot down the commander of our forces at a critical moment in the battle. You were accused of doing that by an eyewitness who is not only an exemplary officer but the son of one of this nation's finest men. You are taken prisoner by the Rebels, but then you're mysteriously let go. And your only explanation involves this peculiar tale of a mounted Confederate assassin, a naked woman in the woods, and a woman serving as a Rebel officer in disguise. If you were an attorney for the defense, where would you look for an acquittal in all that?"

"If I were attorney for the defense, sir, I'd be looking for another client."

At last there came a laugh, but a small one. Leahy joined in it but Pinkerton did not.

"That reminds me of a prospective client who came to my law office back in Springfield," Lincoln said. "He laid out his case and I think it was no better a one than yours, but he said he was sure I could win it for him. I said, 'Well, you have a pretty good case in technical law, but a pretty bad one in equity and justice. You'll have to get some other fellow to win this case for you. I couldn't do it. All the time, while talking to the jury, I'd be thinking, "Lincoln, you're a liar," and I believe I should forget myself and say it out loud.'"

Again the eyes narrowed.

"Is this wild tale all a confection? Are you a liar, Captain Raines?"

It was then that Harry realized this was no conversation. He was on trial—before the most powerful judge in the land.

He thought hard. "Only in the service of my country."

Lincoln studied him for a long moment. "How is it you came back to us, Captain Raines?"

"I crossed the river, sir. By Harrison's Island."

Harry had heard that the gentle "Father Abraham" could sometimes display a bit of temper. He saw a flash of it now.

"I know that!" the president said. "I've read Mr. Pinkerton's report. My curiosity is to why. You brought a wounded man back with you, and the personal effects of several others. You could have been shot by either side crossing the river. You could have skedaddled to your family's plantation in Tidewater. But instead you risked your life to come back to us. Why? More spying for the South?"

Harry shook his head. "I have never spied for the South, Mr. President. I'm for the Union. I work for the Secret Service. I work for you."

"He's likely to be shot on sight by our side, though," said Pinkerton.

"Maybe so," said the president. "Our side's got its dander up, for certain. Bull Run was disaster enough. Now this—and Ned Baker slain. The radicals in Congress are hot for an investigation, Captain Raines, hot for a scapegoat. Couldn't do much better than you, could they? Toss you to those wolves and they'd be fed full at least until the next battle—if General McClellan will ever grant us one."

"Raines'd be well suited to the role," said Pinkerton. "He was there at Bull Run, too."

"Why did you try to free Rose Greenhow?" Lincoln asked. "She's done more damage to our cause than three Confederate divisions. You knew that."

"Friendship, Mr. Lincoln. I didn't want her to hang. Now that she's been revealed as a secessionist agent, she can do no more harm. I meant to get her into Virginia, where she might do nothing more useful for the Rebels than pluck lint for bandages."

"I do not wish to have her hanged, either," said Lincoln. "Such a thing would be a barbarous abomination and earn us the reproach of every foreign government. She would give the South a martyr. I would indeed be worthy of the title of dictator that so many have bestowed upon me. But I wish we were rid of her. Even now she tries to pry secrets out of her guards. I fear she's trying to make an escape on her own."

"She has a small daughter, sir. That would be difficult."

The president pondered this, then put the thought aside.

"What did you think of Senator Baker?" he said softly.

"He was a very brave man, sir."

"Bravest I ever met. I knew him since we were boys. We were lawyers at the same time in Springfield. Served in the Illinois Legislature together. He defeated me for the Whig nomination for Congress. I then took the seat when he went off to serve as an officer in Mexico. He went west after that war, like so many. Was a senator first from California and then from Oregon. I do believe he is singly responsible for keeping the Western states with the Union. But he's lost to me now—to us all—because of that pointless encounter at Ball's Bluff."

Harry could sense that the other two men in the room were fidgeting. Lincoln pulled a folded piece of paper from his coat and then took out a pair of spectacles.

"My son Willie wrote a poem," the president said. "He called it 'Lines on the Death of Colonel Baker.' It was published in the *National Republican*. General Lander wrote one, too. You know him? His brigade includes the Twentieth Massachusetts. He wasn't there that day. He was here, at the War Department. But he wrote a poem about it anyway." Out of another pocket came another piece of folded paper.

"'Aye, deem us proud, for we are more, / Than proud of all our mighty dead,'" Lincoln read. "'Pride, 'tis our watchword: 'Clear the boats, / Holmes, Putnam, Bartlett, Peirson—here.'

"It's not very good poetry," he said, when the reading was done. "But the lines stick to the mind. 'Holmes, Putnam, Bartlett, Peirson.' Those names stick to the mind."

"Yes, sir."

"Holmes."

"Yes, sir. A good man."

Harry suspected there were tears in the president's eyes.

"I am not a vindictive man, Captain Raines. I don't hold the rope or firing squad useful instruments of leadership, as Mr. Pinkerton will attest. I do not wish to see you hang any more than I do that Greenhow woman."

"Yes, sir."

"But it's a hard war. Hard."

His gaze returned to the fire. There was no verdict—not yet.

"All right, Raines," said Pinkerton. "This audience is concluded."

In the coach, Leahy replaced Harry's ankle shackles but left his hands free.

"There's a flask of whiskey and a cigar in that sack next to you," he said. "You know I do not much countenance spirits."

"Thank you." Harry pulled forth the flask and took a drink.

"That is all I can do for you, Raines."

Chapter 13

THE rattling of keys stirred Harry from his slumber. He was sitting bolt upright and fully awake by the time the guard, Corporal Gibson, had the door open. The prospect of hanging—even the scantest possibility of it—did indeed wonderfully concentrate the mind.

"You have a visitor, Raines. A lady."

Very few female hangmen. "I thought I wasn't allowed visitors."

"You're allowed kin, and this lady claims to be that."

Harry took out his watch. "It's past ten."

"She only just arrived. She waits in the big room."

"Her name?" Harry stuck his stockinged feet into his boots and stood up.

"Isabel Boyd. She *is* your kin, ain't she?"

"She does not doubt it."

THERE were some who thought Belle a great beauty. Despite an overly prominent nose and chin, she had large, darkly lashed, fetching eyes and a womanly figure without much equal in the world, though Harry was not much attracted by it.

He found her seated primly on a sofa in the prison's common room, encased in a high-collared black dress and drab shawl with a woolen bonnet over her head. She looked much less alluring than she would in summer or at a fancy dress ball. Smiling broadly upon seeing Harry approach, she leaped to her feet and embraced him tightly. There was an element of pride in her expression, as though Harry had won some school prize.

They seated themselves, glancing about the big room circumspectly. It was the largest chamber in the prison but otherwise was occupied only by a snoring, gentlemanly prisoner who'd fallen asleep over his newspaper and a portly guard standing sentry by the entrance to the prison's main corridor. Harry hoped he was as drowsy as he looked.

"In Martinsburg, Harry," she said, "you are a hero. Your exploit has eclipsed my own."

"Murder is no exploit," Harry said. "And that's what I'm accused of. They say I shot that colonel in the back."

"But you are a Virginia gentleman who would shoot no one in the back."

"The Virginia part is what troubles them."

"So you are to be tried?"

"Doubtless so. Some drumhead military court—the usual preliminary to hanging."

She put her hand to his arm in feminine Southern fashion. "Yankee sons of bitches. When will this happen?"

He shrugged. "How is it you are here?"

"I received a message from a Confederate officer. A black man from Leesburg brought it. When I got to

Leesburg, they said you'd gone, so I proceeded on to here." She leaned back, pleased with herself. "My, but it was hard this time getting through Union lines. And harder still passing into Washington City. I was detained at Arlington for two days. I thought I'd be joining you in this prison, not visitin'. I don't know why I'm being treated with such courtesy this evening."

"Let us take advantage of it." Harry leaned closer, lowering his voice. "Belle, I do not plan to attend my execution. I will not be here when they come."

Her eyes lit up. This war was still a great, wonderful game to her. "They did not search me, Harry. I can come back with pistols in my petticoats!"

"If they found them, you might hang along with me. There are those who are still hungry to have you pay for that dead sergeant."

"I'll take the risk to save your neck. What else do you need?"

The guard at the door had stirred himself and was watching them more carefully now—and listening. Harry drew Belle closer still and put his head on her shoulder, as though in deep melancholy. She stroked his cheek, the dutiful, comforting relation. She smelled of some lemon-orange scent.

"Tomorrow bring me some food and two bottles of the National's best brandy. The food's for me. The brandy will find more useful places. Later I'll want a closed coach, with a fast team, some traveling provisions, and a suit of clothes from my rooms at the National. Can a slip of a girl like you manage all that?"

She pulled back, vastly amused—and excited.

"This slip of a girl could rassle you to the ground anytime she pleases. I am capable of snatching that beast Lincoln from his lair, if necessary. I am General Jackson's favorite spy, ain't I?"

He put fingers to his lips. "No such talk here, please."

"Anyway, I'll do it. I can have all this ready by tomorrow night."

"I would be amazed, but grateful . . . 'cousin.' But there's more."

Harry sat up straight, compelling her to do the same. "Our friend," he said. "Lately imprisoned."

"You mean Rose—"

He raised his hand to shush her again. "I fear for her—and most particularly, I fear for the child. Little Rose must be frightened to death, no matter how bravely her mother carries on. I mean to get them to more hospitable quarters." His voice fell to a whisper. "Across the river."

Belle beamed. "With my help!"

"I mean for you to get them there. I have to go elsewhere."

"Where?"

He shook his head. The guard's eyes were still on them.

"You must speak to her in my place. They allow visitors, though I'm sure you will be searched."

"I will do it. But what am I to say?"

"That we are going to free her and get her to Richmond. Tomorrow night. She must be ready by eleven-thirty. We'll go direct from here to there, and I want to move before they change the guard at midnight. You must be waiting outside this place—down around the corner—at eleven. She and Little Rose must be ready a half hour later. In her room."

"How will you manage it?"

"There is a woman now kept prisoner in that house named Onderdonk—a bawd, by profession. It's said she's a Union spy but her true loyalty's the coin. A friend has bribed her to assist us—to, er, distract Rose's guard."

"What a clever idea. Confound the Yankees with their own whore. But how are we to get her across the lines?"

"There's a man who keeps a boat down by Ripp's Island, where they dump the garbage. That'll get you downriver, till you come to the Confederate battery south of Mount Vernon. He must be paid, also."

"How did you manage all this from prison?"

"I haven't managed it yet. That's why I'm calling upon your help."

"I'll see to it! To everything. You were very wise to have picked me as your confederate." She laughed, and repeated the word.

They rose. As they embraced in farewell, he whispered into her ear once more.

"Tell Rose that if she does not come with me, she will hang and the child will be placed in a Northern orphanage." He thought upon the town she despised most. "In Boston."

WITH breakfast, the guard brought a morning newspaper, as Harry had paid him to do. There had been an article or two about his arrest, short on details as to what was supposed to have happened to Baker at Ball's Bluff, but nothing much beyond that. Instead, this morning Harry found really important news. Winfield Scott, the old Mexican War hero and failed presidential candidate, had retired as commanding general of all the Union armies. That had been expected, though not so soon. What came as a surprise was Lincoln's choice of a replacement. He'd made General McClellan the great chief of all in uniform, answerable only to the president, the same McClellan he'd said had "the slows."

They'd been calling Scott "Old Fuss 'n Feathers," but in his prime he'd been the best general officer America had had since the Revolution. A veteran of two wars, he had snatched victory from certain defeat in a dozen battles in Mexico. McClellan had only a small skirmish in the far-off mountains of western Virginia to his credit.

But that had of course been a genuine victory, however small, and the Union had few to boast about. For the moment McClellan retained some popularity with Congress. His promotion would be a sop to those members screaming for a change at the top because of Ball's Bluff. In politics, at least, Lincoln seemed to know what he was doing.

Harry wondered what the appointment would mean for him. Until Harry's arrest, McClellan had been his boss.

BELLE returned at midday.

"Miss Boyd is here for you," said the day guard, a churlish fellow named Lartner. "She's waiting in the main room."

Harry glanced about his chamber. He'd neatened it considerably. "Thank you, Lartner. I'll receive her here."

"Oh y'will, will ye? How is that permitted?"

"Why, you'll permit it—a wise decision I'll amply reward."

"With what?"

"You won't be disappointed. Don't worry, you may leave the door open." Harry's mother would have countenanced nothing less.

Belle swept in bearing a large wicker basket whose

contents were in great disarray. She gave Harry a kiss
upon the cheek, then sat down upon his rude bed,
looking to the open door. Lartner was still there,
waiting. Harry frowned. The soldier finally turned
away.

"Food for you, cousin," she said. "An army's worth
of fine viands."

He sat beside her, lifting a pastry. "Certainly a general's worth."

"Keep watch," Belle said. She went to the room's
lone window, which had been painted over except for
the top panes.

He saw that she was lifting her skirts.

"Belle!"

"I said keep watch," she said curtly. "Don't watch
me; watch that Yankee guard."

"You'd best hurry," Harry said. "We could be undone
in an instant."

Belle's skirts fell back into place. Flouncing them,
she sat back upon the bed, her right hand going beneath
the pillow.

"It's a forty-four-caliber two-barreled derringer I put
there," she whispered. "Put it in your boot when you
can. It's loaded, but there's no spare ammunition."

"Where did . . . ?"

"You were right," she said. "They searched me this
time. Most places. But not all." She reached into the
basket and pulled out a dusty bottle. "Will this do?"

He examined it with care. "My father's cellar never
boasted a cognac so fine."

"It's on your bill at the National and the price is considerable. Open it now, and I'll join you in a glass."

"I have only a broken, filthy cup. It deserves better
than that." He shouted to Lartner, who poked in his

head. "I have excellent brandy here, Private, but no glasses. Could you fetch three for us?"

"There ain't but two of you."

"Three of us—with you, sir."

"I'm obliged, Mr. Raines." It was the first time he'd addressed Harry so respectfully.

When he'd gone, Harry moved to speak close to Belle. "What of Rose?"

"I talked to her. She doesn't trust you much, all right. She doesn't believe what you say about their hangin' her. They've hanged no woman. But she hates being a prisoner in her own house—and she's scared awful about Little Rose. Harrison, I've never seen her like this. She's almost a crazy woman."

"She'll be ready at eleven-thirty?"

"She promises it. I'll be waiting for you with the coach on Maryland Avenue."

"At eleven?"

"At eleven. I'll hold it there just by the corner." She leaned back a little, studying him with sparkly eyes. "I must confess, cousin, I would not have suspected this of you."

"Do you mean my dauntless courage or my devotion to the Southern cause?"

"I mean a reprobate, skirt-chasing gambler like you caring that much about a little child."

THE Old Capitol Prison had been built as a residential mansion in 1814, the year the British had burned Washington, and had been pressed into service after that disaster as a temporary home for the Congress. When the gutted Capitol building was rebuilt and restored, the temporary one became a boardinghouse, one of the largest and grandest in the city, for a time. No less a personage than John C. Calhoun had lived there.

Its conversion into a prison had involved little more than adding bars to the first- and second-floor windows and breaking through the walls of two adjoining buildings—the Duff Green House and Carroll Row—to add more accommodations. Though they were kept locked, there were outside doors aplenty. Harry hadn't knowledge of all the floors and rooms and corridors, but he'd learned enough.

Or so he hoped.

After Belle left, he had a drink with Private Lartner, then gave the man the bottle, hoping that—in the manner of a rat returning to its nest with poison—he'd take it back to the guardroom and share it with his fellows.

The other bottle he saved for Corporal Gibson, his night guard.

It was a cold night, and Gibson proved very pleased and grateful for the glass of brandy Harry offered. He readily accepted the invitation to return for more each time he made his rounds. By eleven o'clock, he was lying on Harry's bed, snoring loudly. Harry gently relieved him of uniform coat and hat, then pulled a blanket over him. Putting on the coat—wishing Gibson was taller and of higher rank—he pulled the cap down low over his brow, took the guard's keys, and with derringer in hand, left the room, locking the door behind him.

The corridor outside was already dim, but as Harry moved along it, he turned out what gaslights he encountered. Taking what had been the back servants' stairs, he encountered only one other jailer, who paid him no attention.

The guardroom was down by the prison's main entrance, as was the common room, and there were voices coming from it. The soldiers were preparing to change shifts. Harry went the other way, down the servants' staircase to a narrow hall that led out to the backyard. These grounds were securely walled, as they were used for prisoners' exercise, and seemingly offered no escape.

Harry knew better. Unlatching the door to the yard, he swung it slowly open, searched the darkness for a sign of sentries, and finding none, stepped out into the cold. Hesitating, listening now more than looking, he crept along the building wall to a set of double wooden doors that enclosed the cellar steps of the adjoining Duff Green House. This would be the hardest part, for he could not be certain what lay below.

There was no padlock. Lifting one of the doors with an unfortunately loud creak and letting it fall with an even more unfortunate bang, he hurried down the stairs, stumbling and banging his knee as he did so.

Moving through the cellar to the foot of the wooden steps leading to the kitchen above, he paused. He half expected to hear shouting coming from the exercise yard—and cries of discovery. But there was nothing.

Treading as gently as possible on the old wooden steps, he hesitated by the kitchen door, then pushed it slowly open. As he'd expected, the kitchen was empty and dark but for a glow of lamplight coming in from the street.

He hurried forward, past a long table and a large wooden tub, to the door. It was locked, but the key was in the hole. He turned it. The sense of freedom came to him like the cold freshness of the night air. With no further care to anything, he bolted for the street.

Dogs were barking, but they always were. Somewhere over by the Capitol he could hear some sort of noisy commotion, and more noise just as rowdy in the other direction, down by Swampoodle, the city's Irish neighborhood. Here on First Street, it was quiet. There were two soldiers at the main entrance to the prison, just down the street, but they were turned toward each other, talking, hunched against the cold.

Harry headed the other way down First Street, then at the next shadowy stretch crossed to the other side. Reversing direction again, walking along as naturally as possible, he moved on past the prison.

The corner at Maryland Avenue was perhaps a hundred feet ahead. As he drew nearer, he could see the lead horses of Belle's team just beyond the front-yard fence of a house. A few steps more, and he heard the sudden crack of a whip and saw the horses jolt forward. Turning, the coach caught the curb with one wheel as it rounded the corner, lifting, swaying, bumping, and coming down with a jangly thump. Another snap of whip and the team hustled toward him in a fast trot, Belle on the driver's perch wearing a man's overcoat, the coach lurching suddenly to a stop as it drew nigh.

"You're late," she said.

Harry swung open the door. "Make up for it."

BELLE kept cracking the whip. They rumbled down the hill through Swampoodle then took Massachusetts Avenue to I Street and proceeded west to Lafayette Park. Harry had her pull up just shy of St. John's Church, which sat across Sixteenth Street from the Greenhow place.

"Harry, we're a block from the president's house. Another from the War Department."

He dropped quietly to the street. "You're breaking no law. Not yet. Just sit tight. I'll tell you when to be worried."

Flitting along the park and then across H Street, Harry made it to the darkened rear of "Fort Greenhow," looked around carefully, then pulled himself up on the wall and dropped to the garden on the other side. Nothing stirred at his intrusion. Ahead, he could see a few lights in the upper floors of Rose's house.

There were voices coming from the kitchen, soldiers taking refreshment. There should have been a sentry at the rear door, but Mrs. Onderdonk would be attending to him—or so Harry hoped.

Dropping to the ground, he straightened his army jacket, pulled the cap down low, and walked purposefully toward the house. The back door opened at his pull. The soldiers in the kitchen scarcely looked up.

Ascending the back staircase, he saw a guard seated in a chair at the other end of the upstairs hall, but his chin was on his chest. Harry fetched up the derringer that Belle had given him.

At Rose's door, he was about to gently rap when he thought better of it and gently pushed it open, hoping she'd not greet him with a scream or curse. Harry needed her absolute compliance and obedience, qualities that were strange to her.

Alone but for her daughter, not yet taken to her bed, the lady was seated with great, sad-eyed dignity on a chair by the window, with only a candle for illumination. Rose's eyes looked as though they'd been fixed on the door for the entire night. On the bed, beneath covers, the child lay sleeping.

Harry walked up to the woman, looking down into her staring eyes solemnly.

"Did Belle explain it all?" he asked.

"Yes."

"Will you come with me now? I can have you in Virginia before sunrise. Richmond by tomorrow night."

She sighed. "This is my house."

"You said you'd do anything for the Southern cause."

"And so I would."

"Then come now. We are going down the main stairs and walking straight out the front door. All I must ask of you is not to say another word until we are free of this place."

She turned to wake the child. It was well she was being so compliant. The derringer wasn't for the guards. It was for her—persuasion, just in case.

As they prepared to return to the corridor, he offered her his hand, for guidance. She pulled hers away. Nevertheless, she stayed close behind. Her sleepy child seemed much confused, but obeyed her mother's bidding, as always, and kept quiet.

There was a soldier in the foyer below. Happily, a mere private. He looked up.

"Provost marshal's office," Harry said to him. "Secret Service wants to talk to her. Be back later."

He didn't linger long enough to hear the man's reply. Taking Rose's arm now whether she liked it or not, he pulled her along down the stairs, Little Rose somehow keeping up.

Belle, bless her, was alert to all this. There was a slap of whip and the horses jerked forward. The carriage was beside them in a moment.

"Hurry, Rose! Inside!"

She looked at him, looked up at Belle, and then stared at the open coach door.

"Rose, please!"

Her eyes closed in a sudden wince as a gunshot sounded, a whizzing bullet thunking into the wood of the coach just to her left.

Harry whirled about toward the door of her house, his derringer to the fore. Even had he his spectacles in place, he couldn't have hit much with the little gun. All he had in mind was an intimidating shot in reply.

He was suprised to see two soldiers standing in Rose's doorway, staring back at him, looking just as startled by the gunshot. Neither had his weapon raised.

"Rose! Get in! Hurry!"

She was wide-eyed, openmouthed. Frantic, she turned and flung her arm around her daughter, pulling her to her side.

"Rose!"

Another shot. Harry heard this round pass close by his ear. Belle flicked the reins.

Rose screamed. Her arm tight around her daughter's shoulders, she began to run.

Back toward her house.

Harry jumped aboard the coach as a third shot whizzed overhead. He had seen the flash this time.

It had come from Lafayette Park.

Chapter 14

Harry left Belle at Georgetown, wishing her a safe journey to Martinsburg. She was quick of mind and resolute in action. He supposed his concern would be better placed for any unfortunate Union soldier who tried to hinder her.

Belle's considerable efforts on his behalf hadn't been entirely in vain. Harry had officially escaped the Old Capitol Prison—as far as he knew, the first person to have done so. But he was otherwise appalled by the night's turn of events.

He took refuge in one of the federal city's ubiquitous wood yards. Shivering, he struggled to make himself lie there, still and quiet, listening until he was certain there would be no pursuit. Then he crept out of the yard and down a long alley that led to the river. He needed to depart this city swiftly, but there was a stop he needed to make. He wished he could go to his rooms, to fetch new clothing, or to his stable office, where he could procure pistols, some money, and a horse, but both those places would likely have soldiers or the provost guard at them now.

Still, there was another destination where he'd not be expected.

THE black man who opened the door at Mollie Turner's whorehouse did not want to admit him. Standing in the doorway, he studied Harry's appearance and shook his head.

"Only gentlemen callers're welcome here, Corporal," he said. "Try the place around the corner."

Harry had no money for bribes or inducements.

"I'm not here as a patron. I need to speak to Miss Ella Turner."

"The likes o' you got no need for that. She sure got no need o' the likes o' you."

Harry took a deep breath. "Tell her it's her friend the captain. And that it's extremely important."

"What you mean captain? You a corporal."

"Just tell her! Tell her I have what she asked for."

"Then give it to me."

This was taking too long. "That I cannot do." He turned from the door. "And I will tell her later why it is she failed to receive what she requested of me."

He started walking. He kept walking. He was out in the middle of the street when the majordomo finally called out, "Wait!"

Harry looked back.

"Wait around the corner of the house," said the black man. "I will tell her you're here."

He did as bidden. It was many cold minutes before the door opened again. The hooded figure that came to him was not the black servant, however. It was Ella, wearing her long green cloak. Stepping into the shadows beside him, she drew him farther into the darkness.

"Are you crazed, Captain Raines?" she said. "The

house is full of Union officers. General Hooker is in there!"

She had named a brigade commander who had just been promoted to head a division guarding the capital. Harry had observed the general in saloons and did not care for him much.

"I have what you wanted," he said.

She had pulled the hood of her cloak well over her head. He could see only the faint outline of her face—and the gleam of a beautiful eye.

"What is that?"

"The pass. Signed by President Lincoln." He reached into his pocket and then handed the folder paper to her, with great care. It was the one he had carried sewn within his cuff. There was no other name on it save the appellation "the bearer."

She looked at it carefully, holding it toward the faint light from the corner street lamp, then folding it again.

"It was weeks ago I asked for this."

"Yes, ma'am. I apologize. I was distracted."

"You were in the Old Capitol Prison. By what miracle do you come to be here?"

"With great difficulty. Is Booth still in need of that pass?"

"He still desires it. He hasn't returned to Washington."

"Caitlin Howard is still with him?"

"She has not returned either, and I don't know where she is. Wilkes is in Buffalo or Cincinnati, at a theater, I know not which. If she's what you want in return for this pass, I cannot deliver her. And I do not wish him to have it. Not now."

"But—"

"He travels too much as it is. I have no desire to pro-vide him the means to go where I could not follow. He will leave her, someday soon, but when he does I don't wish it to be for some actress in Richmond or Charleston. I want him here."

He stepped close, wishing he could see her better.

"Ella, I'm desperate. I need a horse and some money—which I will repay."

She said nothing.

"I also need the name of someone in Baltimore who would take in a fugitive from federal justice," he continued. "Someone so ardent in their love for the Confederacy they would accept such a fugitive without question."

He sensed rather than saw her smile. "That would be most anyone in Baltimore." She paused in thought. "But, in such a need, I think you would best call on the Cary sisters—Hetty and Jenny Cary. Hetty is held the belle of Baltimore, and Jenny is nearly as comely. They live by Mount Vernon Square."

"Mount Vernon Square. The battle monument."

"Yes, but they will require bona fides before they tender assistance. That Yankee soldier's coat will not do."

"I'll prepare myself accordingly."

She pulled her cloak more tightly about her against the cold. "Why do you go to Baltimore? It's full of federals as well as secesh. After General Dix took command of the Baltimore district, it's said he had a cannon at Fort McHenry trained upon the Cary house."

"I go on business. Business of some urgency."

"As your friend, Harry Raines, I would urge you far away from here. I fear for your life."

"I find myself with the same notion this evening."

She gave him a curious look, but did not pursue the subject.

"Here are a few gold pieces, Captain," she said, reaching within her cloak. "That's all I can give you—except this."

To his amazement, she leaned close, tilting her head, and gave him a soft, sweet, gentle kiss.

"I fear Wilkes would kill us both for that, but you have it coming. So does he."

"I am honored, Miss Turner."

She stepped back. "Indeed you are. As for a horse, you will have to steal one. There are a number in my sister's stable. Officers' mounts. All saddled and waiting. Go now and it will be some time before the loss is noticed. My sister's callers seem to be enjoying themselves tonight."

Now she thrust something else into his hand. The pass.

"You're sure?" he asked. "He has asked for this. You would be denying him. You said he was already angry with you about me."

"I am certain," she said, turning away. "I think you may have need of it tonight, Harry. And other nights. He won't. I do not wish it."

He placed it in his wallet.

Ella smiled, but more sadly than sweetly. "Go now, Harry. Go fast and far. And be very careful. I've learned the name of the party who's trying to kill you. His name is Buckeys, Samuel Buckeys. And he's a Maryland man."

Chapter 15

FROM his window at Barnum's City Hotel, held as the most secessionist hostelry in Baltimore, Harry could see two federal detectives, one lounging by a lamppost on the corner of Fayette and Calvert just below, another across the street, pretending to read a newspaper. That morning, returning to his room after breakfast, he'd noticed two others in the lobby, idly engaged but obvious as well.

The federal authorities now in control of Baltimore certainly knew the sort of people who stayed in this particular hotel. They doubtless tolerated the establishment and its politics because it served their purpose to do so. It was their window on Confederate activities in Maryland. Taken as a sanctuary by Southern sympathizers, the place was useful to the federals to keep an eye on things, to monitor the levels and natures of secret secesh business here.

If only they'd learned to be more discreet about it.

Harry was decidedly not himself, certainly not anyone looking a fugitive from the Old Capitol Prison. He was wearing a very fine suit of clothes—gray trousers, paisley vest, large silk cravat, and London-tailored black frock coat with black silk facings. Black kid gloves; a wide-brimmed, flat-crowned black hat; highly polished black boots; and a walking stick completed the ensemble. He had colored his hair and mustache black, so dark he might have passed for John Wilkes Booth.

In fact, he was registered at Barnum's as "Richard York," a reference to Booth's favorite role—with a "III" attached. Harry was styling himself a professional gambler while in Baltimore. That was true enough. He was gambling everything on a few chance words let slip by Loreta Velasquez.

The stick he carried, in Southern gentlemanly custom, distinguished him as a man who perforce did no real work. In the "slavocracy" of the South, labor was held to be fit only for the inferior classes, beasts of burden, and, of course, Negroes.

There were plenty of the latter to be found in the town, many of them laboring for money. For all its proslavery sentiments, Baltimore had the largest concentration of free blacks of any city in the country, more than twenty thousand. Of slaves, there were only about two thousand. Yet here had been seen ladies of high station parading about in dresses made of the Confederate colors—until the Union Army outlawed the practice. Southerners who complained that President Lincoln was fostering dictatorship were not exaggerating in the case of Baltimore. Yet he had the most excellent reasons.

Harry descended to the bar for a quick whiskey.

There were several well-dressed patrons, one of them a man he recognized from the night before. His name was Charles Langley, and he claimed to be a newspaper correspondent assigned to Baltimore. The fellow was nearly as handsome as Booth himself, with a magnificent mustache to match, and wore clothes that looked far too expensive for a newspaperman. He claimed to be with the *New York Tribune,* though he seemed very much a Southerner.

Harry bought the fellow a generous drink of his own favorite tipple, Old Overholtz 1857, and one as large for himself.

"You found yourself a poker game yet?" asked Langley.

Harry had been inquiring after one the previous evening.

"No, sir. No one has obliged me."

"You'd find a mighty lot of them in one of the federal camps. The soldiers go at it all the time. Never stop."

"The federal camps are not the society I prefer." Harry took a gentlemanly sip of the bourbon.

"I guess not—in your circumstance."

"What do you mean?"

"I believe I know who you are."

"My name is Richard—"

"I believe, sir, your name is Harrison Raines."

Langley produced from his coat pocket a slim, folded newspaper, opening it to an inside page and setting it on the bartop. There was a story about Harry's escape from the Old Capitol Prison, accompanied by a badly done cut of a sketch, with hair and mustache rendered as though light in color. The story seemed to have mostly to do with his theft of General Hooker's own horse from a whorehouse stable, an occurrence apparently greeted with widespread amusement in the capital.

Harry had left Hooker's animal at Relay, the railroad junction southwest of Baltimore, to be recovered by the army. But the general, it appeared, remained highly displeased.

"You recognize me from that crude drawing?"

"Not exactly. I've heard a lot of talk about you, and you seem to fit what is said. I am surprised, sir, to find you in this place."

"It's a place of Southern sympathy."

"It's also a place of much Northern curiosity. You're a damned fool to expose yourself so liberally to watchful eyes. Some mistake you for the actor Booth. Were it not for that, you might this moment be in irons."

"I may have been incautious." That was no lie. He drank again. "But I didn't think I'd be looked for here."

"Not looked for—but now observed. My editor in New York telegraphs me all the time with the complaint that no news ever seems to come from Baltimore. Not since the Union occupation and mass arrests. But here you are to provide for the lack. I'd be pleased to hear whatever you might want to tell me of your adventure— to be published after you have departed from this city and I am sure you are safe. When do you go? And where?"

Harry sipped. "Don't know the answer to either question. I was told I might find friends and a helping hand at the house of a family named Cary. I called upon them yesterday but found no one at home."

"Might have a month ago. And they would have been well disposed to you, I think. Especially Hettie. But it's too late for that. The sisters have gone to Richmond. The brother's in the Confederate Army. The parents have removed to the country. General Dix, who runs this town in the manner of a generalissimo, requires an oath of loyalty to the United States as the price of continued residence. Those unwilling to do that must go elsewhere."

"Does no one simply lie?" Harry asked.

Langley thought upon this, then turned to his refreshed glass, lifting it carefully for a sip, his eyes flicking carefully over the others in the barroom.

"There is someone else here who might offer you hospitality—and assistance. How soon do you depart?"

"Not this day."

"Good. Don't stray from the hotel. The pleasure of your company may be requested this evening."

He would say nothing more about this invitation. They talked awhile longer about the small progress of the war, then Langley finished his drink and took his leave. Harry thought him a smooth fellow and wondered why he didn't move his base of operation to Washington, where his charm and skills might find better purpose.

Harry had no doubt he was a spy.

GOING for a brief walk, playing the innocent when he strolled by the lurking federal detectives, Harry returned to the warmth of his room and lay down. Sleep came quickly. When he awoke, it was evening.

He refreshed himself and went downstairs, but found no message for him at the desk or anywhere else. A glass of whiskey in the bar restored him again but did nothing for the pangs of hunger he was beginning to feel.

Langley's talk of an invitation had not produced one.

Harry waited in the lobby, reading newspapers and lounging, until after nine, then gave in to his appetite, which was raging with some fury. In the dining room, he managed oysters, a beefsteak, potatoes, and an apple pie, washed down with wine and coffee.

There was still no word at the desk. He went to the

room he was told was Langley's, but there was no response to his knock.

Another turn around the streets. The night had become very cold and he walked fast. The detectives had gone but he did have a sense of someone following him. Pausing in the light from a gas-fired street lamp, he glanced back into the shadows and saw a large, squarish, bearded man standing close to the side of a building. For a moment he thought it might have been Samuel Buckeys, but the fellow would have no idea Harry had come here.

He hurried across the street, around a corner, and then down an alley. At the farther end, he stopped and waited for some sign or sound of pursuit. None came. Walking quickly, he returned to his hotel. Once back in his room, he locked the door and turned out the lamp, reclining on his bed with his revolver nearby.

This was no life. He should have taken Saylor up on his generous offer of escape.

The next thing he knew, there was a sharp, insistent rapping. According to his watch, it was after midnight.

With pistol in his right hand, he went to the door, flattening himself against the wall on the other side of it and turning the key and knob with his left. With a quick pull, he swung it partially open.

No one entered. Nothing moved. Then he heard a soft, cool, feminine English voice say, "Harry? Are you there?"

HE pulled the door open fully, so swiftly he startled his caller.

"Kate?"

Caitlin Howard stepped into the room uncertainly, hesitating just inside. Harry went to the gaslight to turn it up. When he looked back to her, she gave a slight shriek.

"What's wrong?" he asked.

She had put her hand to her mouth. She dropped it, leaving a small, embarrassed smile on her face.

"I am sorry. It's just that, with your hair so dark, you look exactly like Wilkes."

Her own copper-colored hair looked quite dark in this faint light as well. But there was a brightness in her gray eyes.

"My apologies." He couldn't keep the edge from his voice. "I'll shave the mustache."

"No, please . . ." She glanced quickly about the room. He pulled forth a chair for her near the little coal stove and poured her a glass of whiskey.

"Thank you." She sipped with trembling fingers. "Winter is almost upon us."

"How did you find me?"

"A friend of Wilkes."

"The name?"

"I don't know. The friend told Wilkes where you were. He knows people everywhere."

Harry leaned back against his dresser, arms folded. This was not good news. He was shivering, but tried not to show it.

"It's dangerous here, Caitlin. Why have you come?"

"Dangerous?"

"Dangerous city. Full of Rebels. I don't know if anyone told you, but I'm a fugitive. I'm charged with murder."

"Yes," she said sadly. "Of course I know. I read it in a dozen newspapers. I've come because you have something for Mr. Booth."

"I do?"

"Yes. A document. Guaranteeing unhindered passage. I've come for it."

Harry crossed over to the stove. "Where is he?"

"He went on to Cincinnati. He has an engagement at Wood's Theatre. *Hamlet, Richard III,* the usual repertoire. The booking's through December seventh. He'll need what you have to give him before he returns to Washington."

"And he has you traveling all over the country on this errand?"

She shook her head. "I came to talk to people at Grover's Theatre in Washington about a part in a new play. I'll be there a few days before, before returning to . . ."

Harry stared at her, but she avoided his eyes. He sighed, then went to a dresser drawer, returning with the carefully folded presidential pass.

"I'm not doing this for him," he said, handing it to her.

She took the paper carefully and placed it in a pocket. "I do appreciate the kindness, Harry—and your friendship."

"I'm doing it for Ella Turner," he said. The cruelty of his words seemed to sting far more than he had intended. "As an obligation. I made a bargain with her. She has helped me in my present troubles. Though it appears she has mentioned them to Booth."

"She . . . I see." Her voice fell.

It was truly cold. Harry went to the scuttle and quickly tossed a handful of coals into the stove. "Have you a place to stay tonight?"

"I came direct from the Camden Station. I'll find quarters. I'm leaving on the first morning train."

"Stay here."

A long pause. "We are friends, Harry, but . . ."

"We shall remain friends. You take your rest on the bed. I'll sleep on the armchair. It's too late and too cold to go searching for an available room."

"You're sure this won't make difficulties?"

"I am sure."

With a rustle of skirt she rose, finished her whiskey, set it on the night table, removed her shawl and bonnet, and then lay back on the bed. He pulled the thick quilt over her.

"There."

Her eyes showed affection, but also wariness. After turning down the gaslight, Harry pulled his greatcoat over his shoulders and went to the only soft armchair in the room.

"Let us talk awhile," she said.

"We used to do that a lot," he said. "Late into the night. Last summer . . ."

"I'm living with Wilkes now, Harry."

"So Ella informed me."

"You call her Ella."

"She's also a friend."

"I see." Icy words.

"He'll leave you, Kate. He leaves them all."

She didn't answer. They remained silent. Harry stared at the glow from the stove. Outside, he heard a faint jangling. It came nearer, a cavalry troop. He sat absolutely still, listening to every ringing fall of hoof until they'd passed by.

"What are you going to do, Harry? This city is full of soldiers and detectives. It's a poor place for someone in your trouble. Why don't you run for the South?"

"My politics haven't changed, Kate. I'm here in the hope of finding the person who did commit the murder I'm accused of."

"How will you do that? You're all on your own."

"Booth could help, were he here," Harry said.

"He has the new play. The play comes before everything." She turned on her side, pulling the quilt closer. "I'm going to sleep now, Harry."

"All right. Sweet dreams, then."

"No one has those now, Harry. Not with this war."

He sat and listened to her breathing for a long time. He could tell she was not sleeping. Harry decided a moment had come he'd put off for far too long.

"I love you, Kate."

She did not reply.

"I needed to say it before you go," he said finally.

A long silence. Then she sighed. There was a rustle of dress again and she was standing.

"I'm going to go, Harry."

"Kate, please. I meant no . . . I wouldn't touch you."

She gave him a weary look. "I shouldn't mind if you touched me, Harry. It's the loving part that's beyond my coping."

"That's the part I can't help."

"I love John Wilkes Booth, Harry. You know that. You know it well. You have always known it."

"And he loves Ella Turner."

She pulled her shawl around her shoulders. "I'm not sure he knows who he loves. He does not love you, Harry."

"He's obliged to me. Especially now."

"As I shall constantly remind him." She gathered up the rest of her things.

"He's for slavery, Kate. You loathe and abhor the institution as much as I do."

"He doesn't know what he's for. He's all caught up in myth and legend. The romantic South. The glorious cause. He's confused, like so many of you Southerners."

"I am not confused."

"No? Then why are you here—a fugitive from federal justice. I know you didn't murder that officer, but the newspapers say you did try to break Rose Greenhow out of prison. What is that if not confusion? It could be called treason."

"Kate, please . . ."

She pulled on her bonnet, tying it tightly. "I'll take a cab back to the station. It's warm there, and it's only a few more hours' wait."

He held her with his gaze as long as he could, then went to his saddlebags, pulling forth a small flat package.

"I need a favor from you," he said. "It's important to me, important to my quest. I know I've made you angry, but—"

"I'll help you, Harry," she said, her voice more gentle. "Any way I can. We are friends still."

He put the package in her hands. "When you can, find out where this came from."

She opened the package carefully, peering at the object uneasily.

"You've seen these before," he said.

She held it up to the light. "Yes. Of course."

"And you will help me?"

"Yes."

"Thank you." He didn't move another inch closer to her. "A good night to you, Kate."

"A good night to you, sir." She moved by him more swiftly than he had ever seen her exit from the stage.

THE cold and troubling thoughts kept him from sleep after she left. At the very first touch of light at the window, he rose and set about washing and dressing, this time choosing clothes for their warmth.

No one was in the lobby except for the night desk clerk, and he was asleep at his post, snoring on a chair. Harry slipped past him, down the corridor that led to the rear door of the hotel. Crossing the yard, he found the stable door closed but unlocked.

A black stable hand was at work with a shovel and rake, cleaning stalls. He gave Harry a quick but disinterested look, without ceasing his labors. Harry went back and forth along the twin rows of stalls, then halted by the stable hand.

"I'm looking for a white horse," he said.

"White horse?"

"White horse. A gray."

The man, who had a white scar running the length of his cheek, returned to his labors.

"Ain't none in this stable—as you can plainly see."

"Are there any in this neighborhood? "

"Mister, there's white horses all over this city."

"But in this neighborhood—owned by Confederate sympathizers."

The groom thought upon this, or upon Harry, then set down his rake and led Harry outside and up the gangway that ran from the yard to the front of the hotel. He pointed diagonally across the street toward the northwest, where the marble column of the George Washington Monument could be seen rising from its hilltop.

"Up there," said the man. "Mount Vernon Square. One of the houses on it. They got a gray."

There were federal detectives on the street again and one now straightened from where he'd been leaning against a tree. He seemed to be watching them.

"Is there a livery nearby?" Harry asked.

"This here's a livery stable," said the black man. "We hire out horses."

"I need one."

"A white one?"

"Any color."

HE rode down to the inner harbor, taking his breakfast at an establishment near the custom house. Afterward, he went on to the end of Long Dock, eyeing the steamers and schooners tied up along it, then crossed the bridge over the canal to City Dock, steering his horse among the stacks of crates and barrels and assorted military equipment piled there awaiting shipment to Washington and the front.

None of the soldiers on guard challenged him. One or two actually called out to him admiringly as "Mr. Booth." Harry decided against shaving off the mustache. If he continued to be taken for the actor here, it could be useful. It pleased him to know how much it would irritate Booth were he to know.

The horse Harry'd rented was responsive and had a comfortable gait. Despite the cold, he decided to continue his perambulation of the city, crossing the Philadelphia, Wilmington & Baltimore tracks east of the station and heading up the hill on Central Avenue. At Monument Street, he turned west again, ascending the hill to Mount Vernon Square. He paused at the starkly Gothic facade of the Methodist church on the north side of the Washington statue, then found his way into the alley that ran behind the houses on the north side of the square.

As he expected, a number of stable doors were now open, as horses were being exercised and stalls cleaned. Halting at the stable behind a large red-brick house, Harry caught sight of a narrow-hipped white mare or gelding being worked over with a brush. The animal had a very long gray tail, much like the horse Harry had seen in the woods near Ball's Bluff.

He moved on. At the end of the alley, behind the yellow house on the corner, he found the stable still closed and locked. Dismounting, he led his hired mount up close to it, peering through a dusty window. There were four stalls along one wall. Two had horses in them—a bay and a chestnut—and the other two were empty.

A man was watching him from the street just beyond. Paying him no mind, Harry remounted and moved out of the alley at a walk, pulling his hat down low and hunching a shoulder slightly so the man would have trouble getting a good view of his face.

Once again, there was a resemblance to Samuel Buckeys.

HARRY took a circuitous route back to the hotel, arriving from the southwest. No one had followed, at least that he had noticed.

A letter was waiting for him at the desk, a brief note from Charles Langley:

> *If you are not engaged this evening, you and I are invited to supper with the Ingraham family. They are very interested in meeting you and I believe you will find them more than sympathetic. Please be ready by eight o'clock. They reside not far, on the Monument Square.*
>
> *Yr. Obnt. Svt.,*
> *Charles Langley*

Chapter 16

THERE were only four of them at the table for the Ingrahams' impromptu dinner party. Mr. Ingraham, the head of the household, was off at his plantation on Maryland's Eastern Shore, where Harry gathered he had been in residence for most of the now many months of war. The father's ailing wife was upstairs, bedridden with a lingering fever and having little interest in descending from her room even if well.

No matter. The masters of this house were obviously the two grown children.

Not yet twenty-five, the daughter, Amalie, was the elder child, a comely and spirited young woman said by Charles Langley to be the reigning belle of Baltimore in the absence of the decamped Cary sisters. Unusally tall, nearly as tall as her brother, with finely brushed light brown hair, bright blue eyes, a small mouth, narrow waist, and a fair complexion, Miss Ingraham had beauty enough to lay claim to that title on appearance alone.

But she had a demeanor and temperament to match. Harry had been born and raised among high-strung, aristocratic women of her type, who abounded in Tidewater, Virginia. But her autocratic manner went far beyond this. The emperors of France or the czars of Russia must have such daughters.

For the moment she was amiable enough, playing the Southern coquette to both Harry and Langley, as if they were beaux.

"We are thrilled and delighted to have you in our house, Captain Raines," she said in a great flutter as the first course was served. "Word of your daring exploit precedes you."

She was wearing a floral perfume. Its scent was beguiling.

"Captain?" said Harry, not wanting to discuss his "daring exploit," as he presumed she must mean the murder of Colonel Edward Baker.

He didn't much want to discuss the "captain," either. His mind raced, wondering how Miss Ingraham had acquired knowledge of this rank—suspicion falling swiftly on Ella Turner. She likely had betrayed his Secret Service role to Booth, and this was the result. Caitlin had not known of his work for Pinkerton. Certainly his cousin Belle did not. He feared he was undone—a marked man now on both sides of the Potomac.

"Oh, I am sorry," said Amalie, fanning herself. "It's your brother James, isn't it? He is the captain in your family—a very dashing captain, in the cavalry. Someone told me that when I mentioned you were coming tonight. But he cannot be as dashing or intrepid as you."

"My brother is in the cavalry, yes, ma'am. He and my father are with General Longstreet."

Her eyes were playful. "You must be very proud—to have the both of them wearing the uniform of your country."

He looked down at his soup bowl. "They are both honorable men—gentlemen true to their beliefs."

She fanned herself again. "And they must be proud of you—even though you do not wear the uniform of their country."

"Amalie!"

The sharp rebuke came from her brother, who was named Robert. A thin, delicate, even feminine fellow, perhaps a year or two younger than she, he looked so much like his sister he might have been a twin—were his hair not so dark and coarse. He'd been drinking wine too heavily, and his cheeks were flushed. His complexion was otherwise quite the same as hers.

She lowered her eyelids. "I am sorry, Robert." A sweet smile now for Harry. "You have served your country well, Mr. Raines—without a uniform."

"Indeed he has," said Langley. "Begging your pardon, sir, but I took the precaution of making inquiries after meeting you. You are in truth considered an enemy of the Union."

"And so you are welcome in this house," said Amalie, all sweetness. "Anytime."

"A toast!" said brother Robert, refilling his glass. "To Harrison Raines. Who joins the ranks of our heroes."

Harry gave a quick, awkward bow of his head, then sipped his wine discreetly. He wondered how much of a mistake he had made in coming here. There was something about this Robert that seemed a little crazed—and dangerous.

"I am very taken with your gown, Miss Ingraham," Harry said, deciding to play the cavalier.

It was in truth a wonder of patriotic design. The bodice was a blue field dotted with the stars of the several Confederate states. The apron of the ruffled skirt was of red and white panels, arranged as the stripes on the Confederate flag. The Stars and Bars as adornment for a woman. She looked a veritable pageant.

"That awful General Dix, our brute of a lord and master, was not taken with it," she said. "He issued an order banning the display or sale of secessionist badges, pictures, flags, songbooks, photographic plates, cravats, jewelry—even children's stockings, if they are of the wrong colors. I stepped out upon the square one evening with my friends Hetty and Jenny Cary dressed in this fashion. We were pounced upon by the Yankee provost guard and told to change clothes at once or be arrested as Rebels! One sergeant threatened to tear them from my body if I didn't!" She looked at each of the men, seeking from them the same high degree of amazement. "What of the federal Constitution? What of my rights? I tell you, gentlemen—this *is* the second American Revolution. King George the Third wasn't half the tyrant that this baboon in Washington City is."

Her brother set down his wineglass—too sharply. Some of its contents sloshed onto the table. He ignored this, as did an elderly black servant who'd been standing in the corner by the sideboard, which had two decanters and an odd small bowl with a dozen or so paper roses in it. A painting of some ancestor looked down from just above, with stern disapproval. The black man had an expression to match. There was no seat for him, and he looked as though he needed one.

"They arrested the mayor, newspaper editors, half the state legislature," Robert Ingraham exclaimed. "And marched them all off to Fort McHenry. They've turned that place into a prison camp."

Harry knew of the arrests. Though he had been off at his farm, as ordered, the midnight raids that had netted all these operatives and suspects had been led by Pinkerton. The Scotsman had been fearful that the Maryland state legislature was preparing to vote secession.

"It sounds an outrage," Harry said politely.

"Sounds? It was, sir, and so it continues to be. If President Davis would send a Confederate army up here into Maryland, the people would rise up and the Union would be finished."

It was in fact what Lincoln feared most. With Maryland lost, Washington would be completely surrounded by secesh.

"The Southern army has had two splendid opportunities to accomplish that," Harry said. "Bull Run. And now Ball's Bluff. The road north was wide open both times. But there was no advance."

Robert Ingraham gave Harry a stern but slightly daffy look.

"Are you questioning, sir, the valor of Southern arms?"

"Their valor is unquestionable. The generalship is another matter."

A flicker of utter fury passed across both the brother's and the sister's countenance, but quickly vanished. A smile on her part followed, and more artful fanning.

"Why, Mr. Raines. In Richmond, such talk would be treason."

The remark brought silence all around the table.

"I'm afraid I have more to fear from that charge in these precincts," Harry said finally.

Her fan seemed a blur.

"Why, of course you must! Poor man, it's a wonder you're not in irons this very moment. That hotel you're in is watched all the time. I do not know how you have escaped their clutches—given the gravity of the blow you struck against them."

"This is not my natural hair color," he said. "I darkened it, and my mustache—with something actors use.

Oddly, some have since mistaken me for an actor—
John Wilkes Booth."

Amalie picked up a small bell near her plate and
shook it almost violently, capturing the elderly black
man's attention. He nodded and mumbled something,
turning toward the serving kitchen of the house.

"I would not have made that mistake," Amalie said,
returning her attention to Harry. "But then, I am
acquainted with the gentleman."

"I was hoping you might know someone who could
find a way for me to get to Richmond," Harry said as the
next course finally began to appear.

"Know someone?" said Amalie. "My good sir.
Robert and I are such someones! But it's a difficult matter. Nowadays it's a difficult matter to cross the street."

"Our father's afraid if he tries to return here they'll
lock him up, too," said the brother. "He's not been home
in weeks."

"I thought my best chance would be to strike west
and cross the Potomac somewhere past Harpers Ferry,"
Harry said. "I have a farm and kinfolk near Martinsburg
and I can make my way south from there. It's getting
from here to there that's the rub. Is it safe, do you think?
The road to Frederick?"

"I don't think so," said Robert Ingraham.

"We really could not say," said his sister. "Frederick
is a farm town, full of Germans, and we have little business there. I would urge you to wait here until I think
it's safe for you to move and then make for the Eastern
Shore. The Yankees control little of that country, and
you could slip by their patrols with ease. We have
friends there, many friends. Get south of the Choptank
River and it should be easy to find a boat to take you
across the Chesapeake to Virginia. The Yankees still

hold Fortress Monroe but we have Norfolk, and the James and the York are open to our vessels."

She seemed almost breathless in her excitement at the prospect of his escape, rather reminding him of Cousin Belle Boyd. Amalie's brother was staring at her raptly.

"How long would that take?" Harry asked. "To get out of Baltimore. To the Eastern Shore."

"Mr. Raines, that's entirely up to the Yankees. But it shouldn't be long. If you stay in that hotel, though, I fear they will get you. You are the murderer of Lincoln's closest friend, after all. If you won't accept our hospitality, sir, then most assuredly you will be compelled to accept General Dix's."

"Please, sir," said Robert. "You must. We insist."

Amalie pushed herself back somewhat in her chair, a queenly gesture.

"She may be right, Raines," said Langley. "A couple of people in the hotel asked about you."

"What sort of people?"

"One was a federal detective. Unmistakable, though he left no name. The other was a horse trader."

Harry set down his fork. "Could his name be Buckeys?"

Langley shrugged. "He didn't give a name."

"What did he want?"

"Didn't say. Asked for you under your registered name—Richard York."

"Who could know that?"

"Anyone who looked at the register, or inquired of the desk clerk."

Amalie rapped her knuckles on the tabletop, just once, but emphatically.

"That does it," she said. "Clearly not safe. You're staying here."

"My things . . ." Harry began.

"We can send servants over for them in the morning. Mr. Langley can settle your bill."

"I really don't want to impose on your kindness this way, Miss Ingraham. I would endanger this house. You've enough hardship with your father away. I—"

"Enough? Men are dying for the cause every day! That poor Mrs. Henry—killed by a Yankee shell in her own house at Manassas. Her own house! Think of Rose Greenhow, suffering who knows what outrages as a prisoner in her own home! No, sir. What we have done is nothing. Nothing. I would harbor a thousand men like you within these walls, if I could. So please. Stay. For our sakes. As well as yours."

Langley smiled. Robert reached and poured Harry more wine.

DESPITE the cold, Harry stripped to essentials, folding his suit and shirt carefully on a chair so he might look his best on the morrow until the rest of his clothing was fetched from the hotel. All he took with him under the covers was his revolver and placed it at his right side.

He needed to think, but the wine had made him sleepy. He was on the brink of succumbing to its effects when he heard a soft sound outside the door. After a moment a dim slit of light became visible, but nothing followed—immediately. It was as though the intruder were trying to ascertain if Harry was asleep or alert.

Apparently, the mysterious figure was satisfied, and the door opened farther. Harry saw the blur of a shadow, and then the door closed again and all was fully dark again.

He now had the revolver in hand. He gently pulled it

free of the covers, holding it upon his chest, barrel toward the door.

"Who is there?" he asked.

No answer.

"I have a pistol pointed at you," Harry said.

"My, my, Mr. Raines. You *are* a desperate man."

He felt the mattress give slightly, and then the wooden frame creaked, and all at once the warm, huddling form of a naked body was at his side, seeking the warmth of his arm and body. There was the smell of lilacs.

Harry pulled the covers fully over them both, keeping the pistol in his hand.

This was no time for fealty to Caitlin. He had no doubt she lay within another's embrace this very moment.

"Good evening, again," Amalie said.

"It's more the dead of night."

"Perhaps we can enliven it."

"Miss Ingraham, I hardly know you."

"Well, I trust you will attend to that." She snuggled closer. "And soon."

He put down the revolver.

Chapter 17

HARRY awoke before her. The windows were rattling with the wind and the air in the room seemed as cold as the out-of-doors. There was light in the sky, the sun just rising.

Amalie was sleeping on her side, facing away from him, her back close against him, her flesh cooler now, only her light brown hair showing above the counterpane.

She had barely spoken to him during the night, and then only in passionate endearments appropriate to the moment—though not at all to their limited acquaintance. He had known her less than four hours before she'd entered his room.

Perhaps it had all to do with his vague and artificial resemblance to Booth. The actor routinely worked such magic on the ladies.

He whispered her name. A wisp of a sigh was the only reply.

Harry slipped from beneath the covers and stood at the edge of the bed, shivering in his nakedness. After putting on his spectacles, he studied Amalie for a long moment, then gently, carefully, and very slowly lifted the quilt and sheeting and held it back to expose the long lovely curve of her back and hip. Lifting it farther, he stared for a very long time, until absolutely certain.

He had not looked upon this woman's nakedness ever before. The woman in the woods had a substantial bosom. He'd been able to see the curve of that. Amalie's was quite modest.

All at once she rolled over to face him.

"Whatever are you doing, sir?"

He smiled. "Admiring." He lowered the covers again. "Very beautiful."

She seemed puzzled, but grew amiable.

"You look ridiculous, standing there rattling your bones in the freezing cold. Come back here where it's warm."

"That's an invitation no sane man would refuse, but I fear for me it must wait."

"Whatever for?"

"I need to go back to my hotel."

He needed to get dressed, lest he perish from the shuddering chills before her very eyes.

"Harry! I said we'd take care of everything."

He began pulling on his clothes. "That's very kind of you, but I'd like to wash up, change socks, make myself more presentable, and do so soon. I feel like some wretch from the street. Also, I left something in my room I don't want to leave there—not even for a few hours."

"What on earth would that be?"

"Let us just say that I wouldn't want any federal detectives to find it."

He had given Caitlin the Union pass signed by Lincoln that he'd carried sewn in the cuff of his best shirt. Still in the right cuff was another pass, signed by Jefferson Davis. The Confederate president knew his father and had the same mistaken perception of Harry's loyalties as these Ingrahams.

"What could they do to you, Harrison, hang you twice?"

"They'd certainly have no qualms about the first time if they found it." He went to the bed and leaned down to kiss her.

She pulled away. "You vex me, sir."

Harry bowed, perhaps too formally. He really knew nothing at all about this woman.

"I'll be back in an hour, Amalie."

She turned away. "I may not receive you."

"You promised to help me."

"The promise remains—if you will."

"Amalie. It's only a few blocks distant. I'll be back before you wake again."

"I don't want you to go out. It's dangerous. You don't know this city. I do."

"Amalie. I must."

He looked back at her just before closing the door. She was sitting up, her arms covering her breasts, and markedly unhappy.

HE walked the few blocks down the hill to Barnum's City Hotel. There were two or three shadowy figures loitering about Mount Vernon Square outside the Ingraham house despite the early hour, but none detached himself to follow Harry downtown. None, at least, that he noticed. And no one seemed to be lurking about the hotel, either.

The desk clerk was asleep. Harry awakened him to ask for his mail, which amounted to two letters. One said simply: *I hope this finds you well. He returns soon. I thank you. Be careful. Ella.*

The other was in a bold, clumsy, and definitely masculine scrawl. It demanded money. A hundred dollars—as supposedly promised—by sunset.

The signature was "Samuel Buckeys."

Both letters were addressed to J. Wilkes Booth, though clearly Ella's message was for him.

"When did these come?" Harry asked.

The clerk, a small man, looked back at the rows of mailboxes, as if they might answer for him. They didn't.

"I don't know," he said, shrugging.

"Anyone else looking for me?" Harry asked.

"Not while I been on, Mister, er, York."

HIS room looked much as he had left it—so much so that Harry was a little troubled. The chamber seemed too neat—too untouched.

He went to his saddlebags, finding a Navy Colt revolver still there, having left its mate at Amalie Ingraham's. Also there was his small leather sack of gold coins. He counted them out, finding none missing. A letter he'd been trying to write to Caitlin still lay unfinished on the little writing desk by the window, his pen lying across it just as he had put it down.

The bed had been made and there was fresh water in the pitcher on the washstand, but that was the work of the chambermaid. He looked through his other small travel bag, once again finding nothing amiss. Finally, he took up the shirt in which he carried his all-important safe conduct.

He'd removed the pass signed by President Lincoln from the left cuff to give to Caitlin for Booth. The pass from President Davis was still in the right cuff, where Belle had carefully sewn it.

But the cuff had been slit open, a tiny cut with a tiny sharp instrument. The pass presumably had been removed and examined, and then returned.

Harry went to the window. Two men who might have been Boston Leahy's brothers were now lounging by a doorstep opposite. He'd seen no sign of them when he'd entered.

The time had surely come to leave the city of Baltimore. He didn't want to do that just yet, but his shadowy adversaries were giving him little choice.

Taking up his remaining Navy Colt, he stuck it into his belt, put the money bag in a pocket, and then departed. Going to the stable in the rear, he asked his friend the groom to saddle him a mount for the day, then returned to the hotel dining room for a quick breakfast. It was of cold beef, cheese, and bread, for the kitchen fires had not yet been started.

Charles Langley did not appear, but then, he hadn't struck Harry as an early riser.

AVOIDING the front of the Ingraham house, Harry rode up the alley behind it, checking at a window of the coach house to make certain none of the animals or rigs had departed. Unable to tell for certain, he then retreated to a vantage point up the hill from which he could observe the rear of the residence clearly. He waited a very long time, suffering bitterly from the cold when the wind rose. He wondered if either Amalie or Robert left the place shortly after his departure, or whether they had no intention at all of going outside of the house that day. Brother Robert certainly was no homebody. He seemed a man with several lives—and not all of them respectable.

The thought of leaving Baltimore there and then, heading north into Pennsylvania and returning to his farm on the Potomac through Hagerstown, began to appeal to him. There was a ford across the river near Sharpsburg and Antietam Creek. If there were troopers watching his farm, he could take refuge with his blacksmith friend Jay Hurley in Shepherdstown. The Underground Railroad could be reopened briefly—for him. From Hurley's, he could send out what messages he had to.

The coach-house door opened. Harry hung back, out of view.

A dark-colored horse appeared, pulling forth a high-wheeled gig with its canopy in place. When the little buggy turned the corner into St. Paul street, heading downtown, Harry cautiously walked his horse back down the alley. The coach-house door had been left open by the Ingrahams' Negro groom, who was busy putting oats into feed buckets. The white horse with the long tail was gone from its stall.

Harry moved on, turning into the street and then urging his mount into a trot to get a little closer to the buggy, which was rolling along downhill at a fair clip.

Across the harbor on the grassy height to the south, the Union Army had installed at least two batteries of artillery. It looked as if the guns were trained directly on Monument Square and could demolish every house around it for a morning's sport. Perhaps their menacing presence contributed to Amalie's ill temper.

Drawing nearer to his quarry, Harry moved his horse over to the left side of the street, dodging a bit of oncoming traffic but gaining a view of the side of the gig. The driver was definitely female, but her face was obscured by a blue bonnet and veil. She wore a gray cloak and blue gloves.

Lest he be recognized himself, Harry fell back and reined his mount back over to the right, falling in behind his quarry and keeping about a block back from her.

She rattled on through the main business area of the city, passing the wharves along Light Street on the western shore of the harbor. After several blocks more, she turned left onto Fort Street, heading east.

Toward, of all places, Fort McHenry.

One of the strongest fortifications on Chesapeake Bay, McHenry had been doing double duty as a federal military prison since the previous September, trafficking more in Southern operatives and sympathizers than in captured Rebel soldiery, though that could change as the war progressed.

The fortress was still a key element in Union defenses, and the facilities for holding prisoners were limited. To accommodate more, a large grassy area to the north of the fort had been fenced off and prisoner barracks were being constructed. From a distance, it looked like some walled, medieval city.

As with the Union Army camp at Poolesville, McHenry could be heard from a considerable distance by the coughing of the soldiers—and, presumably, prisoners. An army's morning cough could sound like a rolling artillery barrage once every man got going. Harry could hear it plainly now, a mile away.

There was not much military posted outside the fort. Stopping his horse by some trees, he watched as she parked the buggy among a small group of other vehicles outside the main gate to the prison compound. She did so in practiced fashion, as though she had made this visit before and knew where to go. As well she must have done. Probably half her friends were in this place. Maybe all.

Harry gave her time to be admitted—or ejected—

then trotted down to the entry port, going directly to the side of her buggy and looking within, as though he fully expected someone to be there. Finding no one, he dismounted, tied his horse near the rear of the gig, then walked up to a lounging soldier at the gate.

"Excuse me," he said, removing his hat in a deferential gesture. "I'm looking for the woman who came in that buggy." He pointed to it. "Do you know where she's gone?"

"Inside." The man spat tobacco juice, then took a bar from his pocket and bit off another chaw.

"I'm her husband. Can I go in after her?"

"As far as the guard office." The man gestured at an inner courtyard past the gate. "Any beyond that, into the fort itself, you got to have a pass."

"Does she have one?"

"Guess so. She comes here every week."

"Every week?"

"That's all she's allowed. All anyone's allowed." The man's eyes took on a suspicious cast. "You're her husband?"

"Been away. At the house, they said she'd gone down here."

The soldier stood more erect, pulling his musket straight. A sergeant was at the gate, watching them.

"Go inside, if you want to find her." He found something far away to look at.

Harry strode forward, noddding to the sergeant, who did not return the amenity. Continuing on briskly, Harry moved through the gate. Inside the compound there were wooden buildings to either side, one marked as the guard office. Behind it was another palisade and a gate leading to the main prison barracks. To the right, a curving road led up to the main fort gates, which were open but well guarded.

He stopped. Two people were coming out of the fort, one a Union officer, the other a woman.

In a gray dress and cloak and blue bonnet. And veil.

Harry was wearing his greatcoat, which Amalie had not seen before. Pulling up his collar, he turned away and walked quickly toward the nearest building, which was a guard barracks. A dozen or more men were lounging within it.

He thought of asking directions, then thought better of it. Instead, he introduced himself as his friend William Howard Russell, the correspondent of the London *Times*. He took out a pencil and the folded letter from Ella Turner, and in an approximation of the stage English he'd heard from Caitlin and other British actors so many times, he began asking reporter's questions about the Confederate prisoners, whether any high-ranking officers had been taken, what the conditions in the camp were like, how the inmates were behaving.

For the most part, he got only banter in reply, some good-natured, some rude. Then all at once there was silence. The sergeant who had been at the gate was standing in the doorway.

Harry repeated his explanation and false identity. The sergeant was satisfied but not pleased. He took Harry's arm and, politely but firmly, guided him back outside.

"Do you have a military pass?" he asked.

"I am a British subject, sir. And we are near no battle lines."

"This fort and the whole city of Baltimore are under the authority of the military department of Annapolis, Mr. Russell. I could have you locked up here for this infraction."

"Only to be quickly released, as soon as General Dix was informed of it," Harry said. "But if it's a pass you require, I'll go get one." He gave a quick bow. "Thank you."

Without further hesitation, he walked on out the gate, fearing that he'd find himself confronting Amalie Ingraham directly on the other side.

She wasn't there. The gig was gone. The horse he had hired remained tied to a post.

HARRY took Fort Street at a full gallop, made a foray through the city center, and then cautiously returned to Monument Square and the alley behind the Ingrahams'. The gig was not in the coach house nor anywhere else he looked.

He was hungry, and it was nearly noon. A quick meal at his hotel and then he'd retreat from this city. There were things to do in pursuit of his ends in Washington— and, if his reputation as a supposed Confederate operative was still valid, in Leesburg. And he needed to enlist Belle Boyd's help again as well. He needed quite a bit of help. On his own, he seemed only to be digging himself deeper into his hole.

A different desk clerk was on duty, but wasn't much more civil than the night man. There was no *billet doux* from Amalie in his mailbox, no message of any kind. The clerk said he'd had no visitors.

But that wasn't true. Opening the door to his room, he was greeted by Samuel Buckeys, sitting in the chair where Harry had attempted to pass the night with Caitlin. He had moved it to face the door and sat with a long-barreled revolver in his lap. There was a faint smell of gun smoke in the room.

Buckeys hadn't fired his weapon, however. Harry picked up the pistol and looked to see a full load of seven bullets in the cylinder.

Using his handkerchief, he tilted back Buckeys's head and examined the man's shirtfront and vest as well. They were not clean, but there was no bullet hole, and no blood. Pulling Buckeys forward a bit, he found both of those things in the man's back. There was a bloody, blackened hole in a very fatal place.

He was examining the black powder stains around the wound when the hotel manager, accompanied by a constable and two soldiers from the provost guard, entered his room without knocking.

Chapter 18

HARRY'S wish to visit the interior of the Fort McHenry prison had now been fully realized. His first day as an inmate, they'd kept him in an empty powder magazine in the bowels of the fort's south-facing bastion—a cold, damp, windowless, brick-walled, half-underground chamber with only a lantern for light and skittering rats for companions.

He'd no idea what the improvement in conditions signified, but the following morning he was moved inside the fort's ramparts to a second story room in the building that housed the officers' quarters. There was an actual bed, and a window overlooking the small parade ground. The view provided only soldiers to see, but they were preferable to rats.

An officer had told him he might be transported to Washington, but for two days, no one came. Then, on the morning of the third day, a black coach with barred windows rolled into the fort and pulled up in front of his building. Hearing the commotion, Harry went to the window. The coachman was a large, powerfully built black man who reminded him of Caesar Augustus. A young Union Army officer sat beside him. Both had their eyes fixed on Harry, as though they knew exactly which room he occupied.

At that instant the door behind him banged open. Two soldiers entered, one of them dangling a set of leg irons, the other, wrist manacles. Harry smiled benignly as they were applied. The discomfort would be worth it, for he assumed the shackles meant some degree of freedom.

THE officer who had been riding with the black coachman had dismounted and now stood holding open the door, a full colonel's eagles prominent on his shoulders. He bowed slightly as Harry put a foot to the step.

"I would have thought you'd be a general by now," Harry said.

Templeton Saylor smiled. "By the end of the war, my father will probably see to it I'm president of the United States."

A strong hand and arm reached out from within the coach and pulled Harry up and inside. Boston Leahy.

"At the end of the war, Abraham Lincoln will be president," said Allan Pinkerton, seated in the opposite corner with arms folded, his bowler hat pulled down close to his small, quick eyes. "And you, Raines, will still probably be in prison. If not in the ground."

Harry sank back against the rear seat as the door was slammed shut. A moment later, with a quick crack of a whip, the team jolted the carriage forward and they rumbled out of the fort at a quick trot.

THEY had stopped after proceeding no more than half a mile from McHenry, on the lee side of a small, sandy hillock, out of view of the fort's ramparts but overlooking the wind-whipped blue of Baltimore's wide Patapsco River and the distant masts of ships.

These were his friends—circumscribed as the relationship might be by his difficulties with the law. Dutifully, he told them all he had learned. Almost.

Without naming her, he now mentioned the Velasquez woman as a possible culprit in the assassination of Colonel Baker, citing her white horse and penchant for attending battles in the uniform of a Confederate officer. He related as well his encounters with Charles Langley and the Ingraham family, and his following a woman he took to be Amalie Ingraham to the McHenry prison on what appeared to be one of a regular series of visits.

"Why do you think this Leesburg woman could have done it?" Pinkerton asked.

"I think she could have, but I don't know."

"Should we be in Leesburg instead of here? Hunting her down?"

"I should be there. There is, unfortunately, only one way of identifying her as the woman in the woods. If I were able to see her . . ."

Saylor laughed, Leahy smiled. Pinkerton did neither.

"You will not have our leave to depart prison for a journey into Confederate territory for the purposes of examining a woman's backside. Tell us more of what you know about these Ingrahams."

"There isn't much. They're friends of the Cary sisters—the 'Monument Square girls'? Amalie Ingraham is very much like them. A Rebel patriot. Her brother Robert is a strange fellow. High-strung. And I think he wears a wig."

"A wig?"

"His hair is too dark for an Ingraham and too coarse

for real. I may be wrong, but I think he otherwise has a shaven head."

"That may be bad news," Pinkerton said. "There's a Rebel outfit on the Eastern Shore that . . . never mind. Go on, Raines. Go on."

"I wasn't there long, but it seems that with the Cary girls gone, it's fallen to the Ingrahams to be the principal mischief makers in Baltimore. They also seem very thick with this fellow Charles Langley, who I am pretty near sure is a spy, and not for us."

"We know him, and his work," Leahy said. "He's a spy for the South but useful to us—as a means of misinforming the Richmond government. We let him find out things we want Richmond to know, or think. Otherwise, Langley'd be behind bars with you."

"I'm sorry, Raines, but you're going to have to get used to bars," Pinkerton said. "The charges against you in the matter of the demise of the late Edward Baker still stand. The president has not been satisfied with anything you or we have had to say about it. He holds you as prime suspect, and for that I'm sorry. But we may be able to introduce some mitigation in your favor."

He paused to look to Saylor.

"I warn you, Colonel. I know you are not a member of the U.S. Secret Service and not bound by our conventions, but if word gets out to anyone about this rendezvous or the conversation transpiring, you'll find this happy detached duty you've come to enjoy at a sudden end. I'll have you with the worst line outfit General McClellan's got in the field."

Small threat, thought Harry. McClellan was putting no one into the field.

"Understood," said Saylor. "I'm only here to help my friend."

"You keepin' your health, laddybuck?" said Leahy. There was solicitude in his countenance.

"Somewhere between poorly and fairly," said Harry. "The other wretches, though . . . It's a hard place."

"Count yourself lucky you're not somewhere worse," said Pinkerton. "There're those in authority who'd have you in an iron box by tomorrow sunrise. I don't blame them much. You've made a shambles of pretty much everything you've put your hand to, Raines. A shambles."

"I'm sorry, Mr. Pinkerton."

The detective rubbed his eyes. He was a tired man.

"That woman whose buggy you followed down to Fort McHenry, the Ingraham woman."

"Amalie."

"Yes, Amalie. You're right. The whole family's secesh. Brother Robert is definitely a Rebel agent and I think an officer of those partisans on the Eastern Shore. Dangerous clan. Dangerous."

"We've learned who she was visiting at McHenry," Leahy said.

"A prisoner of great consequence," Pinkerton continued. "Colonel Richard Thomas."

They were all looking at Harry.

"Who?"

"Colonel Richard Thomas, commanding officer of the Confederate Potomac Zouaves—and a damned pirate!"

Harry blinked. Neither Ingraham had mentioned the man. Charles Langley hadn't either.

"He's the rascal who seized the steamer *St. Nicholas*," Leahy said. "In June. Don't you remember?"

Of course he did. It was the most daring deed thus far in the war. But he recalled no Colonel Thomas.

"You mean 'Zarvona,'" Harry said.

"I do indeed," Pinkerton said. "As that's his other name. And it appears the Ingrahams are his very good friends."

As Pinkerton explained, Thomas was a Maryland man, from the Eastern Shore, the son of a speaker of the Maryland House of Delegates and the nephew of a Maryland governor. His relations' high position had won him an appointment to West Point, but he'd left before graduating and gone off to China, according to legend, to fight pirates. Tiring of that, he'd then turned up in Italy as a volunteer officer in Garibaldi's rebel army, giving himself the nom de guerre of "Zarvona." Sumter propelled him into the Confederate military, where he'd formed a band of cutlass-wielding brigands uniformed in the manner of all Zouave units, in bizarre European headgear, red shirts, and baggy pants. Many of them also shaved their heads, in the manner of their illustrious leader.

Thomas's unit hadn't accomplished a lot—until late in June. He'd been leading his band on raids of Union camps on the Eastern Shore, stealing horses, cutting telegraph lines, and other trivial enterprises. Then he came up with his bizarre idea of stealing a Union warship.

Harry remembered the rest from the newspapers. The warship Zarvona decided to go after was the gunboat *Pawnee*, the biggest weapon the federal navy had against Confederate blockade runners in the lower Potomac. The vessel was regularly supplied by the steam packet *St. Nicholas*, a side-wheeler that made regular runs between Baltimore and Washington via the Chesapeake and the Potomac. The plan had been to seize control of the *St. Nicholas* and then overpower the crew of the *Pawnee* when she came alongside for resupply.

Zarvona got it half right. He put a dozen or so of his men aboard the *St. Nicholas* in Baltimore dressed as civilians. A resourceful fellow, he disguised himself as a woman—from the newspaper accounts, a damned attractive one—boarding the steamer with three large, heavy trunks. Several of the genuinely female passengers were affronted at the brazen way this "lady" flirted with the *St. Nicholas*'s captain.

After a stop at Point Lookout, Maryland, the shameless femme fatale invited several of the "civilians" to "her" cabin, where they fetched cutlasses and pistols from the trunks. They had command of the steamer in a trice.

Unfortunately for the plot, the *Pawnee* had unexpectedly gone to the Washington Navy Yard for emergency repairs and failed to make the rendezvous. As compensation, Zarvona and his men used the *St. Nicholas* to lure and capture three small Yankee merchant vessels, and then took their haul up the Rappahannock to Fredericksburg, where they'd been honored with a festive reception worthy of John Paul Jones or Oliver Hazard Perry.

Zarvona was a man of no little confidence. In July, he made his way north again, boarding the steamer *Mary Washington* for a return to Baltimore and another attempt at the *Pawnee*. He was recognized, and upon arriving in Baltimore, was taken to Fort McHenry and locked up.

"I thought he was moved to New York," Harry said. "Fort Lafayette."

"No, sir. He abides in yonder fortress on the Patapsco," Pinkerton said. "He's a rich man and his father still has a powerful lot of influence—so he's comfortable. I believe they've given him the officer of the guard's quarters just inside the gate. He's kept supplied with fine viands and wine—I'm told quite a bit of the latter stuff."

Harry had walked by the door to that chamber just two days before.

"He tried to escape out a window," Leahy said, "so they moved him to a cell on the other side of the main passage. I'm told it's not so commodious as the previous accommodation."

"And Miss Ingraham visits him there?" Harry asked.

"She visits him. Has since the summer."

"Then there's a lot he might tell us about the Ingrahams. And what they're up to."

"And they about him."

Pinkerton leaned forward.

"Listen to me careful, Raines. What we may have before us is a conspiracy of assassins—led by this Zarvona. People who will wage war, not in open combat, but through stealth and murder. War as practiced by the Cult of Thugee. These sons of bitches tried to get the president when he passed through Baltimore after his election. Now it appears they've killed his best friend—singling him out on a battlefield. If they succeed in getting away with this, no one will be safe."

"Then Mr. Lincoln doesn't believe I did it."

"Maybe he does. Maybe he doesn't. But a mob of them in the Congress do, including this hellish Committee on the Conduct of the War. It'd be powerful convenient to give them you to chew on while the administration gets on with matters."

A steamer was coming up the Patapsco, its dark smoke dirtying the clear blue sky, its paddle wheel stirring up a froth on the river.

"Am I truly in danger of hanging, then?"

"Mr. Lincoln is not a hanging man," Pinkerton said, taking a quick look out the window. "And he has another fate in mind for you. If you're willing to help us, and do not mind abiding awhile longer in McHenry."

"My choice then is between prisons? McHenry or the Old Capitol?"

Harry looked out at the river again. The steamer had passed on up to the outer reaches of Baltimore harbor.

"Your choice, Mr. Raines, is to get to know our friend Zarvona, or find yourself back in Washington becoming well acquainted with Congressman Roscoe Conklin and the Committee on the Conduct of the War."

"What about Samuel Buckeys?" Harry asked. "I am charged with his murder."

"A dreadful fellow," Saylor said. "And a traitor to boot. You did well to shoot him."

"What?" said Pinkerton. "Raines killed someone?"

"No, I didn't. But I am charged with the crime."

"A shambles," said Pinkerton. "A bloody shambles." He shook his head. "Raines, you vex me."

Chapter 19

HARRY had spent so much of this year in cells he wondered if he'd have been more useful to the federal service as a prison warder than as a member of Pinkerton's Secret Service.

His new abode now was the middle cell of a row of three located in the guardhouse just inside the fort's main gate. These were special cells, not designed for the comfort and happiness of the inhabitant. Cold, dark, high-ceilinged, and very narrow, they had stone floors and only a single, small, barred window at the rear that looked out over the fort's covered main entrance passageway, failing to provide even a glimpse of sky.

The hinged cell doors were simply bars and crosspieces, providing no privacy and a view only of the whitewashed brick corridor wall opposite. Harry could hear the chatter of guards in the nearby barracks room but little else. The prisoners in the three cells were free to converse through the bars, but only Harry and the neighbor on his left availed themselves of the opportunity.

Harry's neighbor was a grandson of the very same

Francis Scott Key who, on a prison hulk in the waters just south of this fort, had written the words to "The Star Spangled Banner" a half century before. The irony of his present circumstance had not eluded the descendant, Francis Key Howard, a Baltimore newspaper editor of Southern sympathies. He mused on how they all might have been enjoying a different fate if "the bombs bursting in air" had compelled McHenry's surrender to the British in 1814.

"The British have been no friends to slavery," Harry had said. "The 'peculiar institution' might have perished earlier under their rule."

"But the South would have survived," was the only reply. "There'd be no Yankee nation."

Howard was coeditor of the *Baltimore Exchange,* a newspaper favoring Maryland secession. He'd been arrested on the strength of the editorials he'd written. He was being held without formal charge or trial, but that was no rarity at Fort McHenry, which the inmates were calling "the Baltimore Bastille."

Harry's neighbor on the right was indeed the fabled Colonel Thomas—alias Zarvona—who thus far had not uttered a single peep, or even cough, though this prison sometimes seemed to shake with the racking spasms of its inmates.

Upon entering this establishment, Harry had been allowed an introduction to the occupants of the adjoining cells. He'd shaken Howard's hand, but there'd been no response from Zarvona. Harry had seen only a body huddled beneath a blanket at the rear of the chamber, the head barely visible beneath a thick cloth cap. The poor wretch—for that he seemed—kept his back to the barred door and stayed utterly motionless for long periods of time. In truth, he appeared dead. Here was not the pistol- and cutlass-wielding swash and buckler of legend.

"Is he ill?" Harry asked the guard when Zarvona failed to respond to his greeting for about the five hundredth time.

"Morose," said the soldier. "The place gives him an evil humor. And he drinks to excess, though he'd have none of it when he first came here."

"How does he get spirits?"

"We'll provide whatever you wish to pay for."

The three cells were on ascending levels, each slightly higher than the other. From his middle chamber, even pushing his face against the bars of the door, Harry could see but little of Zarvona's. He could not reach it with his hand, either, though he and Howard were able to pass things to one another on the other side.

During the day, he'd call out to Colonel Thomas, using both the man's real name and his nom de guerre. Never a reply, though at times he could hear the man moving about and making use of his toilet arrangement.

"Truth to tell, I do not belong here," Howard said as they were lamenting their circumstances one afternoon. "Under the dictator Lincoln, I am arrested on suspicion. You, however, are a murderer, and our friend next to you a pirate. I do find myself in odd company."

"Your profession is newspaperman? Then you are right where you belong. I am not a murderer, and it is only the newspapers who say otherwise."

"My paper didn't call you a murderer. You were viewed as a patriot. Until you killed that Buckeys fellow. Why'd you do that? Some say he was a Confederate agent."

Harry heard a slight, muffled sound rather like a stifled laugh. It came from the cell on his right.

"Zarvona?" he called out. "Have you stirred at last?"

There was no reply, and then there was—a low groan, and then a hoarse, "Leave me be, you bastard."

It was the last Harry heard from him for the rest of the day and night.

THE inmates of the main prison compound outside the brick bastions of the fort were allowed ample exercise. Some of the Confederate soldiers had picked up the new Yankee sport of baseball, and set at it so frequently there seemed to be one long, continuous game at play.

Within the brick fort itself, though, the privilege of exercise depended on the friendliness of the guards, which too often depended on the generosity of the prisoners. Harry and Howard were liberal enough with their money to keep their guards extremely happy, and thus were permitted the liberty of the interior grounds within the bastion when those spaces weren't being used for drills or formations.

Zarvona, son of one of Maryland's wealthier and most powerful politicians, should have been able to secure himself the right to promenade along the ramparts if he wished, but though allowed visitors, he was denied such liberty. Harry supposed the *St. Nicholas* episode had stung the North's pride, and this was a way of making him pay for it. When he and Howard strolled in the open during a sudden balmy turn of weather, Zarvona remained in the cell, wrapped in his blanket, face to the wall.

PINKERTON had left Harry with plenty of money, some of it provided by the generous Templeton Saylor.

Harry used a dollar to bribe his guard to let him linger in the passageway outside his cell one afternoon after returning from exercise. Settling down against the wall opposite Zarvona's cell, he didn't speak for a long while, contenting himself with observing the fellow wrapped in the blanket.

At length, Zarvona lifted his head to see if Harry was still there.

"I have a bit of freedom for the moment," Harry said. "Is there anything I can get for you?"

"Who are you?" Zarvona said, the words again spoken in a sort of croak.

His face, half-hidden by the cap, appeared haggard but perhaps handsome, the heavily lashed light blue eyes luminescent even in the shadows of the dank, dark cell. Harry could see a few wisps of hair beneath the cap, though it was hard to tell its color in the darkness.

"My name's Harrison Raines," said Harry. "Of Charles City County—outside of Richmond. I also own property up the Potomac from Harpers Ferry."

"That's Virginia," was the raspy response. "What're you doing here? This place is for Maryland men."

Zarvona sat up, wrapping himself more thoroughly in his blanket in the process. Hunkering against the wall, the blanket obscuring his lower jaw and mouth, his cap pulled down over his brow, he looked like a turtle, or a bedouin.

"I thought you might have heard of me," Harry said. "I'm accused of murdering Colonel Edward Baker, the president's best friend. As well as a horse trader, swindler, and sharper named Sam Buckeys."

The head burrowed still farther into the blanket. "Jefferson Davis is the president."

"Sorry. I meant the other one."

"I never heard of you."

"I thought you might have. A lady of my acquaintance visits you quite regular. Amalie Ingraham?"

Zarvona abruptly turned his back to Harry and lay down, facing the wall. "She never mentioned you, sir."

"And neither did she mention you to me. Is she a friend?"

No reply. No look. No movement.

"Chi trova un amico, trova un tesora," said Harry. It was the only Italian he knew.

"What?"

"That's Italian. It means, 'She's ugly and has a big ass.'"

Zarvona rolled over toward Harry, his eyes blazing.

"If we weren't in this damned prison, you son of a bitch, I'd call you out," he said. "I'd shoot you in the back. If you were in this cell, I'd strangle you."

"Hmm, I gather you and the lady are very close friends. My apologies, sir."

The eyes now narrowed slightly, as if the man were contemplating some action, but he turned back to the wall and withdrew into his thoughts.

The phrase *"Chi trova un amico, trova un tesora"* meant "Who finds a friend, finds a treasure"—as anyone who had fought with Garibaldi would know.

Harry got to his feet and walked down to the end of the short corridor, signaling to the nearest guard.

The fellow pulled out his keys. "You want to go back in your cell?"

"No. I'm not feeling well. I need to see a doctor."

LEAHY, stripped to the waist, was exercising. He continued at it as Harry was escorted into the room by the hospital orderly, who turned about and swiftly departed, closing the door noisily behind him. Harry's manacles had been left in place.

The Irishman performed four more repetitions of his calisthenics, then stopped, resting on his heels a moment.

"I think the time has come for both of us to escape this place," Harry said.

He sat down on the edge of Leahy's bed. Out the window, he could see the Patapsco River and a Union gunboat that appeared to be at anchor.

Leahy stood and went over to his washbasin, splashing himself generously.

"You'll hear small complaint from me on that," the Irishman said. "What have you found out?"

"The man in the cell next to mine is not Zarvona," Harry said. "And he may not be a man."

Leahy toweled off his still quite ruddy face, then peered skeptically at Harry over it. "Not a man? Are you at this again, Raines? Next you'll be telling me Stonewall Jackson is really your cousin Belle in disguise."

"Well, it's not Zarvona. I'm certain of that. He speaks no Italian and Zarvona spent those years with Garibaldi. If not Zarvona, who then? The last person to visit him in his cell was Amalie Ingraham."

"But she left a few minutes later, did she not?"

"Someone in women's clothes did. I of course assumed it was Amalie. But think upon the precedent. Zarvona disguised himself as a woman when he first went aboard the *St. Nicholas*. He fooled everyone aboard including the captain. Why not here? All he needed was to switch clothing with Amalie, and that could be easily done in that cell."

Leahy pulled on his shirt, frowning as he thought upon this. "But he'd have left the poor woman in jail.

For days if not weeks. Would a gentleman willingly visit such horrors upon a lady? Would she tolerate them this long, just so that brigand could go free?"

"You don't know these women. Their patriotism is all hatred. Anything for the cause. Besides, he might well return at the next visiting time and change back with her. He may have done this several times. She might have found the sacrifice worth the while if he was up to some great mischief on the outside."

Harry looked to the window again. The gunboat, a wooden side-wheeler, had turned slightly and was now bow on to them, its two forward cannons seemingly aimed right at them.

"What did you say was the name of the warship Zarvona went after?" he asked.

"The *Pawnee*," Leahy said, combing his hair until every strand was in just the right place. "A converted steam packet. He never got near it because it was laid up at the Washington Navy Yard."

"And it's now repaired?"

"Aye. Back on station in the Potomac."

Harry stared at the gunboat there on the Patapsco, which was continuing its slow circle. Upriver from it, in an office at the Baltimore City Dock, was likely a large entry book that would now very much merit examination. But not by him.

"Mr. Leahy," he said, "I fear I should go right back to my cell. We must get busy. Especially you."

"To go after this Zarvona? He could be in one of a dozen places by now—if you are right. Of course, if you are wrong, then he would still be in his cell."

"We must determine that."

"Have the inmate examined by a prison matron?"

"That would tip our hand, wouldn't it? No, we must come at this more innocently. In about an hour, have a detail of guards search that row of cells I'm in for weapons. I expect you'll find one in mine. An offense worthy of a bit of solitary confinement—or removal to a more secure establishment."

"And your mysterious neighbor?"

"In a search for weapons, prisoners may be required to remove their clothing."

An hour came and went, as did another. Back in his cell, Harry engaged his friend Howard in quiet conversation, explaining his absence by relating how he'd been hauled before federal detectives attempting to make him sign a written confession to Colonel Baker's murder.

Dinnertime arrived, the warder clanging open the iron gate to the corridor with his usual oafishness. The meal was a watery sort of stew served in a metal bowl with a knot of hard bread floating on top of it, plus a cup of coffee that tasted as though it had been brewed from old shoes. The spoon that came with the stew had not been washed. He could not imagine Amalie enduring these indignities for a minute, let alone days and weeks.

The warder stood in Harry's cell a moment, sniffing like a rat, as though he could smell what he might be looking for.

"What you got there, Raines?" he said loudly.

"What?" said Harry. He was sitting on his narrow pallet, back against the door.

"I said what is that? Get up!"

Harry slowly did as bidden. The guard fumbled in the bedding, suddenly producing Harry's small, two-shot derringer.

"You damned Rebel sonofabitch! You got a pistol here!"

The guard stepped back into the corridor, shouting for reinforcements, who arrived very quickly—a sergeant and two privates, one of them carrying a musket. The corridor was so narrow the man couldn't turn the weapon sideways.

"Search the cell!" the sergeant commanded, so loudly he might have been heard throughout the fort. He looked sharply at Harry. "You! Out!"

Harry tried to amble but was grabbed rudely and shoved against the whitewashed corridor wall. He stared at it, an inch away, listening as the paltry few belongings he had in the cell were rudely tossed about.

"The others, too!" shouted the sergeant. "They may all be armed!"

More clanging, banging, and shouting. Frank Howard, thrust against the wall next to Harry, looked genuinely frightened. Harry liked the man and hoped he hadn't been secreting some contraband that would get him in serious trouble.

The occupant of the other cell had to be dragged forth. Hanging limply in one of the soldiers' arms, the prisoner was dumped like a sack onto the dirty floor.

"Strip 'em!" bellowed the sergeant. "Off with their clothes."

Harry suffered the indignity sullenly, hoping at least that a nice hot bath and a change in underwear might follow. Standing finally naked and cold, he stole a quick glance to his right. He had a twofold opportunity here. The search would reveal whether the prisoner was Amalie, and if he had made a mistake in his initial observation. There also remained the possibility that she had been the naked lady in those woods off the Frederick Road.

They had to lift and hold the inmate upright as they

pulled off garments. After Harry had taken a look, they let the poor wretch sink back to the floor. An astonishing sight it was.

"Robert Ingraham," Harry said, with genuine curiosity. "What're you doing here?"

Chapter 20

December 1861

HARRY had been taken with a string of other mana-
cled prisoners to an open wagon for transport to the rail
depot. It was cold and blustery, with a wind off the harbor from the north, and Harry was pleased indeed when
the hard, uncomfortable vehicle finally pulled up in
front of Camden Station.

The other poor wretches in the wagon were less fortunate. They were bound for New York and Fort
Lafayette, a much less hospitable place than McHenry,
and were to depart Baltimore from President Street Station, a cold ride away on the other side of the harbor.
Disconnected from them, but left in wrist and ankle
irons, Harry was led by two soldiers into Camden,
where he was greeted by Leahy, who rudely shoved him
down onto a bench.

"I'll take custody of him," the Irishman said to the
soldiers. "You go on about your business."

"He's a dangerous criminal," said one of the soldiers.
"And a spy. Killed a colonel."

"I'm acquainted with his particulars," Leahy said. "Don't worry. I haven't lost a prisoner yet."

He stood watching as the two passed out the door.

"Well, we're onto your friend Zarvona, all right," he said.

"He's in Washington?"

"No, but we'll soon be. We'll talk about it on the train."

THEY sat side by side in the rearmost seat of the last car, a location that kept them relatively inconspicuous while giving Leahy a view of anyone who might approach them. He put Harry in the window seat, hemming him in thoroughly. The roadbed was rough from the wear of all the heavy military traffic the line was now carrying and the two men were jostled against each other constantly. Leahy's arm and shoulder were as hard as brick.

"Can I have these taken off now?" Harry asked, lifting his wrists and jiggling the chain.

"No. There are likely Southern agents on this train, and you remain an official criminal. You must be treated as one."

"Mr. Leahy, I am tiring of this."

"That's unfortunate, boyo, but there it is."

"What about Zarvona?"

Leahy observed the other passengers for a long moment, then leaned close to be heard over the train's rumble and rattle.

"He's on a steamer—we think headed for the Potomac. We're going after him."

"Just the two of us?"

"Mr. Pinkerton and your friend Colonel Saylor will

meet us at the B and O depot. We'll pick up anyone else we need from the Washington Navy Yard."

"Navy yard?"

"We're going aboard the *Pawnee*."

Harry had more in mind a good meal, a hot bath, and about six weeks' sleep.

"Me, too?"

"You'll do as you're bidden, Captain, or it's back into McHenry."

Harry wasn't completely certain he was joking.

"What happens to Robert Ingraham?"

"That's an easy one," Leahy said. "We caught him in a jail cell. We'll leave him there. Save us the bother of a trial."

"That's a bother you people seem to dispense with pretty regular." Fatigue and lack of food were making Harry feel giddy. "You ought to make him wear a dress."

"Been far too much of that peculiar business as it is."

"And his sister, she wasn't to be found at the Ingraham house?"

"Not there; not anywhere in Baltimore. We think she probably fled south—like her friends the Cary girls."

Harry remembered Amalie's mention of an escape route across the Chesapeake and down the Eastern Shore. She was probably all the way to Easton, if not miles beyond. The recollection of their night together warmed him a little. Had there been no war, their acquaintanceship might have progressed quite differently.

He dashed that thought, recalling the tired old black man who'd been made to stand all through the meal in the Ingraham dining room.

Leahy pulled his bowler hat down over his eyes. Like

Napoleon, who took catnaps in the midst of long battles, the Irishman had the remarkable ability to take his sleep almost anywhere. Harry could not. They had reached top speed—a good forty miles an hour—and the rails were shaking the train as though angry with it.

Harry shook Leahy even harder. The hat came up again, revealing a deep scowl.

"I'm armed, you know," Leahy said darkly.

"What about Zarvona? What steamer?"

They were crossing a long wooden trestle over a wide stretch of shallow water. The sun was down now and the distant shore was dotted with orange lights.

"It's called the *Cacapon*. Left Baltimore two days ago."

Leahy reached into a pocket of his vest, pulling forth a *carte de visite* and handing it to Harry, who had to take it with both hands.

The image on the card showed Zarvona as his real self, Colonel Richard Thomas, resplendent in his Confederate Zouave uniform, complete to shaven head and fez. He brandished a large pistol and gazed at the camera with a leering sort of smile. That he could hold that madcap expression long enough for a clear picture to be taken was impressive. But then, the man was a supreme actor—certainly a much better one than the hapless youth who'd replaced him in his Fort McHenry cell.

"We borrowed this likeness from the commandant at McHenry, who'd confiscated it when Zarvona was brought in," Leahy said, nodding to the image. "We showed it at the steamship offices and along the city dock. Two people there recognized him—by the eyes and the peculiar smile. Zarvona bought a single ticket for the steamer S.S. *Cacapon*."

"Did they see him go aboard?"

Leahy shook his head.

"It probably won't surprise you to hear that when he bought the ticket, he was dressed as a woman. When I showed those people the *carte de visite,* they presumed Zarvona was 'her' brother. I didn't tell them otherwise. This becomes hard to explain."

"But they marked the resemblance?"

"Thought he and 'she' might be twins." He squinted at the *carte de visite.* "Helpful things, these photographic cards. Ought to use them more in police work."

"What's the *Cacapon*? Where bound?"

"She's a Chesapeake Bay passenger steamer, but seaworthy enough for the ocean. From Baltimore, she goes to St. Michael's on the Maryland Eastern Shore, then Annapolis, then Point Lookout, then up the Potomac to Port Tobacco, then the rest of the way to Washington City. Ties up at Georgetown. Same dock the twice-a-week New York steamer uses. The trip takes three days. As she left two days ago, we expect her on the Potomac tomorrow."

Harry leaned his head back against the seat, closing his eyes. "And Zarvona bought just one ticket? What name did he use this time?"

"A French one again," Leahy said. "Madame Revanche."

Harry shook his head. French was a language he knew something of. His mother had been from a Huguenot family in Charleston.

"Perfect," he said. "That's French for 'revenge.' He's out to repeat his earlier escapade in every detail, Mr. Leahy, but this time to succeed." He sat up, blinking. "Did he—as Madame Revenge—bring large steamer trunks aboard? As memory serves, he had three of them last time, filled with rifles and pistols."

"Didn't ask. We must presume that he did."

The train continued chuffing over the cold, harvested farmland at good speed, spewing sparks into the air in recurring billows. Then it suddenly slowed, brakes squealing, and pulled onto a siding and stopped. A few minutes after, another train came roaring up from behind it, passing swiftly and noisily, carrying troops down to Washington. The faces in the windows that passed by in quick succession were of every imaginable sort, but seemed to bear the same curious, apprehensive, innocent expression. These would be new recruits. They'd been flowing into the capital all summer and fall. Come the spring, if McClellan ever got moving, they'd start flowing back in the other direction. Harry knew what they'd look like then.

"I can't believe Zarvona would try this alone."

"Maybe he's having some men come aboard at St. Michael's. No way of knowing till we find 'em."

Another train passed them, this time coming from the other direction. Two of the cars bore white flags with black squares in them—signifying hospital cars carrying wounded. The remaining two cars bore no insignia save the railroad's. Harry could guess what they contained.

He sighed. "You wouldn't have any spirits on you, would you, Mr. Leahy?"

"Captain Raines, that's all the same as asking Mr. Lincoln if he's got any slaves to sell."

"Did they ship Holmes's body back to Massachusetts?"

"Holmes?"

"Lieutenant Holmes—Oliver Wendell Holmes. He was shot at Ball's Bluff. He—"

"The one who accused you?"

Harry nodded solemnly.

"Well, they didn't," Leahy said. He folded his arms, staring straight forward.

"Didn't what?"

"Didn't ship him back to Massachusetts. Leastwise, not in a box. The lad's still alive."

Chapter 21

DESPITE the hour, Washington's B&O depot was filled with soldiery and every type of civilian, including women and children, as well as representations of the lowest orders of society. A few people gave Harry's manacles a glance, but none took particular interest or appeared to recognize him. Out on the street, Leahy pushed him toward a closed coach that waited among a line of others. Inside were Pinkerton and Templeton Saylor, the latter smoking an elegant cigar. Harry entered coughing, taking a rear-facing seat.

"The guards at Fort McHenry are going to think you don't like them," said Saylor, "the way you keep leaving them."

"What you've done has been useful," said Pinkerton, bestowing his highest accolade. "We may put an end to Zarvona's deviltry, thanks to you."

"If he's actually on that steamer."

"Oh, he is. He is," Pinkerton replied as Leahy climbed aboard and pulled shut the door. "I telegraphed our people at Port Lookout. 'Madame Revanche' made the crossing from St. Michael's—she and her trunks. A number of other passengers came aboard there—most of them young men."

The coach lurched forward, moving out fast.

"And the *Pawnee*'s waiting for us at the navy yard?"

"Not much need for her on the Potomac," Saylor said. "Haven't you heard about the great naval triumph of the Third Indiana Cavalry?"

"Naval triumph? Cavalry?"

"The Confederates tried moving a blockade runner downriver—a sloop called *Victory.* The Third Indiana spotted them and gave chase along the bank. They could move so much faster on horseback, they were able to stop along the shore and pepper the boat with musket fire, some of it pretty accurate. After a taste or two of that, the Rebels abandoned her in the shallows and she became the cavalry's prize. Found a load of more than eighty thousand percussion caps in her, plus a lot of brass buttons. Saved some lives with that catch."

"Damned newspapers finally had something good to say," Pinkerton said. "'Victory over the *Victory.*'"

"A toast," said Saylor, reaching into his uniform coat for his flask. "To the mounted navy!"

He took a long pull, wiped the flask with a very clean handkerchief, and offered it to Harry, who lifted his wrists.

"Why do you have him in those?" Saylor asked.

Pinkerton gave a curt nod. Leahy leaned forward and unlocked the handcuffs, slipping them afterward into a side pocket.

"Those go back on when this is done," PinSB Headkerton said.

"Why?"

"'Tis Mr. Lincoln's wish."

THERE were light swirls of snow in the air when they reached the navy yard. The coach stopped close by a long wooden building that seemed a warehouse of some sort. Leahy had a key and led Harry inside while the others waited.

Stacks of boxes and barrels of navy stores were everywhere, some of them containing weapons. Leahy, holding a lantern he had taken from the coach, took Harry to a rear room. Opening a cupboard, he produced a naval officer's uniform.

"Put this on," he said, "and put your other clothes in this bag."

Harry shook out the top garment, a long blue coat with brass buttons and two thin bands of gold on the sleeves.

"You're now a lieutenant in the U.S. Navy—for the duration of this *Pawnee* business," Leahy said.

"A demotion."

"In the navy, that's the equal of an army captain. Be grateful you weren't made an ordinary seaman. Rank is hard to come by in the naval service."

THE *Pawnee* was a ten-gun steam sloop and one of the fastest vessels the Union had on the Chesapeake. At the outbreak of the war, she'd been based at Hampton Roads in Virginia waters near the Gosport Naval Shipyard in Norfolk, and might have been seized by the Confederates had she not been part of the flotilla sent—too late—to relieve the Rebel siege of Fort Sumter.

Returning from that somber disappointment in the Carolinas, she'd found her next assignment in the rescue of the forty-gun steam frigate *Merrimack,* which had been caught by the war while laid up at Norfolk for repairs. Once again, the *Pawnee* had been tardy. The Rebels by then had captured Norfolk.

The *Pawnee*'s commander, Captain Hiram Paulding, was looking forward to the encounter with Zarvona with great relish.

"We'll hang him from the mainmast, Major Allen," he said to Pinkerton, using the latter's nom de guerre.

"Let's get our hands on him first," Pinkerton said, a little grumpily. "Last time, they caught him in the women's toilet, hiding in a closet. Maybe this time he'll put up a fight."

"Let's hope he does," said Paulding. "He's got one coming."

The captain appeared to be well acquainted with Pinkerton, and Leahy was known to him as well. He seemed offended by Colonel Saylor's presence and eyed Harry with undisguised suspicion.

"He's vouched for," Pinkerton said.

"He's Booth, the actor! Masquerading on my ship as a naval officer!"

"Look again, sir. Raines, take off your hat."

Harry did so, grinning sheepishly.

"If he's not Booth," Paulding said, "who is he?"

"A murderer," said Pinkerton, staring forward along the dark river, "helping us in hope of receiving some leniency for his crimes."

IN his first exploit, after having seized the *St. Nicholas,* Zarvona had planned to come alongside the *Pawnee* under the pretense of bringing supplies, and then board and take her before she could stand off and use her guns.

Paulding thought the Confederate daredevil would try something similar with the *Cacapon.* As she wasn't a victualing boat, he'd probably feign some kind of distress, perhaps asking the *Pawnee* to take aboard an injured crewman or assist in engine repairs.

Pawnee would be ready. She had a platoon of marines aboard, plus some dismounted cavalrymen now taking orders from Saylor.

D**AWN** found them in the wide estuary of the Potomac, drifting along in the current with sails furled and only enough steam up to keep them in steering. They were just a few miles overland from the Rappahannock and Fredericksburg, which still held two of the prizes taken by Zarvona in the *St. Nicholas.*

Harry went out on the forward deck, where he was shortly joined by Saylor. The young colonel once again shared his flask, both of them glad of the warmth.

"Are you happy to be returning to Washington?" Saylor asked.

"If that's where this takes us—and as long as it does not mean another jail cell." Harry drank. "But truth to tell, Templeton, I am tiring of the place. There are more welcoming climes."

"I am surprised to hear that from you."

"Then you do not know me well, sir."

"My ardor for the place still abides."

Harry drank again and returned the flask. "Then I do not know you well, sir."

"This is a more suitable way to go to war, don't you think?" Saylor asked. "Warm cabins. Good food. No mud."

"You wouldn't say that if you were belowdecks on a sinking vessel."

"Better that than being slaughtered on the shore the way those poor wretches were at Ball's Bluff."

"It's on the shore where the war's to be won, Templeton. Not at sea."

"The navy's key, Harry. The only way the North's going to defeat the South is to strangle it to death. On land, we only lose. I daresay the president sees that."

The sky was lightening rapidly. It was going to be a clear day, despite the previous evening's flurries.

"Right now I'd like to strangle myself," Harry said, "for not getting onto Robert Ingraham sooner. We might have stopped this Zarvona—and learned what was behind that vile business at Ball's Bluff."

Behind them, men were moving about on the deck. All ship's crew. The marines and cavalry would be staying below and out of view.

Saylor lighted a cigar. The smell at that hour made Harry not want one.

Two small dots appeared in the morning murk downriver. The larger dot seemed to be trailing a plume of smoke. A crewman up in the mainmast called out the sighting. Harry looked to see Captain Paulding step out of the wheelhouse and lift his telescope toward the downriver horizon. He barked out an order, and men forward ran toward the capstan around which was wound the anchor chain. They began to turn it, shoulders into the labor. There was a splash, and the heavy chain began to run out.

Paulding was going to hold to this spot. The river was fairly narrow at this point, both banks well within cannon range.

"That's not the *Cacapon*," Harry said.

The riverboat drew closer, growing larger in their view. At length, as she finally came abeam, Harry could see the name *Belle Haven* painted on her side. Their were a few passengers on her deck, and some soldiers with muskets. One cannon each pointed from bow and stern, the artillery pieces protected by hay bales.

"Government mail packet," said Saylor. "Probably carrying money."

"The next vessel may be Zarvona's."

Saylor glanced over Harry's uniform. "Are you armed?"

"I'm only just free of irons."

The colonel opened his coat. He had a .44-caliber Army Colt revolver in his holster, but produced another from within his tunic.

Harry hefted it carefully. It was an English-made Adams, a five-shot, double action revolver firing a .36-caliber round. They'd been licensed to a Massachusetts firm in hopes of securing a Union Army contract after the outbreak of the war, but, despite their excellence, were rejected as too costly. Many officers purchased them privately to augment their army issue.

"It's a fine piece," Harry said.

"A gift from my father," Saylor said. "So I'd appreciate your not dropping it in the river."

"Steamer off the port bow!"

The lookout's warning was unnecessary. Every spyglass aboard the *Pawnee* was already trained on the approaching vessel—a side-wheeler with a mainsail aloft to catch a following easterly breeze.

"It's the *Cacapon*, sir," said an officer.

"Let's make ourselves less conspicuous," Saylor said, putting a hand to Harry's arm and steering him behind an iron-plated bulwark.

They crouched, revolvers drawn but held out of view. Looking down the deck, Harry saw that some of the cavalrymen under Saylor's command had appeared as though from nowhere and were similarly deployed behind cover. Turning his gaze upward, he noted that Pinkerton had vanished from the window of the wheelhouse. Only Paulding and the helmsman were visible.

Harry raised his head enough to check on the *Cacapon*'s progress, which had been considerable with the strengthening wind. If she was going to hail the *Pawnee* and heave to, she ought to be slowing soon.

Zarvona had had perhaps two dozen men with him when he seized the *St. Nicholas*. If that was all he had with him now, he'd be badly outnumbered—and no cannon to the *Pawnee*'s ten. But the *Cacapon* would have crew and innocent passengers aboard. The Union men aboard the *Pawnee* would have to be very guarded with their fire.

And if some of the Rebels were wearing women's clothing, what then? At whom would he shoot?

Harry turned his back to the bulkhead and crouched low, reaching into his coat and producing his glasses case, then pulling on his spectacles carefully. When he looked back toward the river, the *Cacapon* was almost upon them, moving fast.

He saw Saylor cock the hammer of his Navy Colt with his thumb. The cavalrymen had breech-loading carbines—far more effective weapons.

This could all be a mistake. Zarvona might well be as far from this reach of the Potomac as the Cary sisters and Amalie Ingraham. The Union men could shortly find themselves injuring or killing innocent Northern civilians—another Union fiasco to go with Ball's Bluff and Bull Run.

And his fault.

The lookout in the crow's nest shouted something

Harry could not quite make out. A moment later he heard Paulding calling to deckhands forward to weigh anchor.

The *Cacapon* was so near, its smoke was curling over the superstructure of the *Pawnee*.

Chapter 22

As the *Cacapon* pushed on by, its high paddle wheel making a great, whooshing, sloshing racket, Harry carefully lifted his head, searching the steamer's decks for passengers but spotting only a single sailor, a tall fellow in dark blue jacket who stood aft looking as though the *Pawnee* did not exist.

"That's damned odd," said Saylor. "She shuns us. I certainly wouldn't be so impertinent with a Union Navy warship in these times. A damned good way to get a cannonball through the boiler."

Paulding came out of the wheelhouse, staring after the steamer in amazement and indignation. After a moment more of pointless gazing, he cupped his hands around his mouth and hailed her, but the steamer was too far along and making too much noise for anyone aboard her to hear.

Or so it would have seemed.

All at once deckhands appeared on her deck, several of them going quickly aloft. The *Cacapon* had two stubby masts, tall enough for mainsails and topsails, and a long foresail. The crew busied themselves laying on full canvas.

Paulding was shouting furiously, getting up steam. Harry could feel the deck throbbing beneath him. Free of the anchor, the *Pawnee*'s bow began swinging around.

Saylor was standing fully erect, his revolver still dangling pointlessly in his hand.

"She'll be out of cannon range in a minute," he said.

"Cannon's out of the question," Harry said. "Civilians on board. They're as good as hostages."

"I hazard they *are* hostages. Zarvona's probably got them locked up belowdecks."

"Or Zarvona's not aboard, and the passengers are all snug and warm in their cabins."

"Only one way to find out," Saylor said, holstering his weapon. "As our good Captain Paulding seems to recognize."

IF race it was, it was a losing one. On engine alone, the *Pawnee* was the faster vessel, but the *Cacapon* carried more sail, and with a favorable wind such as she was enjoying from astern, she appeared able to maintain an equal speed or better. Their only hope to overtake the craft was for the wind to shift or die, but it kept coming out of the southeast, brisk and steady.

Harry and Saylor joined Pinkerton and Paulding in the now crowded wheelhouse.

"Went by us as blithely as a Sunday sailor," said the captain. "Damned rascals."

"They might not be on that ship—or any ship," Harry said.

"We should have received some sort of recognition from her," said a young naval lieutenant, the *Pawnee*'s second officer. "The Virginia ports on this river are under blockade and we're a military vessel. She should have acknowledged us."

"Only one seaman on deck—no passengers in view," said the captain. "Too damned suspicious. It's got to be Zarvona."

Pinkerton extended his telescope toward the other ship as it continued to recede into the distance.

"This river's full of shoals and bars," he said. "Reckless to be traveling that fast. Captain could lose his master's certificate for that. No, sir. He's aboard her all right, and we'll catch him—sooner or later." He lowered the spyglass. "Trouble is, if it's later, what mischief is he going to get up to in the meantime?"

THEY steamed upriver all morning. The wind dropped, felicitously for the *Pawnee,* but the advantage in speed this gave them was for naught. The *Cacapon* had too great a lead. Rounding the bluff at Mount Vernon, they came to a long straight stretch of the Potomac with a view so unhindered they could see the squared-off obelisk that was the Washington Monument abuilding on the mall twelve miles away.

But there was nothing of the *Cacapon.* Steaming on past Fort Washington on the right and then Alexandria on the left, they turned their spyglasses and binoculars to every vessel of *Cacapon*'s size they encountered, without success.

At last drawing nigh the city of Washington, they were confronted by the obstacle that was the city's Long Bridge, reaching across the Potomac from just below the capital mall to Arlington Heights. The landing at that place had two navy vessels moored alongside it and there was an assortment of small boats working the river by the Virginia shore, but no steamer of the *Cacapon*'s size.

"She either went up Washington Channel to the Sixth Street Wharves or on through Long Bridge up to Georgetown," Captain Paulding said.

"Georgetown is where she's supposed to go, isn't it?" Harry asked.

"Aye," said Pinkerton. "But look. Only way through the bridge is that one small channel between the pilings—there, where the bridge swings open to the side. The *Cacapon* could get herself trapped on the other side of that pretty easy. But if she went over there, to the Sixth Street Wharves, the moorings are crowded with ships to hide behind. And she'd have a quick passage straight down the Eastern Branch to freedom."

"Right by the navy yard, though," Paulding said. "If we could warn them, there's enough cannon to blow her out of the river before she has full steam up."

"Unless she's bent on some mischief at the yard," Leahy said. "What if he has some gunpowder aboard? Maybe Zarvona's got some idea of blowing up the navy yard."

Pinkerton shuddered. "Very well. Make for the Eastern Branch, please, Captain."

Paulding barked a command to his lieutenant, who barked it to the helmsman. The great wooden steering wheel began to turn.

"But what if he has taken her to Georgetown after all?" Harry said. "By the time we got back to the main river, she could be done with her business and on her way downriver."

The helmsman brought the wheel back to amidships, looking to the captain.

"Hard aport!" Paulding commanded. "We'll drop this man on the Long Bridge and come back for him later."

"Mr. Leahy," said Pinkerton. "You go with Raines. And disabuse him of any ideas of strolling off the bridge to join kith and kin in Virginia."

THERE was a walkway to one side of the lateral planking of the main vehicle roadway on the bridge and Harry and Leahy stationed themselves on that, as the military traffic was frequent, including a line of artillery carriages and caissons that made the bridge rumble and sway as they thundered by.

The day was milder than the one previous, but recurring gusts of wind across the wide expanse of water brought a chill reminder that it was December.

"There's the house of the man we should have instead of McClellan," said Harry, nodding toward the hill across the river and the Greek-columned Curtis-Lee mansion that sat atop it. "Some say General Lee's the best of both armies."

"Maybe so," said the Irishman, turning to look back upriver and resume his search for the *Cacapon*. "Though that ain't saying much."

Leahy was fiercely loyal to Pinkerton, but did not share his leader's affection for McClellan.

"In the Mexican War, Lee led Scott's army through an old lava field in a driving rain in the dark of night to take Mexico City," Harry added.

"But he turned down Mr. Lincoln's offer of the top job, so that's that," Leahy said. "If Lee's so brilliant at making war, why do the Rebels keep him in Richmond, generaling papers?"

"He is Davis's principal military adviser," Harry said. "And I daresay Rebel politics at this point are very much like a lava field in a driving rain in the dark of night."

Leahy snorted. Harry had come to understand that he—Harry—was the only Southern man Leahy allowed himself to like.

"Something you should know, Harry," he said. "Your friend Saylor filed a supplemental report two days ago about that fight at Ball's Bluff. Claims he was near you when Colonel Baker was hit. Says you couldn't possibly have done it."

"Why did he wait until two days ago? It happened in October!"

Leahy shrugged.

"You'll have to ask him about it. Don't know why he didn't tell you about this himself."

"Modesty is not among his virtues." Harry adjusted his spectacles, leaning forward and squinting. "Mr. Leahy, I see a ship."

"What? The *Cacapon*?" Leahy was looking in the wrong direction. "There's nothing between here and Mason's Island. Nothing coming out of Georgetown."

"No. To the south." Harry blinked and looked again. "It's the *Pawnee*."

THEY went aboard as the gunboat chuffed slowly through the opening at the swing section of the Long Bridge, Harry painfully whacking his knee as he clambered over the rail. Collecting himself, he looked to the wheelhouse. Pinkerton had his spyglass raised. A moment later he lowered it.

"She wasn't at the Sixth Street Wharves," he said to Harry. "Must have come this way."

Paulding had kept his glass trained on the Georgetown waterfront.

"There she is!" he said. "Aye. Along the quay, tied up aft of the New York steamer. It's her all right."

"No time for stealth," Pinkerton said. "We'll have to come at her directly."

They made for Mason's Island, which divided the Potomac into a narrow, shallow channel on the Virginia side and a deep, wider one by Georgetown.

There was a plantation on the island. Harry could not remember whether it was still a working one or still home to slaves. It crossed his mind that Zarvona might have Confederates there, or plans to use it in whatever scheme was aborning here.

Paulding knew his river well. Coming just shy of the long shoal that extended from the southern tip of the island, he swung the bow to starboard and disengaged the *Pawnee*'s paddle wheel. Slowly, the ship made a clumsy pirouette, halfway through which the captain resumed propulsion, heading obliquely toward the Georgetown quay aft of the *Cacapon*.

Now no one at all moved on the passenger steamer's deck—a very peculiar sight for a ship just arrived at port. Paulding crept the *Pawnee* close, then reversed engines to come alongside the wharf with its bow to *Cacapon*'s stern. There was a shudder of engine as the wheel was disengaged once more, and then a thump and creak as the *Pawnee* came against a set of wooden pilings.

At that moment a rifleman rose up from behind some bales aboard the *Cacapon* and fired a round into *Pawnee*'s wheelhouse, shattering glass.

Chapter 23

Harry's cheek stung. Putting his hand to it, he pulled forth a jagged sliver of glass with fingers that came away red. Another bullet struck the wheelhouse, above the forward window and into the wooden frame. Then another knocked out more glass.

Saylor and Captain Paulding had blood on their faces, too. Happily, their complaints were the same as Harry's—glass shards, not bullets. All now crouched very low, Saylor and Leahy holding revolvers. Harry was happy to keep the one Saylor had loaned him in his coat. He'd had enough battles for the moment.

Another shot, then three more in quick succession. They came from the *Pawnee*. Several of the marines had come on deck and were returning fire. There was a robust reply from the *Cacapon*. The Confederate rifleman had been joined by friends.

"We must get aboard that steamer!" Pinkerton said. "We must put an end to this."

Saylor kicked open the starboard door of the wheelhouse and, hunched low, peered around it. The shooting continued, but nothing was marked for him.

"I'll get some of my boys and outflank them," Saylor said. He looked to Harry, lifting his brows in query— and invitation.

"All right," said Harry. He was beginning to think fondly of his peaceful jail cell.

Saylor led the way out on hands and knees. Harry followed, taking note of Leahy's presence behind him. When they reached the rear of the wheelhouse, all stood. Without hesitation, Leahy leaned out around it, leveled his huge .44-caliber Remington revolver toward one of the infantrymen on the steamer, and fired it twice, the last shot producing a scream.

"You've improved the odds," said Saylor, moving on. "Let's go."

THE young colonel managed to get a full squad of his horseless dragoons to join him in his enterprise. One man was hit going over the rail and another fell into the Potomac trying to leap onto the quay. All the others made it, assembling behind Saylor and the cover of dock pilings. Harry and Leahy stayed near them, hugging the shelter of the *Pawnee*'s curving side.

The cavalrymen were armed with .52-caliber breech-loading Sharps carbines. Harry hoped they were well trained. A stumble by one of them on the dock and he could have a very large hole in him.

"We're going forward," Saylor said. "Second rank, you fire a covering volley for us. Then we'll do the same for you when you come up."

Harry was impressed. Saylor was becoming a much more accomplished officer than he'd been at Ball's Bluff.

Moving thus along the deck in charge-and-volley fashion, taking cover where they could find it, grateful for the distraction provided by the marines on the *Pawnee*, the small Union force advanced to the side of the *Cacapon* without injury or hindrance. Saylor was the first aboard the steamer, charging right up the gangplank, pistol blazing.

Three cavalrymen and then Harry and Leahy followed, less heroically. A few bullets whizzed and sang nearby, then ceased. Harry saw Saylor pressed back against the steamer's main abovedecks cabin forward of the gangplank, reloading his revolver. Two of his cavalrymen hurried by him, hunched over, firing from the hip. Then all at once it was very quiet, except for a low moaning.

They'd been opposed by only five Rebels. Two stood with hands high. Two others sprawled motionless and bleeding on the deck. Another clutched his thigh, rolling back and forth.

Saylor holstered his weapon, grinning broadly, playing the victorious general. Leahy tugged at Harry's arm.

"We must get below," he said. "The passengers."

Moving swiftly down the companionway, they encountered no more foes, nor anyone. But then came a whimper, and a cry for help.

"Calm yourselves!" Harry shouted. "You're safe. We're Union Army."

"You're Union Navy—sir," said Saylor, brushing by with revolver again to the fore.

Several of the cavalrymen followed, moving along the steamer's central passageway and flinging open doors. People began emerging from them—men, women, and from one cabin, two small children. Some were crying. Most were smiling. A few looked on silently and sullenly. Harry took them to be Southern sympathizers. He was surprised there weren't more.

All of them were in their nightclothes.

"He told us we'd be shot if we changed back," said one still nervous older man. "He said we'd be shot if we left our cabins."

Harry asked himself why Zarvona had kept all these people aboard the steamer. Did he fear they'd spread word of his little invasion through the city? Or did he plan to use this vessel again, with these people serving as hostages to enable his escape?

The answer was likely both.

Saylor had moved on to the last cabin, from which no one had emerged. He hesitated before the door, then backed up and kicked out against it near the latch. When this failed to open it, he kicked again.

The door snapped free and then a shot rang out, the sound sharp in the confined space. Saylor flung himself to the side, apparently unscathed. One of his cavalrymen rushed up, boots stomping, and fired his carbine into the opening—to no great effect, but providing distraction enough for Saylor to lean around the door frame and send two rounds into the room.

Another silence fell, but for coughing. Acrid gun smoke hung thickly in the corridor.

Saylor entered the cabin, Harry coming after him. A figure in a gingham dress lay sprawled on the floor, revolver still in hand and chest oozing blood. The head was completely shaven and a wig lay on the planking nearby.

Harry leaned close. It was not Zarvona. He shook his head. Saylor had already made the same observation.

"One of his Confederate Zouaves," Saylor said.

Leahy was of a sudden standing beside them. He'd already found the *Cacapon*'s captain locked in crews' quarters and acquired from him the passenger manifest. He looked to the cabin door, which bore the number "9," then consulted his document.

"This is Madame Revanche's cabin," he said.

"Is this her?" said Saylor, reloading his pistol.

Harry pondered the lifeless form. Saylor had fired so matter-of-factly, and aimed so perfectly. Harry had killed no one in this war, and neither expected to nor wanted to. He began to wish he were not in this naval officer's uniform.

"Raines," said Leahy. "We'll find no more answers here."

THE marines from the *Pawnee* had come up and had taken positions along the street, which seemed absurd. They looked like an invading force, but were in the capital of their own country.

"The shopkeepers, people on the wharf," said Harry to Saylor. "They must have seen Zarvona and his people go by."

"Well, let's ask them."

Harry had no notion where Pinkerton might have gone, though it didn't much matter. Saylor had taken full command of this expedition, and the role seemed to suit him. At Ball's Bluff, he had been as uncertain as the rest of them.

They sprinted from the dock up the earthen bank to the street that ran parallel to the river. Several of the cavalrymen darted into stores and businesses. Harry and Leahy went on down the wharf to the New York steamer, a vessel named the SS *Bedford*, moored ahead.

Two dockworkers rose from behind a stack of crates at their approach, both as anxious as they were grimy.

"The shootin' over, Lieutenant?" asked the shorter and the brighter looking of the two, a florid-faced man who was missing the larger part of his right ear and a few teeth.

Harry had forgotten his borrowed naval uniform.

"It's over," he said. "Did you see a large body of men come off that steamer? Perhaps a woman with them?"

The dockworkers gave each other looks that strongly implied Harry might be missing significant portions of his brain.

"You mean passengers?" said the one lacking an ear. "They come off, like always."

"And went where?"

"Into town."

"All of them? Together? In a bunch?"

Half Ear stared at Harry as though he might be the thought that was eluding him.

"In a bunch," said the other dockworker, a bent and older man, with deep-set eyes that reminded Harry a little of President Lincoln. "There was someone holdin' horses for them. And a coach." He paused. "And they had no baggage. They didn't wait for their baggage."

"Was there a woman? A large woman?"

"Two women," said the older man. "Pretty women. One of the horses—it had only one eye."

Harry nodded his thanks and broke into a run, clambering up the wooden stairs to the street and pounding along the cold-hardened dirt.

"You know someone with a one-eyed horse?" Leahy asked, running alongside, with far greater ease than Harry.

"I did. But he's dead."

"Dead?"

"Samuel Buckeys."

COLONEL Phineas Gregg, surgeon in charge of the Georgetown Union Hospital, was hard at his work, cutting into the leg of a wounded soldier lying faceup on the table of Gregg's surgery. Two orderlies stood at either end, one holding the man's shoulders and the other his ankles. Harry's sudden entrance startled and displeased Gregg, though they were good friends. He gave Harry the briefest glance, then returned to his labors. Ether was often in short supply and surgeons did not like to waste it.

"I am sorry to see you wounded, Harry," he said. "But I cannot attend to you now."

"Wounded?" Harry's hand went to his face. "This isn't a wound. It's a cut—nothing."

Gregg gave him another quick look, less disapproving. "You look like you've been run through with a saber."

"No. A piece of glass is all. Phineas, I need something else of you. Horses."

"Horses? You're the one with horses. You're the horse trader. I'm the surgeon. Are you confused, sir? Are you drunk?"

"I'm just off a boat. The city's been invaded by a party of Confederates. I need a horse. Horses. Whatever you can spare." He heard noises behind him and looked to see two of Saylor's cavalrymen standing in the doorway, seeming confused as to what they were doing there.

"Your ambulance horses," Harry continued. "Anything."

Gregg stood up straight, holding his surgical knife in one hand and wiping his brow with the other. His patient's leg was severely discolored. It occurred to Harry that something larger than the knife might soon be in order.

"Invaded?"

"A small party, Phineas, but dangerous. That man Zarvona. He's escaped from Fort McHenry. I don't know what he's planning to do here but we'll try to catch him first. If you'll help."

"Yes, yes." He nodded to one of his orderlies. "Take these people to the stable and let them have whatever they want."

"Yes, sir," the man said, dubiously, and started for the door, the two cavalrymen right behind him.

"Harry," Gregg called as Harry turned to follow. "Lieutenant Holmes was asking for you."

"Holmes? He's here?"

"He was, but—"

"Not now," said Harry, going through the door. "I thank you, sir."

THE animals were used to draw ambulances, so there were no saddles. Harry thought riding bareback would present little challenge, but the horses objected, refusing to budge from the hospital yard. Harry swore, then shoved off his beast, looking to the row of three ambulances lined up rearmost to the hospital wall.

There was reason for their idleness. With General McClellan in command, there was little need for ambulances, except to fetch the sick from the camps and transport the dead to their final posts. Harry would endanger no lives in borrowing one.

"Get harness and hitch a team up to the first one," he said, feeling the authority of his naval shoulder straps.

"But, Lieutenant," said a corporal, the most senior of the cavalry troopers in view. "Where're we goin'?"

"To Lafayette Park. Hurry!" Harry said.

He'd thought upon this, not long but well. It seemed to him there could be only four possible objectives at this end of the federal city of sufficient value to the Confederacy to warrant Zarvona's expedition. The Treasury and its stores of gold coin and bullion were one. The President's House and Mr. Lincoln would be another. The War Department with its all-important telegraph room was yet another.

The fourth, just across Lafayette Park from the president's residence, was the Greenhow house, now serving as detention quarters for at least a dozen women Rebel sympathizers and agents. The other three buildings would be as well defended as fortresses. Rose's house would, in contrast, be lightly guarded. Only women to worry about.

Experienced at their work, the cavalry troopers had an ambulance hitched to a team as quickly as they might saddle and cinch their own mounts. Harry clambered onto the seat and snatched up the reins.

"Get aboard!" he shouted.

CAREENING through the traffic of Pennsylvania Avenue, Harry had to swing around a hay wagon as he rounded the bend in the thoroughfare by the War Department. Slowing, he gave the gray-painted structure a hard look. Soldiers were going in and out, as occurred all day long. Sentries idled at the gate. There were a few horses tied to the fence, all of them army mounts from the look of the saddles. No coach stood waiting.

Slapping the reins against the backs of his own team, Harry hurried the ambulance on past the President's House, finding much the same sort of innocent scene. Nothing at all seemed out of the ordinary. If Mr. Lincoln's life was in danger, or that of anyone in his family, it was not from any threat involving a coach and a band of horsemen.

In the next block, the imposing Treasury also seemed

utterly unmolested, and logically so. The building was full of armed soldiery. The ground-level floor was the headquarters of the provost marshal for all of Washington City. Zarvona would dare enter there only if he was on a suicide mission. But there was nothing to indicate that. The two soldiers at the ground floor entrance were alert. Both stared long at Harry's ambulance as it rumbled by.

At Fifteenth Street, slowing to make his way through a stream of pedestrians, Harry turned north, passing the Riggs Bank and then turning left at the next corner onto H Street. General McClellan's headquarters looked busy, but not with unexpected visitors. At the next corner, the house where Dolley Madison had died just ten years before, there were three horses tied up. But here was no target for the Confederacy. Mrs. Madison had come from the Carolinas and been married to a Virginian.

There were a surprising number of people in Lafayette Park for a winter's day, strollers and idlers. Ahead, to the right, at the corner of Sixteenth Street, was St. John's Church. Beyond it, the tall, stately house belonging to Rose Greenhow and now serving as her prison.

The team was moving at a fast trot. Harry yanked back on the reins, pulling on the vehicle's brake and causing the wheels to skid slightly on the hardened dirt. Stopping finally at the side of the house, he flung himself to the ground. The cavalrymen with him came tumbling out the rear, carbines at the ready.

Only one sentry stood at the door. He raised his musket in challenge, but was clearly intimidated to have so much armed soldiery come rushing at him—especially as they were led by a naval lieutenant.

Giving Harry a troubled look, he hesitated, then brought his weapon down to order arms and put the flat of his hand to it. Harry returned the salute, feeling a fraud.

"Sir?" said the guard.

Harry looked up and down both Sixteenth and H.

"We're looking for a party of armed men," he said. "Civilians on horseback. A coach with them. With women in it."

"No armed men, sir," said the guard. "Just women."

"Two women? One of some size?"

"Guess so. Agreeable-looking women. One had on a big hoop skirt."

"Where are they? What did they want?"

"Come and gone, Lieutenant. Brought some fruit for the lady inmates. Got eleven women under house arrest here now."

"Raines!"

Harry whirled about to see Pinkerton running up the walk, his short legs working like steam-engine pistons. Where he had come from, Harry could not imagine.

"How did you get here?" Harry asked as the detective came huffing to his side.

"Horsecar, most of the way," Pinkerton said, catching his breath. "Had to hold a gun to the wretches to make them hurry."

"But . . . ?"

"Zarvona's after Rose Greenhow," Pinkerton said, catching his breath and glancing quickly over the yard and front windows of the house. "Isn't that obvious?"

"Two women have been here. But no men. No horsemen."

"Raines! Let's get inside! Now!"

The sentry, who recognized Pinkerton, hastily

opened the door for them and stepped aside. In the hallway, they were confronted by a provost-guard officer who did not know Pinkerton and objected to the intrusion. They commenced to wrangle, with Pinkerton trying to elicit from the man the same information Harry had already been given by the guard outside. Rose Greenhow had had two visitors, both women, one wearing a particularly voluminous hoop skirt.

In addition to the cavalrymen who had come with him, there were probably a half-dozen armed Union soldiers in the house, plus one or more female detectives. Harry did not want them all bursting in on Rose and Little Rose, fingers on triggers.

Moving away from Pinkerton, he quickly ascended the stairs. He heard someone shout after him, but paid no mind.

A severe-looking woman in black, whom Harry remembered as one of Pinkerton's lady detectives, was seated in a straight chair on the second floor landing. She leaped up at his approach, alarmed, calling out his name.

The wrong one.

"You can't come up here, Mr. Booth!" she complained. "Go back. There are women prisoners here!"

There wasn't time to explain the mistake, or Harry's darkened-hair disguise. He knew the lady would not be armed. Putting a finger to his lips, he pulled out the revolver Saylor had loaned him and went to the door of Rose Greenhow's bedroom. It was locked.

"Give me the key," he said softly.

"No."

Where was Pinkerton when he needed him? There was still an argument in progress downstairs. The officer had foolishly contested Pinkerton's authority and the detective had more foolishly decided to settle the issue before attending to the major business at hand. People were running back and forth down there.

Uttering no further word, Harry turned and aimed his pistol at the woman, again placing a finger to his lips. She surrendered, angrily but quietly. She reached into a pocket within her skirt—he hoped not for any weapon.

Instead, happily, she produced a key. He took it, nodding thanks. Gesturing to the woman to step back, he quietly put the key into the lock, turning it until he heard a sharp click. Taking a deep breath, he wondered what he might say to this Zarvona to forestall any violent response. Perhaps, in womanly garb, Zarvona would have difficulty producing and wielding a weapon.

Harry took his finger away from the trigger of his pistol. There was a small chance he had come here by mistake. This was a city full of Rose Greenhow's friends and they'd been visiting her at every opportunity. The two women might well have been simply that—friends. Perhaps ladies of Harry's acquaintance. Zarvona and his crew might be anywhere in the city at this point—even bound for the Soldiers' Home in the belief Lincoln was there.

Lincoln might in fact be at that place.

Harry had no wish to put a bullet through Rose or her daughter, whatever patriotism might require of him.

He pushed the door open, slowly at first—then, as he came to see the woman seated opposite, by the window, her back to him, dressed in black, as though in mourning.

"Rose?"

She had a pistol in her hand. It came around first as she turned toward him, the barrel seeking him as though it were an eye.

He slammed back the door against the wall of the

room, diving through the doorway to the right, raising his own weapon but unable to take enough aim to fire.

Her gun discharged, the bullet zinging past Harry's left ear. She fired it again, and almost before he heard the sound, he felt a sharp, sudden stinging in his left shoulder muscle. That arm went numb. He hit the floor without its assistance, banging his chin. Rolling to the side, he hit his head on some piece of furniture. She yelled at him, and bolted for the door, making an awkward jump over him, her foot coming down hard near his ear.

That was all he could see of her. A black riding boot—seen in a flash beneath her thick black skirt. Then she vanished.

He heard her screaming something about Confederate assassins. Many footsteps, then people in the room. The noise about his ears became unbearable. He stopped listening.

Chapter 24

HE regained his senses to find Leahy kneeling over him, causing pain as he worried over Harry's wound.

"Is it bad?" Harry asked.

"None of 'em's good, but you're all right. Pity it wasn't your drinking arm."

Harry sat up, wiping his eyes with his free sleeve, as Leahy had cut off the one on his left arm. He pulled out his flask and handed it to the Irishman.

"Pour some of that on it."

"Why?"

"Something I learned."

Leahy shrugged. The pain that followed almost raised Harry off the floor.

"Where is she?" he said.

"Who?"

"The woman who shot me."

"There was a woman who ran down the stairs, but nobody knows where she went, or who she was. The house is being searched. Pinkerton sent runners to General McClellan's headquarters and the provost marshal's office, asking a citywide search for the fugitives. They won't get far."

"Ha."

Harry stood up, found he could remain in that position, and then descended to the main floor, though with Leahy's help. Pinkerton was outside on the house's front steps.

"We guessed right, but got here too late," he said bitterly. "They are utterly fled. Greenhow gone, the little girl gone, Zarvona gone."

Two women had called upon Rose. Two had left.

"One of them had a big hoop skirt," Harry said. "She must have had that child under the skirt, clinging to her leg."

"Not 'she,'" said Pinkerton. "'He.' Zarvona."

"And the other woman, the one who took a shot at me, she stayed behind," Harry said. "If it was a woman."

"Whatever she was—he was—she's gone, too," said Leahy.

"Damnation," said Pinkerton.

He looked across the park to the President's House. None of them spoke for a long time. What soldiers there were on hand stood awkwardly, looking at them.

"Harry says she was in black," Leahy said.

"So was Rose Greenhow," Pinkerton said. "Every day—for weeks."

"I think they've gone to Georgetown," said Harry, of a sudden.

"But we've just come from there."

"They planned to leave on the *Cacapon*. That's clear enough. Left those poor souls behind to hold it for them. They got what they came for without any hindrance from us. We arrived too late. So they will be wanting to carry out their scheme as planned. They'll have no knowledge of the fight on the quay."

"But our men have seized the *Cacapon*."

"They may be discovering that this very moment, but it still puts them in Georgetown. They won't be coming back this way, even when they find they've lost their ship. Zarvona knows he could be running into half the Union Army here. No, sir. He'll take the fastest way out, and there are only two roads leading out of Georgetown to the west—River Road and Canal Road."

A small group of horsemen was cantering toward them, across Lafayette Park. In the lead, waving his hat, was Saylor. He leaped from the saddle before his mount had fully stopped, but kept his feet.

"Is it true?" he asked. "She's gone? Rose Greenhow?"

"Gone with Zarvona, damn 'em both to hell," said Pinkerton. "Why aren't you looking for them?"

"I fear, sir, I did not credit the report. Where have they gone?"

Pinkerton had worked for railroad magnates and was respectful of the kind of wealth and influence a man like Saylor's father wielded. But he did not attempt to disguise his indignation.

"If I knew, Colonel, I'd be there!"

"I think they went back to Georgetown," Harry offered.

"Then let's be after them!" Saylor took a step back toward his mount.

Pinkerton frowned. "I'm going to the War Department." He looked to Harry. "Report to me there. And don't clean yourself up. I want you unrecognizable, and that you surely are."

"I daresay," Saylor said. "He barely looks human. More a specter from the grave."

Time was passing. "I need a horse," Harry said.

"Can you ride?" Leahy asked.

"I'll find out."

Saylor ordered one of his men off his mount, then bowed, gesturing toward it. "Your servant, sir."

HARRY was righter in his guess than he'd imagined. A crowd had gathered on the Georgetown landing. Saylor's little troop pushed their way through it to find Captain Paulding's marines in possession of seven Confederate prisoners and three corpses—two of them Zarvona's raiders, the other one of the deckhands from the New York steamer. There were also a proportionate number of saddled horses, all in lamentable condition. One was missing an eye.

Harry moved his own animal closer. "I know this animal," he said. He examined another, a dappled, swaybacked gray with scarred flanks. "These are Sam Buckeys's horses."

"Lucky we don't need them," Saylor said.

He turned his own mount about, scanning the docks and street. There was nothing to be seen of Zarvona and his presumed traveling companions.

Paulding was on the deck of the *Cacapon,* shouting to them.

"They're in a coach!" he called. "They took the Canal Road!"

Without a word, Saylor turned his horse once more, edged his way out of the crowd, and put spurs to flank. Harry and the cavalrymen followed, but at a distance they couldn't close.

Chapter 25

THE Canal Road was wide and well traveled, following alongside the Chesapeake and Ohio Canal at the foot of high river bluffs all the way to the Chain Bridge and up the Potomac for miles beyond. Pinkerton had sent out an alarm that Harry hoped would reach the pickets guarding all the bridges into Virginia.

But it appeared much more likely that the fugitives were heading into the Maryland countryside, turning north at some point to avoid the federal force still gathered in camp around Poolesville. Several byways branched off from the Canal Road, cutting up into the hills northwest of Washington. The Union Army was busy building forts along those heights, but few had been completed.

To protect the canal, which despite the war was still being used to transport passengers and freight upriver to Cumberland, McClellan had established a string of batteries and sentry posts, but these were along the towpath on the river side of the canal and faced toward Virginia on the opposite shore. They would have offered little impediment to a coach pounding along the highway at their rear.

There was small chance of catching up with Saylor. The colonel had galloped on madly, as certain of his goal as Harry was not. As he had no other ideas to offer, Harry contented himself with his place in the midst of Saylor's cavalrymen, happy at least that the colonel had provided him with a decent mount. He had no idea where Rocket had gone since he'd left him with the army in Poolesville. Perhaps General Hooker had sought the horse out and requisitioned him.

Or had him shot in revenge.

Harry and the cavalrymen thudded by one of the long canal boats, drawn along by a team of mules plodding the towpath. The mule man and the boat crew turned to gaze at the troopers, and one of the deckhands even waved.

Leaving the boat behind, a bit farther upriver they came upon a lock, the whitewashed lockkeeper's house standing hard by it. Harry noticed a woman hanging clothes on a line.

She told him she had seen a coach, which was traveling fast and had almost run down her lockkeeper husband, who now sat planted on a wooden bench outside the door of his little house, quietly smoking a pipe. The couple had also taken note of a farm cart and an earlier line of military freight wagons, plus a bright yellow buggy. There was not a lot to do in their line of work but observe the passing traffic, both waterborne and hoofed.

The coach by then could have been halfway to Rockville.

Harry struggled to keep his animal up with the troopers', then all at once reined him in.

It was sublimely peaceful here. Through the bare trees, the Potomac glittered brightly in the sunshine.

The canal water beside it was a darker, muddy green, but in stretches reflected the light blue of the sky. But for a small artillery emplacement upriver and a strolling infantryman somewhat nearer, one would have no notion of a nation at war.

If Zarvona was fleeing up the Canal Road, Harry had no doubt Saylor would catch him. He recalled the capture of Louis XVI and his family in their attempt to escape the wrath of the Paris mob during the French Revolution. Had they disguised themselves as peasants, riding in a hay cart, they might have made it. Instead, they'd traveled by coach in their finery, and found themselves with an ultimate destination called "Madame Guillotine."

But Zarvona was not so stupid.

Neither was Harry.

He urged his horse into a trot, returning to the lock-keeper.

A𝚃 Harry's approach, the man went back into his little house, reminding Harry of some nervous woodland creature retreating into its burrow. All this soldierly activity appeared to have spooked him.

Too bad. He was going to get some more.

"Lockkeeper!" Harry shouted, halting his horse squarely in front of the door of the house. "I'm Lieutenant Booth of the United States Navy. Come out here!"

The man's face appeared in the doorway. He looked somewhat like a badger.

The lockkeeper stared blankly. "You been shot?"

Harry rubbed at his shoulder. "There's a boat coming up the canal from Georgetown."

"Right. There is."

"You are not to let it pass this lock."

"What do you mean? That's my job here. Get the boats through the locks."

"Not this one. That's a federal order. Do not open the gates."

"What's happened?"

"There was a fight at the Georgetown docks. Rebel raiding party. We think some of them may be in that boat."

"Rebel raiders?" The head withdrew a little.

"Yes. And they're likely armed."

"Armed?"

"Yes. They are not to pass. I expect you to see to it." Harry turned his horse back toward the road.

HE trotted the animal a short distance, halting by a tree and looking back in time to see that the lockkeeper and his wife, the latter lifting her skirts high, were running madly in the opposite direction. The man's absence would serve Harry's purpose. The lock was easy enough to operate, but it would take Zarvona a while to realize he would have to perform the task himself.

Harry had one revolver. There would be innocent passengers aboard the canal boat. Some of Zarvona's men might be with him. However the struggle ended, Rose Greenhow would likely recognize Harry—bloodstained face and arm and darkened mustache or not.

He would need help, and Saylor and the cavalrymen were by then a mile or more away.

But the artillery battery upriver was within shouting distance. Harry spurred his horse in that direction, bearing down on the emplacement at full gallop and reining in his horse so abruptly he almost flew from the saddle. Several of the soldiers looked up.

Unlike the lockkeeper, they would not take orders

from a naval lieutenant—especially one who looked as improbable as he must.

"What unit are you?" Harry shouted.

"Battery B. Company D. Eleventh Illinois. Who're you?"

"Lieutenant J. W. Booth, U.S. Navy. I've a message for you. Confederate infiltrators made a raid on Georgetown. They scattered in all directions and some may be heading your way. Could be on foot. Could be on horseback. Could be on a canal boat. Be alert."

They would not believe any tale about gunmen dressed as women.

"They in uniform?"

"Don't think so. Good luck."

Without further word, he turned his horse again, and made off in a dash back toward Georgetown.

He caught sight of the canal boat just beyond the lockkeeper's now vacant house. Pulling his horse off the road and into a crevice at the foot of the bluff, Harry tied it to a stout branch and then crouched down and waited. The craft took an interminable time to reach the locks.

When no lockkeeper appeared, the boat captain blew a blast of his horn, though a shout would have sufficed. It was not productive. After another blast, he sent a crewman ashore to pound on the lockkeeper's door, again without result.

A male passenger poked his head out a window of the boat. Reassuring him, the captain then ordered the crew to open the lock gates themselves. It took them a considerable time for a task the lockkeeper doubtless handled easily alone, but finally they finished and the captain ordered the teamster on the path to draw them forward. Once they were within the lock's embrace, with the gates closed behind them and water flowing through the sluice from the higher level ahead, Harry fired two quick shots in the direction of the Union artillery battery, then another to make certain. Running low through the brush, he scurried across the road again, rolling into swampy ground next to the canal.

There was a clump of bushes ahead, but leafless, they provided little cover. There was only one real hiding place available to him—the steep wall of the canal bank. Steeling himself for the cold, he held his revolver high, and slid into the water. It came up to his chest, but he was able to wade to the opposite bank, holding himself close to it to avoid being seen from the towpath.

He figured at that moment he was either the smartest man in the federal service or the craziest. Then he heard the little thumps of running feet. Realizing he had only one round left in his pistol, he decided he was probably both.

The sounds came closer. Harry pressed himself against the cold earth, listening intently, then sprang, heaving himself up over the lip of the bank with one hand and grasping with the other at the billowing folds of skirt as they came by.

He slipped back into the canal, but without losing his hold on the cloth. The runner, tripped and yanked off balance, tottered, then regained footing and tried to pull away. Harry gave another yank and the fugitive came sliding into the canal with a big noisy splash. For his part, Harry shoved himself out of the water and rolled up onto the bank, quickly gaining his feet and bringing the revolver to the fore.

Thrashing about for footing, the man in the dress turned to face him, wig and bonnet gone and bald scalp glistening—though not as much as his eyes, which seemed those of a trapped but wily animal, still looking for a way out.

But there was none.

"Colonel Thomas, sir," Harry said, aiming his pistol very carefully at the center of the man's head. "You are my prisoner."

Harry gave a quick glance up the path, relieved to see two Union soldiers trundling along toward him, muskets in hand.

Chapter 26

THE *Pawnee,* with Zarvona safely locked in irons below, headed off downriver with a great chuffing and clanking on its voyage to Fort McHenry, leaving Harry and Saylor on the Georgetown dock, staring after it in some puzzlement.

Pinkerton was notified as soon as Zarvona had been apprehended, as the detective had requested. But inexplicably in this moment of triumph, he had remained at the War Department, sending back only orders. Zarvona was to be returned to his cell in Baltimore as though he'd never left, without official notice or any kind of record of his temporary absence. Mrs. Greenhow was to be treated as harshly— but circumspectly. No newspaper reporter was to be told anything. Rather than trumpeting this close-run triumph, Pinkerton wished to pretend, and have the country presume, that nothing at all had happened.

Zarvona had submitted to his fate peacefully, even philosophically. Rose Greenhow, in contrast, had to be dragged from the canal boat in a fury, her daughter clinging to her skirts in terror. The coach that had been originally intended for their escape took them instead to Fort Greenhow, where Rose was returned to her room as though naught had transpired.

"Pinkerton doesn't want it known we've had our nose tweaked by these people again," Harry said.

"But look how we've tweaked back," Saylor replied. "Zarvona. Rose Greenhow. Only Jeff Davis himself would be a bigger prize. What more could they ask?"

"Some battle victories. Today's adventure is nothing at all like that. This makes it seem that the capital of the republic can barely defend itself against a handful of raiders. That Confederates can come and go from jail cells as they wish, making mischief where they will."

He glanced about the wharf one more time. The casualties of the little engagement, both dead and wounded, Union and Confederate, had been taken off to the Union hospital in Georgetown. Only bloodstains and a few pieces of clothing remained.

Harry had tried to stay out of view throughout the endgame of this sorry affair, observing the capture of the fugitives from a distance. Saylor had talked to Rose Greenhow briefly, causing her to fly into a near-violent rage. She had in fact hit him. There were officers in Washington who might have shot her for that.

"You're sure she didn't see me?" Harry said.

"Not you," said Saylor. "I wish I'd been as prudent."

"She knows you, then?"

Saylor looked at him with some astonishment.

"I don't spend all my time in low gambling dens, Harry. One can't move in the finest society of this city without encountering the lady who commands it."

"One can now," Harry said.

The *Pawnee* was turning slightly, heading obliquely for the opening in the Long Bridge, its smoke a curling smudge across the still-bright sky.

"I don't think she would have recognized you," Saylor said, looking at him with some disapproval. "Your appearance wants attending to, Captain Raines."

Harry shrugged. "As a fugitive, I've not much choice."

He meant the remark as a joke, but Saylor responded with great seriousness.

"I regret that is still your status," he said. "At this point it deserves alteration."

"Mr. Pinkerton seems content to leave me in my predicament."

Saylor frowned. "I think, Harry, that we can at least suspend the law's regard for the time it takes you to return to your quarters at the National and refresh yourself and your clothing. I'll take a few of these men along and see to it you're not disturbed."

"Am I that much in need of repair?"

"Harry, in your present state, you are not fit company for man or beast—and certainly not for the finest society of this city."

"And when I am?"

"As I said, I think your status deserves alteration."

THERE was water in the basin on Harry's washstand. It was cold from the continuing chill of the room and had been standing there for many days, but he was grateful for it.

When reasonably clean, he pondered his image in the mirror. He had wearied of being mistaken for Wilkes Booth. Much as he had been fond of his mustache, he took razor in hand and parted with it now.

His rooms had been cleaned, far more thoroughly than usual. He detected an odd scent of roses, which he realized must have come from perfume. The chambermaids at the National were being paid very well.

He dressed warmly, against the weather he might encounter in the days ahead on the road, and armed himself well. Pinkerton had told him not to leave Washington City, but he would have to ignore that instruction.

Somewhere out there was a woman in a black dress and riding boots. Harry had thought his prey would turn out to be Zarvona, but when they'd captured him, he was wearing ordinary shoes—and of a hefty size. The boot Harry had seen beneath the black skirt had been more diminutive, though very military.

Downstairs, crossing the lobby, he passed by the front desk and saw that his mailbox was stuffed full. His luck had been turning. There might be a letter from Caitlin.

The lobby was crowded, but no one was paying him much mind.

"My mail, please," Harry said quietly to the clerk.

The young man stared, uncertain at first, then showing surprise.

"Mr. Raines? Can that be you?"

Harry put a finger to his lips. "Yes, it can. The mail, if you would."

Moving to the side, he flipped through what looked to be mostly notices from creditors. There was nothing from Caitlin, but there was a most unexpected letter from Boston—from an O. W. Holmes.

Stepping into an alcove, he tore it open and read it over quickly—then again, this time very carefully, as though it were writ in a foreign language, though the young gentleman's English was much superior to his own.

Saylor and his detail of cavalrymen were still waiting in the street outside the hotel's entrance. Harry returned the rest of his mail to the man behind the front desk, then folded Holmes's letter and placed it within his coat. He made a quick survey of the people seated in or milling about the lobby. None seemed to have recognized him, or taken note of him at all.

He darted into a rear corridor and headed out a back door into the alley that led to Sixth Street.

THE door to the office of Harry's horse trading business was locked, and there was no response to his repeated knocking or shouted summons. The paddock was empty of horses. The stable door was locked as well, and he heard no animals within.

He doubted Saylor would come after him—at least not soon—but he feared the colonel might mention his absence to someone else in federal officialdom who would order pursuit. Harry hadn't finished his task. He needed days more to do that.

But days would do it. He was convinced of that.

He waited for a produce wagon to lumber by, then returned to his office door, took a small penknife from his pocket, inserted it in the keyhole, and jiggled it in a remembered manner. The procedure took longer than it should have, but finally there was a click. Turning the knob, he pushed his way in.

The place looked altogether different than he remembered—or had ever seen it. The odd papers and records he usually had piled and scattered on every flat surface had disappeared. The floor had been swept and scrubbed. The entire room was neat and clean, which had not been his habit.

There wasn't time to wonder at this. All he needed from here was traveling funds.

Going to the desk, he lifted it by one end with some effort and swung it aside, then knelt and pulled up a floorboard that one leg had been resting on. He reached within the space below, taking out a small metal strongbox. A low voice behind him commanded him to put it down.

Harry shook his head, sighed, set down the box, then slowly rose and turned.

Caesar Augustus lowered the revolver he held, but not far. He had come out of the tack room that adjoined the office.

"Don't you recognize me?" Harry asked.

"I do now, Marse Harry, but you have changed some," said the other, sticking his weapon in his belt. "I thought you was in prison."

"I may be again, if I don't depart this place soon. Why didn't you answer my knock?"

"Hard to do that when you're asleep."

"Where in hell are all my horses?"

"Sold some to the army. Took the rest back up to Shepherdstown."

"Where's Rocket?"

"Colonel Saylor had some soldiers bring him in. I put him in a stable up the street. Didn't want to keep him around here, where he'd be seen. People were looking for you."

"People like Samuel Buckeys?" Harry began rummaging in a drawer of his desk, looking for the strongbox key.

"He been around a few times, but I ain't seen him for a lot of days. He go off somewhere?"

"He's gone to a place where we don't want to follow. Someone shot him in Baltimore—in my hotel room. Shot him dead, Caesar Augustus."

"Word in Murder Bay was he was lookin' to shoot you."

"Yes, well. He didn't." Harry got the box open and

began taking U.S. greenbacks from it. "I'd be obliged if you could fetch Rocket for me. I'm reluctant to go strolling about the avenue at the moment. I left some Union soldiers there and I expect that by now they'll be looking for me. I don't want to be found."

"Where're you and Rocket planning on goin', Marse Harry?"

"Poolesville. Then Leesburg."

"Union Army's still at Poolesville. And there's Confederates around Leesburg."

"That's why I'm going there. I'm looking for a certain Union Army officer, and also a Confederate one." He looked again at his desk. "You didn't see a letter for me from Caitlin Howard?"

"No, Marse Harry."

"She's in Cincinnati, I think—with that damned Booth."

"No, sir. She's here in Washington City. Saw her yesterday."

"Here? You're sure? Where is she? At her boarding-house?"

"You said you got army soldiers looking for you, Marse Harry. You best leave Miss Caitlin alone for a while. I'll get Rocket. Then we'll go. I'm goin' with you this time. You need keepin' out of trouble."

"Leesburg's in Virginia, Caesar Augustus. You'd have to travel as my slave. There's no other way."

The word gave him an unpleasant taste as he spoke it.

"I'll go with you. This time anyway. I'll fetch Rocket."

WHEN they were near the Union Army camp at Poolesville, Harry sent Caesar Augustus on ahead while he retreated with the horses into a small woods around the shoulder of a hill. Blacks escaping from the South were forever wandering into Union Army encampments, looking for food and ways to make themselves useful and pick up some small money. Caesar Augustus had passed himself off for one of them before in Harry's service, learning much from the chatter of his fellow Negroes and the idling troops.

This time, Harry needed only one piece of knowledge.

"He's there," said Caesar Augustus, much later, returning to Harry's hiding place as the sun was going down. "His company's bedded down over by the river. Most of General Stone's command has moved."

"All to the good," Harry said. "It's across the river I'm heading next. You're still willing?"

"Yassuh." The black man spat.

THEY had a cold supper of bread and beefsteak, then, wrapping themselves in camp blankets against the cold, took their horses around to the south of the camp.

Harry left Caesar Augustus holding the animals, then moved into the assemblage of Union tents, seeking the one that was his goal. When he finally found it, there was still the glow of a lantern within. Moving to some brush at the rear of the shelter, cramped in the cold, Harry sat down and waited for it to go out.

He heard the officer speak to an orderly, then bid the man a curt good night. Shortly after, the lantern was extinguished. Harry waited a little longer, then crept forth, loosening two pegs and a length of canvas on one side of the tent and crawling beneath.

Once fully inside, he slowly got up to his knees and quietly pulled forth a revolver. Edging closer to the officer curled up for warmth on his cot, Harry gently set the pistol barrel against the man's ear, then quickly whispered: "It's Harry Raines, Philbrick. Make a move or call out, and you lose an ear and whatever's on the other side of it."

There was no reply. The silence lasted such a long time Harry wondered if the man was still asleep despite the rudeness of the intrusion.

Finally, the captain turned his head an inch toward Harry, fully awake yet still perfectly quiet.

"What do you want?" he said.

"Only one thing. Why did you file a report with General Stone saying I fired the shot that took down Colonel Baker at Ball's Bluff?"

"You are mistaken, sir. I filed a report saying that Lieutenant Holmes made that observation."

"What?"

"That's what I wrote. The report's with Stone. Take a look at it."

Harry moved the revolver barrel back a few inches. "Holmes?"

"That's what I said. That's what he said."

"Are you aware that Holmes survived his wound and is recuperating now on leave at his home in Massachusetts?"

"I heard he survived. I thought he was in the hospital."

Harry slowly got to his feet, keeping his aim on Philbrick.

"You've known he survived, yet you let your report stand?"

"Of course. It's what happened, isn't it? Now, what do you want?"

"There's a candle beside your cot. Light it, I have something I want you to read."

There was a brief hesitation, then Philbrick struck a
match and put it to the wick of a squat mound of wax.
Harry stepped back from the flickering yellow light.
Switching his pistol to his left hand, he pulled Holmes's
letter from his coat pocket and tossed it onto the cot.

"It's from Holmes," Harry said. "Read it."

Philbrick hesitated, searching Harry's face for a sign
he wasn't about to be shot. Harry decided to withhold
that comfort for the while.

"Read it!"

Philbrick did as commanded, but remained calm. His
nerves had improved since that ill-starred night patrol.

When he was done, he folded the paper carefully and
extended it to Harry, who snatched it back quickly.
Philbrick's gaze fell to the floor.

"It would appear I made a mistake, sir."

"Holmes says he accused me of nothing. He says
that when you asked him what happened to Baker, he
tried to tell you that the shot that wounded the colonel
came from some trees near where I had been standing.
From behind me. He denies that he told you I had fired
it."

"The lieutenant was wounded. Not sensible. I put
down what I thought he said."

"You bear me ill will for our dispute over those
phantom Confederate tents at Ball's Bluff. This gave
you a chance for revenge."

"No, sir. We were all asked to put down what we
knew about Baker's death, and that's what I thought
Holmes said."

There was a camp stool near Harry. He sat down on
it carefully, resting the revolver on his knee but keeping
it pointed at the captain—though he felt the man posed
little threat to him now.

"Did you read what he said about the red-haired man?"

"Yes, I did. He said he saw a red-haired man in shirtsleeves near those same trees. But there were many who removed their coats."

"He said he had never seen that soldier before."

Philbrick sat up, without invitation. He was wearing long underwear and red wool socks. "I didn't notice any such red-haired man. Not at all."

"Did you see the Confederate officer ride up and empty a revolver into Baker?"

"Yes, I did. Most everybody saw that."

"You recognize the man?"

"No, I didn't. Just another Reb. Anyways, Raines, I never said you did that. All I said was I thought Holmes told me you had fired the shot that wounded Baker before that Reb officer come up."

"Why didn't you do something about that Rebel?"

"We were in a bad fight and gettin' whipped," Philbrick said. "I was looking out for my command. My boys were takin' fire."

Harry fought the heavy pull of fatigue. He still had considerable travel ahead of him that night.

"Do you know a man named Samuel Buckeys?"

"Only by reputation. He sells bad mounts to the army."

The time had come for a gesture. Harry needed to depart this camp without half a regiment in pursuit.

He slipped the revolver into his belt.

"Well, I am satisfied, Captain Philbrick. Sorry to have troubled your night. I won't disturb you further."

"You think you can get out of this camp without raising an alarm?"

"That would be my hope."

"You're a fugitive."

"Yes, I am."

"You were in prison. How'd you get out?"

"They brought me to Washington from Fort McHenry and I found occasion to slip away."

"But you're still wanted?"

"Yes. I'm afraid so."

Philbrick appeared puzzled. "I'll let you go without hindrance, Raines. My way of showing I didn't mean nothing personal with my report. But you answer me a question. Holmes says he sent a similar letter to President Lincoln, correcting the record and absolving you from blame."

"Yes, that's what Holmes said."

"Then how come you're still a fugitive?"

"I wish I knew."

Chapter 27

Iᴛ snowed all the next day, but in light fits that the wind swirled away. By sunset it began to thicken and stick. Harry had waited for the dark in a barn west of Leesburg, warmed by the heat of the several cattle it contained. Caesar Augustus came and went, first to forage food and drink with the pretense he was a Confederate officer's slave on such an errand. With sustenance obtained and consumed, he made another foray, returning as the last light of day was leaving the sky.

"She's at home but she ain't alone, Marse Harry," he said, shaking snow from his coat. "She got that big African gentleman with her."

"Bob."

"Right. Bob." He spat. "The loyal slave."

Harry handed Caesar Augustus his whiskey flask. "Did Bob see you?"

"I talked to him. Called to him from the road and we had a talk over the fence. I told him I was a John Henry."

"A fugitive slave?"

"Right."

"Will he turn you in?"

Caesar Augustus scowled. "Ain't many Negroes who'd do that to another black man. There may be such but I don't think him. He told me to move on and stay away from Leesburg, as it's full of Confederates and every kind of rascal, including slave hunters."

Harry accepted back the flask and took a sip before putting it away.

"Probably right about the last part," he said. "But I don't think the Rebels have even a battalion here. McClellan could take the town with his honor guard, if he'd a mind to. But he certainly doesn't have that."

"I'd be just as happy to move on, Marse Harry. Washington City or Shepherdstown. All the same to me."

"Not yet." Harry got to his feet. "I need to see this woman. Quite a lot of her, as a matter of fact."

"From what you told me about her, you'd be better off with an army behind you. What am I s'posed to be doin' while you're seein' her alone?"

"I need you to take care of Bob."

"I don't want to hurt that man."

"I don't think that's going to be the problem, since he's got about six inches on you—in all directions."

Caesar Augustus smiled. "Whiskey's a great equalizer. Let's get us a jug, and I'll come back and trade him some for a night's refuge in his barn. I'll tell him I had to turn back at the river because of Confederate patrols. He's a fierce-lookin' man, but I think he's a kind one."

"Must be—to stick with that lady when he could be a free man in the North."

"Maybe you got the wrong idea about her, Marse Harry."

"Maybe I do. But I'm not betting on it."

THE snow diminished, giving way to a clearing sky and sharp cold. Harry endured it, shivering, in the shelter of some trees across the road from the house. Caesar Augustus had been gone long enough to have succeeded in his ruse. Leaving the horses securely tied, Harry went back up the road to where he could cross it without being seen from the house, then clambered over a snake rail fence and came back toward it, keeping low.

There was smoke from the chimney, and orange flickers visible through the front window, but no light from an oil lamp or lantern. He hoped that meant she was abed and asleep—and that she was alone.

A reconnaissance was in order first, a circuit through the snow around the house and then a pass by the barn, where he heard low voices, one of them Caesar Augustus's. The conversation sounded amiable, something about horses—or maybe women. One of them laughed.

After another survey of the house, and a pause to put on his spectacles, for which he had a most definite need, Harry decided to try a cellar door for entry. The lock would not yield, however. Going to a window, he found it a little loose, opening to a wide crack at the bottom of the sash, but a long, wedged piece of wood prevented it from rising farther. He experimented with several other windows as well, with largely the same result. Finally, desperate, he went to the front door.

It was unlocked.

He guessed she'd left it open for Bob so he might attend upon her until she retired. As such a remarkably loyal servant, he'd be waiting upon her as might an orderly upon an officer in camp.

But she had retired. The only light came from the fireplace.

He pushed the door open a few inches, feeling the

cold air on his back as it sought the interior of the house. It would be stirring the flames of the fire. Hastily, he stepped all the way inside and closed the door behind him. After a quick, deep breath, he turned to pull the latch closed, then took out his Colt revolver, moving on with it preceding him.

The fireplace was in the next room. He gave a quick glance in that direction, then proceeded down a short hallway toward what he assumed was the bedroom. Despite his caution, the floor gave a loud creak. He cursed himself, then realized that the sound had not been caused by him.

"You hold there," said the low but feminine voice. "I got a twelve-gauge here with both barrels full of buck. It's aimed exactly where I might cut you in twain."

The words were spoken quietly, but carried such menace and purpose they halted him as though they'd been shouted in full cry.

"You know me, Loreta," he said finally. "I was your prisoner at Ball's Bluff. My name is Harrison Raines."

"Turn around. Slow."

He had put his revolver back into his belt beneath his coat. He did as bidden. Not knowing where she wanted his hands, he kept them low.

She had not been bluffing. There wasn't much light from the fire, but he could see the metallic glint along both barrels of the weapon, which was now leveled at his middle. Miss Velasquez—also known as Lieutenant Harry T. Buford, CSA—was seated in a rocking chair. There was about ten feet between them. He'd be dead before he reached her if he tried to get the shotgun away.

Shotguns were still the most commonplace arm of the Southern cavalry. In the Union Army, horse soldiers were turning to carbines.

She was wearing a very high-necked, prim dress. He

was curious to know whether she was still carrying on her masquerade as a soldier. He asked her, hoping the question might distract her from whatever she was intent on doing with the twelve gauge.

"I'm still an officer in the 'Independent Scouts,' still with the Leesburg militia," she said. "That hasn't changed."

"Colonel Evans released me, when I was here last."

"That he did."

"I am wanted by federal authorities."

"Is that so? What for?"

"I am accused of the murder of Colonel Edward Baker at Ball's Bluff. I believe you are acquainted with that sad event."

"You know that I am."

"I am also accused of the murder of a horse trader named Samuel Buckeys. I'm said to be a Southern agent. I've been imprisoned at Fort McHenry."

"They set you free?"

"I escaped."

"Hard to do."

The rocker creaked. He wondered if the shotgun was growing heavy in her hands. Perhaps so, for she adjusted it, resting the stock next to her leg. Unfortunately, the twin barrels were now aimed at his head.

"You have a white horse," he said.

"A gray. Light-colored. Yes, I do."

Of a sudden she got to her feet, the shotgun directed again at his middle.

"That chair there, by the fire. Go sit in it, Raines."

He did as she ordered, realizing it put him fully in the firelight, where she could watch his eyes. She retook her own seat, turning it toward him. It seemed she had no wish to shoot him, though she certainly had excuse enough to do so.

"Now you tell me what you come here for," she said. "Slithering into my house in the dark of night."

"The hour was late. I didn't want to alarm you. I feared I might get shot."

"Well, you did alarm me. And you may yet get shot."

They observed each other quietly for a long moment. It occurred to him that she was waiting for someone—doubtless Bob—that she was leery of attempting to conclude matters here by her lonesome.

"Your man Bob will not be coming—not soon," Harry said.

"And how do you know that?"

"Because he is with my man, Caesar Augustus."

"Your man?"

"He is as loyal to me as your Bob is to you, but I pay him honest wages for his labor, and he is free to go if he pleases—to do whatever he pleases."

Harry caught the flicker of reflected flame in her eyes.

"Bob will be back soon," she said.

If she were to cry out, or fire off her shotgun, Bob would be there in about two leaps. Harry had to keep her calm.

"I'm sure they have not gone far. My man posed as a runaway in need of help. Your Bob may be loyal to you, but not to the 'peculiar institution.'"

"I think you had better stop talking about Bob."

It was a small house, smaller than he had thought. He guessed there was only one bedroom.

And she had left the front door unlatched.

He heard a disturbing click. She had cocked the shotgun. It surprised him that she hadn't done that before.

"Tell me quick now, Raines. What do you want of me?"

"I hesitate to say."

"Do not hesitate, sir." Another click. Both barrels now. "Speak."

"What I want is something no gentleman would ask of a lady, but I fear I must."

"Surely you didn't come all the way out here this cold night to deprive me of my virtue. Not when there's so much to be had in Washington City."

He smiled, in a manner he hoped she would take for courtly.

"I mean you no harm," he said. "I wish only to resolve the issue of Colonel Edward Baker's killing."

"Why? He's dead. So are many on that ground. It was a battle."

"His death is held to have been a murder. In Washington there has been a great indignation rising up about it. Some in high office are accusing me, yet I am not responsible."

"But here you are in Virginia—where shooting that officer is judged no sin."

"Miss Velasquez, a Confederate officer on a white horse rode up to Colonel Baker as he lay wounded on the ground and fired five rounds from a revolver into him. I seek that officer."

"I never got near the fighting. They had me and my boys keeping watch on prisoners."

"As you say, the deed could make you a hero in the South—in some quarters."

"None that I'm interested in."

"Do you own a black dress?"

"'Course I do. What woman does not?"

"And are you wearing boots?"

She extended a foot from beneath the hem of her skirt. "Indeed I am not, sir. I am wearing slippers."

"Do you ever wear boots? When not in your militia uniform?"

"Yes. And why not? It's winter. There's snow."

She shifted the weight of the shotgun again, only to hold it more firmly. He had a sense of her rising curiosity. He had no idea how this would end, but she seemed willing to go along with this game, if only to play for time and Bob's return.

"Do you own a revolver?"

"Of course. I am an officer."

"May I see it?"

She laughed. "No."

There was a sound behind him, and a draft of cold wind. She turned in that direction, a happy expression suddenly coming upon her face that just as abruptly vanished. Harry hadn't time to look at the cause, merely to make an all-important guess about it, and act.

Her distraction lasted no more than a second or two, but Harry made the most of it, lunging forward to grasp the barrel of the shotgun and twist it upward, moving inside her arm and pulling her up out of the chair, then falling with her to the floor, emerging with the weapon in hand. She had not had her fingers on the triggers. Otherwise, the shotgun would have gone off.

Before he could savor his good luck, she pulled away from him and hurried from the room. Caesar Augustus, whose appearance had prompted her quick change of expression, bounded after her.

More luck. He returned with both the Velasquez woman and the revolver she had gone for, saving them a search.

He had one hand over her mouth. She struggled a moment longer, then gave up. At Harry's nod, he loosed his grip on her jaw.

"Where's Bob?" she asked, a little fear showing beneath the angry pride.

"In the barn," said Caesar Augustus. "Enjoying some whiskey."

"I don't believe you."

"You can go see."

"No," said Harry, pulling out his own pistol, not certain either of the woman's weapons were loaded. "We have business with her here."

"I answered your questions!" she said.

"I have another question," Harry said, "but words will not answer it. Unfortunately, my curiosity can only be satisfied in a way that no Virginia gentleman would ask of a lady, but I must."

Caesar Augustus had released her. He appeared impatient and kept looking toward the front door.

"You sure got a slow way of talking," she said. "What in blazes do you want?"

"In those woods off the Frederick Road—before I was knocked out, trussed up, and thrown over the back of a horse—I saw a woman, buck naked, faced away from me, and standing by a white horse."

She said nothing.

"I need to know for certain if it was you," he said. "I'm asking you, with all due respect and my profuse apologies for the indignity I am asking of you, to stand up, turn your back to me, lift up your skirts, and lower your underdrawers."

"Sir, I told you I did not shoot that man."

"Marse Harry," said Caesar Augustus, "there's a faster way of doing this."

"Not for a gentleman, sir."

She laughed again. "That's all you're after? You got nothin' more in mind?"

"If you're as innocent as you say—and as I think you may well be—I shall be happy with the merest glimpse, and then be on my way—and out of your life."

She thought upon this, then turned and put her back to him. Caesar Augustus moved away.

"I'm not afraid of you, Raines," she said.

"No, ma'am. Not afraid of much, I'd say."

"I didn't shoot that officer." With a rustle of taffeta, she bent over and threw back her skirt and petticoats. Then she reached for her undergarments. "Glimpse away."

Chapter 28

A Confederate cavalry patrol followed them out of Leesburg on the westward pike, trailing them for more than a mile in the darkness. Fortunately, they never got close enough to see that Miss Velasquez was bound and gagged with a tightly wound scarf. From the distance the soldiers kept, they could perceive only a man and wife and Negro servant—or so Harry hoped.

His principal worry was the man Bob. Caesar Augustus had exaggerated the effects of the whiskey. He hadn't wanted to tie up the man in winter weather, fearing he might not be discovered and could freeze to death. His expectation was that Bob would stir himself soon enough to give them trouble, if he guessed their route and was a good tracker.

And so Bob was. With the Rebel horsemen behind them, Harry had turned off the westerly road and took a wagon track north, reconnecting with the Frederick Road and heading for Nolan's Ferry and the Union lines.

They got aboard the big flat raft without any trouble, but about halfway across, the big black man appeared on the Virginia bank of the Potomac aboard a suitably large horse. He didn't take a shot at them, doubtless for fear of hitting his mistress, but appeared as though he wanted to do that very badly. When they reached the Maryland side, Harry gave the boatman a dollar coin for the promise of tarrying there before recrossing the raft.

There was a Union soldiers' camp on higher ground just above the shore, and guards posted at the bridge where the ferry road crossed the C&O Canal. Separating himself from Caesar Augustus and the woman, he rode up to the corporal in charge, speaking low and correctly identifying himself as one of Allan Pinkerton's men bringing in a prisoner.

"She is suspected of being the assassin who slew Colonel Baker," he said, with great earnestness. "I would appreciate it if we could avoid delay so that I might present her at Washington as soon as possible."

The corporal looked somewhat askance at Harry's appearance, and worried aloud that he probably ought to take him to his lieutenant.

"Where is he, then?" Harry asked. "I'll report to him myself."

The soldier said something about a command post about a mile up the road. Harry saluted and the three of them started that way, but, once out of view, cut into the woods and began heading south along the river again.

When they had gone some distance from the soldiers, he loosed the scarf tied around Miss Velasquez's mouth.

"Where are you taking me?"

"To Washington City, if I have to."

"You're going to have me tried, for the shooting of a Union officer in a battle?"

"I am going to bring you to justice for that act. For it was murder."

"You're going to stand up in a courtroom and tell the world that you compelled a lady to remove her underclothes at gunpoint."

That, of course, he was not prepared to do.

"I don't know that there's going to be a courtroom involved."

They rode on a way farther in silence. She appeared to be struggling with some thought.

"I lied to you, Raines."

"I thought as much."

"Not about that Colonel Baker. But about killing anyone. When I got back to the bluff, the battle was still ragin', but it had moved mostly down to the riverbank. The Yankees were all massed down there, trying to get back across, and our boys were firing at them.

"This horrible spectacle made me shudder. I was willing to fight to death's door in the open field, and to ask no favors, taking the same chances for life as they had; but I had no heart for their ruthless slaughter. All the woman in me revolted at the fiendish delight which some of our soldiers displayed at the sight of that terrible agony."

Harry interrrupted. "You say you saw this upon your return? From where?"

"I told you I killed no one. That was a lie. I fired at a Yankee officer. I thought it was expected of me. There was this other lieutenant—who had been in command of my boys. A skulker who'd disappeared at the first shot. He'd come back at the end, with some wild tale about being taken prisoner. Who'd have taken him prisoner? He wanted his company back."

"And you shot a Union officer to prove yourself?"

"He was about to jump into the river—I guess to try to swim it. I fired once, twice, and saw him spring into the air and fall. I turned my head away, shuddering at what I had done, although I believed that it was only my duty. I was sick at heart, unable to endure the sight of it. Cold shivers ran through me, and my heart stood still in my bosom. I shut my eyes for a moment, wishing that it was all over—but only to open them again to gaze on a spectacle that had a terrible fascination for me, in spite of its horrors."

Harry confessed to himself the same fascination when he'd come upon the bluff—repulsion, deep melancholy, but fascination at so starkly hellish a tableau.

"It wasn't like after Bull Run," she said. "I was not anxious for another battle."

"You were at Bull Run?"

"I am a soldier, Mr. Raines. I see myself as a second Joan of Arc."

He recalled the image of her resplendent in her uniform—and theatrical beard and mustache. Then another thought intruded. He chased it away.

THEY followed a farm road through some small hills near Sugarloaf Mountain, shivering against a cold that grew steadily worse. Caesar Augustus halted to remove his coat and pull on a thick wool jersey shirt over his other one. When it was in place, he put the coat on again, his numb fingers struggling with the buttons.

At a crossroads just beyond, Harry pulled up. The thought had returned, and this time refused to budge.

Caesar Augustus looked at him, then back up the road they'd just come down, then once again at Harry.

"Somethin' wrong, Marse Harry?"

"Maybe there is."

"You sick?" Caesar Augustus asked. "You cold?"

"It's worse than that."

"How's that?"

His friend and occasional drinking companion Matthew Brady had made an observation to him one night about his camera.

"The photograph," Brady had said, "shows you what you see. Not what you think you see."

Harry turned his horse to face the other man.

"I'd like you to go on up to the farm and find Belle," he said. "If she's not there, she'll be at her mother's in Martinsburg. She has to leave there. Tell her I want her to go to Front Royal—into Rebel territory—as soon as possible. If she stays, she may have Union cavalry after her. Use her word, 'Yankee' cavalry. Tell her she must go."

"She's not goin' to take that kind of instruction from a black man. And she's not much for takin' it from you, either."

"Tell her if she does as I wish, I'll make her the gift of a rose."

Caesar Augustus stared. "You been out in the cold too long, Marse Harry?"

"Just tell her."

The sun was lowering to beneath a layer of cloud, lightening the sky over the Blue Ridge.

"You still taking her to Washington?" Caesar Augustus asked, with a nod to a now very glum-looking Loreta Janeta Velasquez.

"I'm going back to Washington. Join me after you've talked to Belle. I'm going to need you in the federal city—if you'll oblige me."

"Very well, Marse Harry, where'll you be?"

"Probably in jail—at least until Pinkerton finds me. Maybe I'll be there after he finds me. But try the National."

He flicked Rocket's reins, turning him again as he moved the big animal into a rhythmic trot, keeping Miss

Velasquez's lead in hand. When he felt certain there was enough distance between the two of them and Caesar Augustus, he halted, turning his mount to come next to hers. Leaning in the saddle, he undid her bonds.

She pulled away her scarf, taking a breath of cold air much like someone rising from under water, then rewound it around her neck.

"What're you doing?" she asked, eyeing his revolver.

He looked at her sadly. "Tell me again, and truly. Were you at those woods north of the bluff—during the middle of the battle? Just tell me the truth."

She folded her arms across her chest. "Are you fixing to shoot me?"

"Just tell me."

"Well, I was there. But only for a brief time. And I wasn't skulkin'—like that other lieutenant. I went under orders."

"And when you came back, it was as a soldier."

"Yes. I'm a soldier—an officer of the Independent Scouts."

Harry shook his head and sighed.

"Madame, I owe you the most profound apology. I hope someday to earn your forgiveness."

"Sir?"

"You are free to go."

Chapter 29

LEAHY was a master of stealth and always likely to be alert to others practicing it. So Harry approached the door to Leahy's rooms in his boardinghouse with some apprehension. There were thumping sounds coming from inside—in a regular beat.

"One"—*thump*—"two"—*thump*—"three"—*thump* . . .

Harry calmed himself. The Irishman was performing his nightly calesthenics. He would be focused on the routine, at his most vulnerable.

Harry pulled out his long revolver. Leahy was his friend, but Abraham Lincoln was Leahy's god, and Mr. Lincoln still viewed Harry as a criminal. Harry was of no mind to go back into a jail cell just yet.

Twisting the knob, he discovered, naturally enough, that the door was locked. If he was going to catch Leahy by surprise, he would have to shoot it open. He cocked the hammer of his weapon, staring down at it. His need for sleep was showing. This was daft.

He knocked, loudly, to overcome all the thumping.

It stopped. There was a long silence; then, so swiftly it startled Harry, the door opened.

No one was there. The lights had been turned out. Harry stood there quite dumbly, still holding the revolver but pointing it down.

"Raines, you idiot. Why have you come back to Washington?"

Harry hesitated. All at once a hand shot out from the darkness and gripped his arm, yanking him inside. The door shut and all was dark. An instant later a candle came aglow. A moment after that the gaslight was turned on.

"I have orders to arrest you, Harry. We all do."

Leahy was wearing only trousers and a pair of thick white socks. Despite the cold in the room, his bare chest and arms were glossy with sweat. In his right hand, he carried a heavy-looking weight, but with as little effort as Harry expended simply holding his pistol.

"I think I know who killed Colonel Baker," Harry said.

"Do you now?"

"And I wasn't the one who did it."

"That's not a commonplace opinion. But I for one have good reason to agree with it."

Leahy pulled on a thick wool shirt, then went to a table, opening a drawer, from which he took a brown cloth bag. Untying it, he noisily emptied its contents onto the wood.

Harry came closer. There were six bullets. Some were misshapen.

"All forty-four-caliber," Leahy said. "The five from Ball's Bluff. One from the remains of the late Samuel Buckeys. You carry Navy Colts—you've got one in your hand—and they're thirty-six-caliber."

Harry picked up a bullet, then another. "They're all mixed up. How can you tell which is which?"

"Doesn't matter, laddybuck. What matters is that they all came from the same revolver—and not yours."

Harry set the bullets down on the tabletop, then turned and sank into a chair, the only one in the room.

Leahy was content to remain standing. He probably was able to sleep that way.

"Dr. Gregg examined these rounds and determined with his mastery of the French science of ballistics that they were all fired from the same weapon. He'll swear to it."

"Did you find the weapon in question?"

"No. But it wasn't one of your Colts."

Harry sighed. Then pulled forth the pistol he had taken from Loreta Velasquez. He had intended to return it to her when they'd parted by the Potomac, but it had slipped his mind.

"What's that?" Leahy said.

"An English-made Kerr five-shot percussion revolver, commonly carried by Confederate cavalry-men." He paused. "And, I suppose, cavalrywomen."

"What'd you say?"

"Never mind." He handed the weapon over to the Irishman. "You may want to fire a round—and have Dr. Gregg compare it with the others."

"Is this yours?"

"I'm afraid not."

Leahy's forehead became creased. "Can you prove that?"

Harry frowned at the question. "No."

"That's unfortunate," said Leahy, hefting the weapon, "because I find it now in your possession."

His meaning came uneasily to Harry's mind.

"You are a lawyer now, Mr. Leahy?"

"No, and I wouldna be. But Mr. Lincoln is. And he's going to be the final judge of this mess." He hefted the weapon. "And that includes the evidence of this pistol. If a round fired from it matches these others—"

"It's not my weapon."

"Do you want to tell me whose it is?"

Harry had compelled the poor woman—a better "man" than many he'd encountered in uniform—to disgracefully expose herself, had dragged her out tied and gagged into a cold night, and then left her on a colder morning alone and without provision in Union territory.

"No," he said.

A gust of wind rattled the window, stirring a draft against Harry's face. It was as though the glass did not impede it.

"There's more to this," Harry said. "I need some time. More time."

"Then you should have gone to your farm and not come to Washington."

Harry studied the other's face, finding it as impossible to read as always. Leahy looked upon gambling as disapprovingly as he did John Barleycorn, which was a pity. He had the makings of a better poker player than probably could be found in any card parlor south of the avenue.

"You fellows would only have come after me," Harry said.

Leahy shook his head for emphasis. "Not so long as we knew where you were. But you come back here, where all the world can see you. Then you've got to be locked up. Mr. Lincoln's orders."

"I need time. I must meet with some actors."

"If you're after visiting Caitlin Howard, she's here. Rehearsing a play. Not Shakespeare. A comedy. *Our American Cousin.* At Grover's."

"I know. She hates that play."

"Not partial to it myself. But it's work."

"Is Booth with her, do you know?"

"We haven't seen Mr. Booth yet. His presence is customarily advertised by swooning ladies."

"Give me a day. Just one day."

"Major Allen—Mr. Pinkerton—he's sent instructions to every Secret Service agent in the federal city to bring you in. There'll be someone watching the National—and it won't be anyone so ready to indulge you as I am."

"You mean you'll grant my wish?"

Leahy thought upon this—as though for a second and more useful time.

"Yes, of course. If you'll promise to be at the War Department by sundown tomorrow."

"Very well. I will."

Leahy stood. Harry did the same.

"I think you're innocent, Harry. But I've got to do my job."

"I know. Thank you, Joseph."

"I will see you tomorrow."

GROVER'S Theatre stood at the intersection of Pennsylvania and an angled side street called Rum Row, which formed a small, open triangle. Avoiding the National Hotel, where he knew the loungers inside and out would include a Pinkerton man or two, Harry spent the night in the hayloft of Nailor's Livery directly across from Grover's, took a quick, furtive breakfast in an oyster bar a few doors down the avenue, then settled in for the morning in the deserted little Fourteenth Street office of a newspaper correspondent of his acquaintance—a fellow who slept late and worked little—just around the corner from Grover's.

Around noon Leonard Grover opened the back door

to his theater—out of habit, leaving it unlocked. Harry waited a few minutes, then crossed the alley and slipped inside. A quick reconnaissance found Grover at work in his office, located on the second floor at the front of the building. Without disturbing him, Harry went backstage to the long room where the actors and actresses applied their makeup. He searched through it, without success, then discovered an adjoining chamber with shelves running along three of the walls, each piled high with hats, wigs, beards, mustaches, swords, doublets, and all manner of other disguise and costumery.

He found what he sought very soon. Taking the red-haired wig to a window, he noted the same craftsman's mark as before, the same stains on the lining. The shelf might well have been the proper place for the hairpiece, but putting it there was not what he had asked of her.

He wondered why she hadn't destroyed it. But of course, it was sacred. It belonged to *him*.

Stuffing the wig in a pocket, Harry took a chair and sat down to wait. Pinkerton's men would not be looking for him in a theater. Once Caitlin was on the premises, she would have small opportunity to retreat.

But she never arrived. Stagehands did, descending to the well beneath the stage and commencing a noisy bit of work with saws and hammers. A charwoman with a bucket glanced in at Harry, but went on to other business. Leonard Grover wandered backstage, fiddled with some props, then wandered away again, taking no notice of his uninvited guest.

Stiff, tired, hungry, and in need of a chamber pot, Harry finally crept out of his lair. There was a board on the wall of the dressing room with paper notices on it. One explained the reason for his unsuccessful wait. The rehearsal for that day had been canceled.

The visit was not entirely a loss, however. Finding a very old-fashioned torn and ragged frock coat among the costumes, along with a Shylock's cap from *The Merchant of Venice,* Harry assembled the wig and these garments upon his person and walked blithely down the aisle and out the theater's front door.

Outside, on the avenue, lounging against the entrance to the National, Harry caught sight of a Pinkerton man he knew. Affecting a limp—but preparing to run for his life—Harry deliberately headed for him, passing close enough to pick the man's pocket, yet the fellow hardly gave him a glance. The disguise was masterful.

After that, fully confident, he walked more nonchalantly, making his way to Sixth Street and the high, long building that was Mrs. Fitzgerald's boardinghouse, home to a number of actors keeping permanent residence in the federal city. Caitlin had a bedroom and sitting room there, to which Harry had been no stranger.

His disguise worked no magic on this lady.

"She ain't here," said Mrs. Fitzgerald. She threw her slops into the street, then remounted the stoop and turned to face Harry, squinting at him. "You become an actor, Mr. Raines?"

"I would if I could, but I haven't," he said, looking up to Caitlin's curtained window. "It's merely discretion that dictates my appearance today."

"You could use more of it." She disappeared through her front door, which she shut firmly behind her.

There was a rough-looking man in a dark coat and cap loitering across the street, but out of earshot. Harry got a sharp, quick study from him as he departed, but there was no pursuit, nor any further attention.

HE finally came upon her where he least desired—entering a building just across the avenue from Center Market that housed Matthew Brady's photographic studio, Thompson's Saloon, and a drugstore.

It was the latter place that Harry feared was her destination. Caitlin was no great drinker, but she had a most destructive affinity for laudanum, a drug she normally resisted but succumbed to quickly in her recurring interludes of depression—usually precipitated by Booth casting her aside, as was his frequent wont. Harry had stayed with her night and day through two of her worst episodes, one of which had nearly killed her. He couldn't afford the time to do that now.

He didn't want to have a row with her inside the shop, especially if that led to his being publicly recognized. He'd wait. He entered the warmth of Thompson's and took a place at the corner of the bar that gave a good view of the street.

She remained in the building for the time of two whiskeys. When at last he saw her pretty bonnet-topped head passing by the grimy window, he gulped down the last of the second glass. He caught up with her at the next corner as she waited for a barrel-laden freight wagon to rumble by. Harry leaned close to her ear.

"Why are you back in Washington?" he asked.

He spoke in a gruff voice. Her head snapped 'round and her face performed a swift repertoire of expressions—irritated at being accosted on a public street by a stranger, startled to see such a bizarrely garbed person at her elbow; then recognition, then anger.

"You offend me, sir," she said, her eyes searching the street traffic around her. "I am unused to being greeted in this manner."

"I am sorry. What were you doing in the drugstore?"

"I was not visiting the drug shop."

If this was a lie, he'd gain nothing quarreling about it.

"I'm sorry, Caitlin. I am not myself these days." He reminded himself of his appearance. "I dare not be."

She continued avoiding his eyes. "They say you were in jail."

"In jail, escaped—now a fugitive."

Now she looked at him. He removed the ridiculous cap. At the sight of the red-haired wig, she flushed.

"Walk with me," he said.

She was nervous now. "Where?"

"To Carusi's Hall, by the canal. It won't smell so bad in the cold."

She started forward, head down. "Very well."

When they had turned down a side street, Harry removed the wig, dangling it before her.

"This snatch of hair has been on quite a journey," he said.

"How did you get it?" she asked.

"I took shelter this morning in the back of Grover's. You promised me you'd find out where it came from."

"So I did."

"And so?"

"It came from Schultz's, a costume shop near the Front Street Theatre in Baltimore."

"And who bought it?"

She bit her lip, still looking down, as though transfixed by her dainty feet as they peeked from beneath her skirt at each step.

"Caitlin, please."

"I cannot answer you, Harry. Do not press me."

They moved along Ohio Avenue, which led diagonally down toward the canal and the boat basin, where there were a number of sailors and dock folk moving about. As they came closer, Harry took Caitlin's arm, pulling her around to face him.

"Would you hurt me, sir?" Her gray English eyes had a sudden darkness to them. And a flash.

"Never. But I would have an answer from you." He examined her face more closely. "Or have you given me it? Wilkes Booth bought this thing, didn't he?"

"What does it matter if he did?"

"It matters little. What matters is what he did with it."

She jerked her arm from his grip and hurried on. He caught up with her, keeping pace with her quick step.

"Please, Caitlin. I have to know where this wig next went."

"I cannot tell you."

"Can Booth?"

"He knows nothing of this. He's done nothing wrong. He's been away from Washington. He's caused no trouble. Please don't involve him in this."

Harry was as armed with threats as General McClellan was with artillery. Caitlin knew very well that a few words from him, whether from a jail cell or no, could have Booth's pass rescinded. He had evidence of the actor's having been involved as a go-between in a conspiracy to divert shipments of Union Army shoes into the hands of the Confederates, evidence he had promised Caitlin he'd keep secret only if Booth would curtail his seditious activities. She swore that he would.

She was, in effect, swearing that now.

"Caitlin, I retrieved the wig from Ball's Bluff, from among the Union dead."

They continued on, Caitlin quickening her pace.

"He was not there, Harry. There's ample proof of that."

"Then . . ."

She stopped, taking him by both arms, her eyes now imploring him. "I know what you're about here, Harry. Wilkes is not your man. He does not go to battlefields. Don't you understand? He hasn't the will. He fears—he fears something might happen to his face. Look elsewhere, please!"

And then she came into his arms, holding him tightly. He felt her tears against his cheek.

"Caitlin, I—"

"Don't say it, Harry. I know your feelings. You know mine." Standing back from him, she gave him a long, sorrowful look. Then she reached into a pocket of her coat and withdrew a small flat package, unwrapping it carefully.

He thought, oddly, that it might be a deck of playing cards—though that was certainly improbable, much as she enjoyed poker. Then he saw the elegantly printed name "Brady" on the paper band. She broke it, removing one of a stack of *cartes de visite* bearing her likeness and placing it gently in his hand.

Brady was perhaps a genius. The art of photography was not always kind to its subjects, but he had contrived to have his lens embrace all her beauty, and transfer it intact to this cardboard-mounted paper image. Whatever happened between them, Harry knew he'd never part with this object willingly.

"Take care, Harry. I wish you well with all my heart."

He watched her till she reached Eleventh Street and turned north at the Washington Library.

There was one place left for him to go.

HE'D used this ruse before, but it worked again—with the aid of the red-haired wig and the odd cap. The cheapest of the slatterns available at that hour—a some-what older, thin-faced woman with damp, dark hair—led him up the stairs like a farm maid attending to the last of her daily chores. In her small chamber, she went quickly to her bed, seeming more interested in sleep than her trade.

"You are tired," Harry said, putting two dollars on the nightstand, twice what she charged. "And so am I. I'll leave you to your rest."

"You sure, mister?"

"You sleep. I'll come back some other time. Keep the money."

"You're crazy."

"Possibly so, but it's your profit. I'll let myself out."

Instead, he made his way along the upstairs hall to the rear of the house and the "apartments" of the proprietor's beautiful young sister.

He rapped twice, quickly. Then called her name.

"Ella?"

For a long time there was no response. He was reluctant to speak out loud again, but was about to when the door abruptly opened to a vision of blond hair, green eyes, and pale luminescent skin. There was no recognition at first, then there was—accompanied by no happiness.

"You are mad, Harry Raines." She gave a quick nod for him to enter, closing the door quickly. "I heard you'd escaped from Fort McHenry. Why do you come here? I can't help you."

"Yes, you can. I need the answers to two questions. I promise you no harm will come to you or Booth from this."

"Harm may come to you, Harry. Wilkes had word of your visits to me and this vexed him sorely. You've already humiliated him in that business about shoes for the Confederates. And he suspects you were involved in the arrest of Rose Greenhow, on whom he doted. You are not safe. If this house learns of your presence—"

"I am disguised. No one took undue note of me."

"Then you must go now, before someone does take note."

She stepped forward, touching his arm.

"The last time you warned me about something," he said, "you said Samuel Buckeys was out to kill me. That someone had hired him to kill me."

Ella shrank back, looking away.

"The someone was John Wilkes Booth," Harry said. "Isn't that so? That's one of the things I'm here to ask you. Was it Booth who hired Buckeys?"

She returned to her chaise longue, as though it were a sanctuary—a rampart. Then she surprised him by patting the space next to her, inviting him to it. He was at this point quite numbingly weary. He accepted, easing himself down beside her.

Surprising him more, she took his hand, holding it in both of hers.

"Poor Harry. You've been through so much. What you must understand about Wilkes is he's not a violent man. He is no man to be involved in murder. Yes, he hired Buckeys, but only to scare you. It was all dramatics. Playacting. He'd no idea that poor wretch would be killed. By you, they say. Wilkes hadn't expected that of you. Now he is doubly mad. He still owed the man money, and you know he is punctilious about his debts."

"Not killed by me. Buckeys expired in my Baltimore hotel room, is all."

Harry put on his spectacles, to allow for a quick perusal of the room.

"You have your answer, Harry. And as all is now said and done, you need not worry yourself any longer. You must go. The federals present another danger more compelling."

"You have no roses," he said, looking about the room.

"What? It's December, Harry."

"No paper roses."

"That is not my flower."

"I have another question, Ella."

He'd removed the wig before knocking on her door. He took it from his pocket.

"This belongs to Booth," he said. "He bought it in Baltimore. It was retrieved by me from the battlefield at Ball's Bluff. I know Booth was elsewhere, but I must know to whom he gave it. This is the last piece of my puzzle, Ella. I must have it. I promise you, no harm will come to him because of it."

She frowned, an unseemly expression on so young and fair a countenance.

"He told me about it," she said, finally. "But I was to say nothing. I promised him. I have never broken a promise to him."

They sat side by side quietly. At length, Harry rose and, with a gentle touch to her elbow, bade her to her feet, then escorted her as though on a promenade to her writing desk.

"Say nothing."

She didn't. She wrote no word, either, but drew a picture. He pondered it, then folded it and placed it carefully in his pocket.

Chapter 30

HARRY had now become a sergeant, wearing a great-coat that was a bit too wide and a bit too short for him, and a forage cap he kept down low on his brow. The corporal who had admitted him led the way up the stairs, nodding to the woman detective seated on the landing, and then unlocking the door to the room they sought, having some difficulty with the key.

The room was dark. Harry went to the window curtains and pulled them farther apart.

"We been over this place a dozen times," said the corporal. "They had a seamstress here taking apart her clothes."

Rose and Little Rose had been taken downstairs, the excuse this time being an examination of the child by Surgeon Gregg. He'd been advised as to what was afoot, and would be detaining the two as long as possible.

But Harry didn't need very long at all. What he'd sought had been there all the while.

"All right," Harry said. "I have what I need."

"That's all you come for?"

"It's enough."

THEY hurried back down the stairs. At the bottom, Harry caught himself up, hesitating.

She had already formed her firm conclusion about him. Nothing he did, one way or the other, would alter it. There was risk in doing this, but he'd accept it. He had no choice—not if he was to be absolutely certain.

"Corporal," he said, "where is she?"

"In the back parlor."

He didn't knock. The scene within was almost a tableau—a scene from a staged version of the life of Rose Greenhow. A soldier armed with musket and bayonet stood just inside. Another of Pinkerton's female detectives sat by the window. Dr. Gregg and Rose were seated facing each other by the fire, with Little Rose standing between.

Upon seeing Harry, Gregg shook his head slightly and sighed. Harry strode forth, resolutely, but not so briskly as to frighten the little girl.

He stood looking down at her mother, waiting until there was full recognition. She said nothing, her eyes speaking for her.

"I know everything, Rose," he said. "I want you to know I know."

Her lips flared back as she saw what was in his hand, revealing long teeth.

"Harrison Raines," she said. "There's one for you. If someone will perform the favor."

He smiled. "I know that, too."

Harry bent a trifle nearer, searching her eyes one more time. The hatred there was as deep as a well.

Now he was certain.

OUTSIDE, near the alcove where the three of them had hidden that fateful rainy night in October, Harry rejoined Leahy.

"Thank you for the indulgence," he said.

"It's not out of our way. The President's House stands before us just across the park."

"Did you locate the visitor list from October?" Harry asked.

"I did indeed." Leahy held up a thin sheaf of ruled paper, on which were recorded a list of names.

"May I see it?"

Leahy thrust it at him. "Don't tarry. We are overdue."

The name he sought was on the second page. He kept going, though, on to the third and last page, examining that final one more carefully than the others, then handing it back.

"I am obliged."

"Did you find what you were looking for?"

Harry shook his head. "There is no entry for Amalie Ingraham, or anyone else who might be Zarvona in disguise. At least as far as I can tell." He stretched out his sleeves. "May I be free of this uniform now? I looked in on the Greenhow woman. There's nothing now to hide."

"Yes, there is, Harry. We don't want you recognized by anyone else—not yet."

"Very well. Let's take our walk across the park."

HARRY was by now familiar with the inner recesses of the White House, to which he and Leahy were led. This time, however, they were not kept waiting in the upstairs lobby but led through the alcove directly into the president's office.

He was at his desk, writing. He offered a greeting, but did not look up. Harry and Leahy remained standing. Nicolay, who had ushered them in, exited and then returned with Pinkerton, Colonel Saylor, and a tall, full-bearded man named Ward Lamon, a Springfield lawyer now with the provost marshal's office who was said to be one of the president's closest friends and advisers. Saylor, inexplicably, was wearing civilian clothes. Harry wondered if a uniform coat would show he'd been promoted to general. It felt odd for Harry, stubbornly civilian, to be seated here in uniform when this officer was not.

Lincoln set down his pen, sitting a moment reflectively. Retrieving the writing instrument, he quickly added a line, returned the pen to the desktop, and turned in his chair, removing his spectacles and placing them carefully within his coat.

"Attorney General Bates is downstairs," said the president. "I don't know if it would serve a useful purpose to have him here for our little talk. But he may be called upon if needed."

That, Harry knew, would mean a criminal proceeding—or a referral to the now very active Congressional Committee on the Conduct of the War. However things turned out, Harry would at least then have a determination and explanation of his fate—an accounting of the price he'd have to pay for persisting in this matter.

He had returned to Washington in the still-abiding faith that Mr. Lincoln was a good man—perhaps one of the few truly fine men in American politics—a man who routinely and happily commuted the sentences of deserters.

But he was also a man for the greater good, a wily politician who understood that the path to his goals would have to be littered with the sacrifices of others and even his own principles. After the rats, the most unpleasant and chilling aspect of Harry's incarceration at Fort McHenry was the brutal swiftness with which his fellow inmates had been shorn of their rights under the Constitution.

These were howling times. The government was as much motivated by fear, distrust, anger, and hatred as it was by wisdom and a sense of fairness. Harry realized that the greatest danger before him came not from Mr. Lincoln but the president's willingness to place his fate in the hands of unjust men for the sake of his ultimate designs.

"I had hopes of having this conversation earlier, Mr. Raines. I trust I haven't taken you from any important business."

"The only important business I have is this, Mr. President. I'm sorry it took a while longer than I expected to prepare for it."

"Well, I seem to have a commanding general taking that long to commence his business, so I suppose patience will have to be among my few virtues."

He grinned, but not at Harry. Pinkerton was impassive, staring coldly. Saylor's eyes sought Harry's, looking sad.

Lincoln rose from the desk and seated himself in another more comfortable chair among several arranged in a circle around a small table. He motioned to Harry to seat himself next to him. Lincoln had been a circuit-riding defense attorney for much of his career. Harry realized he was taking a witness chair.

"All right," Lincoln said, nodding to Leahy. "Let us have the proofs."

The Irishman produced the sack with the bullets he'd shown Harry and the Kerr revolver of Loreta Velasquez that Harry had surrendered. Then he added a bouquet of paper roses—which Harry had taken from the Greenhow house.

"That's all?" Lincoln asked, his eyebrows rising.

"That and Colonel Saylor here," Pinkerton said.

The colonel gave a half bow.

Lincoln took up one of the roses.

"So light," he said. "As delicate as the real thing. Yet a piece of weighty evidence, is it?" He returned the artificial flower to the table and then leaned back, extending his long legs. "I'm reminded of an old fisherman who had the reputation for stretching the truth. He got a pair of scales and insisted on weighing every fish he caught in front of witnesses. One day a doctor borrowed his scales to weigh a new baby. The baby weighed forty-seven pounds."

There was a smattering of laughter around the circle, but not from Harry.

"Should I explain, Mr. President?" Harry asked.

Lincoln put a hand to his brow, as though shielding his eyes. "Yes, yes. Proceed, Mr. Raines."

Harry cleared his throat. "I have a cousin—not blood kin, but through family marriage—named Belle Boyd."

"We are familiar with the lady," said Pinkerton. "Too familiar."

"She killed an army sergeant in her house," Lamon explained to Lincoln. "Mitigating circumstances. He was a drunken lout or some such. Threatening and abusing the girl's mother."

"I recall," Lincoln said. "She was set free. But we came to regret it. The Southern newspapers made a heroine out of her—inciting other Virginia women to follow her example."

"The Boyd girl's part of Rose Greenhow's circle," Pinkerton said, with something of a hiss.

"Secretary of State Seward is one of Mrs. Greenhow's friends," countered Harry. "So am I—or so I was. I am not her favorite nowadays. But don't be troubled by Belle. I've sent her away from Martinsburg. I have a friend in Shepherdstown—a loyal Union man who ran a stop on the Underground Railroad there—Jay Hurley.

He reports Belle has gone away, deep into the Confederacy—which is where we should send all such women until this conflict ends."

"Get back to your point, Raines," Pinkerton said. "The paper roses."

"Belle had one," said Harry. "She had it with her when she was staying at my farm last fall. Hetty Cary, ringleader of Baltimore's Monument Street girls who's since fled to Richmond, she was said to have worn one in her hair. Amalie Ingraham—"

"That's the woman implicated in the Zarvona plot to free Rose Greenhow," Pinkerton said.

Lincoln nodded.

"She had a paper rose," Harry continued. "She had it framed. On the wall of her bedroom. There were more in the house—in a bowl downstairs—I think to honor her brother."

The president smiled, as did Lamon and Saylor. Pinkerton did not. "Get to your point, Raines. Mr. Lincoln has other business."

"Belle explained her rose to me out at my farm," Harry said. "She spoke of it proudly, as though it were a badge of honor."

"Like the Medal of Honor that the Congress has just instituted for the navy?" said Lincoln. "I would like it also applicable to the army, were General McClellan ever to bring his soldiers to a place where there might be occasion for it."

"Yes, Mr. President," Harry said. "Very much like that. But not awarded for valor."

"They're the mark of spies and assassins," said Pinkerton sharply.

"Belle received hers for killing that sergeant in Martinsburg. I don't know how many of these false flowers have been given out, or for what reason, but I don't doubt that there are many, and for much the same thing."

"And those there?" the president asked, pointing to the table.

"I just now fetched them up—a full bouquet of them—at Rose Greenhow's house, now serving as a women's prison."

"For her spying?" said Lamon. "For the secrets that won the Rebs the Battle of Bull Run?"

"She didn't receive them," Harry said. "She gives them out."

There was a very long silence.

"Assassins," observed Lincoln, nodding as though to his own thoughts.

"Sounds to me like that Cult of Thugee in India," said Lamon.

"And one of those was for Ned Baker?" Lincoln asked.

"I presume," said Harry. "But I don't know whose."

"I warn you," said Pinkerton. "That woman warrants hanging. We have to do something about her, no matter what. She's been writing letters to Richmond. Letters they put into the papers. Lies about being abused."

Lincoln shook his head. "I want to know about the bullets."

He took his spectacles from his pocket and leaned close to the table, but did not touch the expended rounds. As Harry knew the president was fond of firearms and enjoyed practicing with and testing military weapons, he could only assume an aversion here to touching an object that had passed through human flesh, bringing death.

"Seven bullets," he said.

Harry blinked. "Seven? There were six."

"The seventh is from that Kerr revolver you handed over to me," Leahy said. "There wasn't a match. A proof on your side of the scale, Raines. Five of these rounds you see, Mr. President, were used to slay Colonel Baker. Another was taken from the body of Samuel Buckeys, a sharper and Confederate agent who'd been hired to harass Mr. Raines out of Washington."

Leahy explained to Lincoln what Dr. Gregg's findings had been as concerned the ballistics examination and the common source of the bullets.

"This other weapon," Lincoln said. "Of forty-four caliber. The one that fired the six bullets. It's missing?"

"Yes, sir."

"Could it have been Zarvona's?"

"Could have been Jefferson Davis's, for all we know," said Pinkerton. "But we don't know. We just know it doesn't seem to be among Raines's considerable personal arsenal—and so is probably not his."

"We searched the Ingraham house," Leahy said. "No weapons. Zarvona had on him a Spiller and Burr thirty-six-caliber. It's of Confederate manufacture—Macon, Georgia, I believe. There were no weapons at the Cary house in Baltimore. We also searched the rooms of a journalist mixed up in this—a Charles Langley, who purports to represent a New York paper. He had a rifle and two small pocket pistols."

Lincoln pondered all this with extreme concentration, as though he were weighing matters of great national importance. When he spoke, it was with a mournful tone, as he repeated the word, "Assassins."

"Mr. Lincoln?" said Lamon.

The president looked at him, as though Lamon's face held some key, then returned his attention to the others—all business again.

"This newspaper spy, Langley," he said.

Lamon came forward in his chair. "We'll telegraph Baltimore and have him arrested!"

Pinkerton shook his head. "No. He was in Baltimore at the time of Ball's Bluff. Couldn't have done it. Besides, he is very useful to us. We feed the enemy much wrong information through him."

Lincoln's eyes, now bearing no trace of either humor or melancholy, fixed sharply on Harry.

"You are charged with the killing of a man named Samuel Buckeys—a supplier of horses to the army."

Leahy picked up a bullet. "He wasn't killed with any of Raines's weapons, Mr. President. We've examined them all."

"There's a peculiarity here, as I recollect," Lincoln said. "According to your report, Mr. Pinkerton, Buckeys was shot in the back of the head while sitting in a chair in Raines's hotel room. Raines told you Buckeys had followed him to Baltimore and had previously fired a shot at him outside some bawdy house here in Washington. The murder was done in the hotel room, is that not correct, Mr. Leahy? The shot was fired from inside?"

"The only window was closed on account of the cold weather and there was no bullet hole in it," the Irishman said. "According to the army surgeon at McHenry, the hair around the entry wound was singed with gunpowder."

"Let's think upon this," said Lincoln. "He was cheating the army with bad horses and Raines knew about it. He was trying to take a stake in your livestock business, Mr. Raines. You had some good reasons to kill him."

"Yes, I did," said Harry. "But I didn't."

"I'm not suggesting that you did," the president said. "I'm discussing this peculiarity. I won a capital criminal case or two on the Illinois circuit arguing such a point of logic. If a man is your enemy and he believes you may be willing to kill him, and he is waiting in your hotel room, seated in a chair facing the door with a pistol in his hand, why would he let you enter and walk behind him without stirring an inch? Makes no sense. No sense at all."

"But whoever shot him must have been someone he knew, someone he knew and trusted," Pinkerton said. "A man like Buckeys isn't likely to let just anyone go behind his back."

"A bucket," Harry said. "A charwoman's bucket—with water and a scrub brush in it. I thought nothing of it at the time, but when I left, which was almost immediately, I passed a charwoman in the hall—on her hands and knees, with a bucket. Why would there be two buckets?"

"Was she pretty?" Leahy asked. "Our detectives outside saw a pretty woman run into that hotel, wearing shabby clothes. They took note because they wondered if she was a common prostitute, and if she was how she could be plying her trade in such a respectable hotel in the most respectable neighborhood in Baltimore."

"The woman I saw in the corridor was not pretty," Harry said. "Nor was she young."

"That Zarvona could make himself pretty," said Pinkerton. "We remember that from the *St. Nicholas* affair. We don't know if he was in his cell at McHenry or not. I explained to you his curious ruse, Mr. President. A variation on his *St. Nicholas* theatrics."

"That's why I don't think it could have been Zarvona," said Harry. "The *St. Nicholas* affair was a bold, public escapade—a daring deed. It made a hero of him. Wearing women's clothes to sneak into a hotel room and shoot someone in the back is neither heroic nor public. It's sordid and secret. Not Zarvona's style at all.

He deems himself a liberal patriot, fighting in a revolution."

"But why would this pretty charwoman go to Raines's hotel room to shoot Buckeys?" Lincoln asked. "How would she know the man was there?"

"She didn't go there to shoot Buckeys," Leahy said. "She went there to shoot Raines. When she found Buckeys there instead, another idea occurred to her. Murder the man and make Raines pay for it. Send him to the gallows and so discredit anything he had to say."

Lincoln cleared his throat, leaning forward. "Only one question remains. A crowded hotel. A gunshot in the middle of the day. Whoever fired the shot, why'd no one hear it?"

The others looked on blankly.

"The square there is paved with bricks, is it not?" Lincoln asked, preparing to answer his own question as both judge and defense attorney. "There would be freight wagons, the coach from the station. Quite a clatter." He leaned back. "Now let us return to the matter of my dear and good friend Colonel Baker. And the matter of the undressed woman in the woods."

"Two of them," said Harry. "One that I saw, and was able to identify later. Another who was not revealed to me. They were changing clothes. One of them putting on a Confederate officer's uniform."

"The shooter?" said Lincoln.

"Quite possibly, sir. Probably. But the shooter was definitely not the unclad woman."

"How are you so sure of that?"

Harry ran it through his mind again, but nothing changed.

"I came upon her in those woods, sir, off the Frederick Road, standing near a white or gray horse, with her back to me. She was entirely naked, and in the act of changing clothes. There was a uniform jacket on the ground. And a pair of boots. When I saw her, she had a man's shirt over her head."

"Exactly what you'd expect for a woman who'd gone into battle, posing as a man—as an officer."

"But this was after the battle, sir. After the shooter had run from it. Upon reflection, thinking back on it all, I realized that I'd got it wrong. She hadn't been taking the uniform off—as the shooter would be doing after committing that felonious act. She was getting back into it. She was pulling that shirt—a man's shirt—back on. She was dressing in that uniform. She had traded it with someone else. And that person is the one we seek. The woman I had in mind—I've identified her as the one I saw naked. But she could not have been Baker's killer. She is innocent. It was someone else. The other person to wear that uniform."

"Names," growled Pinkerton.

"The naked one—in uniform, she went by Lieutenant Harry T. Buford. That's how I know her."

This time Lincoln did pick up one of the rounds, forcing himself to examine it carefully. Then, one by one, he looked over the others. The sadness returned when he set the last of them down.

"Might it have been this Zarvona?" asked Lamon. "Wearing a dress again?"

Harry considered this, then shook his head. "He is a colonel of his own regiment—his own very colorful regiment. Why would such a man disguise himself as a mere lieutenant—a very anonymous officer? Why would he limit his conduct on the field of battle to one quick, murderous, dastardly dash—and then be gone and barely noticed? If he was going to appear on that field in uniform, it would have been his own—the red shirts, a uniform he designed himself."

Lincoln looked to Saylor. "And what of Lieutenant Holmes's statement?"

"Withdrawn from the record, Mr. President. He was misunderstood as he lay wounded. It was my error, and Captain Philbrick's error, for which we apologize and recant. It was powerfully confusing on that bluff. You could have said most anyone had shot Colonel Baker, and be hard put to find anyone to deny it."

"With the exception of Lieutenant Holmes," Lincoln said.

"He says only that Raines did not do it," Saylor said. "Smoke, confusion, what Clausewitz called the 'fog of war.'"

"Clausewitz. You take your soldierin' seriously, Colonel," the president said. "Though you seem to be out of uniform."

"I'll attend to that presently, Mr. President."

Lincoln abruptly rose—a surprisingly swift motion for a man of his years, height, and general ungainliness. Harry was startled.

"I must deal with the 'fog of Congress,' gentlemen," he said, walking to a window that looked out over the south lawn and the Washington Monument building in the sunlight in the distance. "I must deal with Senator Benjamin Wade and his Committee on the Conduct of the War. They must be fed. They've been put off too long about this."

The president put his hand to his brow. Harry wasn't sure if he wasn't wiping his eyes. He thought he saw the broad shoulders shudder or shiver.

But then Lincoln turned to face them, returning to his chair, but remaining standing, his long hands on the back.

"When I was a young lawyer, and Illinois was little settled except on her southern border, I with other lawyers used to ride the circuit, journeying with the judge from county seat to county seat in quest of business. Once, after a long spell of pouring rain which had flooded the whole country, transforming small creeks into rivers, we were often stopped by these swollen streams which we with difficulty crossed. Still ahead of us was Fox River, larger than all the rest, and we could not help saying to each other, 'If these streams give us so much trouble, how shall we get over Fox River?' Darkness fell before we had reached that stream and we all stopped at a log tavern, had our horses put out, and resolved to pass the night. Here we were right glad to fall in with the Methodist presiding elder of the circuit, who rode out in all weather, knew all its ways, and could tell us about Fox River. So we all gathered around him and asked if he knew anything about the crossing of Fox River. 'Oh yes,' he replied. 'I know all about Fox River. I have crossed it often and understand it well. But I have one fixed rule with regard to Fox River. I never cross it till I reach it.'"

He walked over to Harry, put his hand on his shoulder, and shook it slightly, then returned to his chair and seated himself in it.

"Raines," he said, "I never for a moment thought you guilty of anything more than service to your country. All this conversation we've just had, that was for the benefit of me, Mr. Pinkerton, and Mr. Lamon when we make known our disposition on these matters to Senator Wade and his infernal committee. I can't think of a judge or jury in Illinois who would find you responsible for both poor Ned Baker and Samuel Buckeys's deaths, given the facts of the case."

Lincoln picked up one of the paper roses, eyeing it curiously.

"Rose Greenhow, whose mad passions lie at the root of all this—well, I guess she vexes me more than Jefferson Davis himself. Pinkerton, I'm going to give in to you and have Mrs. Greenhow transferred to the Old Capitol Prison. After Christmas. And once there her communication with the Southern Confederacy is to cease. She's to have her daughter with her, and a physician in attendance, but no one else. Does that please you?"

"It certainly does, Mr. President."

Lincoln wasn't through. "I want that damned Zarvona transferred to New York—Fort Lafayette—and I want him treated like a criminal, not a soldier, because that's how he's been behaving. Soldiers don't terrorize civilians the way he has."

"I'm in full agreement, Mr. Lincoln," said Pinkerton.

"Ward," said Lincoln to Lamon. "You tell Attorney General Bates I want all the charges withdrawn that have been placed against friend Raines here. I want it done at once."

"Consider it done already."

For the first time in weeks—months—practicable thoughts as to his own future came rushing to Harry's mind. Presuming the war was still paying Shepherdstown little attention, he decided he might well pass the rest of the winter at his farm. He might have Caitlin there, once her play was done, or go with her to New York or Boston. He could do with a liberal dose of civilization—and a vacation from all things military. The sergeant's uniform he was wearing had begun to itch.

Lincoln was still speaking. "But I want him kept on the fugitive roster—for the time being."

The happy prospects washed from Harry's mind as though through a sluice. He sank back in his chair. The others seemed just as stunned.

"Is there need of a judicial proceeding?" Ward Lamon asked.

"I need Raines," Pinkerton said. "We need every man."

"And so you shall have him," said the president. "I hope." He paused. "Gentlemen, if you could leave Mr. Raines and me for a moment, he'll join you presently. Downstairs."

They all stood, Harry staying fixed in his place as the others filed out, Saylor giving Harry a look of friendly bewilderment and a shrug before going out the door.

Nicolay closed the door from outside. Lincoln rose and put his hand on Harry's shoulder again, then led him to the map he had mounted on a wooden conductor's stand. It showed Washington and Richmond, the Eastern Shore and much of Chesapeake Bay, as well as the Potomac Valley far up into the mountains. Colored rectangles were pinned to it to denote military units. There was a wall of them forming a crescent in northern Virginia at the approaches to the capital. In and around Washington itself were many rectangles, signifying McClellan's idle forces.

"I need you, too, Raines," he said, his voice sounding a little tattered now.

He dropped his hand from Harry's arm, leaning down and adjusting his eyeglasses to ponder something on the Virginia portion of the map.

"Your old *friend,* Lafayette Baker, the State Department detective, he made it to Richmond and back," Lincoln said. "He was captured, escaped—a remarkable exploit."

"Yes, sir. I remember."

"Unfortunately, though, he didn't learn very much. He couldn't confirm or deny the numbers of the enormous Confederate troop strength Pinkerton and General McClellan keep insisting is there. We've no idea of Confederate plans—whether they might be itching to invade. We don't know if Davis is happy with his commanders—as they expand their army, who's going to rise. Most of the good ones are in that army, I'm sorry to say."

His finger went to the south end of the Chesapeake, sticking like an arrow to a spot at a confluence of rivers. Squinting, Harry saw that it was Norfolk.

"There's our biggest loss of the war," said Lincoln. "We've held on to Maryland, Baltimore, the western mountains of Virginia and Harpers Ferry, Fortress Monroe. But we lost Fort Norfolk and the Gosport Navy Yard there. Before it was abandoned, we burned and scuttled the USS *Merrimack,* but the Confederates have refloated her. We've no idea why."

Back came the presidential hand to the Raines shoulder; this time the grip was very hard.

"I need a good man down there in Virginia to find out these things. It occurred to me right off, Raines, that there might be great advantage in your fix. You've got the best possible reason now for being in the Confederacy. You've got people to vouch for you. Your father's a friend of Davis. You know the ground. Powerful useful, Raines."

Harry felt numb. He'd been in Richmond once since the war began, not for purposes of espionage but to see to the safety of a young woman—an actress friend of Caitlin's.

But he'd not been with his family since Sumter. They lived in Tidewater, in the deepest enemy country. This would be the only way.

"For how long?"

"That'd be entirely up to you—whenever you'd think best. You won't be much good to us caught and put to a rope."

"May I think about it awhile?"

Lincoln nodded, let his hand drop again, and began walking back to his writing desk. "Certainly. Certainly. But no more than a day." He turned to look at Harry. "This war's not waiting for any of us."

Harry of a sudden found himself unable to speak. He was going to need all of that day.

"I'll leave it this way, Raines. You've earned your right to your own wishes here. If you'd prefer to move back to your farm and work for us out there in the Potomac Valley, that'd be fine. That country's important to us. If you think you've done and risked enough and that this might not work—that you'd rather go to New York or California or Europe or someplace, well, you're entitled. But if you'd do this, I'd be eternally obliged."

"You'd want me to go alone?"

The president nodded. "Colonel Saylor has volunteered to go with you, but I think that'd attract too much attention and is a bad idea."

"I think I'd agree."

"You have your man, the stable hand. We of course have friends in Richmond you could call upon if needed."

"Stable manager, Mr. Lincoln. Caesar Augustus. More my friend than my man, and free to do as he pleases—especially in this."

"Well understood." The president continued moving toward his writing desk, halting at the chair. "If you choose to go back to your farm or want to go north or abroad, tell Mr. Leahy or Mr. Pinkerton by noon tomorrow. If you choose to go south, I want you simply to vanish between now and tomorrow noon."

"Very well, sir."

Lincoln had seated himself and returned to his melancholy correspondence, pen in hand.

"One point on the matter of Colonel Baker, Mr. Raines."

"Yes, sir."

"You ever get a tick of hay or a biting bug down the back of your shirt? Must happen fairly regular in the horse business."

"Yes, it does."

"What do you do to get rid of it?"

"Remove the shirt and shake it out."

"And then what?"

"Put it back on again."

The president continued writing.

"You've got to look at the facts from all directions, Raines. Not just the one that pleases you. I think this woman pleases you—or did. I would suggest you go find this 'Lieutenant Harry T. Buford' of yours and have one more conversation. I don't think you necessarily got it right, what happened out there in those woods. You don't know for sure how long she'd been wearing that shirt."

Lincoln's words came at him like rocks.

"Yes, sir,"

"Thank you, Raines. I am obliged."

HARRY stayed away from the National until dark, and waited longer until most of the hotel staff and guests would be preoccupied with supper. Entering finally through a cellar door and using back stairs, he reached his door without significant encounter. He'd already thought out what clothes and saddle baggage he'd need. The main thing was to rid himself of this ratty sergeant's garb and return to a state more resembling a gentleman.

Remembering the Baltimore episode with the deceased Samuel Buckeys, he turned the key with great care and quiet, pushing the door very gently—at first only a few inches.

There was no sound. Expanding the opening, he crouched down a little, looking quickly to where the street window put his two parlor chairs in silhouette. Nothing broke their line. Opening the door fully then, he stepped inside, closing the door softly behind him.

All was silent, except for the noise from the street. He went to the gaslight to illuminate the bulb, but before his finger touched the valve, he heard what sounded like the merest wisp of a breath—as though from a zephyr. It seemed the slightest exhalation.

Then came a more audible inhalation. From the doorway to his bedroom.

His eyesight improving in the continuing darkness, he went to the side of the passage, taking one of his Navy Colts in hand. There was another chair in the second room, also by the window, and evidently empty.

Another faint sound, too familiar. Harry realized he had only a few seconds to live.

It could be only one of two people. Everything depended on his decision as to which it was, and that depended on a judgment of character—how far a person would go in pursuit of revenge.

"Loreta?"

As he guessed, his voicing of that name caused a pause, which he took advantage of—in that instant flinging himself into the bedroom, but low, onto the thinly carpeted floor, averting his eyes to escape the flare of the expected gunshot.

It came when he expected, an explosive, skull-rattling report and a humming whine near his head.

He rolled farther, weapon still in hand, raising himself on his elbow. The shadowy form on the bed rose up, sitting, leaning quickly forward, perhaps momentarily put off by the bright flash.

At that moment, he knew, Leahy would have fired. So would have Pinkerton, Templeton Saylor, Oliver Wendell Holmes, and every other sensible man. But Harry could not.

He sensed himself targeted once more. He had to shoot. What came was a foolish, idiotic, probably suicidal notion, especially given the quality of his eyesight, but he thought he might be able to shoot without killing. Instead, he'd shoot to disable and disarm. Ludicrously, he fired at what he guessed was the intruder's revolver. It was an impossible feat.

But Harry had learned to shoot from his father, who even now was held to be the best shot in the Confederate cavalry. He had taught Harry to fire fast by pointing his weapon as he might a finger, rather than taking aim.

Harry did that now, pointing at what he took to be the other pistol. Two gunshots rang out, almost simultaneously, followed by a sort of yelp.

The other's pistol went spinning, falling to the floor in front of him with a thunk and a clatter. He knew his had been the first shot. He was just as certain that it had hit the mark. The bullet had struck either the weapon or hand, throwing off the other's aim and shot.

The shadowy figure had fallen back—collapsing as might a marionette with cut strings—and now lay with head and an arm hanging off the bed. Leaping up and turning on the gaslight, he saw through the gun smoke a broad crimson stripe running down his victim's neck.

It was not Loreta Janeta Velasquez. He had called out that name in odd compulsion, but he had already decided it was someone else. Loreta, he figured, would want to talk to him first. She might want to talk to him and care for nothing else.

Not so the woman he had shot—Amalie Ingraham.

He came close, sitting on the edge of the bed, lifting her into his arms, cradling her head and ignoring the spreading blood.

Her eyes were open—on him—but she didn't speak. There was a red-flecked froth on her lips. Looking close, he saw a terrible hole torn into her neck just beneath the line of her jaw. What had done this? He'd hit the revolver.

"I meant you no harm," he said.

A rough male face appeared in the doorway, another behind it.

"What's happened?" said the first.

"Go downstairs. Ask for Joseph Leahy. Bring him here."

There was hesitation, then one of the faces vanished.

He held her close. She was still breathing, but without words. Shudders seemed to go through her—struggles without strength.

"Amalie. Amalie."

A strong hand gripped his shoulder.

"What have you done, Raines?"

"Get a doctor!" Harry said.

Leahy leaned close, then shook his head. "No point, Harry. God rest her soul."

"Please!"

Leahy shook his head once more, then went to the corner of the room where the other pistol had gone. "The wound is mortal, Harry," he said.

Harry turned back to the woman in his arms, holding her more closely, wiping what appeared to be tears from her cheek. He had some in his own eyes as well.

"Amalie," he said. "Why?"

Her eyes were fixed on Harry's. He could not decide whether they were full of pain or malice. Probably both.

She was trying to speak. He put his ear near her lips, but heard nothing. Drawing back, he saw her form a single and quite obvious word.

Leahy was watching. "What did she say?"

"'Yankee,'" Harry said.

She spoke no more. The look in her eyes had turned vague. Harry could feel convulsions going through her body. Her arm jerked once, then again, then again quite violently. There were two more pulses, then none. And then she was utterly loose in his arms.

He laid her carefully back onto the counterpane and wearily stood. His clothes were stained with her blood.

Leahy was holding her pistol. He looked it over carefully, then offered it to Harry for examination.

"A French-made LeMatt five-shot revolver," he said. "When we searched the Ingraham house, we found a receipt from a Paris gunsmith in her father's desk. I guess this is the item."

The barrel had a sharp indentation on it, deep enough to have cut the steel raw. It was skewed slightly to the side.

"Ricochet," Leahy said. "You hit the weapon. That's what got her."

Harry looked down into her blank eyes. "Killed her," he said.

Leahy took back the revolver. "Can't ever be fired again," he said. "It'd blow up. No way to test the rounds for the ballistics."

Harry sighed. Their work still wasn't done.

"She fired twice," he said. "If the bullets didn't go through it, one or both should be in the wall behind you."

Leahy turned about, then made a happy sound. Taking out a long pocketknife, he uncased the blade and commenced to dig at the first of two holes he'd spotted.

"You know, Raines, I'd given up all hope we'd ever find Colonel Baker's assassin," he said, commencing his labor. "Now you've gone and done it." Leahy's probing and scraping of a sudden produced a successful result. "Though I must say, laddybuck, your methods are surpassing strange."

Chapter 31

As Harry requested, Saylor agreed to meet with him the next morning outside the Corcoran Art Museum on Eighteenth Street. With his wide-brimmed hat and cape-shouldered greatcoat, Harry was not much recognizable. He was enjoying at least the acting part of the grim business that had befallen him.

The day was warmer than the last, though hardly balmy. He needed his riding gloves.

Saylor was waiting on the museum's front steps, so lost in thought he didn't take notice of his friend's arrival until Harry was standing before him.

Once again, Saylor was in civilian clothes.

He brightened. "Buy you a drink, Harry?"

"Never say no—especially to a man who can so well afford it—but the hour's early."

"Let's go up to Gadsby's Row. The hour's never late in there."

Whiskey was in fact not an unwelcome notion. The dominating feature of Harry's dreams all through the night had been Amalie Ingraham's dead face.

They began walking up Pennsylvania Avenue toward the George Washington statue at Twenty-third Street. Gadsby's Row, a hotel and bar formerly known as the Old Franklin, was on the corner just before it.

"What are your plans?" Saylor asked. "Are you going south?"

"You know about that?"

"Mr. Lincoln told Pinkerton."

"Haven't decided. Thought you might help me do that."

"Your obedient servant, sir."

"I am surprised to find you on another day without that splendid uniform."

"Gave it up."

"You gave your uniform away?"

"Uniform, shoulder straps, sword." Saylor smiled, though not too happily. "I've resigned my commission."

"You're leaving the army?"

"'I have touch'd the highest point of all my greatness, / And from that full meridian of my glory, / I haste now to my setting: I shall fall, / Like a bright exhalation in the evening, / And no man shall see me more.'"

"Shakespeare?" Harry asked.

"*Henry VIII.*"

This was one of Shakespeare's lesser plays. Harry didn't know if it had ever been performed in Washington, but Saylor was a New York man, and educated in Boston. He had doubtless seen every Shakespearean work.

At Twentieth Street, there was a small triangle of open ground with a few trees. Just beyond it, on the corner of I Street and Twentieth, was a long, narrow house. Saylor looked to it, then stopped, staring.

"Harry," he said softly, as though he could be heard within the house. "I do believe—yes, there she is."

"She?"

There was something familiar about the house, but the memory of it eluded Harry. He had never been in it.

"Peggy Eaton."

Harry had taken off his spectacles. He returned them to his nose. Saylor was correct. In an upper window on the left was a seated figure. Harry sensed she was observing them as intently as they were her.

"I haven't encountered her on the street for months," he said. "I thought she'd gone away."

"She had a young man she kept company with," said Saylor. "I think it is he who has gone. That's why she sits there."

The Eaton woman was one of the enduring legends of the city—as befitted a lady who had managed to bring down a president's entire cabinet.

She was the daughter of the innkeeper who had owned Gadsby's when it was the Old Franklin. As little more than a girl, she'd been a beauty without peer in the federal city, winning her first husband—a navy purser—when she was only fourteen. Among a hundred other ardent hearts, she'd also won that of a Tennessee senator named John Eaton not long after her marriage. When he became Andrew Jackson's secretary of war, the navy purser found himself on a long cruise, from which he never returned—falling victim, some said, to despondency and suicide.

Shortly after that, the beauty became Mrs. John Eaton—scandalizing Washington and offending Floride Calhoun, wife of Jackson's vice-president, John C. Calhoun, and the ruler of capital society. At Mrs. Calhoun's instruction, the other cabinet wives had shunned pretty Peggy.

Jackson, a man of no small temper, was outraged. He had himself been a victim of calumny owing to his inadvertently having married his wife, Rachel, before her divorce had become official. He demanded that the cabinet wives receive Mrs. Eaton, but Floride Calhoun still refused. Jackson's wily secretary of state, Martin Van Buren, produced an extraordinary solution. He suggested that the entire cabinet resign, including himself.

And so they did, with Van Buren moving on to the distant post of minister to England. Calhoun and his other enemies declared him politically dead, and chortled. But when Jackson ran for his second term, he dropped Calhoun and selected Van Buren, who became president in his own right four years later.

Pretty Peggy had survived them all. She still walked the streets of Washington, haughty and proud, often in the company of some handsome young man—like Rose O'Neal Greenhow, a strong vestige of her early beauty abiding with her into maturity and old age.

"I never met her," Harry said.

"I have," said Saylor.

"You know her well?"

"I did. Quite well indeed. But she is a difficult woman to bear."

"She seems . . ."

"Too old for me? Oh no, Harry. With women as with fine wine. 'Age cannot wither her, nor custom stale her infinite variety.'"

Two doors farther along was Gadsby's. They entered, surprised to find no one in the public room but a sleeping drunk and a dozing bartender. Wakened by Harry's thumping once on the bartop, the man stirred himself to produce a proper brandy for Saylor, and Old Overholtz for Harry.

They went to a table by the window. Harry looked at his watch.

"How long do you have to make up your mind about where you're going to go?" Saylor asked.

"Not long," said Harry.

Saylor raised his glass. "At all events. My congratulations on the success of last night."

"'Success' hardly seems to be the word for it."

"Why not? The assassin of Colonel Baker caught in the act of trying to kill again, and bearing proof of her unmistakable guilt in her own hand."

"And dying for it—by my hand."

Saylor drank. "I suppose that must be hard—shooting a woman."

"It's hard shooting anyone, Templeton, as you must know."

"Still. She had it coming. An assassin, after all."

"What makes it hard for me is that I don't think it's really that. Amalie's misplaced patriotism got the better of her. She was not content to keep to her skirts and wage this war on the edges. She wanted a taste of the real thing, so she arranged a trade."

"With another woman."

"An opportunity. And I think that's all Colonel Baker was for her. A sudden chance to make her mark—and earn her paper rose."

"You see no plot beyond that?"

"Not to assassinate Senator Baker. No, I do not."

Saylor started to speak, hesitated, then thought of something else to say.

"The bullets matched?"

"Every one," Harry said. "This science of ballistics is an amazement."

"Mr. Leahy said the revolver was French."

"A five-shot LeMatt. There was a paid bill for it from a Paris gunsmith among Mr. Ingraham's papers."

"And the naked woman you saw in the woods?"

"Utterly innocent, and officially declared so, I am gladdened to say."

"And so ends the tale."

"Not quite."

There was no putting matters off any longer. Harry reached into a side pocket of his coat, fumbling a moment, then took out a lead bullet with flattened point. He set it down gently on the table, unintentionally aiming the flat nose at Saylor.

"What's that?" Saylor asked.

"A single bullet that did not match all the others from the LeMatt," Harry said. "It was taken from the upper thigh of Colonel Baker. A disabling wound, tore a lot of flesh, but not a fatal one. Struck him from behind."

Saylor started to pick it up, but stayed his hand. He stared at it morosely.

"It's forty-four caliber," Harry said. "Leahy thought it was from an Army Colt, standard officer's issue. But my guess is that it came from a five-shot Adams revolver."

Saylor leaned back, his chair creaking, and looked out the window. "Why do you think that?"

"Because someone loaned me such a weapon when I was in need."

"Do you have it still?"

"I gave it to Leahy to hold for me until such time as it can be returned. I do not believe he knows its significance—yet."

Harry reached now into a breast pocket, carefully withdrawing a single crimson paper rose. He gently laid it down beside the bullet.

"This was with the others, from Rose Greenhow's little arsenal of flowers," he said. "I believe that it should go to you, Colonel Saylor."

"I thought we performed this little theatrical in the president's office."

"Not this scene."

Their eyes met. Neither looked away.

"No," said Saylor.

"No?"

"No. It should not go to me. I am not entitled to it."

Harry guessed that Saylor would be armed. The man kept a number of personal weapons in addition to the Adams revolver. Harry kept his gaze steady on his friend, watching.

"Templeton," he said slowly, "Lieutenant Holmes was a witness. He saw a soldier with bright red-orange hair, wearing shirt and braces but no tunic. Holmes saw the man fire in the direction of Baker as the colonel fell. You were seen near there, in shirtsleeves—as I admit were many of the men. It was hot, and in the smoke and confusion, the gray uniform coats your regiment wore last fall looked much like the enemy's, so you discarded them."

He stopped to drink some whiskey. Saylor remained motionless.

"I retrieved the red-orange wig—from the area where you were standing," Harry said. "I traced its origin. It was purchased by the actor John Wilkes Booth from a costume shop in Maryland. He then gave it to a friend—a lady he much admired. I don't know if she asked him to purchase it or if she merely asked him to bring her a wig. But her name is Rose Greenhow and it was in her possession several days before Ball's Bluff."

He paused, but Saylor made no response.

"Pinkerton has had her house under surveillance all the autumn," Harry said. "You were a visitor—several times."

"So was Secretary of State Seward."

"You visited her late in the evening. And you visited her after she took possession of the wig—and after she was placed under house arrest." He leaned forward a little. "And before Ball's Bluff."

Now Saylor's eyes cast down, flickering, then went to his brandy glass. He drank it, slowly, all of it. Coughing, covering his mouth in gentlemanly fashion with the back of his hand, he set down the glass.

"I am not entitled to this paper flower," he said. "It was not my intent to shoot Colonel Baker or any other man in the federal army. No one asked me to do that. He was struck and wounded by a bullet from my revolver, but it was in accident—a ridiculous, ironic coincidental accident, worthy of Shakespearean tragedy—if not comedy."

"Who, then, did Rose ask you to shoot?" Harry asked.

"She never outright asked anyone to shoot anyone. These paper flowers were an honor she bestowed on those in her service—and that often meant the Confederate service—who performed some valuable and exemplary deed for her. The agent who informed her of McDowell's advance to Manassas, for example. Or your cousin-in-law Belle Boyd's shooting down a Yankee sergeant in her mother's house. If Rose wished someone dead, she would declare that she desired it—but she never specifically and deliberately asked for a killing before, not to my knowledge."

"Then . . . ?"

"There was someone she wanted dead—a traitor to the Southern cause, she said. The man who betrayed her and brought about her arrest, she said. She sought a hero who would avenge her and the Cause—a hero who would hold her affections forever. She talked about how much it would mean to her to hear that this traitor was dead."

His eyes returned to Harry. "You," he said.

Harry drank more of his whiskey, wishing he'd not been so stupid to play out this scene without benefit of a weapon of his own.

"This is very hard to believe."

"I loved her, Harry. You know what that is like."

"But still. You had no idea I'd be going out to Poolesville."

"No. But when you did—well, there you were."

"There were easier opportunities. That night, when we were in camp. When I was out on that patrol with Captain Philbrick."

"Harry. I wouldn't have shot down any man like that. The only time I allowed myself even to think about carrying out her request—and it was only for an instant, Harry, a few seconds only—was in the chaos at Ball's Bluff. It was an impulse—a swiftly passing impulse. I had this odd thought that this would be my only opportunity, that in all that mad confusion, the unceasing gunfire, people dying all around us, it somehow would be permissible. This was in my mind. All that was in my mind. I had out my revolver. There you were. I pointed it at you. All this occurring within a few ticks of a clock. Then I realized what I was doing. I felt ashamed, ridiculous in that way—and afraid. I pointed the pistol away and fired, toward the Rebels—just in case someone had seen what I'd been doing."

He was staring at the tabletop so intently it almost seemed he could see through it.

"But the bullet never reached the Rebels," he said, his voice rasping. He cleared his throat. "The round struck Colonel Baker and knocked him down. Before I could do a thing about it, that hellish horseman—that woman—came galloping up and finished the work I'd inadvertently begun."

Harry finished his whiskey.

"You love Rose Greenhow that much?" he asked.

Saylor sighed. "I don't know, Harry. Perhaps I did at the time. Must have. And you?"

"What?"

"You loved her. She said so."

"And that made you jealous? Enough to kill me?"

"Enough to think upon the prospect."

"She called me a traitor to the Cause and a party to her arrest. How would she come to know any of that? Did someone inform her?"

Saylor smiled now. "You did, sir."

"I?"

"You lied to her at a particularly wrong moment. When you visited her at her house, after her arrest, you told her you were detained downstairs because the detectives searched you for arms."

"Yes."

"Yet you went to her with a pistol in your coat pocket, hard as a rock against your breast—and, more particularly, hers. She has a sharp mind, Harry. Sharper than yours. Certainly than mine."

Harry tapped his finger idly on the tabletop, then rose and went to the bar, procuring another brandy and whiskey. Returning, he gently set the brandy glass in front of Saylor. The man hadn't moved an inch.

"I didn't love her, Templeton," he said, after a sip of Overholtz. "I was charmed, and admiring. But it's Caitlin Howard I loved—and still love. That is who I thought you meant when you said we both loved the same woman."

"Caitlin?"

"Your jealousy was misplaced, sir, as regards Mrs. Greenhow."

"Harry . . ."

Raines lifted his hand to stay further word. "I do believe you've lied to me, Templeton. I do believe your conduct out there at Ball's Bluff was no passing impulse. That telegraph you delivered to me all the way out at my farm. You were not only the deliverer, but the sender. I imagine if we questioned every army telegraph clerk between Poolesville and the War Department, we'd find one who might recall the message—and the real sender."

"That doesn't mean I meant you any harm. And at all events, everyone knew how much Mr. Lincoln was worried about Colonel Baker."

"That isn't why you lured me out there, Templeton."

"Harry, I have told you—"

"A lie, sir. You fired more than a single haphazard bullet. There were two shots. The second may not have been intended to strike human flesh, as you have said. But the first went through my sleeve, Templeton. I have that garment still."

He paused. "It serves to instruct."

Saylor contemplated his brandy glass—and perhaps something else.

"What will you do, Harry?"

"I'll do what I think's for the best."

"As you must." Saylor shook his head. "This is a last drink?" he said finally, with great seriousness.

"If you want to call it that," Harry said. "I have much business before me. I can't tarry much longer."

Saylor sipped. "So you will turn me over to the provost marshal."

Harry thought upon this, then spoke the truth. "I could. I probably should. But I don't think that's quite what Mr. Lincoln had in mind as resolution of this matter."

He leaned back in his chair, eyeing Saylor over the top of his spectacles.

"What were you in mind of doing, Mr. Saylor—having resigned your commission?"

"If you hadn't laid down this paper flower, I was going to go west."

"West? To hide from us?"

"My mother is from Chicago. I have relations there. They'd have taken care of me. But, no. I was going to go out there and find an Illinois regiment."

"You want to be colonel of an Illinois regiment?"

"Not colonel, Harry. Private. I was going to enlist— to see this war through as a man in the ranks. Beyond the reach of my father. There's fighting out in the west, Harry. It's not like it is here with General McClellan. The armies out there are trying to settle this thing. I hear they have good generals."

Harry tried to imagine such a thing as a Private Templeton Saylor, Harvard '58. "I don't understand. You're an excellent officer."

"There's a lot you don't understand, Harry."

Saylor's movement was so swift that Harry didn't take note of the gun until it was out of the other's coat and in his hand, the barrel raised high but in Harry's general direction.

"Are you collecting your rose?" Harry asked, feeling a cold runnel of sweat run down his back.

"No. I want no more of roses." Saylor set the revolver—an Army Colt—on the table, turning the handle toward Harry. "I'm surrendering to you, Harry. I'm your prisoner, sir. Whether you want that or not."

Harry gathered back his nerve, then pushed the pistol aside. "Finish your drink, Templeton."

They raised their glasses almost simultaneously. It seemed almost a toast.

Harry set down his empty vessel, ignoring the pistol.

"They're all busy men, Templeton," he said. "Especially Mr. Lincoln. I don't think he wants to be further bothered about this business. From what I know of his mind, he would see that your wounding of Colonel Baker was an unfortunate accident of war. As for the colonel's death, justice has surely been done in the case of the unfortunate Amalie. As for the thoughts you harbored of killing me, you are not the first, and you no longer harbor them." He paused. "Or do you?"

Saylor seemed puzzled, and did not speak.

"I tried to free Rose Greenhow myself," Harry said. "I almost succeeded."

"She didn't trust you."

"There were two shots fired at us on that occasion, from Lafayette Park. They came close, but missed. Was that you, Templeton? Trying to impress the lady? You're a good enough shot at least to attempt something at that range."

Saylor nodded. "Yes. That was me. I was in the park, just across the street."

"Were you trying to kill me, then?"

"No, sir, I was not."

"Scare us, then? Scare her? Foil the plot?"

"No, Harry. At that point I was thinking to kill her."

After a long silence, Harry rose.

"Go west, Templeton. Find a regiment. Serve and fight. No one could ask more of you than that. And as far as I'm concerned, no one will."

"This is your wish? You're certain?"

"I am."

"You're a gentleman, Harry."

"That has nothing to do with it."

Harry turned and walked out of the room. On the street, passing the window, he saw Saylor sitting motionless, the revolver still on the table before him.

STILL unrecognized, Harry walked back along Pennsylvania Avenue past the President's House, then turned south and crossed the canal to the mall, from which was emanating the low groans of cattle in the new enclosures built west of the unfinished Washington Monument.

Tents were growing on the ground beyond like wildflowers. He moved closer to them, following Fourteenth Street, then, hearing a noise behind him, turned to see a column of soldiers approaching, two mounted officers at its head.

As they drew near, he nodded to the officers—a major and a lieutenant—then stood as the rest of the men came by at route step—young faces, a few older ones, some clean-shaven, many with beards. He caught himself looking to the hairless, more youthful faces in search of some hint that they might be females in disguise.

It was a foolish notion. This was just another of the new regiments, still arriving in Washington almost daily. He could see nervousness, fear, fatigue, agitation, discomfort, pride, and elation. But withal, he could see seriousness of purpose. These were volunteers. These were Mr. Lincoln's men.

Just like him.

When they'd passed on, the ground ceasing to reverberate from their many feet, Harry looked back to the city going about its busy day.

Then felt a tug at his sleeve.

There stood little Homer, ill-dressed for the cold.

"Been lookin' for you all over, mister," he said.

Harry shook his head. This would mean a summons from Leahy or Pinkerton. Perhaps he'd taken too long to decide. Perhaps they'd changed their minds about leaving him at any kind of liberty.

"How'd you find me?" Harry asked.

"Way you walk. Saw you way back up the street." He took a small parcel from his pocket and handed it to Harry. It was wrapped in elegant paper. "The pretty lady say to give you this. She gave me a dollar; said you'd give me another."

Harry smiled, then gently opened the package. Inside were three things: a brief note, a small square of paper with a Richmond street address on it, and a *carte de visite* bearing Ella Turner's mesmerizingly beautiful visage.

A sanctuary, if you've the need of it, said the note. *Return to me.*

Those few words, and nothing more.

The boy was waiting.

"She said a dollar?" Harry asked. "And not a penny?"

"She wanted me to find you."

"Very well," Harry said. He took a small leather bag from an interior pocket, removed a ten-dollar gold piece, and gave it to Homer.

"Mister?"

"That is what your message is worth to me." He leaned closer. "You take off with it so it doesn't bring you harm. I must go away for a while, but I will see you in the spring."

"Okay, mister. Thank you."

And with that he was soon a skipping, hopping figure, moving away across the mall.

An odd sense of liberation came over Harry, much as he imagined might be a bird's as it took flight. He put the *carte de visite* in his wallet, next to Caitlin's, realizing he'd be carrying them as soldiers do. Then, with brisk step, he started off obliquely toward an assemblage of tents that had been there for months. Finally, after a small search, he found the section he'd sought, marked by the presence of a number of high-ranking officers.

There were also privates.

"This is General Hooker's headquarters?" Harry asked.

"Aye," said a private, a Massachusetts man by the sound of him. "They're in there drinking."

Harry nodded, thanking the man, then ambled over to the rope line where the officers' mounts were tethered. He waited until the soldiers took themselves to other business, then, recognizing Hooker's chestnut gelding, slipped free the reins and walked him away, turning a corner of the tent street.

Walking as casually as possible, he led the animal out onto the mall and swung up in the saddle, moving on at a casual trot. In a few more minutes he was clear.

He'd head east, then down into the no-man's-land of southern Maryland.

Stealing General Hooker's horse would make it perfectly clear to Leahy, Pinkerton, and Mr. Lincoln what he'd decided to do.

Author's Note

THIS is a mystery, a work of fiction—but historical fiction. The author, like anyone else enthralled by this extraordinary period of our nation's history, owes an allegiance to fact. Every effort has been made to present these Civil War times and circumstances as accurately and authentically as possible. And real persons have been used wherever possible.

The actual people involved in waging this war on both sides were often far more interesting than anything even a novelist's imagination might create.

Those with a passing interest in the Civil War will, of course, know that Rose Greenhow was an actual Southern spy credited with making possible the Confederate victory at First Manassas. Belle Boyd, Allan Pinkerton, and the Monument Street girls were just as real.

Incredibly, there was also an actual Zarvona, who did in fact capture the steamer *St. Nicholas* and try for the Union gunboat *Pawnee* in the manner described here; an actual Loreta Janeta Velasquez who dressed as a man and fought at Bull Run and Ball's Bluff; an actual General Stone, Colonel Evans, and Captain Philbrick.

Oliver Wendell Holmes was indeed present at the battle as a young lieutenant and was wounded as described. Colonel Edward Baker was indeed one of Abraham Lincoln's best friends and he did fall victim at Ball's Bluff to what amounted to murder—the identities of the Confederate cavalry officer who did it, and the red-haired enlisted man seen nearby, remaining mysteries to this day.

And if Harrison Raines and his friends had been as real as these others, the mystery might well have been solved as it is in this novel. It was that kind of war.

Michael Kilian
McLean, Virginia